# THE BELOVED CHILDREN

This edition first published 2020 by Fahrenheit Press.

ISBN: 978-1-912526-93-2

10 9 8 7 6 5 4 3 2 1

www.Fahrenheit-Press.com

F 4 E

# The Beloved Children

## By

## Tina Jackson

## Fahrenheit Press

*For Kirstin. Wot larks. Thank you dear birdie.*

*TAKE YOUR SEATS PLEASE, AND AS YOU WAIT FOR THE SHOW TO START, CATCH A GLIMPSE OF THE MYSTERIES THAT WILL UNFOLD BEFORE YOUR VERY EYES*

*Miss Maude's hand slices through the air above her head. A pair of flies drop to the table. They join a debris of scraps of skin and fur, small bones, hair, thread and the remnants of a hot water bottle. As if briefly mourning the loss of two of their number, the mass of bluebottles surrounding Maude's black bonnet pause in flight, silently hovering, before the interminable buzzing begins again.*

*'Were you seen?' Miss Maude holds up her handiwork to the candle, examining the fine stitches that connect five clawed digits to what look like rudimentary limbs. Two small flames illuminate the embers of her yellow eyes, glowing through the thick veil that conceals her face, giving the woman – just for one fleeting moment, just long enough – the impression of sympathy.*

*'I came the way you said. No-one saw me. The whole world is sleeping.'*

*'Except in here, where the ways of the world are not ours.' Miss Maude's chuckle sounds like rustling leaves. The woman forces herself to look into the black hole of the bonnet's frame where Miss Maude's face is concealed. It's not the first time.*

*'You will take the child?' Miss Maude's voice counters any notion of warmth.*

*The woman shivers as the flat syllables echo round the small, gas-lit chamber. 'Yes. That's why I'm here.'*

*'It's best done now.' As Maude speaks, she lays down the thing she has been making, and rises.*

*The woman swallows, and nods. Her eyes are drawn to the thing on the table: a mannikin with the body of an infant, the tail of a fish and the head and upper limbs of a grotesque, stunted beast.*

*'What is it?'*

*'A mermaid such as Mr Kingsley never wrote of, and you never saw, except in the dead of night, when such things come in nightmares and may be discounted by daylight. I am – as you know – handy with a needle.' Maude leaves the woman to understand that no mention of the mermaid – or other matters – must be made once she leaves this strange, close room. 'Unless, of course, this is the child you would prefer.'*

*The woman shakes her head. There is no question.*

*'The choice is yours. You may take, or not take, either child, as you please. The mermaid will thrive here and earn its keep but the human child will not. So as we discussed...'*

*Maude stands, and then, in her skirts from the beginning of the century, seems to skim the floor as she moves noiselessly to the back of the room, where she bends, and lifts a silent bundle from a drawer. Maude is next to the woman, startling her, before she realises she is there.*

*Maude holds out the bundle. 'You will take this child,' she repeats, lifting a corner of the blanket to reveal skin like a lily and a mouth shaped like the bud of a new rose. Greedily, the woman reaches out her hands for the baby, pulling her from Maude's grasp – from hands covered in black mesh mittens and sleeves of sooty bombazine – into her own arms.*

'My only grandchild.' The woman's voice is as devoid of emotion as if she was reading the card at the optometrist. As devoid of emotion as she had been when... but Muriel could not let herself dwell on that. It was years ago, in another life, long before she was a married woman. A respectable wife. And mother, now.

'Born in the early hours of this morning. She is not like her kind, and she would not thrive here.' Deliberately, Maude removes the thick black veil that shrouds the bottom half of her face, and strokes the glossy black tendrils of beard and moustache that curl around her mouth and chin. 'Her birth mother does not want her, and she has her keep to earn. There are no passengers in a life such as ours.'

'No-one will know? There is no need for anyone to know she has not always been mine?' The woman can barely keep the greed from her voice as she gazes first at Maude, veiled and dead-eyed, and then at the perfection of the newborn baby's face.

'I am not the only one whose lips will be sealed.' The woman remembers the fearful looks she encountered the first time she came looking for Miss Maude; the persistence and persuasion she had needed to employ before she had finally been ushered into the room in the bowels of the theatre where Miss Maude entertained those occasional clients who wished to learn the time and manner in which they would meet their death.

'The money.' The woman hands it over – everything she has been able to amass, and worth every sacrifice she made to gather it. Maude's mittened hands barely show against the dull black cloth as she stashes her gains in a pocket hidden away in her skirts.

'Beyond her name, which is the only thing her mother has given her apart from the fact of her existence, the child is entirely yours.' The woman feels her heart expand as she looks into the baby's eyes. The years of shame, of humiliation, are over. No matter where she came from, this child is her daughter, and she is a mother now.

'You will leave this way. No-one will see you. Tomorrow morning you will present your new baby to the world as your own. No-one will suspect that she is not your natural child.'

'She is the child I have longed for. Thank you. Thank you from the bottom of my heart.'

'Do not be too sure, or expect too much.' Maude opens the door and holds a candle aloft so that the woman can see her way down the unlit passage that leads from it. 'The other child' – Maude points at the mermaid – 'if you had chosen her, may have brought you greater happiness than this one.'

'I don't think so. This girl is every happiness I ever sought.' With one arm, the woman clutches the baby – her baby! – to her body, and with the other, winds her coat around the child to protect her from the freezing night air. She thanks providence for the drop-waisted fashions that have allowed her to conceal both the child, and the fact that she had not been carrying it before this night.

'We are not made for happiness and we would do well not to expect it. We will not meet again.' Maude bows slightly and her shadow looms above her, dancing on the wall behind. 'I will not see my grand-daughter in the flesh. But one day, she will see me.'

The door closes behind her. The night air gathers. Beneath her shawl, the swaddled baby is snug and warm, but her new mother shivers all the way home.

*ACT ONE: STEP RIGHT THIS WAY*

Chapter 1

Chrysanthemum finds two bundles waiting for her on the doorstep when she goes to put out the rubbish at the end of the day. The first is Rose, folded into the far corner of the porch, knees tucked under her and a turquoise velvet hat tilted like a crest over a crumpled handkerchief face. A gaudy little homing pigeon with raggedy, moth-eaten old feathers. Chrysanthemum's heart lurches and lifts at the sight of her.

'Bad penny. Can't get rid of you, can I?'

'Hello stranger.' Rose smiles, and sixty years fall away. 'Not worth even trying. Kettle on? Perishing out here. I'm dying for a nice warm wet.'

'I had a feeling in my waters you might be on your way. In you get.' Chrysanthemum has been expecting Rose to turn up for a while now. *Saw her in the teapot the other day. Not the leaves, no-one does that now it's all bags. But she opened the lid to fill it with hot water and there it was. Rose's face. Funny, that. Nothing along those lines for years, but then even when she was a child it always did come and go. And it was time she came back. Sixty years. A lot of time and no time at all.*

'No point asking where you've been all this time?'

Rose isn't listening. She's wandered off: picked herself up, shaken herself down and trotted inside the front door. Always was light on her feet. Light in the head and all. Light-hearted too, which was catching. Chrysanthemum barely notices the drag on her shoulders as she lifts the other bundle, bulky, wrapped in brown paper and tied with hairy string. *Not many like that these days. Most of the offerings left on the doorstep are in plastic bags. This has her name – first and last – on the outside in careful lettering, so no question of it not being intended for her. There's something about that handwriting. Old fashioned. Look at it later. Under the counter, that'll do for the time being.*

With it out of sight if not out of mind, she makes her way to the kitchen. *Old bones need warming up. Hers and Rose's. A cup of tea. Nice bit of toast. Heaven only knows where Rose has been. Tea and toast'll set her up, that's for sure. Marmalade, with nice thick peel.*

Rose has got her coat off. She's fluttering around, touching things, making sure everything is where she'd left it. Chirruping. 'I remember this. You've still got that, then.' *Not a pigeon, a bloody budgie. Cheep cheep cheep.*

'Fancy, you still being here. I always hoped you might be. What is now? Not still a boarding house?'

'For clapped-out old chorus girls? Not that many of us left these days. No, upstairs is private now. Downstairs is a charity shop for down-at-heel theatricals. Pals. That's why I chose the name. We had to be pals in them days, didn't we? All on our lonesomes otherwise. Well, some of us.'

'Always the best of.' Rose smiles. Drops a creaky curtsy. 'Even if a bit skew-whiff.'

Hauling herself upright, Rose spots a small, battered wooden chest whose paintwork has faded. She's next to it faster than you might think, what with her being so old and frozen. 'What's in there now?'

'Old newspapers.' Chrysanthemum picks up the kettle.

'I used to get inside that box'.

Chrysanthemum plonks the kettle down. 'You did, an' all. When you were Mervyn's magical assistant. Bet you couldn't these days.'

'I bet I could you know. Like riding a bicycle. Oof.' Rose's bones crack as she bends down to unbuckle her shoes. Her clothes are rags and tatters but her high-arched feet are shod in reinforced t-bars with a two-inch heel. An old-fashioned style, and worn, but good for their age.

'I tell you what. You being back. Shall we light the samovar?'

'I didn't see it. It's still here?' She spreads her palms on the table. An excited child might do the same.

'Course it is. Dolores would reach out from the grave and have my guts for garters if I ever tried to get rid of that samovar. It's in the glory hole.'

It takes some effort to heave out the brass samovar from where it's gathering dust at the back of the pantry and place it on the table. Time was it would have had pride of place. Time was it would have felt as light as a feather. That and a lot else. Not now. It's to be hoped it's only her girdle creaking as old bones take the strain. Rose might not give a monkeys how cracked and creased she is, but it's a point of pride. Then there's filling it with water. Rummaging for charcoal at the back of the cupboard under the sink. *What a palaver to get a cup of tea.*

The words are about to fly out and dampen the atmosphere when she spots two figures on the table that weren't there when last she looked. A wooden nesting doll, and a china bear, chipped and faded. Chrysanthemum reaches out an unsteady fingertip to stroke two little, worn faces. *Where have you been? What have you seen? Oh, the stories you could tell.*

'Still got them then?'

'Wouldn't be without. Been everywhere with me. And that's some miles in shoe leather.' Rose puts down a square of threadbare floral fabric, crumpled like dead petals, fragile as a butterfly's wing – *it can't be, but it is, Janna's skirts* – and reaches out a finger to the two toys. It meets Chrysanthemum's, still resting on the head of the little wooden doll.

'They used to frighten the living daylights out of me.'

'Always loved them. Start of the story, really.'

'And now they've come home. Like you. Have you come home, Rose?'

'Not to die, if that's what you mean. Life in the old dog yet. But if there's a corner for me to curl up in.'

'I'll squeeze you in.' Chrysanthemum bends to light the charcoal. Reflected in the tarnished brass, there's a face that looks like someone she used to know. A younger, smiling version of herself. 'You know I will. Stories need endings.'

'And beginnings,' says Rose. 'I do look back.'

The samovar begins, gently, to hiss and gurgle.

'Remember what Janna used to say? "It has stories to tell".'

'I do. It did.' The hairs prickle on the back of Chrysanthemum's neck. 'At a price,' she adds, jowls quivering. There are reasons she keeps it where it is even if she couldn't bear to get rid of it. But her eyes go to it nonetheless.

'There was, and there was not.' Under her breath, almost as if she doesn't dare say it. How long since she'd heard those words? Is that a tremor in her voice?

And as she looks, the brass surface appears to steam over, and as it does, Chrysanthemum sees figures beginning to form. Just as they...

*Sas tai nas... It's her, there she is in her hat and coat, gas mask over her shoulder, hair newly bleached and waved, look at that face, bright as a new penny, gazing at the door of an old theatre, in a town she'd never been to before all this happened. Only her third audition, though she'd been lucky to be pulled out of the line and matched up with two others. Not that they were a match, but they worked. The end of line duchess, the talent and the one that held it all in place. They'd stuck together. Formed an act. And there they were, that first afternoon. The three of them. The Three Graces. Right at the bottom of the bill. Butterflies in the stomachs. Hearts in their mouths, and maybe – well, they were very young hearts after all – waiting to be given away. The world may have been at war, but it was still spring. A time of beginning. And there they were. Waiting for the show to go on. Wondering when their real lives would start.*

*But I'm getting ahead of myself. What was it Dolores used to say? Never rush though a number. Don't give all the good stuff away at once. Let it build. Hold it back. Make them wait.*

*So there she is. Standing outside Fankes' Music Hall. Waiting for the door to...*

THE LIGHTS GO DOWN. THE BAND STRIKES UP. THE CURTAIN RISES.

The smell is the first thing to strike Chrysanthemum. Feet. Bodies. The air in the rehearsal room feels like a well-used flannel: damp, sticky, distinctly whiffy. She grips her attaché case's handle, takes a breath and walks in. She can't help looking over her shoulder. *Don't be ridiculous. She can't possibly know you're here.* The newspaper advert is in her case, under her shoes. She hasn't said a word about where she's going. Like the last two auditions. Waited until her mother went out and then buggered off by the back door.

'Three Graces audition for Fankes?' A woman with graying hair in an immaculate chignon drags her attention from a newspaper and peers at her through cigarette smoke. Chrysanthemum nods.

'Over there.' With her cigarette, the woman signals the far wall, where girls are lined up. 'Get changed behind the curtain, then go to the end of the line. Name.'

'Chrysanthemum Landry.'

'Chris?'

'No. I've always been Chrysanthemum.'

*I never liked that name, her mother always said. Too showy. And it doesn't suit you. So why did she call me it? I'd have liked to have been an Audrey. I should have said that was my name. Audrey, or maybe Peggy. New name, new life. If I get in. I could have had a stage name. Too late now.*

'Oh. Well, on you go.'

The smaller, prettier girl doing the splits in her camiknickers behind the curtain makes Chrysanthemum feel like a carthorse.

'Rose.' The girl extends a hand and smiles with her whole face. 'Been to many of these?'

'Chrysanthemum. Bit of a mouthful I know.' She returns the smile like an apology. 'This is my third time. You?'

'More than I can count. In-the-family kind of thing. You've got a flower name too. But mine's so common. Ten-a-penny, Roses are. Yours is unusual. You are lucky.' *Perhaps not Peggy, then.*

Rose peers out from behind the curtain. 'I wonder what that one's called? She ought to be Greta or Marlene. Look at her. No-one else will stand a chance.'

Chrysanthemum looks. 'I might as well put my coat back on. Who's going to hire anyone else when she's here?'

'You never know. I bet she can't do this.' Rose flips onto her hands and executes a perfect backwards scissor kick to bring herself upright.

'I absolutely can't.'

'I expect you've got other skills then. Everyone in this line of work has got something. My ma always said you do better if you've got something that could be a turn. What can you do?'

Chrysanthemum keeps her mouth shut. She isn't ready to tell a new person about the things her mother always told her to keep quiet about.

'Are you ready? Let's wait together.

'Orage Meacham.'

The stunning blonde girl is being called. 'I bet that's not her real name.' Rose watches through the gap in the curtain. 'She ought to be in the films.'

'Age?' The director looks bored, then looks at Orage and sits up straight. Orage looks at him as if he's turned up on the bottom of her shoe.

Chrysanthemum can't count the times she's wished that look was part of her own repertoire.

'That's for me to know.' Orage leaves off 'and for you to find out' as if she can't be bothered wasting words on him.

'Begin.' The director sits forward in his chair.

The pianist thumps out a tune that might have been catchy the first time she played it. Orage walks through a brief routine that involves three dramatic poses and relies on an innate capacity for languor.

The director stops her. 'Can you actually dance?'

The woman with the cigarette looks wearily in his direction. 'Does it matter? Look at her.'

The director rolls his eyes. 'Orage Meacham. In. Next.'

Next is a sturdy redhead who fluffs her turns, and the girl after that is so out of time that the director motions her to stop mid-bar.

'Rose Brown.'

'Age?'

'Seventeen,' chirrups Rose. *She never is.*

Rose performs with vivacity. Her technique is impeccable. Winsome, the only word for her. A pleasure to watch.

*I wish you wouldn't gush. You show me up something rotten. There's her mother again. Snidey. Sly drips of poison, that's her mother's way. Sticks and stones, she'd mock. But it hurts, because it's meant to.*

'In.' The director doesn't even ask her real age. 'Haven't I seen you before?'

'You might have. I've always lived in Middleton. But it might have been my Mam. Or even my Nanna. There's more of us than you can fit in our house and lots of them have been in the shows.' Rose smiles, and drops a curtsey. 'My Nanna said she'd tan my hide if I didn't get in. Thank you.'

Then it's Chrysanthemum's turn.

It seems as if the pianist goes deliberately slowly, and every step drags painfully, but then it's over.

'Not bad.' The director looks as if he's seen it all before. 'You'll do. Perhaps a bit more work on the corner steps. You look the part, as long as you remember to smile. Over there with the other two.'

Chrysanthemum sits on the bench. At one end, Orage's limbs seem to go on forever; at the other, tiny Rose. Almost a whole foot shorter. *And me in the middle, to even things out. Piggy in the.* Chrysanthemum always knows just what Muriel would say.

'Are there any more?' Weariness makes the director hoarse. 'Send them away Peggy. We've billed them as The Three Graces, we've got three, and I'm on ARP patrol at four. You three, it's £1 and six shillings weekly for twelve shows, two slots in each, you pay for your own shoes and tights, there's digs with Mrs Biswell at 38 Richmond Terrace and there's a full run-through on Monday morning, you can come to that and then up to Wardrobe. Mind your Ps and

Qs when you get there, that's all I'm saying. You'll only have me for that afternoon to get the routines down, so make sure you pay attention, but you'll get a few days to rehearse before we put you on.' Without a backwards glance, he leaves the room.

'Mr Digsby's got a reserved occupation. We're very lucky to have him.' With that, Peggy follows in his wake, ushering out the unpicked and the unauditioned in a trail of cigarette smoke. *Definitely not Peggy. Stuck-up cow.*

That leaves Chrysanthemum, Rose, and Orage.

'Looks like it's us, then girls.' Orage has a rich, velvety drawl of a voice, affected but undeniably glamorous. Chrysanthemum is too dazzled by her beauty to look her in the eye, so she examines her own feet, amazed that they've got her the job.

'You don't have to rush off do you?' Orage makes quite a show of getting out her compact. 'We should toast our success in gin and orange. There's a Red Lion at the end of the road – I saw it on my way up here.'

'I'm in,' chirps Rose. 'As soon as I've got my civvies back on. Come on Chrysanthemum. You're one of the Three Graces now.'

Flushed with success, the three girls are tiddly before the gin touches the lips they'd showily painted on for their auditions with precious cosmetics. The Hollywood glamour of a Hunters Bow in Regimental Red turns Orage into the nearest thing to Joan Crawford the Red Lion has ever seen. Just a smear of Vaseline puts the shine on little Rose. Tangee's Uniform Lipstick changes colour to make even more of Chrysanthemum's full mouth and she can hear her mother hissing *wipe it off.*

'A pound and six shillings.' Rose makes it sound like a fortune.

'That won't keep me in nylons.' Orage waves a leg in the air.

'I was earning that as a hello girl at the telephone exchange.' Chrysanthemum know she's babbling but she needs to make herself understood. 'I did the training after I finished school. They tell you exactly what to say. "Please insert two pennies in the box but do not press button A until your number answers." I did that for a year and a half. And then I just couldn't face it. I was that desperate to get out I'd have done anything. But I always wanted to do this. It can't be anything like as hard.'

'You can't make the dances up you know.' Rose's face creases with concern. 'You'll have to learn the routines. It's a nice steady job, being a hello girl. Inside, and all.'

'They wouldn't have me.' Orage doesn't sound a bit sorry. 'They said I didn't have the right voice.'

'Far too sultry.' How does Rose know a word like that? 'You'd give the gentleman callers all sorts of ideas.'

'I expect they'll get them wherever she goes.' Chrysanthemum's attempt at sounding sophisticated is spoiled when she giggles and chokes on a mouthful of gin and orange.

Orage ignores the spluttering and preens. 'I do hope so. It's an absolute duty to keep up morale, in my book.'

'I've never heard it being called that before.' Chrysanthemum tries the words for size. 'Keeping up morale. I like it.'

'I expect you do dear.' Orage raises an eyebrow in a complicit way that suggests something shared. 'But we've only just met, so why don't you carry on with your story. About the telephone exchange.'

'Anyway. If I'd carried on being a hello girl I'd have had to stay at home. I desperately wanted to do… well, this, or something like this, before I got called up. My mother works in munitions, she's a widow and I wanted… before it was my turn…'. She struggles to find the words and gives up.

'Me too.' Orage, for once, sounds serious. 'I know we'll all have to do our bit, but I'm not twenty yet. Time to live a little before that!' She raises her glass with a flourish. 'Soon it will be clogs and snoods and brown overalls for the lot of us but here's to life before the Land Army! Or munitions, or wherever the fates decide to send us!'

'Isn't there room for you?' Rose doesn't seem to have noticed that the two older girls have got their eye on a near future where they won't be able to choose what they do. 'There wasn't for me. Like I said, too many of us, spilling out all over the place.'

'It's just me and Mother, at least since my father died. She doesn't know I came here today, she's on days at the moment so it was easy for me to get out. There is room for me, in that I've got a room. But she's never liked me very much.' Chrysanthemum makes herself stop talking. The whole point is to get away from Muriel, not bore her new pals by talking about her.

'I got told never to darken their door.' Again, Orage doesn't sound sorry.

'With a…?' Rose inhales the rest of her sentence.

'Gentleman? I wouldn't go that far. But he did me a favour getting me thrown out, I'll give him that much. It was high time I did things my own way.'

'Here we all are, then.' Rose makes it sound such a grand adventure.

'All three of us on our own.' Chrysanthemum is pleased that they are all, in their way, in the same boat.

'But we aren't now, are we? We can look out for each other – we've got each other now.'

'I thought I was joining a variety show, not the Girl Guides.' Orage sticks her tongue out at Rose to show she is only half-joking. 'Just promise you won't give me a bloody badge for anything.'

'To us.' Rose raises her glass. 'Fast friends and all the fun of the fair.'

'To fame and fabulousness. And a fling, before our country needs us. And fortune – that goes without. Once the war's over I'm going to drip in diamonds if it kills me.' In one dramatic gesture, Orage poses her glass next to Rose.

'Should be a martini, really. What is it you want, Chryssie? I'm going to call you that. Has a ring to it. Chrysanthemum's too much of a mouthful. Come on, let's drink to it.'

Chrysanthemum flushes. *Chryssie. It's not Audrey, but… but yes, Chryssie.* 'I'm not really sure what I want.' She hates herself for stammering, and for not knowing. But she hadn't expected to get this far, and wanting that has taken up weeks…no, months, of yearning. Getting in, all her dreams have been fixed on getting in. Getting away. She has no idea what she wants next. 'I just hope I fit in.' It sounds a small hope when she says it but it is such a big thing she doesn't dare to want it. She doesn't belong at home. Her mother has made it quite clear, over the years, that there were things she was not to speak of. Things that nice children didn't do, or say. Nice children didn't talk to imaginary friends they met in the attic, or adopt a family of invisible puppies. And now her mother is convinced she's no better than she ought to be, because there have been a few young men; quite a few, if she is honest, and they've been nice enough, but not for her. Apart from when she's dancing, she's never belonged anywhere, except once, just for a few minutes, before her sixth birthday.

'You are a funny thing.' Rose says it with so much kindness that Chrysanthemum has to look at her shoes again.

Orage spreads her arms.

'Cheers my dears. And bottoms, very much, up.'

Chrysanthemum's heart lifts. And then plummets. She has to go home now, and tell her mother.

Chapter 2

## NOTHING LIKE THE OLD ONES

*There is Rose, still in her coat, padding about. Flit flit flit. Into the lounge. That used to be a room that people kept for best. Hated that. Sunday afternoons, if there were callers, perched on the edge of the settee, balancing a cup and saucer and making polite conversation. You could see their breath because the room was only heated if someone who wasn't family came to sit in it. Sit nicely, Chrysanthemum. Not like that. And in the corridor, the quick, sharp pinch of Muriel's manicured nails in the soft flesh above her elbow. Stop showing me up in front of people. They'll think I haven't brought you up to behave yourself. The smile was for other people. They thought Muriel was a wonderful mother.*

'Quite a lot of new things.' Rose perches her backside on the very edge of the padded chartreuse velour four-seater parked squarely in front of the big telly. 'That was never here. Homely. I'm sure it wasn't this cosy before.' Rose edges herself back so that she's sitting comfortably. 'But then, it was a bed and breakfast. And after the war. No money for new things.' She pats the faded impression left by years of being squashed to the springs by someone's substantial behind. 'Someone's been sitting in my bed.' *She was a sweet little dicky bird. Tweet tweet tweet. Softly she sang to me.*

'And look at all these!' Rose flutters over to the mantelpiece with her fingers outstretched to the gallery of photographs. 'Is everyone here?' *Nearly everyone. But not quite.*

There is a photograph of Chrysanthemum and Muriel, taken when the girl must have been about two, that very clearly shows that mother and daughter are not a natural fit. Muriel, despite the drop-waisted coat she is wearing, is visibly thin, and her prettiness has a nervous, brittle quality. For this picture, she has arranged herself neatly, both in clothes and in posture, her wispy hair carefully drawn back from her face with clips and tidied into uniform curls in front of her ears. The small Chrysanthemum is sturdy, with thick blonde hair and a handsome face for a toddler. She is captured sideways, in the throes of essaying a curtsey, beaming cheerfully up at her mother and showing too much of her nice strong legs. Muriel is smiling politely – tightly – but at the camera, not at her child.

Half a century on, this picture isn't on display amongst the ranks of framed photographs stacked up on the sideboard and hanging on the walls that Rose, still in her hat and coat, picks out and points to. It's been stooshed, tucked away, out of sight but not entirely out of mind, in an envelope in a box in a drawer. The pictures on show – the ones that Chrysanthemum dusts on a regular basis – conjure memories of a full, busy life where the same faces crop up, over and over.

Maurice is a constant presence, his friendly, freckled face – his teenage spots hid another dappled crop – getting wider and more froglike over the years. There's a lovely one of the pair of them, on stage at Blackpool Tower Ballroom, holding their trophy between them the night they won the Ballroom Dancers of the Year 1963 award.

Orage, barely seeming to age, is as impossibly gorgeous in the pictures of her middle years as the ones of her as a young woman. Framed in silver, she's 1950s glamour incarnate, satin evening gown and chandelier earrings, on the arm of her suave tailcoated husband. She's in black and white, a press shot this time, swanlike with a beehive and a slender cocktail gown being presented to the Queen at the Palladium. A snapshot this time, a relaxed family portrait with Rosemary, eating sardines under an umbrella in the Mediterranean sun. Rosemary crops up again as a serious, angelic toddler, and in her graduation photograph: a dainty, solemn face framed by blonde curls under the mortarboard, clear eyes looking out with fearless resolve. Dolores appears several times, including a disconcerting Polaroid taken late in life, iron-grey curls ruthlessly arranged, hands clasped fiercely on her handbag; the 1960s colour processing turning her eyes scorching yellow. There is even Janna's old, hand-tinted cabinet card advertising *Anna Ludmilla Ivanovska, World famus dance cigene,* its colours fading and the tiny sequins glued by Dolores onto the coins in the long plaits tarnished. Chrysanthemum has framed it and placed it next to the most splendid picture of all of Dolores, lording it out of a bevelled 1930s glass frame, clad in gauze and dripping in diamonds, a plumed headdress towering a good two feet over her peroxide head. *But we're getting ahead of ourselves. Who are these characters, some of whom have yet to make an entrance? All in good time they'll reveal themselves. Think of it as seeing their names in a programme, or on a poster, and knowing that they will play their part in the show. What matters, for now, is that in the middle, at the heart of all the other pictures, are* The Three Graces.

'Here I am. I was looking to see if I'd be there, and I am.'

'Where else would you be?' Chrysanthemum doesn't tell Rose that it is the only picture she has of her. This is the picture that draws Rose, now, and Chrysanthemum too, as she stands by her returned friend and sees her life as it might look to someone who has come back after a long time. *It was so long ago that they looked like that. Time has its way of playing tricks and seeming to concertina, or fall away. Was it such a very long time ago that they stood in the wings: costumed, curled, arms round each other's shoulders? Standing together, smiling into a future they couldn't even begin to imagine.*

## SHALL WE DANCE?

Where did it come from, this dancing? She's always loved to dance. As a child, hurling herself into the sounds of the music. Any music. On the gramophone. On the radio. *Stop it Chrysanthemum. You're showing me up.* At school, of course, and in her dance classes, where it's allowed. Encouraged, even. *Don't they look lovely, all your little friends? I expect their mummies are proud of them, too.* Ballet practice, clinging to the edge of the kitchen table as a barre, and tap, which Muriel approves when it's exercises and dislikes intensely when there's any attempt at expression. *No-one likes a show-off, dear.* There are shows, too, when she's small, with Muriel enjoying making the costumes and watching with the other mothers. As she grows into her teens, though, there's something showy about her – something that makes Muriel angry with her. *You should have grown out of that at your age. Great big girl, making a spectacle of yourself.* But she doesn't grow out of it. She grows more into it, at dances where she's on the floor with the first boy who asks, not caring if the lads think she's forward and the other girls tut at her behind their hands. And later, in secret, in her bedroom, trying to replicate the steps she sees in films. She hates it, when she can't do it properly, and loves it when she does, and whether she loves it or hates it, she keeps at it, going back to it and doing the move, or the sequence, time and time again, until she gets it right. And gradually, there's the dawning possibility that those girls she sees on the stage, in the variety shows – they aren't a different species. They're girls, like her, who can dance, and do it for a living. Some are good, most are OK – like her. She knows she'll never be Alicia Markova. She loves ballet but she knows it's beyond her reach. She doesn't have it in her to be a swan, or even one of the corps de ballet. And swans don't have a bust, or a bum, or the sort of mouth that looks as if it's wearing lipstick even when it isn't. But the leggy girls in spangles dancing together in the backline become something to aim for. And when the music starts up, even if it's only a remembered tune running through her head, she finds herself dancing.

It was – is – has always been – the place where the rest of the world falls away and she becomes herself. Only herself. Not the daughter who isn't up to scratch, or the showoff who should have grown out of making an exhibition of herself, or the girl wondering about the woman she will become, or the oddity who sees things that aren't strictly speaking there, or who has the peculiar – and it has to be said, useful – knack of lifting, and carrying, heavy objects. When she is dancing, she is utterly and completely herself even if, as soon as the music and movement stop, she wonders what has taken her over. It takes her a while for her to recognize that it is her, and that she is never more entirely Chrysanthemum than when she dances.

And now her dancing has landed her a job, and she has met girls who feel as if they will be friends. It is the most exciting thing that has ever happened to her but she knows her path is not clear ahead of her and she has to break the news to the person who has always wanted to see something else when she looks at her. Someone neat, and tidy. Someone who does not spill out and spill over. Chrysanthemum returns home after the audition with her hopes sky high and heart in her mouth, and her fears are realised as soon as she says the word 'theatre'. Muriel, grim-faced after her shift, locks her in her bedroom and shrieks though the keyhole.

'You will stop this ridiculous idea immediately and go back to the telephone exchange. Or I will take you to the Forge with me. That way I'll be able to keep an eye on you. I know you've been sneaking off. You can't pull the wool over my eyes.'

'All I want...' Chrysanthemum draws as much air into her lungs as she can to stop her voice wobbling. 'Before I get called up...'

'We all know what you want. Widows have to do war work, whether they like it or not, to make ends meet, but madam here thinks she can leave me on my own while she goes gadding about... sneaking off to go gadding about. And I know just what you've been sneaking off for.'

Unable to contain herself, Muriel twists the key and flings the door open.

'Look at you.' She's twitching with spite at the girl on the bed, just a gawky teenager in a print dress and socks, at least until you see her bonny, frightened face and her mouth, still smeared with traces of Tangee, trying not to tremble. But Muriel has to say her piece. 'No better than you should with that hair and lipstick and I've seen the boys giving you the glad eye. I've seen you looking back too. Anything could happen to you and it would serve you just right but I'm not having it. This is not that kind of household. For once you will stay in your room and do as you're told. And read that, you stupid, foolish girl. Don't think it couldn't happen to you. It's not just other people. You used to show me up with the things you saw when you were a kiddie but now it's my turn and I'll tell you exactly what I can see. It's girls like you that come to a bad end.'

The newspaper, ominous headline folded so that 'Vanished without trace – the mystery of the dancing girl who disappeared' is the first thing she'll see, is flapped in her face and flung into her lap. The date is several months back. Muriel has kept it on purpose.

When the house is silent and Chrysanthemum is sure her mother has taken herself to bed, she lowers her suitcase out of the window with a rope made from a ripped-up bedsheet, and climbs down the drainpipe after it. She's ready to jump at her own shadow and her heart is pounding so loudly it beats a tattoo and she can't believe Muriel can't hear it, but down she goes, only thinking about where she's putting her feet, one step after another until she's at the bottom. She knew she had the strength in her arms but didn't know she was so agile, or so steady, or that she had it in her to do something so reckless but this is her chance and she has to take it. It's not the idea of the Forge, she could manage that if she had to and she will when it's her turn. But even though

Orage and Rose are new, they saw her, Chrysanthemum, and they liked her, and this night-time flight is her chance. Not to be somebody, but to be herself. And to dance.

She spends the night in the air raid shelter, fizzing with too much energy to sleep, and when she telephones the following day, her mother tells her she is no longer welcome at home.

'I am very disappointed in you, Chrysanthemum. You've always been a disappointment. Well, you've been my cross and now I don't have to carry you any more. You can do what you like. I don't care.'

'I'm sorry.' She isn't sorry but she is a kind creature, and in the habit of trying to be a good daughter.

'Sorry isn't good enough. And neither are you.' The receiver clatters into its holder. Those are the last words Muriel says to her.

Chapter 3

By arrangement, the Three Graces meet by the war memorial so they can arrive at their digs together.

'Best to present a united front.' The purr made it immediately apparent why Orage would not have been suitable for work at the telephone exchange. 'All for one and one for all, and all that. TTFN, then.' The telephone amplified her sardonic drawl but couldn't obliterate the kindness. Chrysanthemum imagined her gracefully packing her things, picking out the nicest, layering them in her case in tissue paper. A bit different from her own undignified scramble, locked in her room, waiting until her mother was out to shove everything in that she thought she might need and then hide her case under the bed.

And now there she is. Orage in person, and what a person she is. Lounging on the bench next to Middleton's memorial to the fallen, she draws all the light, Hollywood glamour shining against the soot of a northern mill town, enjoying a cigarette whilst the afternoon sun plays on her cheekbones and turns her golden hair into a shining crown. She waves, and Chrysanthemum's heart leaps. Someone is pleased to see her! *Mustn't snivel.* But the last few days – the night in the air-raid shelter, then the journey and another night in the cheapest B&B she could find, have been lonely and so dispiriting, not to mention cold, that putting on a brave face is harder than she thought it might be. *A whole lifetime of not being the right person.*

But there is Orage, standing up to welcome her, standing up and waving, and there, staggering under the weight of a case almost bigger than she is that she's trying to haul along with both arms, is little Rose, her sweaty, flushed face wreathed in smiles.

Chrysanthemum rushes over. Rose, panting, drops the case and flings her arms round her new friend.

'Oh I am glad to see you, Chryssie! Your hair! I love it!'

The hair – lightened and styled into a Veronica Lake peekaboo wave – appalled Muriel. *Tart. If your poor father could see you now.*

'And you, Orage! I was so excited I couldn't sleep, and what a good idea to all go to Mrs Biswell's together! I wonder what our room will be like? Horrible I expect but we can make it cosy. Is it far?' Rose barely draws breath. 'I hope not, I can hardly even lift this, our William came with me to the corner with a wheelbarrow and I've had to drag it.'

'What have you got in it?' Orage puts down her own case and grasps Rose's by the handle. She barely lifts it a few inches before dumping it back down again.

'I didn't ought to tell you but you're bound to find out, my Nanna has been keeping tins from her rations so I won't go hungry before we get paid, but it's so heavy, I really hope it's not far.' Rose, out of puff now, sits on her case as if she is never going to move again.

'Here, give it to me.' Chrysanthemum takes the handle from Orage.

'No honestly, you've got your own. I'll mana…'

As if it weighs no more than an evening bag, Chrysanthemum raises the case in her left hand.

Rose and Orage stand, open-mouthed, as she lifts her own case with her right hand, and stands there, expectantly.

'Does anyone know the way?'

Orage and Rose, instead of moving, stare at Chrysanthemum. The surprise on their faces makes her glance at the suitcases.

'Oh, that? It's just one of those things I can do, I suppose. I always could, even from being a child. There was a clock, once, that nearly toppled on my father and I saved him from being squashed, though I was only five. Ma used to find it quite useful, when she wanted to move furniture, though she didn't like me doing it in front of people because she didn't think it was very ladylike. Well, who am I following? Is it far?'

Mrs Biswell's boarding house is only a few streets away. Mrs B, a grumpy soul in a pinafore, glowers at the Three Graces and their luggage before handing over a key in exchange for their deposit.

'Just the one?' Orage says what the others are thinking. 'We're not joined at the hip, you know. We might need to come back separately, sometimes.'

'Just the one. Like it or lump it. You're up four flights, in the attic. I've been up there once and it's set my back off so you'll have to make your own way. It's one bath a week, up to the line, and breakfast is at seven. If you're not there you'll miss it. There's a po each under the beds but if you use it, don't put it back under or the steam rusts the springs. And no gentlemen callers. I'm not having it. If there's anything amiss, I'll more than likely be in the scullery.' She turns away and shuffles towards the back stairs as if daring them to follow her.

Chrysanthemum transports all the cases upstairs. Four steep flights. The smiles and exclamations she gets in return do more to warm her than any fire. They're right under the eaves, three brightly feathered dicky birds in a dingy nest. The attic, drearily furnished with old Edwardian iron beds and worn servants' furniture, smelling of must and mothballs, draws a horrified gasp from Orage, and a dull 'oh' from Rose. To Chrysanthemum, looking round with shining eyes at her two new pals, it's a haven.

'My lord this is grim. Still, needs must. Let's bags our beds and wet the baby's head, so to speak.' Orage delves into her case and draws out a bottle – where has she got that from? – of whisky.

'I can't match that! But I have got this.' Rose pushes her case open on the floor, where it takes up most of the available space, and pulls out a fruit cake. Unimaginable luxury. 'My Nanna spoils me something rotten. Always has. Orage had better have that bed by the door because it's ever so slightly bigger, and she's the tallest. And that one in the corner is the smallest, and so am I, so I'd better have that one. Chryssie, will you mind being in the middle?'

Chrysanthemum's eyes blur and she can't speak, but she nods instead, and tries not to cry.

'My bed's awfully lumpy… It's like the three bears… Only I hate porridge.' Giddy Rose is sitting upright, bouncing her wiry little body against squawking bedsprings. She stops, mid-flight, and notices. 'I say, is everything alright?'

Chrysanthemum nods again, but the tears insist on falling. Orage leads her gently to her bed and Rose scrambles to pass her a clean handkerchief.

Eventually, Chrysanthemum is ready to blow her nose, and feeling silly and embarrassed, looks through wet eyes at her new friends.

'Now what was that all about?' All the archness in the world can't hide Orage's concern.

'It's just that…well, it's been a bit awful. My mother didn't want me to come and she locked me in my room.' *It's too much effort to stop her voice wobbling. Deep breath. No good.* 'All that stuff in the newspapers didn't help. She said it would be me next and it would serve me right. I had to climb out of the window.'

A tear drops from her eye and slides down her nose. Lands with a plop on Mrs Biswell's nasty patchwork bedspread. Then another. Plop, plop, plop.

'Oh dear.' It seems like the most natural thing in the world that Rose should put her arms round her shuddering new friend. 'It is awful, the dancer that disappeared, but it's not going happen to you, it was the other end of the country. Still, no wonder she didn't want you to come. Are you all she's got? But we're here now. We'll take care of you. Won't we, Orage?'

'Of course. But this really won't do.' Orage doesn't move to join Rose in the comforting. 'I think, Rose, that we are going to have to sit on her.'

'And tickle her?' Rose's giggle is infectious. Chrysanthemum catches herself mid-sob.

'To death, I imagine. Can you imagine Mrs Biswell's cross face, if she saw what Chryssie was doing? All over her beautiful patchwork. She might burst.'

Another great tear rolls down Chrysanthemum's face, but the edges of her mouth can't help twitching.

'I saw that. She's nearly laughing. Come on Orage.'

The tall girl and the small one launch themselves at Chrysanthemum. Eventually, pink in the face, all three throw themselves backwards onto Chrysanthemum's pillows.

'My gosh that's lumpy.'

'You can have it if you like. Go on, I'll let you.'

'That's more like it.'

'You mean lump it, surely.'

A thump through the floor interrupts the giggling.

'I can hear you,' Mrs Biswell informs them at the top of her voice from the room below, 'two storeys down. And so can the other lodgers. I hope you're not going to be flighty. That one with the peroxide hair looks flighty, and the one with the legs. Young girls today, I don't know. I did tell the theatre I preferred the older acts.'

They wait until the slip slop sound of her carpet slippers on the landing has vanished before speaking again. Naturally it is Orage who breaks the silence.

'Three bags full, Mrs Biswell.' Orage sounds very solemn. 'Huff and puff and blow the house down. Silly old boot. Blow your nose, Chryssie. I see very clearly that we all need a nice glass of this whisky, and a slice of Rose's grandmother's cake, because although to all extends and purposes this looks like a poky attic, it is in actual fact *The Palace of the Three Graces*. If only Mrs B could see through floors. What would she think? Three fast showgirls, living it up in the Palace, knocking back the booze like sailors on shore leave.'

There are three tooth mugs on a shelf by the door and Orage fills them to the brim with whisky.

'I'll be tiddly!' Rose looks at her glass as if its contents might bite.

'None of that. It's good for you. Here, Chryssie. You'd had a cry, so it's medicinal. Anyway, Mrs Biswell thinks you look flighty, so you have a reputation to live up to. Get it down you.'

Orage knocks hers back in one. 'Now, to important things. What do you think of this scent? It's a new one. Gay Diversion. My friend brought it back from America.' As she wafts it round, the mothball-smelling attic is transformed into a boudoir.

Orage will discard the scent bottle without thinking as soon as it's empty – there will be replacements lined up, at least one already opened – but Chrysanthemum, who finds it in the bin, will wrap it carefully in a handkerchief and treasure it. Decades later, if she puts her hand into her underwear drawer and encounters the bottle, she always takes it out. Even without the scent, it brings it all back, as she looks back down the years. That moment in the attic – the glamour! The fun! The laughter! – is when her life is transformed. Even as it is happening, she recognises it for what it is. Even after everything that occurred afterwards, she would never have changed it. *So here it begins. It is the best of beginnings, and the best of friends.*

Chapter 4

'Ah, the new dancers. Come in. Yes.'

The Three Graces receive the summons from Mister Digsby as soon as they arrive at the theatre. 'Mister Chairman's office. His Gillpots. Straight there. Don't go keeping him waiting. No dawdling. It's about this.' The word 'disappearance' in headline type flash before their eyes in a blur.

'It can't be that. Everyone knows about that. Even my mother. He's going to get rid of us. It's my fault, Mister Digsby must have told him, I should have worked on those corner steps.'

'Belt up, Chryssie, he hasn't even ever seen you, and try and keep up with me.' Feather-light Rose moves at such speed she's practically airborne.

'We mustn't keep him waiting.' Orage's heels are a staccato clack and with her long legs, she is in the lead, until Rose catches her up on the stairs. 'Come along Chryssie, he doesn't want to see us tomorrow.'

She's panting by the time they reach the cubbyhole under the stairs where His Gillpots has his office. Stuffed to the gills with bill posters, flyers, ledgers, half a Punch and Judy stand, a coconut shy and a tarnished howdah, it barely contains the enormous roll-top desk from which His Gillpots conducts operations.

How did that get in there? It's the size of the room. Bigger than the door, and there isn't a window. But seeing is believing and The Three Graces have to stand in the doorway because the cubbyhole isn't big enough for them to go inside.

'Mister Fankes? Mister William Fankes?' That's the name on the plaque on the door. The name over the theatre door.

His Gillpots scrutinises the Three Graces over the top of *Variety Times* as if it has only just occurred to him that theatre's three new dancers are young women, and then looks down at a folded newspaper on his desk. His eyes, glinting in his fleshy amphibian face, return to the girls, deliberately measuring each of them from the crown of her head to the insteps of her shoes. They are, after all, his to do with as he pleases, at least when they are in his theatre.

'Ah. The new chorines. No point beating about the bush. It is the unfortunate way of the world that there are villainous types abroad who delight in taking advantage of young ladies, particularly those who disport themselves on stage for the delight and delectation of the masses.' His Gillpots has the

Chairman's delivery of a person used to his patter coming over loud and clear even in the cheap seats. 'It is the theatre's responsibility to make sure its staff does not take unnecessary risks. None of you are to go anywhere on your own. Is that understood? The only vanishing acts we require are the ones on the bill. Do I make myself clear?' He taps his finger on the newsprint word: *disappearing*.

His Gillpots sucks a mouthful of smoke into his wide, wide mouth and ash from the end of his cigar falls with a soft plop onto the paper. 'There have been reports of… terpsichorines coming to what can only be a sticky end. No-one knows what has become of them. Southend this time. Now you may think that's a long way from here but this is a family business where we take care of each other. So there's to be no wandering off. Stick together and remember you are under an obligation to please the audience, not flirt with any flatties what gives you the glad eye. Which, given half a chance, is what they'll do. Human nature, you see. Well, I see, and that's what you have to consider. In this gaff, I'm the gaffer and it's gaffer's rules. You're here for joggering, not getting up to mischief. Am I making myself clear? You're to keep kushtie. Now buzz off and mind your backs. Maurice – that's young Mister Fankes – will be along to look after you.'

He shoos the Graces away from the doorway with a flick of fat fingers that sends cigar ash spilling on the desk.

Rose shudders, and pulls her coat round herself.

'Don't be scared, Rosie.' Orage pats the girl as if she is a quivering lapdog. 'Middleton's in Yorkshire. We're miles way, almost the whole country, and is your journey really necessary? If anyone so much as looks at you the wrong way Chrysanthemum and I will whack them with our handbags. I've got half a brick in mine. A young women's essential accessory.'

'My mam tells me to take care every time I see her. And my Nanna. She says I should hit anyone who tries anything on with a shoe.'

'You can't believe everything you read. Of course there are rotters and no-one's saying you shouldn't be careful but Rosie, don't let him scare you. There's some lovely young men out there.' Chrysanthemum tries to hide her blush under her hair. Perhaps Rose doesn't need to know about young men in the way she does.

'Aren't you scared, though, Chryssie?"

'Of course I am.' But she isn't. Not really. *Not nearly as scared as I was of staying at home with Mother.*

Mr Digsby, the shape of a question mark, scuttles past the Three Graces to His Gillpots' office without acknowledging them and none of the girls know where they are supposed to go in the backstage warren. Chrysanthemum, still hiding her blushes, is rummaging in her bag for a gasper when a young man materialises in the corridor. He smiles widely, heading straight towards them. Bows at them with a flourish. Bad skin. Nice teeth. A dead ringer for his dad, only with kinder eyes. Not exactly the nice young man she'd been hoping for.

'The Three Graces? Our new dancers? Maurice Fankes, assistant stage manager. I'll show you to your dressing room first.'

The Three Graces' dressing room is at the end of an upstairs corridor where each door has the name of an act on it. It is too small to swing a cat but it has lit mirrors, three seats in front of them, and – best of all – their name on the door, even if it has been written in leaky fountain pen on a piece of cardboard tacked to the door. Orage bags the seat in front of the mirror with the best light. Rose claps her hands, all thoughts of His Gillpots' warning blown from her brain, and Chrysanthemum shows that she is thrilled to bits by sitting down heavily on the seat nearest to her, and taking a deep breath.

'Just the three of you in here.' The spotty young man waves his hand round as if he is showing off the splendours of Versailles.

'It's lovely.' Chrysanthemum lowers her eyes and smiles. *And wouldn't Muriel hate it.*

'It's not really a dressing room is it?' The room shrinks as Orage speaks. 'More a cupboard really.'

'His Gillpots – my old man – asked me to settle you in because he's got better things to do like bollocking Mister Digsby, but he thought you'd be better off here, three young ladies, rather than in the big room.' Maurice is unperturbed by Orage's scorn. 'It can get a bit lary in there. The regular speshes are all good as gold but the touring ones can be a handful and they tend to go in there. Don't say I never warned you.'

Maurice winks broadly and stands with his hands in his pockets, looking blatantly at Orage.

She couldn't be less interested even if he is the boss's son. 'You'll catch flies.' And a moment later: 'Are you still here?'

Maurice still isn't bothered. 'I'll be back in ten. You don't want to be late for the run-though.'

'That wasn't very nice of you Orage,' sniggers Rose after he slinks away. 'I'd never dare.'

'He didn't give a hoot.' Maurice has evidently passed some sort of test with Orage.

'Speshes?' That's a new one for Chrysanthemum.

'Speciality acts,' begins Rose, as the door opens.

'He means us, duckie. Us what makes up most of the bill.' A mannish middle-aged woman shoulders her way in, with a smaller, rounder, slightly younger woman hot on her heels, whose pretty, feminine mouth is decorated by a thin moustache drawn in eyebrow pencil.

'We're Duckie and Dora, dearie. Male impersonators and purveyor of saucy ditties about how much we like the ladies. Third on the bill, above the talking sponge. That's Varney the Ventriloquist to you, and his barking chum Barney the Beagle. He'd be here to say hello in person only he's taken his puppet to the pub. Hair of the dog he calls it.'

'Duckie, don't be… '. Dora pats Duckie on the arm and giggles, and Duckie sticks out her tongue affectionately.

'Awful? Anything for you my love.' She turns back to the girls. 'Then there's Stella Maris that sings and thinks she's a cut above because she was a Gibson Girl a very long time ago, and Sid and Joey who do as much of a bit of knockabout as their ageing knees will allow, and Albert Emery the comedian whose line in pork pie jokes is wearing a bit thin if you ask me. Most of them was with Jeffcocks in the old days and they'd have been at the knackers if the war hadn't come along and saved their bacon. But obviously you can't get the acts these days, not when they're all doing their bit. And then you get the touring acts and the guest artistes.'

'Ooh, you mean Mervyn.' Dora flutters her eyelashes at the girls. 'Mervyn the Magus. Top of the bill. Not that he's turned up yet. But I've seen the posters. He was in York last season. Very popular. You'll like him, girls.'

Duckie gives Dora a fierce look. Dora shrugs.

'He's just the sort to appeal to young ladies. Ones without much sense, which is the bulk of them. Not to me though. I've got the most handsome chap I could wish for. Right here.' She lays her hand possessively on Duckie's arm and pulls her towards the corridor. 'Come on. We've got time before the matinee.'

The run-through could be worse. Mr Digsby, chastened after his bollocking, is even more twitchy than he was at the audition. Stella Maris, rendering her celebrated ballads, may have had a voice once, but it was probably before the last war. Sid and Joey might have been funny a long time ago. 'We're a pair of clowns from the old jokes home,' says Sid, and even Chrysanthemum, trying to look interested and learn from her veteran colleagues, has to groan. It doesn't get any better with Albert Emery either. 'Mind you don't get into a fight on the way home,' says Joey. 'They won't get the better of me,' retorts Albert. 'I'll give them a punchline.'

Duckie and Dora's double act raises a twinkle though, and Mister Digsby can be seen scratching notes on his call sheet. 'Family audience ladies, keep it clean.'

'Ooh, we're lovely and clean, aren't we Duckie? Pride ourselves on it, we do.'

'The soap we get through. You'd never believe what a lather we get into.'

'That'll do ladies. Next, please.'

Varney the Ventriloquist raises a smile, or at least Barney the Beagle does it for him by raising a paw and promising to roll over and die for the King. The Three Graces don't yet have any numbers to scrape through but Mister Digsby brings them up, hands each of them a birdcage made out of a lampshade frame and puts them through a few moves. 'Eyes and teeth, girls, that's what the punters want to see, you're good looking girls, and remember they've paid, so give them something for their money. The numbers aren't hard and we'll work on them this afternoon. Try not to look like dying ducks. And keep the small one at the front. She knows what she's doing.'

'Not out on our ear then.' Orage doesn't look as if she actually cares either way.

'Went OK I thought.'

'Oh Rose. Didn't you see me nearly drop that sodding birdcage, or go left instead of right on the crossover step.'

'But at least no-one fell over.'

After that there's a gap. Mister Digsby clears his throat crossly, and looks at his watch.

'What are we waiting for?' Orage makes it clear that she isn't used to hanging around for no good reason.

'The star turn, dearie,' says Duckie, in the tone of someone unimpressed by a colleague's billing. 'You've no idea how tedious it gets.'

Right on cue, the famous Mervyn appears as if out of nowhere. No-one has seen him make his entrance into the theatre, or heard a muff from his dressing room backstage, but there he is, waiting in the wings.

'Now you see him.' Chrysanthemum giggles behind her hand to the other two Graces as the slender, dapper figure in full evening dress materialises on the stage. Not quite a young man, but one that draws the eye for certain.

'Good afternoon ladies and gentlemen.' Mervyn doffs his topper at the assembled artistes.

'Cutting it a bit fine,' mutters Dora.

'Smarmy git,' adds Duckie.

'Bleeding conjurors think the world owes them a living,' slurs Sid, who has evidently been for lunch in the Red Lion.

'It's not the same when you're the headline artiste,' sniffs Stella Maris, in the voice of one who knows.

'Bet he goes off in a puff of smoke.' Orage gives him a lengthy once-over before conceding: 'He'll do. In a blackout, anyway. I expect he's older than he looks.'

Rose doesn't say anything. As Mervyn runs through a series of tricks that culminate in a feather duster turning into a pigeon and flying round the wings, she looks and looks, and her eyes get bigger and bigger.

Finally, when the pigeon has turned back into a duster and been stashed in a black box, Mervyn looks round, expectantly. His eyes seek the Three Graces. *Most men look twice at Orage. Some men look at me. Mervyn didn't even look once.* Instead, he looks straight at Rose, and his grey eyes gleam.

A chill settles over the little theatre. Chrysanthemum wishes she'd worn her cardigan, and wonders why she suddenly feels out of sorts.

Chapter 5

'On your best when you get up to Dolores,' warns spotty Maurice, ushering the girls to Wardrobe. He motions Chrysanthemum up first, then Rose, and finally Orage.

'He's looking at your BTM,' hisses Rose.

'He can look all he likes, it's all he's getting.'

'Stop it you two,' snaps Chrysanthemum. 'Don't be…'

"Rude?"

The word echoes startlingly down the stairwell. The figure who speaks it is poised in the doorframe as if making an entrance. Her iron-grey hair is arranged in immaculate rolls and her eyes are a strange yellow colour, but the thing the girls can't take their eyes off is the beard – a luxurious full-face affair, neatly trimmed, with curling moustaches that she strokes with strong, heavily jewelled fingers.

The woman bares her teeth in something that looks like, but definitely isn't, a smile, and beckons with the other hand.

'I've been waiting for you.'

*Murderer's hands.*

'Staring's rude too, as if you didn't know. Now stir your stumps. It's to be hoped you can move faster than that when there's an audience.'

The old wardrobe mistress spends her days cocooned with the old fortune teller in a warren of rooms on the third floor of the theatre. It may be up three flights of stairs but it feels as if it's underground: musty and fusty, cramped to busting and with the only daylight coming in through a skylight with a blackout curtain dangling as if waiting for a stockinged leg to stick out from behind. The whole place overflows with costumes, parts of what had once been costumes and costumes in the making. Boxes are stacked on top of boxes, each labelled, contents busting out, wantonly seeking attention, 'ladies' evening shawls' crammed indecently beneath 'surplus pirate shirts.' There are shimmering piles of shot silks and spangles, middens of rags and tatters, and a suit of armour topped off with a mangy courtier's wig.

Dolores makes short shrift of measuring and marking and fitting the girls into scratchy spangled scraps that have seen better days. 'Stop fidgeting,' she says to Rose, and to Orage, 'stand up straight.' Then it's Chrysanthemum's turn.

'Need a bigger bodice for you.' It's true. Rose is straight up and down like a washboard and Orage impossibly slender. And there she is, sticking out front and back.

'For this one you need make darts. But is nice shape all the same.'

The Three Graces, full of pins and barely daring to move, jump. 'Hihihi' – a rusty, clockwork laughter. A strange, soft sighing sound moans and groans from an ornate, heavy brass urn, and as it does, a fluttering, heavily accented voice adds to the chorus of noises the three dancers have never before heard in their young lives.

'The samovar is singing. It has its stories to tell. Come, sit by the samovar.'

There's the sound of snapping fingers.

As one, the Three Graces turn round to find that the heap of floral fabric they have taken for costume scraps is in fact an old lady: an old lady with the dark, watchful face of a hawk, lined eyes blackly beady above her bony nose. Of one accord, the Three Graces shiver in their cami-knickers, and a handful of pins flies to the floor.

Dolores bends to retrieve them, with much creaking of stays.

'It means self-boil, I think you'll find. You silly girls.' She tuts, threading pins deftly into her beard and giving Rose what Chrysanthemum thinks is an unnecessary pinch as she reinserts them into the seams of the spangled bodices. 'Manners. I despair, sometimes. Janna, set the teacups out.'

Back in their digs, getting rehearsal-sore legs comfy in the three lumpy beds lined up against the attic wall is a task in itself. Rub, shift, fidget. Of course no-one thought to pack embrocation. After Wardrobe, Mister Digsby devoted a couple of hours to putting them through their paces. A bird dance with a vaguely Chinese theme makes the most of Orage's ability to strike a pose whilst Rose and Chrysanthemum hop around her trying desperately not to scratch themselves as they wave birdcages made from old wire lampshade frames. A cheerful, patriotic dance about keeping busy whilst they wait for the brave boys to come home. It is an act, if not yet by any stretch of the imagination a turn, and Mister Digsby has set the date for their debut for next Tuesday's matinee.

Their legs ache and their heads are spinning.

'I'll never remember the steps for that. Not by next week. And my legs won't move anyway. Probably not ever again.' Chrysanthemum would give a lot for a basin of hot water for her feet but it is too much effort: three flights of stairs down, bearding Mrs Biswell in the utility room and then three flights back up.

'You will. It's easy: two dig-lifts on the right, with birdie hands, two on the left, then tap behind right, tap behind left, tap behind right, heel heel, then tap-slide left…'

'Rose, I am going to murder you if you don't shut up straight away, and Chryssie, no-one will be looking if you get it wrong, because they will all be admiring me, posing in my bower, and if either of you come anywhere near me with those moulting old budgies in those appalling lampshades, I will pay Mrs

Biswell to turn you both into my breakfast.'

'But it is easy. And Duckie and Dora were lovely, and Maurice, though he was a bit naughty looking at your behind, Orage. We've got lovely costumes, too. Dolores is awfully clever.'

'Rose, stop gushing. You're like a tap with a broken washer. And the costumes are one thing, I'll give you that, even if they do smell of mothballs, but Dolores and her pikey sidekick are quite another. Those two give me the willies,' sniffs Orage. *She is so perfectly beautiful that the thought of being any less so is unthinkable. As far as Graces go, she is Hope. You just have to hope that, with looks like hers, trouble doesn't take a shine.*

'Don't be rotten,' retorts Rose. *She is Faith, living on a wing and a prayer, the one who can do impossible backbends and spins that defy gravity.* 'We'll be them, one of these days. I'm sure I can hear rats in the skirting board.'

'Well I won't,' says Orage. 'Not on your nelly. Not as long as shops sell tweezers anyway.'

'At least they gave us a hot drink. And jam.' The jam counted for a lot, even if it felt odd to eat it from a saucer, with tea. What with rations, they go hungry most of the time. *And I am Charity, because someone has to be.*

'If there is a rat,' says Orage, 'it won't stay long when it finds out what Mrs Bisworth's cooking's like. We're four flights up and it still smells of cabbage.'

'And damp,' says Chrysanthemum miserably.

'It's warm in the theatre,' offers Rose. 'It was lovely and snug in Wardrobe. You could make a nest in all those bits and pieces. And no rats.'

"Too right,' yawns Orage. 'One sight of Dolores would scare them right off.'

'I don't know if I'll be able to make it through the practice.' Chrysanthemum clutches her hands to her stomach. 'I haven't been for an hour now but what if I need to go midway though?'

'You'll just have to put a cork in it. Anyway you've only got yourself to blame. I'll lay money that whatever she put in them had been dead for ages. She probably found it by the side of the road.'

Janna has been wandering the theatre corridors with a metal bucket full of misshapen home-made dumplings, cornering people with a whispered 'pirogi, pirogi,' until they buy one. Orage, who spat hers into her handkerchief, and Dolores, whose innards must be made of cast iron, are the only people in the building who have been spared a gippy tummy. Maurice has had to ask His Gillpots for two extra rolls of Izal to cope with the demand.

'I expect Rose is in the lavvy now,' groans Chrysanthemum. 'I hope there's still some roll.'

'She should get a move on.' Orage has her mouth full of pins. 'There's a rehearsal to get on with whether the entire cast has got the runs or not.'

But seconds later, Rose skips into the dressing room. Whatever is preoccupying her, Rose's face gives away long before she opens her mouth that it is nothing to do with her digestive system. Orage rolls her eyes and yawns stagily.

'Which particular paragon of perfection has turned our Rosy-Posy such a fetching shade of beetroot?'

Chrysanthemum raises her compact nearer to her mouth so Rose can't see it twist in a smile. *Orage is too much and she goes too far, but my goodness she's good for a laugh.*

'It's bound to be a man, isn't it? No-one gets that look because Janna's terrified them into buying her unspeakable cooking.'

Rose's toes turn inwards and her blush rises to her roots, suffusing her soft blonde hair with a tint of pink.

Chrysanthemum looks up from her mirror. 'Promise me it's not spotty Maurice of the wandering hands, Rosy. Or Sid or Joey.' Joey and Sid, the two decrepit Augustes from way back in the days of Jeffcocks Jollies, are too doddery these days for much actual clowning but their knockabout double-act is as a pair of drunken odd-job men and they earn the rest of their beer money doing odd jobs. Sid has no teeth and Joey's ear-hairs sprout a good inch from either side of his face.

Rose twists so her knees touch. 'Mervyn,' she whispers. 'Magical Mervyn.'

On his first night, Mervyn the Magus repeated his rehearsal party trick and turned a feather duster into a pigeon. From the wings, Rose squeaked so loudly with joy that Orage hissed they'd have heard her in the cheap seats.

Orage's pencilled eyebrows shoot up towards her hairline. Mervyn may have arrived on the same day as the Three Graces, but whereas they are at the bottom of the bill in very small print, he is right at the top, his name in three-inch letters right below the words 'Fankes Variety Show.' *Had she earmarked the suave conjuror for herself? He's definitely a cut above. With his swarthy skin and pencil moustache, Mervyn looks a bit like Errol Flynn – well, a slightly leathery Errol Flynn if Chrysanthemum is being frank, but still – and unlike Sid, Joey and Maurice, he is neither past it nor juvenile.*

If she were really being honest, she'd admit that at the run through she hoped she might catch him looking in her direction. But then she'd caught sight of Orage standing in the wings with her endless legs and perfect face, and dismissed that particular hope out of hand.

But all Orage says is: 'It's a bit odd he's here – well, that he isn't in uniform, fighting somewhere.'

'Maybe he's in ENSA. Or failed his medical. I don't expect being a conjuror is a reserved occupation.' Chrysanthemum racks her brain for other reasons a youngish man might not to be in the forces.

'He shared his apple with me.' Rose's voice is a happy whisper. 'He was ever so nice.'

'Well just you be careful he doesn't try to share anything else, Rosy.' Orage's voice is surprisingly kind. 'You've got a job to do, after all. You don't want to be forgetting your steps because you've left your brain in your drawers. And he's top of the bill, so if he slums it with a chorus girl that's all he's doing. Slumming it.'

Chrysanthemum raises her compact again but she can't stop the snort coming out.

'I'm sure not everyone's as bad as you think they are, Orage. Or as His Gillpots thinks, either.'

'I'm sure they're much worse,' retorts Orage.

'He didn't do anything,' says Rose. 'He gave me half his apple, that's all. I was sitting on the fire escape and he came out for a breath of fresh air and sat down next to me.'

'With an apple up his sleeve.' Orage looks at her nails, and frowns at the sight of a chip.

'No he was holding it. He cut it in two with his penknife and offered me half and I took it. It was a beautiful crisp red one. We sat on the steps and ate our halves and then he said could he have the core please for his rabbit. So I gave it to him and then I came here.'

'And that was it?' Chrysanthemum glances in Orage's direction but the other girl is bent over her nails, painting over the chip.

'Yes. Well, he did say he'd show me the rabbit later. He was ever so friendly and polite.'

Orage meets Chrysanthemum's eyes. Two pairs roll simultaneously as Rose blushes again and her pale hair turns a deeper shade of flamingo.

Mister Digsby's bollocking from His Gillpots has evidently been repeated to traumatic effect because he has vanished as effectively as one of Mervyn's rabbits. Dolores, standing in for him as rehearsal master, is a martinet, rapping out the beat with a stick and giving the Three Graces the most withering of looks when they mess up the cannon-shot finale where they are supposed to be poised on a railway platform waiting with their hearts in their mouths for their returning soldiers. Orage gets very short shrift when she fluffs the step-ball-change and reverse turn.

'Call herself a dancer,' Dolores remarks in an aside to no-one in particular. 'I've seen more life in a tramp's vest than in those lallies.' Orage wilts visibly, just as a daffodil will when deprived of light, air and water – all of which are lacking in the empty theatre.

'Can't we call it a day?' chirrups Rose. 'We'll be better after a breather.' She hasn't said a muff to anyone just as he warned her, but earlier on Mervyn the Magus kissed her behind the flats when no-one was looking. His moustache tickled her, and she liked it. She is desperate for the rehearsal to end so she can find out what time he's due in.

'Dance again.' Janna's voice echoes spookily through the auditorium as her great bell of skirts glides towards the stage. 'With more joy. When life is sad, that is when people sing. When they are full of joy, they dance.'

Dolores rolls her eyes. 'Tah-rah-rah-boom-de-ay,' she sings, each syllable a ripely rude oompah. 'My knickers flew away...'

Janna beckons the Three Graces with a conspiratorial finger. 'Then I think she is also sad, because she has lost her underwear.'

'They came back yesterday,' sings Dolores, carrying on as if she hasn't heard. But her timing, and the way she stands and the way she sings, make the Three Graces look at her in an altogether different light.

'I didn't known you'd been a dancer,' says Rose.

'Or a singer,' says Chrysanthemum.

'In a freak show,' says Orage, but under her breath, so that Dolores can't hear her.

'She was at the top of the bill of the Hippodrome,' says Janna, in a thrilling tremolo.

Dolores stops singing. 'Isn't it time you went and put that fancy tea urn of yours on to boil? I'm spitting feathers after a morning with this shower, and I'm not having them in front of an audience until they've got this to my satisfaction. Go again, girls. And don't make a barnes of it. There's dogs' legs straighter than your line.' She fingers the beads round her neck. They're a match for her amber eyes, with old, dead things trapped in them.

'We wouldn't dare,' mouths Chrysanthemum behind her back, and glares madly when Rose gets the giggles.

Dolores evidently did overhear the freak show remark, because just as the Three Graces get to the fast mid-section of their waiting for returning heroes routine in the rehearsal, a rogue pin jabs itself into Orage's hipbone and spikes her viciously on every off-beat. She gets through the number but as soon as she reaches the wings she sucks in her breath and winces. 'Evil old bitch,' she gasps, scrabbling to remove it.

'Got on Dolores' bad side?' Spotty Maurice is still looking for an excuse to start a flirtation with the owner of the best BTM he's seen in seasons. 'You want to take care of that. She's famous for cutting out the gussets of her enemies. Esme the Undulating Escapologist got renamed Esme the Excessive Exhibitionist after you-know-who took her revenge. She didn't take kindly to being called Dolores Dogface. Esme's working in a chip shop in Scarborough these days.'

At Chrysanthemum's suggestion, the three girls pool their coupons and buy a packet of fig rolls to take round as a peace offering.

'Look what the cat dragged in,' sniffs Dolores, but she takes the biscuits faster than you can say Jack Robinson, and squirrels them in her pocket. Drawn by the warmth of the little room and the soft sigh of the samovar, the Three Graces hover in the doorway, shivering in their thin dresses. Their digs are a long walk away, sleep is hard to find in the lumpy iron beds lined up against the attic wall and Mrs Biswell has made it clear that there is no chance of hot water after dark.

'Well don't just stand there,' says Dolores, with a look that could be intended for anyone. 'Shut the door. You're letting a draught in.'

There is nowhere to sit apart from the floor, by the low chair next to the samovar, occupied by Janna and her skirts and shawls that give off a musk of earth and woodsmoke. So despite the foul-smelling fug from the pipe Janna clenches between crooked brown teeth and shiny gold ones, they perch there, warming their hands round glasses of tea, lulled into a soporific trance as Dolores runs lengths of fabric through the sewing machine and the mechanical rattle of its treadle adds to the rhythms from the crackling wooden radio and the strange sounds of the samovar.

In its burnished brass, Chrysanthemum finds herself looking at mirror images of a little Russian nesting doll and a china bear in an embroidered jacket, which stand on the shelf where Janna keeps her tea glasses and the tiny painted wooden saucers for jam.

They are nothing but shabby old ornaments, faded and worn, but as Chrysanthemum looks at their reflections through the steam from the hot tea, she sees them alter, transforming hazily into the figures of a girl whose skirt flowered with roses swishes above bare brown feet, and a bear with a gallant, jaunty air, walking on his hind legs and wearing a colourful coat. She leans in, like a child, like the little girl she used to be, the one who got into trouble talking to people no-one but she could see. They stopped coming as she got older, but Chrysanthemum remembers, how they felt as real as anything in her everyday life. And now… this feels real, too. She leans closer, peering to look, to see if the picture will solidify, clarify, and as she does, the figures appear go together deep into a forest filled with flowers. The bear bends his head to the girl and she raises her face to smile at him, as if they are the happiest creatures in the world.

Dolores notices her looking, and stops treadling her machine. 'Janna, tell these girls a story. This one's nodding off.' Chrysanthemum shakes her head, jerks out of her trance, sits upright, conscious of minding her manners.

Janna glowers. 'Pigs' arseholes, you tell yourself, I have no stories to tell.'

'Language. There's young ladies present. Tell them a bleeding story.'

So with a baleful glance in Dolores' direction, Janna spreads out her jewelled brown claws, and gathers the Three Graces round her as if they are children, into the musty folds of her woodsmoked skirts. She cocks her ear intently and listens to the sounds of the samovar, considering for a moment what it wants to say.

'Sas tai nas,' she croons, making music with the strange words. 'Sas tai nas. There was, and there was not.' And then she tells them the story of Kalo Dant, a boy who loved travelling so much that he found a way to visit the lands in the sky. Halfway through the tale, Chrysanthemum glances over her shoulder, to see what she can see in the samovar. But it is just the reflection of two old ornaments: a battered wooden doll and a chipped toy bear.

Dolores takes the next rehearsal too, and is even more of a slave-driver than the first time. Orage in particular comes in for the rough edge of her tongue.

'Handsome is as handsome does, and you, missy, may be very ornamental but you're not a lot of use unless you put your back into it and learn the steps. Tomorrow is the day you make your debut and we'll have Mister and Missus Wood and all the little Woods front of house if word gets out that the dancing in this establishment is of a less than acceptable standard. And then you'll be out on your ear and it'll be munitions work for you, which is all you deserve on the strength of what you've just shown me.'

'What we thought would be best is if she strikes a pose and we dance round her,' says Rose, trying to be helpful. 'She'll be the one they like to look at, you know.'

'I'll be the judge of that,' says Dolores, and she changes their positions in the line so that Rose is in front. 'Now let's see if you can convince me you have any talent. I've seen carthorses that can dance better than you lot.'

'Carthorses is like. Hihihi.' Janna's laughter, from up in the balcony, is like an old, rusty door, creaking in the wind.

'She means well,' says Rose afterwards, as Orage slumps dramatically on the floor, tears of anger glittering in her eyes.

'No she bloody doesn't. It's OK for you, she's put you where everyone will see you. But she's got in in for me. First she puts pins in my costume and now she's trying to make me look bad. She's just a spiteful, jealous old cow who can't stand the sight of a pretty face.' *Modesty is not one of Orage's qualities.*

'She's trying to get the best out of us,' replies Rose. 'It can't be much fun looking like that – don't be too hard on her.'

Chrysanthemum doesn't say anything. If pressed, she'd have to admit Dolores is right. Orage goes a long way on her looks whilst she and Rose do the bulk of the work: Rose doing the fancy stuff, Chrysanthemum making sure the space is filled. Orage is so dazzling that nobody has yet realised she's mostly marking time. But Dolores has noticed. And Chrysanthemum, who is beginning to have a sneaking suspicion that there very little escapes the attention of the beady-eyed wardrobe mistress, would very much like to know what else Dolores noticed, when she saw Chrysanthemum looking in the samovar, and why she changed the subject before it had even been mentioned.

Chapter 6

Sunday afternoon. Rather than spending her day off reading a book on her lumpy bed at Mrs Biswell's, Chrysanthemum puts on her hat and coat and finds herself drawn to Fankes. You never know if there might be a eye to be gladdened at the sight of a pretty face, and she might as well go somewhere, but there's no-one around, so she mooches outside the stage door and wonders what has happened to all the johnnies, or at least to the ones who by rights should have been keeping her company. She tries a sultry pout though her Veronica Lake peekaboo, but it's wasted on thin air. Not a fellow in sight, they're thin on the ground anyway and any possibles have evidently been bagged by the other Graces. Orage was very secretive about where she was going, which means a man, and Rose, despite being sworn to silence, gleefully informs her new pals that she's going on a date with Mervyn the Magus and then makes them promise not to say a word.

'He said I was to keep it a secret but I can't. But you won't tell, will you? He says it's no-one else's business, you see.'

'Keep it under your hat. It's all the rage these days.' Orage, on her way out of the door, shoots the well-worn phrase over her shoulder.

'Is your journey really necessary?' Rose nearly folds herself in half with the giggles.

'Keeping up morale? Ooh, I'd say so,' smirks Orage, and then she's off in a mist of Gay Diversion.

It's too late for Chrysanthemum to say 'don't do anything I wouldn't do' as Rose overtakes Orage all in a flurry not to keep Mervyn waiting.

Dolores, laden with brown paper parcels, finds a despondent Chrysanthemum smoking her solitary cigarette next to the back stage door. 'Oh dear, what can the matter be? All on your ownio?' Chrysanthemum nods glumly.

'You can come along with me, and make yourself useful. We've got The Rhythmettes in and that Phyllis will be chasing me round with her trombone if one of her girls shows what she didn't ought to while she's blowing her instrument because I haven't strengthened those seams before tonight's get-in. Here…' Dolores dumps most of the packages in Chrysanthemum's arms, and sails up the twisting stairs and through the corridors to her lair without a backwards glance.

They've been working for the best part of an hour, Chrysanthemum tacking and Dolores machining, the Home Service on the wireless because Dolores doesn't like to miss it even though she never has a good word to say about the acts unless Sylvester Sheridan is presenting, when there is a high-pitched whirring nose and the Jones grinds to a halt. Dolores, singing along in a powerful vibrato to She Was A Sweet Little Dicky Bird, tails off on 'tweet, tweet, twe…'.

'Dratted thing. I'm halfway up an inside leg. Bob down and put the kettle on whilst I get it threaded up.'

Dolores fishes out the empty bobbin from the base of the machine.

'Not the…'

'Samovar. Don't be daft. Kettle's much quicker.'

'Then why…'

'Makes her happy. Reminds her of where she came from. Heaven knows why she wants to think about that. She used to dance for the Tsar, but it didn't make any difference. What Hitler and his rotten sods are doing isn't new you know.'

'Where did the samovar come from? She can't have brought it all that way, can she?'

'You know what curiosity did. Now get a move on. We haven't got all day and these costumes won't make themselves.'

As Dolores bends her head to peer at her machine, Chrysanthemum glances quickly at the samovar next to Janna's empty seat. There they are, the doll and the bear, reflected in the copper. But as she looks, the picture changes, and Chrysanthemum watches the bear stand proudly to one side as the girl dances, just for seconds, like a stereoscope, whirling in spins so fast her skirts are a blur. So it was there all along. It isn't tiredness, or a trick of the light. She looked. She saw. Now, as then, when she was small, though it was more vivid then, an imagining so bright it was part of her real life. Now it's a fleeting glimpse of something not quite out of sight. A seeing that is almost a remembering.

'Stop daydreaming and pass us those bodices,' says Dolores, and the next time Chrysanthemum looks, the figures have gone.

'He asked me if thought I could fold myself up inside his box, and when I said I could, he kissed me right outside the teashop!' Back at Mrs Biswell's Rose in her nightie is beside herself with happiness, the sheet pulled up almost to her nose. 'His moustache doesn't half tickle! He bought an iced tea-cake and said it was all for me because I was his fairy princess! I did share it with him though.'

'You do set your sights low.' Orage, languid in her negligee on top of her bed, hasn't told anyone where she got to, but her cheeks are pink, and her eyes glitter. 'Half an iced bun and it's love. Switch that light out or Mrs B will shop us to the Warden. I can just see her gloating because she's got friends in the ARP.'

'Well at least I got something to eat.' If there is a bright side, Rose will look on it. 'What did you get up to, Chrysanthemum?'

'Nothing much. Helped Dolores a bit.' Chrysanthemum is glad the light is out and she can keep her thoughts to herself as the other Graces rustle and settle themselves in their beds. She doesn't say it, but the hours she spent with the grumpy old wardrobe mistress had been oddly companionable, and in a way she can't quite put her finger on, comforting. And the figures in the samovar, they'd appeared in front of her eyes, like a picture, a pretty picture, like something from an old fashioned magic lantern, but one just meant for her to see. It's coming back, she can feel it. Rising in her like breath. Like bubbles. Like hope. Perhaps here is something she is meant to see, something she is meant to know. That will make sense of her. She fingers the flannel of her nightdress, which is too short and makes her feel about twelve, and not at all a nearly grown woman. Wondering if she is about to step from one world into another, she closes her eyes, and as she drifts into sleep, it crosses her mind that she might have had the best afternoon of the three of them.

In time for Tuesday's matinee, the dingy little theatre transforms itself, as it does daily, into a glittering palace of wonders. Under the sparkling stage lights, the mangy velvet curtains seem sumptuous. The auditorium is packed with expectant faces happy to park their cares outside the stage door for the price of a ticket. In the auditorium, inside a low-lit booth draped with tattered lace and strings of beads, Janna does a roaring trade as women with their hearts in their mouths cross her palm with their hard-earned so that she'll look into the future and tell them whether the men they love will come safely home to them.

At the end of the last run-through – a mess of missed cues, Chrysanthemum's total inability to remember an eight-bar section in the middle and increasingly irate direction – there seemed to be only one thing for it and that was to hurl herself off the roof of Fankes' Music Hall rather than perform in front of people. But now she is here, in the wings, in a real theatre with real bums on real seats. Not in a cinema, dreaming of dancing with Fred Astaire. Not in her bedroom, practicing step combinations on a breadboard. Gussied up in tulle and sateen like the fairy off the top of the Christmas tree, with a face full of what Orage has taught her to call 'slap', watching Duckie and Dora perform the last moments of a skit that no-one will ever remember. *Except me, because these are the last moments when I will be old me, who dances in her bedroom and practices routines in her head whilst waiting for a tram, and dreams of one day standing here…*

There's Orage, mouthing her way through a sequence of steps, and Rose, stretching out, her face a mask of determined concentration. *And me, peering through the wings to see who has come to see us, on a wet afternoon in March… I thought I'd be terrified but it turns out I'm not…*

'Chryssie! Get your head back in! They'll see you!' As ferocious as her whispered command, Rose yanks her back into the wings. 'They're coming off any minute! Right, are you ready girls?

Rose may be the smallest and youngest but she is also the one who knows what she's doing.

'I'm in front. They're bowing... If you miss a step, follow me, though try not look as if you are... right, here they come, no, wait for His Gillpots, he'll announce us, then the music, here he is, yes, yes, la la la Mister Chairman, what a lot of big words for three young girls, okay, us now, deep breath, remember eyes and teeth, point your feet, keep smiling if you make a mistake, they'll never know.' The music – the tinny, shoddy music of their horrible tune, plinked out by Maurice on an upright in the wings opposite – pipes up.

'We're on!'

Carried out of the wings and onto the stage by the throwaway song they'll probably remember even when they've forgotten their own names, there is no time, only motion. Chrysanthemum doesn't have a chance to feel sick or scared because her feet take over, seeming to know what they're doing without the agency of her brain. Rose seems six inches taller and made of air as she leads them out. Out of the corner of her eye she sees a blur of moving feet at the end of Orage's legs. There is a sickening moment of cold clarity when Chrysanthemum realises she's spun to the left instead of the right and is now on the wrong foot. *Miss a beat, back in sequence. Phew.* And the next thing she knows, Rose has cartwheeled into the splits with her hands above her head for the finish and it's over, Chrysanthemum and Orage with their arms outstretched on either side as if to seize every scrap of the applause – the amazing applause.

'They're clapping.' Chrysanthemum can't believe it. But they are.

'Sssh!' She might have forgotten they're in front of an audience, but not Rose.

Chrysanthemum never remembers coming off stage that first time. Perhaps she floated. But she remembers the Three Graces, coming down the steps from the stage, then arms round each other, not being able to wait until they got back in the dressing room, jumping up and down and squealing. 'We did it! We did it.'

'I remembered it, well most of it!'

'We didn't fall over! And they liked it!'

The Three Graces are so wrapped up in their excitement that it takes them a while to realise that Maurice, Duckie, Dora, Varney, Albert, Sid and Joey are assembled in the corridor, clapping. Behind them, Phyllis Proudfoot and the rest of her Rhythmettes, five study ladies of a certain age, are beaming over horns varying from trumpet to tuba. Even Stella is there, wafting her palms languidly together. The only cast member not present is Mervyn the Magus, who is appearing on stage for his first set to a thunderous welcome.

'Well done kiddos. You were terrific.' Maurice bows, sweepingly, at Orage, and shoots his kindly frog smile at Chrysanthemum. 'First time on our stage, theatre tradition. At least, Fankes tradition.' He winks at her. 'You looked a piece of alright up there. I had my eye on you.'

Oddly, this makes Chrysanthemum blush.

'Very good, very good indeed. You merit a lemonade shandy, dear girls. After it opens, on me.' Joey shambles up to shake a hand, scrabbling in his oversized pockets for shrapnel.

The backstage door opens and a blast of cold air comes in.

'Look what the cat dragged in.' Stella turns her nose up but no-one is looking at her. The assembled crowd part as Janna glides up the corridor. 'You dance so nice.' The tiny, proud old woman touches her glittering paw briefly to her chest, then pats Rose's cheek. 'So next time is better.'

Dolores, bringing up the rear, marches to the front. Without saying a word, she casts a critical yellow eye over the costumes she's made, pulling Orage's headpiece into position, shifting Rose's waistband and yanking Chrysanthemum's bolero where it has come adrift.

'That'll need a stronger fastening before tonight's show. Look at you, bursting out. Now go get into what you're wearing in the next half, and get me that sharpish so I can put a stitch in it.'

She pulls her musquash coat tighter round her shoulders and turns to go.

'Dolores.'

As she hears Chrysanthemum's voice she looks back over her shoulder. It's not a friendly expression.

'I can read you like a book. You're fishing.'

'I'm not, honestly, it's just that…were we…?"

'You weren't bad.' Dolores licks her little finger and runs it over an arched eyebrow. 'Not too bad anyway. For jossers.'

Chapter 7

Next morning is a bright and breezy day that blows three rosy-cheeked Graces, flushed with their success, to the theatre. 'Lovely day for some,' remarks a woman with a worn face, pushing a pram into the wind. *Yes, it is. I have found my feet.* The tricky corner step is no trouble at all when she tries it out on the pavement, so she does it a few more times, Rose and Orage joining in and not one of them caring that they are making a spectacle of themselves in the street. *The thing Mother was always so fearful that I would do.*

As they bounce round the corner, Janna is an altogether peculiar figure outside the theatre, crouching on the floor over a box so that from above, her outstretched arms in her shawls resemble a great, brightly coloured, fluttering butterfly crash-landed onto the pavement. As they get nearer, she kneels up, clutching something to her chest. In the daylight, her wrinkled brown skin has the texture of old paper, and the wispy plaits looped beneath her headscarf are the colour of carrots, as bright as the shiny coins threaded through them, where the henna has dyed her hair orange.

'What have you got, Janna?' Rose kneels next to her, and holds out her hand. When Janna turns to her, it is with faraway eyes. In a rapture, she places a beetroot in Rose's outstretched palm.

'Look!' Janna points at the box, piled with enough beetroots to feed a small army. 'They leave for me to say thank you! So kind! Tonight there will be borscht and we will make feast!'

'Tonight there'll be pink poes, and doubtless sore heads,' grumbles Dolores, weighing up like a barge in full sail and taking in the whole sight. 'Don't touch them girls. Those stains won't come out and if you're dancing with red hands you'll be the three disgraces and small wonder if you're out of a job.' Dolores points at Chrysanthemum, who obediently lifts the box as if it weighs nothing and follows Dolores to the kitchen.

Rose picks up the note that dropped from the box.

> *'He has come home at last and thanks to your words I never gave up hope even in the most troubled times,'* it reads. *'God bless you and your kindness, and I hope these beetroots will warm your heart as well as fill your stomach. Yours, Mavis.'*

'D'you think she can? Really? See the future?'

'Rose, you really must stop being so gullible. She's a big old charlatan, that's all.' Orage steps round a fallen beetroot. 'I'll admit she's utterly and completely spooky, but it's all bogus. Just because someone looks the part doesn't mean they can actually do it. There's no such thing as seeing the future.'

'I'd rather be gullible than cynical, Miss Snooty-Pants.' Rose bends down and carefully picks up the beetroot. 'I bet she can. Why shouldn't she? There's something about her. I wonder if she'll tell me my fortune.'

'I expect she will if you cross her palm with your hard-earned. I'll look into your future for nothing, Rosie-posy.' Orage waves her hands as if parting the waves. 'Oooh, the mists are clearing…I can see…a tall, dark, handsome…magician. He's got his magic wand in his hand…he's waving it about…Rose, Magical Mervyn is going to have his wicked way with yooouuuuuuu.'

'Tell us something we don't know,' says Chrysanthemum over her shoulder. 'I'd best wash my hands. I've got beetroot stains all over them. I hope Dolores is wrong and it does come off.'

'What do you think?' Rose trots to catch up with her friend. 'Do you think she can? Do you think anyone can? See the future? I wonder what they'd see in store for us? Do you, Chryssie?'

'Honestly Rose, you do go on.' It isn't a conversation Chrysanthemum particularly wants to join in with, or at least not yet. Her mother might not be the only person to look at her askance. But she smiles to let her friend know she doesn't want to hurt her feelings. 'There's no reason why she shouldn't. There's loads of things we can't explain. Like where people get to on their afternoon off. Can we, Orage?'

After the second show finishes and the audience all make their way though the blacked out streets to their beds, word gets round that there is a party, and the air hums with excitement. Mervyn the Magus produces a bottle of whisky from his hat, and winks at each of the Graces in turn as he tips a tot into their teacups. 'Watched you in the wings ladies. A very pleasurable sight to behold.'

Mervyn isn't the only one who has found a bottle. It seems as if each of the Rhythmettes has secreted hooch in her instrument case, and it's produced with coy winks and a lot of elbowing as the five old girls egg each other on. Janna presides over a cauldron bubbling with hot, sour, rich red soup, which she ladles proudly into tin bowls, tea mugs and even jam jars as word goes round the theatre that there is enough for everyone, and all are invited. A little worse for wear, the Rhythmettes play and sing jazzy tunes from their glory days, and Dolores, who has been drinking whisky from a teacup as she vamps along on the piano, gets up and dances a very showy black bottom to rounds of applause.

'You know that is dance based on cow who is stuck in the mud.' Janna points proudly at her friend. 'I think she does just like.'

'Don't let her get too tiddly or she'll do her party piece,' whispers Maurice. He's been on the receiving end of a rebuff from Orage, who called him 'the hand-wandering ASM,' so he's sidled up to Chrysanthemum instead, and topped up her glass from the bottle in his hand.

'What's that then?'

'Well, these days if she's had a few she can pamp Colonel Bogey. But, and we're going back a long way here, when she was with Jeffcocks Jollies, she used to be famous for what the Yanks called cooch-dancing – like a shimmy, only more rude. And then right at the end, she used to get this chair in her teeth – just an ordinary chair mind – and swing it round. She'd definitely got the moves. If it hadn't been for the face fur, she'd have gone to Hollywood. That and the business with Tira and Mustapha. Blimey, have you got hollow legs? More?'

'Tira? Who's Tira? Yes please. I love cherry brandy. Mustapha?'

'Bert from Barnsley really. Snakecharmer. Back in the old days. She was a terror. Well, she still is. And she'd never have left Diddikoi Dora after Medved went.'

'Medved?'

'Sock in it young man.' Dolores, who appears from nowhere, grabs Maurice by the ear, and twisted it hard. 'You know what careless talk costs.' He yelps, and she twists it again. 'In this case, yours. And I don't care if your Pa is His Gillpots. Bugger off back to whichever hole you crawled out of, and if you so much as say one word out of line, I will grind you into the ground like a tent peg. Isn't it time you were in uniform? Oh I am sorry - you need to be a man for that. Chrysanthemum, you've had too much of that cherry brandy. Sit down next to Janna, and behave yourself. I've got my eye on you.'

Fuddled enough to be careful about doing as she's told, Chrysanthemum sits quietly next to the gas ring, where the old lady guards the remains of her borscht like a hawk.

'She give him thick ear?' Janna smiles proudly. 'Must be he deserve it. He may be big boss's son but blabbermouth still.' It's on Chrysanthemum's mind to ask Janna about these new names but it's warm near the stove, and what with that and the whisky, and the cherry brandy, Chrysanthemum finds herself drowsily drooping towards sleep. Struggling to sit upright and stay awake, she peers at the gas ring. Where the air meets the heat, lines of haze appear and as Chrysanthemum's heavy eyes follow them, form into shapes. Dreamily, she tracks the patterns, *like when I was small and I used to see things, gosh that used to get me into trouble*, and then shoots bolt upright as the tiny blue circle of burning gas turns to fierce flames. Through the mist she could swear she sees the girl and the bear running, running wildly, running into a forest as sabre-wielding men on horseback strike down any figures that try to reach screaming figures trapped in burning wagons.

'Everyone went home after that. They heard you shrieking over the music.

Janna slapped your face to make you stop and Mervyn helped me to get you home. It wasn't real, Chrysanthemum. You probably had a bit too much, Mervyn said you were mixing your drinks which is never any use. You must have been seeing things.' Rose wraps her arms round her friend and rocks her as they sit on one of Mrs Biswell's lumpy beds. 'It was like a nightmare lovey. You just had a funny turn. Look, drink your cocoa. It's not very nice because it's mostly water but it's hot and I braved waking up Mrs Biswell to go down and make it.'

'No.' It comes out half wail, half moan. 'I thought it was real. It wasn't just that I should have stuck to the cherry brandy. It's why Janna came here. Chrysanthemum sort of said, though she wasn't going to tell me. I just never realised it was so terrible.'

'Then we must be extra kind to her.' Rose hugs her friend fiercely. 'It probably is just you imagining things but even so, poor old thing. She's about a million years old, isn't she? I noticed when we saw her in daylight. And it probably was cherry brandy on top of everything else. You should see my Nanna when she's had a few. She'd swear black was white. I bet your ma never let you near anything stronger than sherry did she? Now get in that bed or you'll be like a rag tomorrow. I wonder where Orage hopped it to? I hope it's fun, whatever she's up to. I bet she's in a nightclub, with an older chap. Wouldn't it be more useful if you could imagine that, instead of awful things that happened before you were born?'

Chapter 8

In the first half of Friday's matinee, Rose makes her debut appearance as Magical Mervyn's glamorous assistant. She lays herself in his magical box as if she has been doing it all her life, and emerges unscathed and beaming after he withdraws each of the 24 lethally sharpened blades that he tests by slicing a wisp of gossamer silk in mid-air before slotting them into the box's sides with ferocious elegance.

'That was a right laugh,' she whispers to Chrysanthemum as she wriggles out of that costume and into her Three Graces outfit in the interval. 'He gave me a little kiss in the wings after, and said he knew I could do it. I'm glad he didn't do it before I went on or I'd have been all of a-flutter. Orage is cutting it a bit fine, isn't she? If she doesn't make it before the half do you think you could...?

'Sorry, sorry, sorry, got the wrong tram.' Despite her words, Orage doesn't look the slightest bit repentant, or flustered. In fact, she looks like the cat who's got the cream. The slight smile lingers entrancingly on her face throughout their number, softening the glances of the audience when they see her and increasing the applause. After the show, and with a pretty, dismissive wave of her nicely manicured fingers, she leaves the theatre without a world of explanation.

'TTFN.' There's no response as the door closes on Orage's departing back. 'I said, toodleoo!' Rose erupts into giggles.

'What shall we do now Rose? See if they've any elastic at Rowbottoms? Or have you got to practice slotting into small spaces? Talking of, my liberty bodice is getting terribly on the saggy side.'

'We'll do that tomorrow. Let's go and see Janna.' Rose uses any excuse she can think of to seek out the old fortune teller. 'I want to tell her about being Mervyn's assistant. There might even be a wet if we're lucky.' She sets off towards Wardrobe. When she gets there, she doesn't beat around the bush. She's like a puppy. 'Hello,' she says brightly, nodding to the bundle of flowery rags. 'We liked your story so much the other night, Janna, that we hoped you might tell us another one. Is Dolores not here? May we come in? I've just debuted as Mervyn's magical assistant, and it went ever so well. It's a good job I'm so bendy.'

Beaming, Janna gets up, beckons the two girls to her, then fusses over the samovar, which quickly begins to hiss and moan and bubble.

'No, she is looking for elastic. Always Dolotka is looking for elastic, she walks miles looking for elastic and today she has heard that there is some at Rowbottoms. So she go. I think she will get, or there may be some trouble. So Chrysanthemum, is sore head today? Is probably not only one. And Rosie is making two jobs now in show, dancer and also something else, very good, very useful, is never in show only one act, you do what needs, sing, dance, sell tickets, feed monkeys even. I also. Come, sit, sit, and listen to the song of the samovar. Its stories are old, and have been told many times, so is better. Much better than the crackling of that … box of bengorros over there.' She points in disgust at the radio, then busies herself with the whole ceremony of jam and glasses and saucers, until everything is ready and she can settle down, and draw the girls to her.

'But first you give to me.' Janna looks beadily at Rose, who immediately scrabbles in her bag and comes up with a sixpence.

'Is all?' wheedles Janna. 'For you I make special. Is worth sixpence only?"

Chrysanthemum delves into her purse and finds a shilling. An enchanting smile spreads over Janna's features, which so beguiles the girls that neither notice that their fingers no longer hold the proffered coins.

Like a vixen running its tongue round its snout after a feed, Janna licks her lips and tucks her booty into a money belt hidden at her waist under layers of greasy floral fabric.

'Now I will tell you good story.'

Her voice takes on a dreamy quality.

'There was and there was not, a long time ago, a king who had three sons,' she begins, in low, sing-song tones. 'And then he had another son, and the king called him Kalo Mitras, because in the language of the people, Kalo means black, and this boy had brown skin and his hair was as black as the night and his eyes sparkled like the stars.'

Lulled by the sing-song cadences as Janna tells her tale, Chrysanthemum nonetheless notices that Rose has folded herself into Janna's skirts and is leaning against her, listening to the story like a child. And she notices the wooden doll and the china bear, but she can't see their reflections, because Rose has sat in such a way that her body blocks Chrysanthemum's view of the samovar.

'That was nice,' says Rose afterwards. 'And perfectly normal, considering. I bet you feel better now. It must all have been a figment of your imagination.'

And Chrysanthemum smiles, and hopes her friend was right.

Orage pulls the same stunt after the next day's matinee, but this time Rose has a plan. 'Shall we follow her? Instead of your elastic. Dolores will have got it all anyway, even if she hasn't got coupons. Let's see where Orage goes.'

She's definitely up to something. Chrysanthemum can feel it. But what would be worth keeping from her and Rose? The only thing she can think of would be Mervyn. Surely she'd never do that to Rose?

'She always leaves by the stage door and if we go by the fire escape she'll never even think of looking for us.'

Swiftly swapping stage clothes for day clothes, the two leftover Graces push open the fire-escape just in time to see Orage's blonde head disappearing round the bend. She's walking fast. Scurrying to match the pace she sets with legs so much longer than theirs, and ducking, giggling, into doorways when it looks as though Orage might be glancing backwards, they keep her in sight as she marches to a street full of handsome houses, and looks around. As she does, a long grey automobile draws up beside her. Its passenger door opens from the inside, Orage gets in, and the door closes. Chrysanthemum and Rose duck behind a handy hedge.

'Did you see who it was?'

'It must be an officer, Rosie. Must be.' At least it's not Mervyn. But who is it? 'Only officers have cars like that.'

'Well if it was me keeping up morale with an officer I'd want everyone to know about it. Wouldn't you? Why couldn't he meet her outside the theatre? That's what I'd do.'

Chrysanthemum shakes her head. 'She doesn't want anyone to know, though, does she?'

'Maybe he's married. He must be older. She is bad. I bet he's rich though. She'd never be interested in anyone that wasn't.'

'Rose, you think someone's rich if they buy you a bun.' The sight of her friend's eager face makes Chrysanthemum smile. 'Thank goodness for you, Rose. Everyone's got things they don't want people to find out, except you. You are a nice change.'

'If you look for that stuff, I'm sure you'll find it. Did I tell you Mervyn had invited me to tea with his mum? He said she used to be a chorine too, so he said we'd have loads to talk about. He said he's got something he wants to ask me. I think I know what it is, too. I think he's going to ask me if we could be a double-act.'

Something has been bothering Chrysanthemum for a while and as she can't get the answer to the question about Orage she's going to ask it. 'Rose, why isn't Mervyn in the forces?' He is the only young man Chrysanthemum knows who isn't in uniform.

'Oh, he's got bad feet,' replies Rose happily. 'I bet you anything you like Orage's gentleman hasn't got bad feet. I bet he's a Yank though.'

Rose's dual role as Mervyn's assistant means a rushed change for her during the number that separates the two acts. It has become usual for her to join Chrysanthemum and Orage in the wings, flying up the stairs with seconds to go before their entrance. But if she is out of breath, the audience never notices.

'He reminded me about the red apple,' she hisses this time as she slots into her place ready to lead them on.

Chrysanthemum only has time to wonder what she means before their music starts. And once they're safely back in the wings and in their wraps, Rose rounds them up and shepherds them towards Mervyn's dressing room.

'He asked me special, for you to drop in.'

'Blimey, that was tight. I thought I'd lost the furry little sod for a moment there.' Mervyn, appearing in front of them from out of nowhere, clasps a rabbit firmly by the ears and raises it until he's looking into its startled eyes. 'You stay with me sunshine or they'll lose all their illusions. No running off or you'll be Irish stew and I'll be joining the ranks of Mister Churchill's unemployed.' He plonks a kiss on the rabbit's furry head and tucks it under his arm. 'Fancy paying a social call, ladies? It won't take the whole half to get changed, will it? Refreshments on me.'

Clutching the scrappy crepe kimonos Dolores has provided as backstage coveralls over their sweaty sequins, Three Graces trail after Mervyn and his rabbit.

'You can tell he's top of the bill because he's got a primus.' Rose's stage whisper carries. Chrysanthemum's eyes shoot towards her hairline. 'Rose how do you ...' until Orage rams an elbow in her ribs. 'Do that backwards step?' she squawks, and Orage pretends to trip her up so that she crashes through the door into Mervyn's dressing room and has to save herself from falling onto the rabbit's hutch.

'Make yourselves at home, ladies.' The Three Graces squash themselves into the corner and Chrysanthemum wishes she could make herself invisible. *There's too much of me, no wonder I'm so clumsy, don't know what to say or where to put myself, look at Orage, all bones, and Rose who's barely there and then me all bristols and bum and belly and thighs, what was I thinking, coming here. It's different when people look. Well, men. That makes it alright if it's admiring.* She could make sense of herself then, know what she was for. But Mervyn doesn't look, or not in that way. *You clumsy great gawk.*

The Three Graces are expecting tea at the most but with a great flourish, Mervyn produces a shiny silver cocktail shaker. 'Now you see it,' and it vanishes behind his back. 'And what have we here? Well I declare. Sidecars, by the look of them. We'd better polish them off before they turn into lemonade.'

'That's awfully jolly. Bottoms up.' Orage, completely unphased by being offered strong drink in the interval by the star at the top of the bill, winks over her glass.

'Not for you, Rosie-Posey.' She whisks the glass out of the girl's hand before her lips touch the rim. 'Chryssie and I can lump along even if we get tiddly but we need you to know what we're all doing.'

*There really isn't a single fly on her.* Chrysanthemum sips her sidecar and otherwise keeps her mouth shut.

'What do you think of it here, girls?' Mervyn perches on his dressing stool as elegantly as if he'd been on a film set.

'It's lovely. We're having such a nice time.' That's Rose, of course.

'Our digs are appalling and it's a miracle we don't reek of cabbage and mothballs. Still, mustn't grumble.' Orage tips her glass again.

'You certainly all look the part. Dolores hasn't lost her touch, then.'

'Do you know her?'

'I wouldn't say that, Rose, but I know about her. My mother was a chorine, you see, in the Jeffcocks days, so she used to tell me all the stories. Dolores, and Tira, and Janna and the bear. She told me all about them. Even Miss Maude, though I don't know as she ever clapped eyes on her. It was her reputation that went before. I was glad to land the gig here, just to be able to see it all for myself.'

Mervyn smiles, and Chrysanthemum finds herself liking him. *He's eager… something curious about him which makes him… Not quite one of us, but not that different either.*

'There's a lot of Jeffcocks people here, aren't they? Can you fill us in a bit on who's who?' Orage makes it sound as if she's at an elegant soirée.

'Jeffcocks was a circus, just a small one but it had some good acts, but when old High Lee passed on he was the last of his family and Billy Fankes from the music hall took most of its acts over. Of course my ma had long gone by then, she'd got married and moved down south, where I was born, but she used to tell us all the stories. To be honest with you they were such tall tales I think she made a lot of it up, but it was her bit of excitement, dancing in the circus. Travelling around, meeting all those people the flatties don't get to meet. There was even a tiger, at one point. I used to love all her stories, even if I didn't believe the half of them once I was old enough to see sense. You can see why I was glad to get the booking.'

Travelling around. Just a small circus. There was even a tiger.

Chrysanthemum had only been small but she remembers that circus.

She remembers that tiger.

## THE GRAND PARADE

What with Rose turning up, and the samovar being brought out of retirement, its song is being sung for the first time in a long time.

'We should have jam, really. Is there any going begging?' *Trust Rose to remember the jam. She always did have a sweet tooth.*

'There's marmalade. Will that do?' Chrysanthemum makes the journey to the larder, roots about, dumps a jar on the table.

'And plates. And spoons. We might as well do it properly.'

'Get her, Lady Muck. Swans in after all these years and she wants plates and spoons. '

'And stories. What's the point of the samovar if it doesn't tell us stories?' *I stopped looking for the stories because I only ever knew the middles. Not the beginnings, or the endings. Or how they fitted together.* That's why she buried the samovar out of sight in the glory hole. But there is Rose, who has been missing for all those years, and has walked in and made the years fall away. And maybe that is an ending, or a beginning, because aren't they, in a sense, the same? And because of Rose the samovar is there, in front of her, on the table.

'I can do without a plate. We can eat it from the jar. Save washing up. And you can start telling me a story. Now it's boiled. And we've got the marmalade. Come on Chryssie. Let's have another cuppa.'

So because it's Rose, Chrysanthemum refills the teapot from the samovar, and when she looks through the layers of grime covering the brass, she's searching to see the reflection of the Three Graces. But even though she gives it a rub with a tea towel, all that comes to her is a pair of legs – sturdy, small-girl legs, running. And when she starts to talk, it's to tell a story that has to start somewhere, if not at the beginning.

*Her own story.*

'When I was small – no, when I was just about to be six, because I begged to be allowed to go for my birthday – the circus came. I'd never seen a circus, never been inside a big top – it was something Mother made it clear we didn't do in our family. The next-door neighbours' kiddies asked if we wanted to go along with them to see the parade. "I don't think so," she said. You'd think they'd asked if we wanted to go and sit in the coal hole. "It's my birthday," I wailed, but there was no budging her.

'More than anything I'd ever wanted, and without knowing why, I wanted to see that parade, but I knew if I asked again, there'd be no arguing with her. So I ran away – not very far, because I was little, but running, all the same. They told us at school that the parade would come down Hardcastle Lane before it went into the park, so on Saturday morning I said I was going to the shop for some sweets and I ran all the way there. I didn't stop to think about what I'd say when I got back. I was that desperate to see it. And I did. I got a leg-up from some lads so I could stand on the wall and I saw it all, and I never forgot it either.'

Rose is giving her full attention, just like always. 'Go on,' she sighs. 'What did you see?'

'There were horses, with girl riders glittering with spangles, and little dogs in red coats, and clowns, and a ringmaster, of course, in his bright red coat and a high top hat, which he lifted to the crowds, as if to say, welcome, welcome. I saw six elephants, each one ridden by an Arabian dancer. Right at that moment I knew that it should be me, up on top of one of those elephants, in a dancer's costume. I swore to myself that as soon as I was able, I would run away to join the circus, or – as it turned out – the nearest thing I could get to it.'

Rose, who has been quietly spooning marmalade into her mouth, nods her head. 'You did as well.'

'After the elephants, there were two wagons with a tightrope between them, and a dancer in a fluffy pink tutu doing arabesques on the wire. A pierrot lolloping along with a sweet, sad face – I liked him much more than the other clowns, pulling silly faces, falling over their great big stupid feet. Everything I saw made me sure that this was where I belonged. There was a great bear, a huge brown thing, dancing at the end of a lead held by a tiny woman in the widest skirt I'd ever seen, all covered in flowers. And best of all – there was a tiger on a string, and it was being led by a woman in a cape made of silver and gold, with white hair, and although I couldn't see her face because she was wearing a veil, she had the same eyes as the tiger, yellow and fierce. I knew I should have been afraid, but I wasn't, not a bit of it. And even more than I wanted to see the parade, I knew I wanted to get closer to that woman. And that was when she spotted me.'

'The woman?'

'No. My mother. She must have followed me, and come up behind me on the wall. I felt this hand on my ear and as I turned round she twisted it so hard I yelped, and pulled me out in front of everyone who was watching the parade, and dragged me home. It wasn't just the pain. It was the worst thing that had ever happened to me. She didn't say anything, which made it worse, because I knew when we got home it would be added to everything else I'd ever done that she didn't approve of, and that she'd never forgive me for.

'And then this strange thing happened. The woman with the tiger came out of the parade, they both had the same walk, more a lope really, and she stood right in front of my mother, and she didn't say anything, she just looked at her, and then at me, and then at the tiger, and my mother let go of my ear, and took my hand, and we walked home without her saying a word. She must have been terrified, when I think of it – a tiger, after all, though you don't think that when you're a child, that it could eat you, you just think it's wonderful. But she never mentioned it again. It was never referred to, any of it. It was as if it never happened, and so I began to think I must have imagined the whole thing, or dreamed it maybe. But I've never forgotten it.'

Chapter 9

Even lounging on the narrow attic bed, Orage makes a glorious sight, all elegant peach limbs and elegant peach crepe teddy. *That mess she's made, discarded nylons and underwear, cigarette boxes and sweet wrappers, would turn Muriel's stomach.*

'Thought you were out.' Chrysanthemum is annoyed that Orage is keeping things from her, and annoyed to find there is someone else in the room. She came back early on purpose to have it to herself so she could have good look at her chin in the mirror. She distinctly felt a couple of new hairs when she powdered her face for the matinee and she wanted to given them a good tweezering before anyone noticed.

'I was out. But I came back. As you can see.'

'Gentleman caller not very exciting then? Who is he anyway? When are you going to tell us about him?'

'Who said anything about a gentleman caller? Idle talk costs lives Chryssie, you know what they say.'

Orage winks enormously, raises herself on her elbow and waves a box of confectionery towards Chrysanthemum. 'I've eaten most of them, you'll be doing me a favour.' She swings herself upright, levering herself off the bed in a single motion and going to the small wardrobe. 'Best get dressed. Can't turn up for showtime in my smalls.'

'Bet there's a good few would have their day made if you did.' Chrysanthemum mentally contrasts her sagging liberty bodice with Orage's handmade underwear, and tries not to wonder how she came by it, or the rose and violet creams.

'Who have you been seeing then? You didn't get these from the corner shop.'

'That would be telling. And not nearly so much fun. Anyway, time to get on.'

Unable to stop herself, Chrysanthemum picks up the mirror.

*They were definitely there.* Whilst Orage's back is turned, she quickly makes a grab for the longer one, and pulls. It brings tears to her eyes, and she dabs at them with a handkerchief.

'Aren't they buggers?'

Chrysanthemum does her best to pretend she'd been tweezering her eyebrows and isn't flustered at all.

'I get them too sometimes too,' smiles Orage. 'Buggers, aren't they?'

Chrysanthemum defiantly pulls out an eyebrow hair that has done nothing to deserve its removal. 'I've always had untidy eyebrows.'

'Eyebrows,' replies Orage, raising hers: two sleek arches, not a straggler in sight. 'Like I said, Chryssie. Buggers.'

There is no sign of Dolores the next morning, let alone the vanished Mr Digsby. 'We have come down in the world.' Orage arrives late as per, but it doesn't stop her from looking down her nose when she saunters onto the stage to discover that Janna is standing in as rehearsal mistress. 'She's practically geriatric. I'm going to phone the agency to see if there's anything going in panto.'

Janna, though, makes Dolores look like a soft touch. 'I don't see any dancing, I see only steps.' Her eyes flash as she says it and she is nothing like the sweet, smiling old soul who flutters round the theatre making borscht for everyone and his dog and telling stories from another time while the samovar sings its strange song. 'What I am watching? Is exercise only, not dance. You listen to the music and you dance to it. Again.'

Again and again the Three Graces put their best feet forward, and each time, Janna increasingly smoulders with disappointment. 'Until you show me what is inside, what you do is not dancing.'

'Show us then.' Orage, flushed and insolent in all her blooming youth, has never looked more beautiful. 'Show us how it's done.' Next to her Janna seems dried with age into a brittle twig. 'Go on then, you dance,' she taunts. 'Then we'll know how. Won't we?'

Rose pulls at her arm. 'Stop it. Stop it. You horrible thing.'

Chrysanthemum joins in. 'Just because you don't want to do it again. Stop it. I don't know what's got into you.'

'A lot more than has been getting into you, I can tell you that. At least some of us are making the most of being young. You can end up like them if you like, but I never will.'

'I will dance.' Janna's voice is no louder than the rustling of a dried up leaf but it commands attention. Brittle twigs and dried leaves start fires. It only takes a spark for the light to catch. 'You will watch me. And then you will know what it is to be a dancer.'

Slowly – so slowly that Chrysanthemum is convinced she can hear Janna's bones creaking and cracking – the old woman pulls herself upright. Shoulders stretch down, back, and then jerk forward. Head sitting proudly atop a neck that now seems impossibly long, her black bird's eyes flash as she raises her arms above her head. Then, with no accompaniment beyond the snapping of her fingers and the tapping of her feet – one-two, one-two – she begins a slow, rhythmic dance, on the offbeat, like no other the Three Graces have ever seen. Janna's many layers of fabric seem to crackle, lit from within. The girls don't know whether to draw closer or stand back. They might get burnt. They can't stop watching.

'That made me feel a bit shaky,' mumbles Chrysanthemum. 'Nobody will ever watch me like that.' Orage looks down at her feet. 'Me neither.' *From her, what an admission.* Rose has tears running down her face.

'They didn't let just anyone dance for the Tsar you know.' Dolores has appeared in the wings and looks more than usually boot-faced. 'I need all of you. Fourteen suits of chain mail for the Lyceum for Henry V have got moth in them. They'll want boiling, unravelling, then re-knitting and spraying. It's all hands to the pumps, ladies.'

Janna brushes her fingers down her skirt, appearing to send sparks of electricity through the material, and looks up brightly. She smiles, all sweetness, and is transformed again into the old lady who nurses her samovar. 'We come,' she says, and sets off briskly towards Wardrobe singing 'A Long Way to Tipperary' as if it were a Russian march. Rose falls into step next to her and joins in. Chrysanthemum looks at her friend's apple-blossom face smiling next to Janna's wrinkled windfall one, catches a glimpse of the future, and feels wistful.

'Chin up, droopy-drawers.'

Dolores struggles to heave a hairy, lumpy sack towards Chrysanthemum. The girl picks it up absent-mindedly, easily, stands with it in her arms, but doesn't make a move. She hasn't come back to earth yet. She's somewhere in the woods, in the dark, staring into the embers of a fire that only moments before was dancing flames.

Dolores leans in close enough for Chrysanthemum's nose to prickle with a waft of stale grease and Ashes of Roses, and prods her with a fat, beringed finger coated in grime.

'No time for dawdling. I've told His Gillpots they'll be ready for the dress, and they aren't going to launder themselves. Stop gawping, you'll catch flies. And get a move on.'

The Three Graces have never seen anything quite like the suits of chain mail that Dolores pulls, one at a time, with tongs, from the sack. The girls have never worked so hard, either. Orage is in charge of the kettle, boiling and reboiling it as each suit is placed in a tin bathtub and covered in scalding water to kill the moths. Janna, armed with a stick, stands over the tub, adds paraffin and stands in the steam, swirling and poking each suit. Dolores wrings them out in her strong hands without taking her rings off and Rose and Chrysanthemum hang them out to dry, empty the tub, and repeat the process until all fourteen saggy, soggy suits are flapping in the breeze of a blustery day.

Dolores sits down heavily. Usually immaculate, her apron is damp and her hairnet has come adrift. 'That was the easy bit,' she says, ominously.

'Do you want us to come back after the show?' Chrysanthemum pipes up.

'Goody-goody,' hisses Orage. 'Teacher's pet. She'll be getting paid for this, it's an outside job, not work for Fankes. You can count me out. Some of us have got lives to lead.'

'I can't,' whispers Rose. 'I promised Mervyn I'd meet him after the get-out.'

'You'd better unpromise him then.' Chrysanthemum surprises herself with how cross she sounds. 'And you, Orage. It needs doing, we agreed to help and I don't see why it should be just me. I'm off for toad in the hole at the café, if there's any left.' She stumps off, leaving the others looking at each other in surprise. Rose and Orage pull a face at each other, and laugh.

'No rest for the wicked I suppose.' Orage swings gracefully to her feet. "Come on, let's tell Mother Superior she won't be doing penance on her own.'

All the blackouts are down when the Three Graces make their way to Wardrobe after the show. The big room is spookily dark, lit only by candles in jam jars, and filled with a percussive clicketty-clacking: Dolores and Janna, crouched over big wooden needles, knitting at top speed. Their eyes are ferocious in the low light, as if all the energy in their old bodies is concentrated, stitch by stitch and row by row, in creating the new suits. The girls are set to unravelling the remaining twelve suits and working the horrible, harsh, hairy painted wool into balls. After a couple of hours, Mervyn pops round the door with a tray of mugs of tea and slices of hot cheese and potato pie. 'Room for a little one? The Lyceum sent it over, tuck in, it's not half bad.' Dolores and Janna down tools for refreshments but as soon as the mugs are empty and the crumbs have been cleared, they're off again, working up to such a relentless rhythm that it makes the Three Graces pick up speed as they unravel and roll.

'It's like being in a fairy tale – one of the Grimm ones, where things aren't nice at all,' says Rose. 'We're going to be stuck here forever unless one of these suits magically contains a handsome prince who comes along to rescue us.'

'And if he does come it won't make any difference because the two old witches who have kept us prisoner have cast a spell that means we can't leave until we've turned this nasty string into suits of finest cashmere.' Orage looks in anguish at her hands, beginning to chafe with the hairy wool.

'If there was a handsome prince he wouldn't fancy me anyway.' *Perhaps she should admit that she's miffed that her friends have got gentlemen callers but not her? Not that there is anyone to fit the bill, but wouldn't it be nice if there were, and after everything Muriel threw at her?* 'It'll do you two good to have a night off.'

'What, trapped in the witches' lair with only fourteen suits of armour that aren't going to turn into princes for company? Precisely how the rest of the world live. Sometimes, Chrysanthemum, you are strange.'

'And you with your mystery gentleman caller that no-one ever sees,' says Rose protectively. 'That's not strange at all, Orage.'

Chapter 10

'It'll be all eyes on you tonight girls.' Dora's face is lit up with mischief as she comes off stage, lips twisted with mirth under the pencil moustache, which has smeared. She winks: mucky face and a mucky mind. 'You'll be a proper sight for sore eyes.'

'Why? Who is it?'

'Chryssie, ssshh. We're on in a sec.' Whispering in the wings is not allowed and Rose is strict at showtimes.

'Well who is it then?' It's unusual for Orage to sound flustered.

Duckie shoves Dora towards the steps down from the stage. 'The Tommies are in,' she mouths, and winks. 'Give 'em a good show, Graces.'

'I love a man in uniform.' Orage recovers her equilibrium, and her voice carries.

'They'll hear you!'

'Be quiet! That's our music!'

Rose may be out of the wings with perfect timing but Chrysanthemum is a half-beat out and as she looks at the stalls she can see why she's lost her focus. As the Graces hoof their way forward to the footlights you can feel from the stage there's a charge in the air. Friendly, boisterous, and male; quite enough for there to be a head-turning whiff for a young dancer on heat. They've crammed out the first two rows, a whole battalion of them in front of the usual crowd of women and children and old folks. They're bright-eyed and Brylcremed and some of them a bit boozed up, shuffling forward in their seats to get a better gander at the three young dancers.

'That's a bit more like it! After all them old codgers!'

'Bring on the dancing girls!'

'Eyes on the prize boys!'

They may be in a pack and a few may be a worse for wear and on the sweaty side but they're all cheerful and some are handsome fellows and every one of them is grinning up at the Graces as if his face is about to split. It's enough to make a young girl's head spin.

The soldiers' faces merge into a blur as the Graces go through their routine but every time Chrysanthemum spins and spots her eyes land on a face that sharpens into focus with each repetition: a clean-cut, square-jawed, moustached young face, whose light, clear eyes lock onto her as she goes round. When the number comes to an end and she glances at the audience from under her lashes as she drops into a curtsey, he's still looking. This time, though, he smiles and as he does something starts to fizz in her, and when she's back in the wings she crosses her fingers that she's right and he'll be looking again when it's time for their next number.

And he is, and this time she smiles back. She watches what that does to his expression, how a kind of dazzled hope turns his expression into one she wants to see again. She remembers this, this version of her, the effect she can have, and she dances the rest of the number for him, and drops her curtsey right in his direction.

'We saw that,' grumbles Rose as the Three Graces make their way from the stage. 'The whole bloody audience saw that. His Gillpots won't want you flirting with the soldiers, Chryssie. Not on stage. Don't you remember what he said?''

'She doesn't care, Rosie. Look at her. She's not listening. One sight of a young man with a Clark Gable 'tache and she's gone with the wind.'

Still, she knows her moves. Keep him waiting, just long enough for him to wonder. Orage and Rose have both disappeared into the night before Chrysanthemum leaves the theatre. He's there at the stage door like she knew he would be and she's glad she's taken the time to re-do her lipstick and arrange her hair prettily.

'What's your name then? Johnny?' She hopes she sounds just a little bit like Orage.

'Reginald actually. Reggie. Would you like one of these?' He's younger than he seemed from the stage, but still handsome, and the look of admiration in his eyes reminds her what she's been missing.

He proffers a pack of Woodbines and she notices his hand shakes slightly as he lights their smokes. It makes her feel warmly towards him as well as excited.

'You were awfully good. All of you, I mean. But you in particular.'

She knows that can't be true but she likes him for saying it. She likes him for being there. She likes the version of herself his liking her is letting her be. She likes the fizz and fun of being flattered and flirted with. She squints at him through the smoke of their shared cigarettes, and there is no reason she can think of not to like him. So they find a pub and get in a couple of drinks before closing time, and he makes her laugh, and their hands somehow meet across the table, and he tells her that this is the last night of his leave, and asks her would she walk round with him a bit, only instead of walking it turns to a bit of a cuddle, and what with cuddling and giggling the next thing you know he's gone in for a kiss. And there's no reason Chrysanthemum can think of, no reason whatsoever, why she shouldn't kiss him back.

'Aren't you lovely?' Reggie comes up for air. 'Aren't you something a bit special?' He takes Chrysanthemum by both hands and twirls her in the street, round and round, so that her head's spinning again, and she can feel herself getting carried away and not wanting to do anything to stop it. As he comes in for a hold, her arms go round him and without even thinking about it she's holding him by the waist, the great strapping soldier boy, holding him and lifting him and picking him up, as if he weighs nothing. As if he's as light as a feather.

'I say. I've never met a girl could do that before.' She realises that she's standing in the street with a young man aloft in the air, and hurriedly puts him down as it crosses her mind that nice girls don't kiss Tommies they've just met, they don't go walking in the blacked-out streets with people who've waited for them by the stage door, and they certainly don't pick them up and whirl them around in the street, but Reggie grabs her even closer and kisses her again. 'I want to do this all night. I want to get on that train tomorrow and think of your lips every inch of the journey.'

This time it feels as if Reggie is embracing the strange, devouring Chrysanthemum in mouthfuls and she, pressed up against him, is just as hungry. It's not precisely about Reggie, but it is because of him, or more precisely because of the version of herself she is with him. And if she wants to, and she does, she can be that version for the rest of the night. Orage has gone off with her fancy man, and Rose has made her way to Mervyn and his magic tricks, and there is no reason why she shouldn't do as she pleases. It's gone to her head, the whirling and the flirting and the kissing.

'There won't be... anyone else. Where I live. You could...'

That's a thought to make Reggie's eyes light up. An invitation he isn't at all inclined to refuse. They make their way at full tilt on sure feet through the darkened streets, quickening their steps until they're inside the door, then up the stairs, two giddy kippers, Reggie carrying Chrysanthemum in a fireman's lift so there's only one set of footsteps. She tries desperately not to giggle until he almost drops her on the second landing so without thinking she picks him up and slings him over her shoulder and carries on up to the attic landing.

Once inside the room they're on top of the bed and all over each other, clothes scattered across the floor, arms and legs and hands and knees and all sorts of bumpsadaisy, Chrysanthemum down to her cami-knicks and Reggie saluting like a proper trooper, and who knows how far it might all have gone, when the door is flung open.

Chrysanthemum looks over Reggie's shoulder to see Mrs Biswell standing in the doorway with a nightlight illuminating a face like a hen's bottom.

'I knew it. From the first time I clapped eyes on you. You disgusting little trollop. You can sling your bloody hook. Immediately.'

Reggie sits with Chrysanthemum on the pavement as dawn breaks but as the cold light filters across the sky there isn't really been anything to say to each other and although he gallantly asks for, and writes down, her name, she's been thrown out of the address she could have given him and it's almost a relief that he has to go.

'I'll write to you at the theatre,' he promises, but she knows that even if he does, it won't matter.

'It was lovely,' she says kindly. 'You were lovely too. And they were ghastly digs. Now off you go, you mustn't keep them waiting.' She watches him walk away from her, and waves when he turns around, before he goes on his way, getting smaller and smaller and less and less important in her life. And then she is on her own, and no idea what she is supposed to do next.

At daybreak, Mrs Biswell comes out and waits on the step for Orage and Rose to return, arms grimly folded, pointedly ignoring Chrysanthemum, who is smoking and trying to make it look as if there is nothing unusual whatsoever about sitting on her suitcase in the street.

'I am not running a bawdy house and I made it perfectly plain that gentleman callers are not admitted, and certainly not in the bedrooms.'

Mrs Biswell motions Orage and Rose through her door with her thumb. The disgusted expression on her face warns them not to say a word.

'You've got half an hour to clear out and I'm not tarring you all with the same brush but I won't have a mucky trollop under my roof and that's all there is to it. There are some sights that the Lord did not intend me to see. I knew it from the start. You'll all be as bad as each other. So out with the lot of you.'

Chrysanthemum follows them in and carries their cases down from the attic, belongings stuffed in willy-nilly, and plonks them on the pavement.

'Girls, I'm so sorry, really I am. We thought the coast was clear.' She can barely look them in the eye. *What was I thinking, what on earth was going through my mind, and now we have nowhere to go and it is all my fault.*

'Did she?'' Orage and Rose blurt it in unison. 'See him? I mean, all of him?''

'Most of him. And quite a bit of me as well. Are you shocked?'

'Well a bit,' admits Rose. 'Was he the one from last night? That was flirting with you from the stalls?

'I am, but not because you were keeping up morale. Only because whoever he is has left you to deal with it.' Orage's worldly wisdom has never been more welcome.

'He only had the one night and his division were off first thing. It's not his fault. He was a nice chap.' Chrysanthemum can barely remember what Reggie's face was like and she can feel the anxiety stirring as if it's something alive inside her that's waking up. *They must think I'm awful. I am awful. First the drama of running away and now this.*

Rose sits down next to her on the case. 'It's not really worth making a fuss about. I don't really care that we can't stay in that horrible B&B anymore.

Theatricals are always getting thrown out of their digs, it's just one of those things. But we are in a bit of a spot.'

'I wish we could have seen her face.' Orage joins them on Chrysanthemum's other side. They are sandwiching her with kindness. 'I bet she looked fierce. It must have put him right off. No wonder he legged it back to the boys.'

It is the first time the Three Graces have really laughed together in days and as long as it lasts, the anxiety balling in Chrysanthemum's stomach subsides. Clustered together on her case, they cling to each other, setting each other off until their sides hurt.

'What a spot I've got us into.' Chrysanthemum shudders once they've laughed themselves out and the fluttering anxiety returns. 'I really am sorry. Where on earth are we going to go?'

'I expect I can manage to wangle a hotel for tonight.' The other two's ears prick up.

'Does this mean we get to meet him?' Rose is ever hopeful.

Chrysanthemum answers for Orage, whose silence speaks volumes. 'No,' she says. 'It doesn't.'

Orage's eyes are suddenly downcast. 'I'm sorry girls. I shouldn't have. I wasn't thinking. I'd better go.' She stands up and picks up her case. 'I'll see you at Fankes. I really am sorry.'

For the second time that morning Chrysanthemum watches a person walk away from her. This time, she feels a part of her heart going with the retreating figure, and it hurts.

'Should we go… ?'

'No, Rose. We shouldn't. It's my fault anyway. She'll tell us if she wants to, and if she doesn't, we can't force it out of her, can we?'

'But what if he's dangerous? Chryssie, everyone knows about…'

'I don't know, Rosie, I don't know what to think about that, except that if he wanted to, he's obviously had lots of chances where he could have, and he hasn't has he?'

'I suppose so.' Rose furrows her brow. 'That does make sense. But the rest of it doesn't. She knows we're all worried about that. It is a bit rotten of her. I wish she'd tell us.'

'Me too, but we'd best leave her to sort out her own mess, if she's in one. We'll see her in a bit. At least she's got somewhere to go. And in the meantime, we'd better find somewhere too.'

'I bet he's married. He's bound to be. Oh, poor Orage. She deserves better than that.'

'She does. But it would explain. Yes, of course it would. Anyway, she knows where we are.'

'And we've got to go to…'

'Work. I know. And if it comes to it, we can probably sleep in the dressing room, at least tonight. I'm sure we'll be able to lump it.'

Rose's face beams at her, not a trace of rancour or resentment, and Chrysanthemum gratefully passes over her gasmask case and handbag.

'Don't think I'm not dying to know too. You take those. Leave the cases to me, Rosie.'

They plod along in silence for a moment until Rose pipes up. 'Cheer up Chryssie, we'll be OK. We can kip down in the dressing room tonight and see about finding somewhere else.'

Chrysanthemum's heart may be lighter, but there is a sudden downpour so they're drowned rats by the time they reach the theatre. Dolores, clad in voluminous oilcloths, is furiously hammering at the stage door, which is hanging off a hinge. Janna is attacking the edges where the new hinge should join with a rasp. She shows brown and gold teeth in a crooked smile at the girls. 'Lasharas o wudar.' She gestures proudly at their work.

'That'll be double Dutch to them,' mutters Dolores through a mouthful of nails. She eyes the suitcases. 'As Madame Maximova has just explained, and any fool could see if he had his eyes open, we're repairing the door. Don't tell me you've got chucked out of your digs.'

'How did you know? Did Janna see it in the future?'

'She didn't need to. Never mind crystal ball, you could see that one coming a mile off. You want to watch it, giving the boys the glad eye. You wasn't exactly keeping yourself to yourself last night, was you, Miss Muck? You'd be best off coming back with us. We'll show you the way after the evening show.'

Dolores gestures that they should go through the door. 'I'll finish this. Go inside with Janna and get dry.' She gives the hinge a determined thwack with her hammer.

The sound of her braying echoes though the corridors as the girls go with Janna. She appears to glide though the theatre's passages, and where her headscarf and the top layer of her shawls and skirts have got wet, there's the illusion of a rising film of steam, as if the moisture were being chased away by fire.

'I never even thought they might live somewhere apart from Wardrobe.' Rose whispers as Chrysanthemum heaves their cases after the two old ladies through a tangle of backstreet terraces and into the wasteland that borders the woods nearby. Dolores' coat of squashed blonde musquash, topped with a diamante-encrusted velvet turban that, like the coat, has once been splendid, give them something to follow in the unfamiliar darkness. 'I thought they were just... part of the theatre. There stopped being any houses a while back. I wonder where we're going.'

They soon find out. A path, veering off the main road with a roughly painted old sign saying 'Egypt Lane', leads through the woods to a clearing. A half-moon casts a silver glow that blackens the outlines of trees into silhouettes, and illuminates a crow that flies down and wheels round them in a circle, cawing on its approach to Janna, before taking off again. Chrysanthemum and Rose shudder as they peer round.

'They call this Devil's Kitchen,' announces Dolores over the hooting of an owl. 'No-one comes here. Just us.' She gestures round the clearing as their eyes adjust. Parked to one side is an enormous showman's wagon, gleaming with paint and polish so that it glistens in the moonlight. Beyond it, barely visible in front of the trees, is the tiniest, most rickety bowtop the girls have ever seen.

'Rose can go in the vardo with Janna and you, Chrysanthemum, can come in with me.'

Chrysanthemum watches as Rose skips happily towards Janna's caravan, then follows Dolores up the trailer's steps, and catches her breath as the door opens and a stale fug of Ashes of Roses invades her lungs. Once inside, she looks around in amazement. As Dolores lights the lamps, the yellow glow reveals a long, narrow living area surrounded with bevelled mirrored cabinets that reflect the ceiling of duck-egg blue paint embossed with birds and garlands of flowers. Shelves heave with crystal glasses and gilded china. There's no blackout paper but not a chink of light escapes though kippered swags of heavy cream damask over the windows. Any unmirrored surface is lined with posters, handbills and old framed photographs, presided over by an imposing portrait of a much younger Dolores, in diamante-encrusted satin and a feathered headpiece. Next to it, a framed oil painting shows the rear view of Dolores waiting backstage to make an entrance. Every possible surface is covered in a lifetime's collection of costumes: spangles, sparkles, fishnets and fleshings, all tumbled together. Dolores sweeps an armful off what is revealed as a chaise longue.

'We'll make you up a couch here, you'll be nice and comfortable. I can't be doing with lumpy beds.' Dolores pulls out an armful of bedding from one of the mirrored cabinets: a quilt in salmon satin; flannel sheets; a tartan blanket. All smelling of must and mothballs, but still, luxurious. *No lumping it here. Blink and life changes. The world turns upside down. Surprises pile upon surprises.*

'And if you get cold in the night, we'll leave this out for you.' Dolores picks up a heavy red velvet cloak from the chair opposite. It's lined with thick black silk padding, only slightly shredded. 'I used to wear this when I was waiting to go on at Ringling's. Second half. I was the attraction. Sideshow – not the big top. Still. It used to get ever so chilly in those tent shows.' Dolores shakes her head as the memories fall out. 'You won't feel any draughts through that. Japanese quilting.' She disappears through a door that leads to her sleeping area, and reappears shortly afterwards in an apricot lace negligee and curlers, waving a bottle of gin. 'We'll have a little nightcap, shall we?'

*Sometimes life alters as suddenly as scenes change in the theatre. In a sudden twist of fate, Chrysanthemum and Rose are removed from the world of flatties and ticket buyers. The curtain falls, and rises again, and there they are, in the world within the woods which is where*

Janna and Dolores pass their time. A world with its own ways. A world where unreal things are everyday occurrences. A world where seeing is believing.

And here we still are. We think it's the past but. After all these years. The show has moved on but look at the evidence. The way the set has been dressed. There is the portrait of Dolores, over the mantelpiece now, which an art gallery came asking after, though I soon told them to mind their own. They were offering quite a bit, but how could I part with that? Though I might leave it to them. She'd like that, being admired by the punters. But it's part of my life. All her pictures. All her things. There is Janna's cabinet card, which catches, even though she has faded, enough of the essence of her I can see what the Tsar must have seen when she danced for him. I'd never dare get shot of the samovar. And now, all these years later, here is Rose, making her entrance again. We have never quite left the world that we found in the clearing in the middle of the forest. So here we are again. Waiting for the next act.

*ACT TWO: BEFORE YOUR VERY EYES*

Chapter 11

Chrysanthemum watches out of Dolores' etched glass windows before bedtime to see the fire still burning outside the bowtop. On any night she might see Janna sitting on her haunches, smoking her pipe and watching, beaming and clapping, whilst Rose practices acrobatics and a new scissor-kick that looks as if she's doing the splits in mid-air. Sometimes a crow flies down from the trees and settles on the bowtop, for all the world as if it, too, wants to watch Rose. Such a thing wouldn't be out of place, in this strange new environment. Sometimes she catches glimpses of a little fox, its mask and brush disappearing into the undergrowth. Sometimes Chrysanthemum thinks she might see other things too, and seeing has a way of turning into believing.

Changed circumstances swiftly become everyday life. Reunited for the first time in the dressing room, Orage looks oddly tentative until Chrysanthemum pointedly asks to borrow her Max Factor and Rose follows it up with a request for a squirt of scent. Orage hands over both with grateful haste, and The Three Graces patch things up without a word being said about Orage's gentleman.

'Is your hotel nice? It's lovely and snug sleeping in the vardo.' Rose rolls up her much-darned stockings and puts them in her attaché case. 'Much better than in that awful bedsit. I used to hate Mrs Biswell. And Bibi sings songs and tells me stories while I go to sleep.'

'Bibi?' Rose has started to smell of woodsmoke. Orage, in contrast, obviously has access to a bathroom with hot water, and is even more expensively fragrant than before. She wrinkles her powdered nose.

'It means auntie,' explains an unperturbed Rose. 'And she's going to show me how to cook over a fire. She says there are all sorts of things to eat in the woods if you know what to look for. Go on, give me another squirt of your Je Reviens then.'

Orage holds the atomizer at arm's length and sprays her friend liberally. 'Now you,' she says to Chrysanthemum. 'I'm the only one of the three of us who smells like a woman. She smells like a bonfire and you smell of carbolic. Is Dolores turning you into a skivvy? Come here, let Monsieur Worth work his magic. It's very effective – I can vouch for it.'

'You'd better be taking precautions,' mutters Chrysanthemum, blushing. The words 'is he married?' are on the tip of her tongue and she swallows them.

'No need to worry on that front.' Orage sniggers, and follows up her perfume assault by attacking Rose and Chrysanthemum with a giant swansdown powder puff.

'She still hasn't told us where she's staying,' hisses Rose when Orage nips off to spend a pre-show penny.

'And neither will she, til she's ready. But from the look of her, she's not roughing it. So put a sock in it before she gets back. She can piddle faster than you say Jack Robinson.'

It's all so much fun in the daytime, dancing and giggling in the dressing room between shows with the Graces, that what she's started to see in the woods almost slips Chrysanthemum's mind. Always when she's tired, or during the times between night and day that are either the end of one thing or the beginning of another. On the way back to Devil's Kitchen, in the dark, or when she nips out of the trailer in the night for a pee, or first thing, when she wakes up, and looks out from the trailer window. Sometimes it's just the night creatures: badgers, stoats and owls, stripped of their colour and silvered in the moonlight as they go about their business after darkness falls. Sometimes she's thought she's seen Janna, moving silently beneath the trees, blending into the foliage as the night light strips the faded tints from her patterned clothes, only the glint of her gold coins giving away that it's a person. Sometimes, when she's looked again, all she's seen is the small, brown fox whose eyes glow gold.

Once or twice, when the moon has been full and the little fox has enticed her into following, she's let herself be drawn further than sense would suggest. In the silent spaces between the sleeping trees, she's cast around to make sure she's far enough into the woods not to be spotted, except by the vixen, and given herself over to the moonshine, and danced. Throwing herself from tree to tree, whirling with her face turned to the stars, raising her arms above her head, and dancing to music only she can hear as a strange, wild energy thrills through her body. She loses herself in this dance in a way she never can on the stage, and after the surge has passed through her, she feels strangely calm, and oddly elated. She knows that this dance is only for herself and, perhaps, the brown fox, and when she is fully awake she remembers it as if it was part of her dreams.

Sometimes, though it's usually after Dolores has slipped her a nip of bedtime gin that makes her head spin, she'd swear blind there she's seen other things. Not dreamlike at all. More solid than suggestion. First of all, a ghostly form resembling a swaying figure in a ballet tutu, high in the air between the trees, almost invisible, coming in and out of focus. As she peered, it seemed to hold a parasol aloft and attempt to walk in a straight line en pointe.

Maybe that time it was a bird, the crow that sometimes comes and settles on the bowtop, or maybe she needs spectacles, or perhaps her imagination was playing tricks on her. That, or the gin. But the wispy apparition of a sad-eyed clown, perching on the trailer steps? He looked up with a winsome expression aimed directly at her. Then the insubstantial little figure gave her a gentle smile that stretched until – as, with perfect balance, he lifted a leg to demonstrate – he could put his foot in his mouth. There was something so harmless about him, as if he were asking her to like him, that Chrysanthemum found herself smiling back, not frightened at all, but bubbling with laughter. The little clown dissolved into nothingness, fading away until only the shadow of his smile remained, leaving her wondering if she'd conjured him.

They aren't all endearing though. A brassy blonde makes the hairs prickle on the back of her neck when she shakes her fist in the direction of Chrysanthemum's chaise-longue bed. The apparition's expression is of such unmistakable rage that Chrysanthemum is unable stop herself squealing in fear.

At the sound, Dolores materialises from outside, where she's been stashing off-ration groceries in the belly box, solidly alive and reassuringly dismissive. 'Here. Have a boiled sweet. Residents been making your acquaintance? Don't worry about them. They can't get in and they won't do you any harm. It's because you've been touching their things – they can come through now. The quilt was Tagalong's and you're sleeping under Tizzy's comforter.'

'Tagalong? Tizzy?'

'Clown and tightrope walker. As for Tira, that's my own fault. I shouldn't have given you those old drawers of hers to clean the windows. I'll give you a duster, then she won't come through. But don't you worry about her.' Dolores places such emphasis on the word 'her' that Chrysanthemum startles.

Dolores glowers venomously at the corner of the trailer next to the door, shaking her fist in the direction the blowsy blonde appeared. Setting her jaw, she turns back to Chrysanthemum as if nothing untoward has happened.

'It's not always a blessing, having an imagination. What you need is a nice knitting pattern to stop you lollygagging. Look though that lot and see if there's one you like.'

She removes the polishing cloth from Chrysanthemum's hands and replaces it with a stack of patterns.

Chrysanthemum, who has spent her whole life walking on eggshells around Muriel, isn't used to sticking up for herself, but it's not every day that you find out you're being visited by the spectres of bygone circus performers. It's far too significant for her to be fobbed off with a knitting pattern.

'Who are they?' She hopes she doesn't sound truculent, if only because she doesn't want to get Dolores' back up. Or further up. 'I mean, I know who they are – they're in the photographs on your wall, or at least some of them are. But why are they here?'

'They may be shadow people now, but in their time they were show people.' Strong teeth flash through Dolores' beard in a grim smile. 'They don't feel they're themselves if no-one's looking at them. You know the saying: the show must go on.' She looks closely at Chrysanthemum. 'You're not frightened of them are you? It's not the first time for you, not by a long chalk it's not.'

Chrysanthemum looks back at Dolores and realises that the old lady isn't mocking or incredulous or disbelieving, just paying attention to her. Dolores bares her teeth. 'Seeing is believing, that's what show people say. Believe me, I've seen a lot of things. You do, in this line of work, and you're in it too now, so you might as well start getting used to it.'

'It's not the first time.' *What a weight off to say it. Imagine the relief when you don't have to hide something you've kept under your hat for the whole of your life.*

'I've been seeing things I can't explain ever since I was small. But no-one ever believed me so I stopped saying anything. There used to be a litter of puppies in the attic. When I was little. They were adorable – I used to go and play with them. I thought everyone could see them. I got walloped to within an inch of my life when I told my Ma. She said I was a cuckoo in the nest and I must never tell anyone what I saw. And I never did, and then until I came to Fankes it sort of went away, and I thought it was just something that happened when I was a kid. But now it's started happening again. I don't know what I'm supposed to make of it.'

'We've all got secrets,' said Dolores. 'It's the way of show people. Everyone's got a story that they might not want to tell. Don't worry, I'll keep yours. And don't you be in too much of a hurry to find out what you don't need to know.'

'But if they let me see them, then perhaps they do want me to know. I wish they didn't. I didn't want to see the figures in the samovar. That was the first time.' *What a relief to talk about it.*

'In general, if people want you to know something, they'll tell you. Or not, as you well know, with your fancy friend and whoever it is that's keeping her in cosmetics and the rest of it. Otherwise, keep your eyes open and your thoughts to yourself. Janna came from the Carpathians a long time ago because the Cossacks burned her settlement. She had a dancing bear with her. It's not uncommon, with her sort. That's all you saw, so you can put it out of your mind. And while we're at it, what about one of these?'

'Why didn't you tell me earlier?'

Without prompting, Dolores has just answered her unspoken questions about Janna, entirely matter-of-fact, when she'd previously been so cagey. And it's wrong-footed her. But she hasn't told her anything Chrysanthemum doesn't already know – just confirmed it in a way that firmly closes the door on that subject. *Now I don't know what to think.*

'No one likes a nosy parker. And only a fool tells their business to any Tom, Dick or… Chrysanthemum. Now chose a sweater or it'll get chosen for you.' She stands over Chrysanthemum like a hawk whilst the girl thumbs through the patterns.

'I like that one.' It takes a long time to decide so she picks the third pattern in the pile. 'But it's too complicated for me.'

Dolores looks disgusted. 'You're not going to let a knitting pattern get the better of you, are you? Show some ambition for goodness' sake. I'll give you some wool and get you started and if you get into difficulties you can ask me about it. You could do with brightening up - you'll look nice in apricot.'

As Chrysanthemum sits through Monday morning's weekly run through, Mervyn – fingers all a-blur as he flips cards from a deck Dolores has already taken great pleasure in pointing out is 'rough and smooth' – emanates something electric that makes her giddy.

'Madam, the card you are holding is the ace of hearts,' he says, and tips a wink in the direction where Rose is standing, and whose heart wouldn't be set fluttering, just a little bit?

Even Orage, who isn't the slightest bit inclined in his direction, has to admit something strange flows from Mervyn.

'It's only table magic,' remarks Dolores in a stage whisper that for once doesn't carry. 'I can see right though him. I've had better than that with liver and onions. If he's got the fluence I'm the next Empress of China.'

She pronounces the as 'ver' and draws herself up into a tight, cross bundle when she realises no one's paying a blind bit of notice. All eyes are on the main event, which is Mervyn, and to Chrysanthemum, watching not just from the wings but at his effect on Rose, it's not just on stage but off as well. And if she's really honest at close quarters there's something about him that's just a little bit head-spinning. Tilts the world on its axis so that everything around him is transformed. The same, but somehow different. A little odd. A little charmed. Perhaps, even, a little enchanted. Whether she likes it or not, and right at the moment she's not at all sure she wouldn't, if he was to turn it in her direction. Johnnies are all very well but, well, they're johnnies. It's not at all the same as being singled out by the star.

She knows she's being wretched. And he's not all that, not really, just that he reminds her a bit of Errol Flynn and that there hasn't been anyone since Reggie. And it's only hand tricks, now you see it, sleight of hand and cards that have been treated with gum Arabic and soap powder to make them textured or slippery. Before the war a good magician would have had assistants to bring his tricks to life and don't think Dolores hasn't regaled her with the stories. Whilst he was doing one thing, making passes in the air, diverting the audience's attention, a top-of-the-bill stage magician would have other forces at work to create the illusions. The Indian Rope Trick. Levitation. Escapes. Human forces; mechanical forces.

But the world is at war and has fallen on hard times. Making do and mending, not just with clothes but with everything else too. Duckie and Dora, Sid and Joey, Albert Emery and ghastly old Stella Maris, all brought back from the knackers' yard to tread the boards. And there Mervyn is, the shining star set off by a batch of old has-beens, out there on his own producing rabbits from hats and charming the birds, if not from the trees, then from the back of the stalls, and bringing feather dusters to life. But even so there's something about him that's binding, like the beginning of a spell. You can't not watch.

Magician, though. His stock in trade is things done for purposes of concealment. What's he really up to? Where did that thought come from? But he's not in the forces, which is in itself a peculiar thing, and even though he seems happy with his lot, with his rabbits, with helping out behind the scenes, he must want more. Of course he must. What is revealed, in his line of work, is of necessity a long way from what is true. His stage name is Mervyn the Magus, and a magus isn't limited to parlour tricks. Magus means master, and Chrysanthemum is wondering what direction he sees his mastery taking him.

Of course there's Rose, and where does she fit in? She looks at Rose, who is looking at Mervyn, who is looking at the strings of sausages that he's producing from his hat, and the penny drops in its slot. Who wants to pull bangers from a topper for the rest of your days? No wonder he's so taken. The smaller the better, Mervyn says, so open and admiring as he looks at her. Sizing her up. The key to a better life. Rose so doll-like, as light as wire and just as flexible. Rose who could fold herself small and disappear, or reappear, at will. Rose so fearless that she could take any risk, and with so much sweetness that her being lifted by her hair, or at the end of a fingertip, or folded into a box and run through with swords before emerging alive and smiling, would seem like a miracle. Rose, the perfect assistant. With Rose at his side, Mervyn could be the Magus of his dreams, and cast a real enchantment. But she'd have to be the keeper of his secrets. And if she isn't? Will she get magicked away, like the rabbit and the pigeons?

If she knows too much. If he lets her into his secrets. Is that a risk he'll be willing to take? If she knows how a trick works. And threatens to give it away. His secret. Perhaps all Mervyn sees is what he wants in Rose, and who he can be with her by his side. He sees that she's small, and sweet, and light, and pliable. He can't see that she's made of will, and wire. He doesn't look, and so he cannot see what Rose is really made of. He sees a means to his end. He sees that with her, he could have power. Presence. Prestidigitation.

Chapter 12

Dolores may not have let Chrysanthemum in on any secrets, but there is an odd comfort in the way the bad-tempered bearded lady so matter-of-factly accepts what other people find strange. Cleaning out Dolores' prized Spong of what looks like scraps of fur after Janna purloins it for her latest batch of pirogi, Chrysanthemum looks down at the unlovely mincing machine and realises she feels more herself here than she ever did with Muriel.

No-one would ever describe Dolores as maternal, but she's oddly companionable. Every night after the last show, Chrysanthemum scurries down Egypt Lane and through the unlit woods, in a hurry to be back in the trailer. She waves goodnight to Rose and then climbs the steps, opens the door just a chink and slips from the wild wood into an Abdulla and Ashes of Roses-scented fug that feels increasingly like somewhere she might belong. Dolores, splendid in her apricot lace negligee, with a teacup filled with gin in her hand, invariably reads the riot act about something – the Spong night it's all aimed at Janna: 'I could be doing with the dozy bint if for once in her blasted life she took her head out of the clouds and bothered to think about what the gristle does to my blades' – but once she's got whatever it is off her chest, it never takes much to get her going.

Like Janna, she always begins her stories the same way. Unlike Janna's stories, with their incantatory 'sas tai nas...', Dolores' always start with an obscenity, or an insult. 'That effing tightrope walker.' 'Stupid sod of a clown.' 'Great nelly of a liontamer.' Regularly enough for Chrysanthemum to suspect Dolores might have been fond of him, there is Usnavy, 'that bleedin' tiger,' who'd been given, as a kitten, to the show when it travelled to South Africa.

'He used to sleep on that sofa where you are now. And wherever we went, we used to take 'im into schools so the kiddies could look at him. Ever so good he was, he never had one of their heads off in all the time I had him. Never even tried. He was ever so good-natured.'

There are a couple of snaps: Usnavy, rolling on his back on the sofa with his giant paws in the air, and Usnavy, on a lead held by Dolores in her blonde musquash, with a schoolboy's head between his jaws. 'Not one of them he ever bit, though I would have done. Little bleeders.' It doesn't come as much of a surprise that Dolores isn't fond of children.

'But he was a devil for escaping.' Sweet-tempered even as he sought his freedom, the Usnavy who pads his way through Dolores' memories would seem to smile as he tried, and often succeeded, in slinking away from the circus.

'I used to get him back with a bun. It was his weakness, a nice bit of cake. Still, bleedin' thing, he'd run us a right old dance.' There is a note of approval in Dolores' voice as she says it.

Then there are the characters from the glory days of Jeffcocks Jollies. Dolores was born into the touring circus and now that she has, in her way, made their acquaintance, Chrysanthemum particularly welcomes the stories of 'dozy sod' Tagalong the clown who kept putting his foot in his mouth, and Tizzy the 'pie-eyed tightrope walker', who learned the art of balancing when she was a child in Donegal, by keeping her eyes firmly fixed on heaven in the hope of being granted a vision of the Blessed Virgin.

'That was before she turned to the hooch instead of the holy water,' snarks Dolores.

Then there is Glaswegian Joan, who chain-smoked, drank gin and kept the books until showtime when she transformed into Farah Shahani the Persian Queen, so graceful she appeared to float on air, and her sidekicks Ruby Floozie the Little Egyptian, a cheerful, chatty, foul-mouthed little soul who came on directly after Joan for contrast, scowling furiously as she whirled and swirled with knives sharpened to a razor's edge in her hands, and the fiercely beautiful Little Rahnee, who didn't need a weapon of any kind because in her jewelled hands a silk veil turned into a lethal weapon of seduction. There is High Lee the ringmaster, in his stacked shoes and spangled red coat ('soft sod he was').

Though there are many stories, one that is never mentioned is the provenance of the samovar. And what you are not told then becomes what you are most anxious to find out, but Chrysanthemum knows better than to push for tales that are not offered freely. She enjoys listening when Dolores is in the mood for telling. And despite Dolores' continual assertion that it is only going to be good for a dishcloth if Chrysanthemum doesn't try harder, the cardigan is coming along nicely. And then, perhaps as a reward for Chrysanthemum's efforts, out of the blue there is the story of how Janna came.

## FUN FOR ALL THE FAMILY

*Janna was picked up at the docks when the boat from Hamburg came in. Found in the hold, no more than a teenager, a stowaway with a mangy, famished bruin wearing a ragged Russian officer's coat for company. Word of their arrival spread on the wind. Ma told High Lee what was coming, and sent Cyril the strong man with a chinking purse and two tentsmen to secure her release and bring the pair of them back to Jeffcocks. She howled as if the undead were on her tail when they parted her from the bear and tied it to a stake in the lot, and the bear roared fit to frighten away even the most stouthearted beastman.*

*Half-starved she might have been, and tired to the bone, but she hissed, scratched, spat and clawed as we tried to hold her down and strip her of her clothes. As the rags were torn away, the sheet beneath her turned black with lice.*

The tentsmen were outside, stationed by the tent flaps, puffing their pipesmoke into the autumn air, billyclubs at the ready if Ma's new acquisition tried to take off.

'Ma. She'll scratch my face. I thought you said she was worn out with wailing. She's filthy. She's like an animal. What d'you want her for? Why can't we just leave her?' She could have had her own act, the Little Whinger, my sister.

My ma stood like a pillar, taking as much notice of Tira's objections as she did of the flies over her head. She looked at the girl on the pallet at length, taking in the rags and filth, just a bag of bones with burning eyes she was. Ma must have seen something to her satisfaction cos she nodded to herself as if she'd made up her mind. When she finally turned towards us, all you could see through her veil was a dull topaz gleam where her eyes might be. She never needed to raise her voice, Ma.

'I've had her feet tied so she's not going anywhere. Tira, take these shears. As you appear to dislike her so much, you can have the job of shearing her. She won't scratch your face when you've got these in your hand. And burn the hair. It's riddled with eggs. Dolores, once her hair's been cut off, you pour that kerosene over her and rub it in.'

Petulant and truculent she might have been but Tira still took the shears. Notwithstanding the brandished blades, the girl turned wildcat, flailing, kicking and scratching as much as the ropes that bound her to the pallet allowed, until she managed to sink her teeth into my sister's forearm.

'Ma!' There was blood as well as toothmarks where she'd been bit.

'Dirty diddikoi look what she's done. She's wild, Ma.'

'That, Tira, is why I am going to so much trouble.' The quieter Ma spoke, the more you knew she meant it. 'I know what she is and I have a good idea of what she can do. She — and that bear — will be a draw. A big draw. You are looking at Jeffcocks' new attraction. And you, my girl, will never amount to more than a pretty face in a mirror until you learn how to see, rather than simply look.'

Ma advanced towards the bed.

'I'll do it, seeing as you seem to have lost your wits. Watch.'

She picked up the shears where Tira dropped them and advanced. Again, the creature on the bed writhed, grappled and clawed. With her free hand, Ma slapped her round the face. When the shock of the slap made the girl pause, Ma grabbed both her wrists. She was strong, my ma. The girl stared directly at the yellow eyes and spat into the mesh veil, then sank her teeth into Ma's black bombazine cuff.

Ma dropped her as if she'd been singed.

'You have only made things worse for yourself.' The flies buzzed round her head so loudly that her words are all but muffled. 'I'll be back tomorrow.' She swept out of the tent, dragging Tira, who was cowering next to the flap like the little coward she was, by her ear.

I'd been squatting by the pallet, watching. I stood up and crept nearer.

'You bit my mother.' Even I'd never dared.

The dark girl's expression softened for a second. Maybe she was curious because no-one had spoken to her nice up to then. She must have been scared out of her wits but I'd never seen anyone with the guts to stand up to Ma like that.

*'I'll cut it off for you. She'll make you have it done and it'll be less horrible if you let me do it.' I went a bit nearer.*

*She hawked and spat, but at my feet rather than her face.*

*'Well you obviously like me more than Ma. I'll come back later, after my spot. We're a song and dance act, me and Tira. My sister. You bit her an all. Kushtie, that was. The gaff's on and Ma'll be working then, she's the tober omi, so she won't miss me. I'll feke it.'*

*She stared at me with her great black eyes and I knew she hadn't understand a word I'd said.*

*'You don't rokker me, do you? Not a word of it. Where you from? Are you a flattie? One of the tentsmen said you was an Egyptian.'*

*She shook her head and turned away.*

*'You'd better get used to it. We've all had to.' I thought I'd leave her to it before I got on Ma's bad side. Two tentsmen were still there, next to the flaps, sucking on their pipes, billyclubs by their sides. 'You best not try to do a runner, cos Ma's told these not to let you out of their sight. No one goes against Ma. Except you, biting her. She won't like that one bit.'*

*Before I headed off, though, I turned back to the pallet, and pointed at myself.*

*'Dolores.'*

*Then I pointed at her. 'Come on. If I'm going to be your pal you better tell me what to call you.'*

*It was a whisper the way the she said it. 'Zha' and 'anna.'*

*'I'll have a look at that bear an' all. Get 'im some mangiare. There's probably some condensed milk I can shush. I'll be back after the gaff.' I was nearly though the gap in the wallings before I turned round, and when I did, she was staring at me. She didn't flinch, or smile, but when I looked she looked right back at me.*

*'I may be just a little tawnee at the moment but now you're here we'll flash and dazzle 'em,' I said. 'We'll show 'em. Won't we. Janna.'*

Chapter 13

'I've arranged for you to sit in with Janna.' Dolores hasn't mentioned Chrysanthemum's sightings from the trailer for weeks, or told her any more about her younger days. Recent conversation has consisted of a frankly terrifying lecture about the best way to darn stockings without wasting thread, and forthright grumbling about her lodger leaving streaks on the mirrors when she polishes them. 'All you're doing is showing it the cloth. Put some elbow grease into it. Like this.' Dolores rubs a mirror until it squeaks, then licks her finger and deliberately smears it again. 'Now you.'

So this comes out of the blue. Dolores never brooking a refusal, it isn't an offer that can be politely turned down, either.

'What should I…?'

'Just turn up and sit quietly. She's expecting you after the matinee.'

Chrysanthemum is all of a flutter as she approaches Janna's booth. The sign is out, shabby in the daylight, ill-spelled and unconvincing without the mystery of evening or the anticipation of showtime to lend it an allure.

> *Gipsy Maximoff. Romany Palmist 100% genuine. Your conseller and friend Advises you on matters which may seem dark and doubtful if you are Not Afraid to Face facts A reading may enliten you on matters which at present seem Dark and Doubtful.*

*Dark and doubtful is how I feel.* But when she looks tentatively round the curtain, Janna is singing softly to herself – 'tura-lura-lura, tura-lura-lura' - and marking out a little dance in the minute space. She stops when she sees Chrysanthemum and looks up at her, scrutinising her as minutely as if she was a bird in search of worms. Then she reaches up and pats Chrysanthemum's cheek.

'I like this umbrella song, is clever to make a sad, pretty song about such a thing of everyday. Now you must not be scared. I can tell you are a good girl and think very much about things. Too much think. So now you will sit there and be very quiet and you will watch, and listen, but not think.'

She gestures to Chrysanthemum to sit in the corner.

'But won't I be in the way?'

'If you do as I say no-one will know you are even there. They come after all to think about themselves and so they are not looking for what is not the things they want to know.' *Lesson number one. All my life I've worried what people are thinking about me. And people are mostly wrapped up in their own concerns, and not thinking about you at all.* Then she realises she is thinking, which Janna has said not to do, so she sits on a little stool at the back of the booth, and looks round.

'And now we wait, and see if anyone come.'

From the outside, the booth is nondescript: covered in tarpaulin decorated round the entrance with a ragged brocade curtain, some tattered bits of discoloured lace, and a few strings of beads. Inside, though, richly bedecked with strips of shiny fabric, glittering beadwork and draped scarves, it is hard to tell where Janna's multi-coloured clothes end and the furnishing fabrics begin, and her face swims, apparently disembodied, in the sea of patterns and textures. She sits, so still that Chrysanthemum is not even sure if she is breathing, at a low table covered in an old shawl, her hands folded in her lap. Chrysanthemum finds it almost impossible not to glance around, but although Janna is facing in the opposite direction, she doesn't dare fidget.

Eventually, a gloved hand timidly parts the curtain, letting a shaft of light fall into the booth just sufficiently to illuminate Janna's jewelled claw as it beckons the woman inside.

'Madame Maximova?'

Chrysanthemum hardly dares to breath as Janna gestures, slowly, to the women to sit. No-one speaks. The tiny, birdlike woman singing about umbrellas is nowhere to be seen. She's disappeared. In her place is a presence of concentrated energy that fills the small space to such an extent that the air feels heavy. Chrysanthemum wriggles as the hairs rise on the back of her spine.

'Cards, or crystal, or palm?' The words fall into the humming silence.

'Palm.'

'Your gloves. Take off. Both.' The woman peels them away from her hands, and surrenders them – *and her spirit* – to Janna. Chrysanthemum cranes to see what Janna is looking at, but the ray of light that falls only shows her the rings glittering on Janna's fingers as they hold the woman's rough, pale hands and raise them so they are palm upwards.

Janna moves so that she is slightly too close to the woman, who freezes. Janna smiles confidingly up at her.

'You not come from here.'

The woman shakes her head.

'Your lucky colour is blue.'

'No.' The woman shakes her head again, and holds herself as distant from Janna as the space will allow. 'It's just the only coat I've got.'

'You don't like liars.'

The woman cranes forward slightly, closing the gap she's made between her and Janna.

'And now I see.' Janna leans in even closer, but this time the woman bends slightly towards her.

'You have known adversity.' *Haven't we all.*

The woman nods.

'Fortune looks brighter after hard times.' The woman nods again. This time, Janna points at a line on the woman's hand, as if she is pointing at a route on a map. 'I can see you on a beach with two children. But it's not this time.'

Afterwards, she motions to Chrysanthemum to sit at the table, where the woman has been.

'So now you tell me what you have seen.'

'The woman was nervous when she came in, and smiling when she left. She didn't want to believe you at first, and yet she really did, too. You told her things that she didn't think you could have known. Like that she had lost a child and hoped for another, and that she'd have to wait a while for that because her husband had died, three years ago, but there would be a new house with a new family in it if she was willing to look at who really cared for her rather than the man who gave her presents but not what was in his heart.'

'So you do well, and you listen. And now, what do you think?'

'I don't know what to think. I mean, you knew things she didn't tell you. How could you know?'

Janna pauses before she replies, and as she does, she takes Chrysanthemum's hand. The girl feels a crackle of electricity, and then heat spreads from her palm all the way up her fingers. 'Is some of show, but for only one person, not theatre. And I am…phuri dey…very old lady, so many years of show. And people like book if you know how to read. But when you look without thinking is many things that you see. That is why I tell you not to think, so you see things clear. And now I look at you. And I see that where I see the present and the future and the past that are connected to it, this is not the same as you. What you see, or what you think you see, are things that have been gone for a long time. That only you see, or so you think. But Dolores know. I too.'

As Janna speaks, Chrysanthemum is distracted by seeing, and as there is nothing for her to do but look she begins to make out the outline of a large bear becoming visible in the corner of the booth. A nose. An eye that might be a trick of the light. Whiskers that could be dust caught in a ray of sunlight. Brown fur like brushstrokes. A paw, unmistakeably, whose shiny claws are the length of her fingers… Chrysanthemum pulls her hands sharply away from Janna and tries to back away, but Janna is stronger than she seems, and forces Chrysanthemum to stay where she is.

'Everyone can see what is not there if it is their will to see. Or to be seen. This is very terrible for you, I see.' Janna looks into the corner where the bear continues to materialise, smiles gently and waves her hand so the figure Chrysanthemum could swear she sees gradually disappears. Then she looks back at Chrysanthemum. 'But it need not be so. We all carry our stories with us. You see them. This is your fortune. Some creatures can see spirits whether they wish it or no. Like you. For you to decide if is bad, as it seem to you, or maybe not so bad after all, or real, as it may seem, or maybe also not real at all.'

Then she lets go Chrysanthemum's right hand, but keeps hold of her left, and gently, begins to swing the girl into a waltz step.

'He'll mend your umbrella…

'And go on his way… singing… '

Chrysanthemum falls into step and as her feet follow Janna's lead it feels as if she is dancing her way back into her body.

She stops when she hears Janna's voice, and suddenly realises that she has been dancing on her own. 'And now you see also that you are more nice dancer than you imagine,' says Janna. 'It is clever what happen when you no think.'

The next few hours are spent helping out in Wardrobe. Chrysanthemum's mind is happily elsewhere as she runs through the highlights of her extraordinary morning. So much of her life has been spent feeling odd and awkward. Other people – normal people, as Muriel puts it, always in that tone of voice that implies that she is bearing a wound that Chrysanthemum is in some way responsible for – aren't blessed – by which her voice implies the exact opposite, cursed – by the ability to see people who aren't there, or lift ridiculously heavy objects. But now Dolores seems to get it. Even with Rose and Orage, who feel like sisters, or at least what she imagines sisters might feel like, there are things she's never said, for fear that their new-found friendship will fizzle if they find out what she really is. And then, within the musty confines of Janna's booth, all that fell away. "*My mother said, I never should, play with the gypsies in the wood.*" *And now I am doing. And there's nothing you can do about it, Muriel.*

'You're off with the fairies,' grumbles Dolores. 'And you'll never be a singer, I can tell you that for nothing. What I did tell you was to put those wigs in the second hatbox to the left on the third shelf down. Do it properly. I'm not wasting my time with you if you're going to make a muck of things.'

Janna wanders in and wanders about, skirts swaying, pipe clenched between her brown teeth. Chrysanthemum beams at her.

'Thank you Janna. I had a wonderful morning.'

Janna executes two perfect heel turns that make her skirts spin out, then peers at Chrysanthemum through clouds of evil-smelling pipe smoke as if she isn't quite sure who she is.

'You nice face. You give to me maybe one shilling,' she suggests. She moves closer and peered upwards, searching Chrysanthemum's face before exhaling a cloud of smoke that makes her cough. As she splutters and wipes her eyes, Janna examines her curiously.

'You kind girl. Always you help. This makes luck.' She pats Chrysanthemum's sleeve in the manner of a cat that wants you to part with a tidbit. 'For other people.'

'But not for Chrysanthemum.' Dolores' stage whisper is meant to be heard. 'Go and sit down Janna. Or put the samovar on. Chrysanthemum, don't give her anything, she's just cadging. And Chrysanthemum, if I find you've put those hairpieces where they're not meant to be, I'll play Hamlet with you.'

Smoke and mirrors, thinks Chrysanthemum. She saw what she saw, and felt what she felt. When Dolores' back is turned, she tries a couple of Janna's heel turns. On the second one, encouraged by Janna winking at her through the pipe-smoke, she loses her balance and topples into the box of hairpieces, scattering them like so many mangy scalps over the floor.

'I've got eyes in the back of my head you know,' but when Dolores turns round there they are, her old friend and her new lodger, creased up laughing and striking an identical pose, arms outstretched with a toupee in each hand, and her bellow turns into a bark that might be laughter.

'I bet she can't.' Pulling herself out of her fishnets once the matinee's over, Orage pooh-poohs Chrysanthemum's account of her morning with Janna. 'And I don't believe for a single second that she will. But I'm going to ask her.'

Orage has to bend down to get inside Janna's booth, and once inside, like a giraffe being crammed into a everyday room, she has to bend even further to approach Janna. Before she folds her limbs onto the low chair she beckons to Rose and Chrysanthemum to come in. As all the Three Graces squash themselves into the booth, Chrysanthemum looks embarrassed and Rose's face reveals how unhappy she is about being in a situation where her loyalties are divided.

'You all like sardine what is in a tin.' Janna draws her shawl over the bottom of her face to hide her mouth but it is obvious from her eyes that she is laughing at them.

'Is it something you want? Or just to see what small space can you all fit in?'

'I want you to tell my fortune.'

Janna bends across the table and looks into Orage's face so intently it could strip wallpaper. She holds Orage's gaze for a long, claustrophobic moment that makes the close booth feel airless, until the girl's face turns the colour of beetroot and her forehead is faintly beaded with sweat. *There are too many people in here. There's not enough oxygen, that's all.* But that isn't it at all.

Eventually Janna releases her. Orage, visibly drained of bravado, pats her hair to restore her sense of herself.

'OK I do. But you pay.'

'I…' *That's taken the wind out of her sails.*

'How…how much?'

"Seven shillings.' Even Chrysanthemum gasps. 'And sixpence.'

'That's a lot of money, Janna,' pipes up Rose.

'What you think, that I do for nothing because I am silly old woman?' *Yes, that's exactly what she thought.* 'She want, I do, it price, she pay.'

Orage, though, has composed herself, and her face, and is neither going to make a fool of herself, nor be made a fool of.

'No, if that's the price, that's what I'll pay. She unclasps her handbag and draws out first her purse, and then a crisp ten-shilling note, which she passes to Janna with an airy grace she can't possibly feel. *Where did she get a new ten bob note?*

'And now I tell you. For you, a golden life. Good luck, good fortune, and money. All you wish.' Janna folds her shawl around her as if to make the point that the show is over.

'Is that it?' Orage, who has just parted with seven shillings and sixpence, feels short-changed.

'All you wish.' There is a finality to Janna's voice, and her expression darkens. 'Trouble ahead is not for you.'

# Chapter 14

Seeing is believing down Egypt Lane and Chrysanthemum has never seen such a rusty old death-trap as the machine Dolores is dragging out from underneath a tarpaulin concealed beneath leafy branches behind the trailer.

'Don't just stand there like Marsden's monument, you great gawk. Give me a hand to get this thing ready for the road. Put your back into it – it weighs a ton.'

She sets to and helps Dolores haul away the branches until the bashed up, dented metal contraption is revealed as a BSA motorcycle, complete with sidecar.

'There's a cloth there. Rub the seat down, and inside the sidecar. You don't want to get all that muck on your derriere.'

'Get what? What?'

'Do you want to come with me, or not?'

Chrysanthemum realises that Dolores is wearing a leather coat, jodhpurs and a leather flying helmet that looks as if it has been in the wars.

'Go where? What about petrol? Where are we going to get that? That's if we ever get this thing started.'

'Less of your lip, I don't know what's got into you these days.' She's never heard Dolores sounding so jovial. 'Janna's wandered off again, and is now mistakenly in police custody. One of her clients was so kind as to let Mr Fankes know she'd spotted her in the custody of an ARP warden, and he sent young Maurice with a message. As for the petrol, never you mind where it came from, and you can be putting it in the tank whilst I go do my business.'

Dolores lifts up a tank, which sloshes as she dumps it at Chrysanthemum's feet.

'Back in a jiffy.' Dolores practically dances as she strides into the woods and disappears into the undergrowth. Her swaying rear, in jodhpurs and leather coat, conjures the Pink Elephants on Parade sequence in Dumbo.

After a couple of farting refusals, the rickety old motorbike behaves like most other things in Dolores' vicinity, and does as it's told, sputtering into life. Sitting astride the juddering monster, Dolores lowers a pair of goggles over her eyes and brushes her beard down rakishly.

'Hop in.' She gestures at the sidecar with a gauntleted hand.

Chrysanthemum clings onto the sides like grim death. Dolores is aiming the vehicle between her thighs at the road rather than steering it. But as the road straightens out, she realises she's exhilarated. She raises her head; the rushing wind makes her eyes water. Dolores in profile is grimly piratical, bent low over the handlebars, the leather helmet emphasizing the determined thrust of her jawline.

It's only when they draw up outside the village police-station and she tries to move that Chrysanthemum realises her bones feel as if they have been shaken up inside the bag that's her body. Dolores strides into the station.

The desk sergeant barely looks up. 'Can I help you sir?'

Dolores doesn't say anything, but poses regally, before removing the goggles, then unzipping the jacket and making an upwards, jutting motion with her chest that makes her sex perfectly clear.

'Can I help you…madam?'

'That's better. I am Dolores Pickles. From the theatre. I've come to collect Madame Maximova. I gather you have been very kindly taking care of her until I arrived.'

'Madame Max…no-one here of that name. Are you sure of the person's identity, Miss… Pickles.'

'Mrs. And yes. There's no mistaking her. The Russian lady.'

Dolores is putting the dog on. 'I have been given to believe that Madame Maximova is awaiting collection.'

'We haven't got no Madame anything. Not any Russians neither. I am sorry Madam. It looks like you've had a wasted trip.'

For a split second, Chrysanthemum notices an expression of uncertainty flicker across Dolores' features. It isn't a look she'd seen before. Oddly touched, she steps forward.

'Who do you have here?' she asks politely. 'In the way of ladies, I mean. We have come quite a long way.'

The sergeant gives her almost a smile, which might be relief. He scratches his right ear with a considering air.

'We haven't got anything in that line,' he says after a long pause for thought. 'We've just got a dirty old thing what was found grubbing in a vegetable patch near the railway station. The ARP warden that apprehended her called us in on account of him believing she might be an enemy alien. I soon put him right on that one. She's just an old diddikoi, I told him. Brought her in to be on the safe side.'

'Did she give a name?'

'Nelly Kelly something she said she was called.'

Chrysanthemum can feel Dolores glowering behind her.

'Where is she?''

'She's out the back.'

'What have you done with her?'

'That dirty thing? We put her in the kennels so she wouldn't give her fleas to the men.'

The desk sergeant returns, accompanied by a senior policeman.

'Can you vouch for the fact that the woman who calls herself Nelly Kelly whatever-it-is is not an enemy alien?'

'I'll vouch for you,' begins Dolores, and 'kennel!', but Chrysanthemum steps in front of her. 'Mrs Kelly has been Mrs Pickles's companion for years,' she says gently. 'She's not a German, and she's lived here for most of her life. They're both old ladies and it would be very kind if you could just let us collect her so we can all go home together.'

The senior officer looks gratified, and smiles modestly at Chrysanthemum, who looks at him out of the corner of her eye in a way that makes him blush. 'Go and get her.' He shoves the desk sergeant towards the door. 'Do you live local, Miss?'

'I'm at the theatre too.' Chrysanthemum smiles at him through her Veronica Lake fringe. 'In the show. I'm one of the dancers. You'll have to come and see us… officer.'

'I'd like that, young lady. I'd like that very much.'

'What's got into you?' mutters Dolores. There's no hiding the note of admiration. 'Well I say. Something has rubbed off.'

Chapter 15

First there's a rap at the door, a gentle, insinuating rat-tat-tat that cuts through Chrysanthemum's sleep. The sound of someone with a secret she wants to share. She rolls from the couch into Dolores' sideshow kimono and stands up, lifts the curtain, peers through the window. The bevelled glass turns Janna's peering face into a close-up hawk's beak. Chrysanthemum stands there, stupid, not yet out of her dream-world and plunges into a hall of mirrors as a jewelled twig of a finger beckons her. Into the forest? Into the house made of candy? Into the oven?

'It's rude to leave people standing on the doorstep. Let her in. And put that on properly, state of you, it's not decent.' Dolores, out of nowhere, stands in full splendour, buckled shoes and musquash coat glittering with brooches of faceted stones that catch more light than mere diamante. Topped off with a stained turquoise turban, she is ready for all comers. 'Well open it then.'

Despite her instructions, she doesn't wait for Janna to come in, and sweeps outside, looking neither to left, right, nor downwards either as she sails down the trailer steps. She makes as much of her exit as she would an entrance, trailing charisma and such a head-turning waft of Ashes of Roses that she is halfway across the clearing before the half-awake Chrysanthemum realises Dolores is clutching a breadboard under her arm.

Not at all sleepy now, Chrysanthemum wriggles into her clothes and coat, and flies over to the vardo.

'Rose. Rose.'

Rose peers round the door. She is learning mannerisms from her landlady.

'What is it?'

'Come on. I want to see what they're up to.'

'It's …'

'Early. Tell me about it. We'll get breakfast later. Come on. Janna came knocking, and Dolores is dressed up like a dog's dinner and carrying the biggest breadboard I've ever seen. I want to see where they're going.'

The two Graces keep their distance, tracking their landladies from a distance until they reach the churchyard.

'She looks as if she's going to church.'

'She never goes to church. Well, maybe if she thought she could nick the collection.'

'Sssh. Don't make me laugh.' Chrysanthemum struggles to keep speaking in a whisper. 'She's got ears like rashers of bacon. If she hears us, she'll murder me.'

'Which one? She knows what I'm doing when she can't even see me. The other night she said 'Put that teacup down, before you break it,' when I was inside and she was still sitting by the fire. I was only having a look. I jumped so much I nearly did break it, I can tell you.'

'Ssssh. If they know we're here we'll never find out what they're up to.'

It is an adventure, and Chrysanthemum and Rose, only in their teens, are like children. Ducking between and behind the headstones in the overgrown churchyard, they track Janna and Dolores to the furthest edge of the cemetery, to where a lone, black marble headstone stands in isolation, overhung by a willow. She can hear crows calling and cawing, and one of them flies down and perches on the headstone. It feels distinctly colder here, and uninviting. Chrysanthemum shivers. Rubs goosebumps. 'I wonder whose that is. All on its own all that way from all the others.'

'I'm not going any nearer. It was fun but now I don't like it.' Rose bites her lip.

'Come on, duck down behind this tree. We can go in a moment. I just want to see what they're up to.'

Rose looks doubtful, but huddles next to her friend. They watch as Dolores places the breadboard on the grave, just below the headstone. Then, with great ceremony, she removes her coat, lays it carefully on the ground, unpins her turquoise velvet turban and places it on top of the musquash. Holding onto the headstone, she flexes her ankles and executes a few creaky warm-up circles with each foot, then steps onto the breadboard and arranges herself as if she has heard the words 'positions, ladies.'

'Janna. Accompaniment.'

Janna pulls herself from her haunches. She starts to clap a rhythm, slowly at first, as Dolores began to dance. At first it is just a basic toe-heel shuffle, but as Janna's rhythm picks up speed, Dolores' feet fly faster and faster, landing with furious precision so that the taps add to the strange music. The rhythms become faster and more complicated, and Janna accompanies them with strange yelps and cries, and then dances herself, still clapping, but swirling in a swift polka round the grave whilst Dolores hoofs unholy hell on top of the breadboard. The crow, unperturbed, watches the strange antics from its perch on the headstone.

It isn't long until they stop, and stand gasping until their old lungs let them draw breath. The crow dips its beak, spreads its wings and takes off. Dolores reaches into her handbag and pulls out a hip flask. Janna lights her pipe, and sniffs the air.

'Shit for heads you think we pigging stupid? We know you're there.'

'She's really going to give me what for.' Chrysanthemum is, all of a sudden, terrified.

'They must think we were born yesterday. What do you think is worse, Janna? Spying or sneaking away?'

'You come out or we give you thick ear.'

'Oh lord. We're for it now.'

'It'll be much worse if we slink off. Come on Chrysanthemum. Best face the music.'

Rose pulls Chrysanthemum to her feet so they stand in full view of the two old ladies.

'I'm not going down there though.' Rose makes herself solid, like an animal that doesn't want to be moved.

'We only wanted to see what you were doing with the breadboard.'

'And now you've found out. This is where they buried my bitch of a mother, on this day thirteen years ago, and may her bones rot.'

'Pigs' arseholes she send Medved to the army. She say not enough food in circus to feed one bear. So he fight in trenches with men and he go mad.' Janna's eyes burn black fire as she spits on the floor. 'Bitch. And that not half of it. We do every year this.'

'She didn't have a soul so it couldn't go to hell, but the world's a better place without her in it.'

Chrysanthemum has never heard Dolores sound so chipper.

'Might as well face the music. Come on.' Chrysanthemum takes Rose by the hand and pulls her towards Janna and Dolores, and the grave they've been dancing on.

'Go on. Have a look.' Dolores points at the headstone. 'That'll teach you.'

There's only a name: Maude Devell. 'You'd have been better off not finding out. But now you know. Not that I approve of you creeping about the countryside poking your noses where they're not wanted. If you want to know something, you only have to ask.' *And if we asked you'd either tell us what you want us to know, or a clever version of nothing at all. If you see something for yourself, at least you can make up your own mind whether you believe it or not. There is the samovar, sighing and hissing and singing its song. Sas tai nas, sas tai nas. Seeing is believing when you are looking for something, even when the show is over and the flatties have all gone home.*

## Chapter 16

'It's this afternoon and I can't go out dressed in these old rags!' Rose, the least bothered about her clothes of the three of them, is frantically going through the contents of her case.

'You could borrow my tea dress, and maybe if Orage...'

'It's ever so nice but you do have a bust and if I get jam on Orage's good things she'll kill me.'

'It's not that.' Orage looks up from her movie magazine. 'You'd be welcome. But I'm a good seven inches taller than you.'

'With no bum, to speak of. Your frock is pretty, Chrysanthemum. Maybe it might work.'

'I am more padded than you. But perhaps we could pin it.' Chrysanthemum sounds doubtful even as she says it.

Dolores walks in uninvited and catches Orage and Chrysanthemum folding the cloth round Rose's tiny body. She laughs so hard she has to sit down.

'Good Lord,' she splutters eventually. 'My eye and Peggy Martin. You'd need clothes pegs to fasten that. Or bulldog clips. Fisherman's socks in her liberty bodice. Oh Lordy. Is she supposed to sleep in it?'

'Mervyn is taking her out to a restaurant in a hotel. She wants to look nice.' After the episode in Janna's booth, Orage is very much on her dignity. 'She doesn't want to show herself up.'

'Unlike some I suppose. I haven't had such a good laugh since that bleedin' tiger put himself to bed in a pram at the church mothers' meeting. Come upstairs. Just for that you can come with me and I'll sort you out, though what she sees in that streak of piss is beyond me. Bleedin' magicians, they're always less than what they make themselves out to be. I've got my eye on that one, though more than likely it'll be now you see it, now you don't.' She sticks another Abdulla between her teeth, sparks it up and splutters gleefully until she gets her breath back.

'Come on then, get up them dancers, let's see what we've got.'

She pulls out three dresses from a closet at the back of Wardrobe. They are all in pretty, pale shades of crepe de chine, but they are from before the war, for evening, and far too long for daytime.

'I think she just wants to look like a normal girl,' ventures Chrysanthemum.

Dolores looks withering, but doesn't bother to reply.

'Pick one,' she orders Rose, who points at the blue. 'What are you going to do for shoes?'

'I wondered if Orage's might...'

'Don't be ridiculous.' Dolores points at Orage's feet. 'Look at the size of them. Kipper boxes.'

Orage scowls.

'I suppose she'll just have to make do with her own. After all there is a war on. Come back after the matinee and I'll have your frock ready for you.'

Rose looks a picture as she sets off. Orage has loaned her best hat, and prettily arranged Rose's curls underneath it. Chrysanthemum has shined Rose's old shoes as best she could. And Dolores has worked a minor miracle with the old tea dress, cutting more than a foot off its hem, shaping the bodice into a sweetheart neckline and trimming it with velvet ribbon bows, and shortening the sleeves into gathered puffs. Rose is so pleased with it that she kisses Dolores on her hairy cheek.

'But shukar,' Janna appears, and takes in Rose at a glance. 'You look a picture. But is waste on him. No good is that one.'

'Oh Bibi. You and Dolores. What have you got against conjurers?' Rose kisses Janna's windfall cheek with her applebossom lips. 'Honestly. He's being a friend to me. Look, here he is.'

Mervyn smiles cheerily at the assembled company, then proffers the bag he's holding behind his back.

'Eccles cakes. I thought you could have them with a nice cuppa. I'd take you all with me if I could. Rose, you look splendid and I shall be proud to have you on my arm. Whoever made that frock knows a thing or two, I can tell.'

After Rose has gone, waving happily back at her friends as she skips off with Mervyn, Janna's face darkens, and her hands move down to grip the sides of her skirt.

'That's right dear, you shake your skirts at him.' Dolores herds Janna, who is standing by the door, back inside Wardrobe. 'And if he does anything to deserve it, I'll teach him a lesson. But he hasn't yet, so do leave off.' The comment about the frock has clearly put her in a good mood. 'Put the samovar on and let's have a brew.'

Janna does as she'd been asked, but although Chrysanthemum and Orage are invited to stay, refuses to be drawn about whether the samovar has any stories to tell, and sits stonily in her chair, still gripping the sides of her skirt, until it is time for her to go downstairs and sit in her booth. She even turns down her Eccles cake, and refuses to be drawn about the black cloud that has settled about her.

'Is there anything the matter, Janna? Has someone upset you?' tries Chrysanthemum. Janna doesn't even look in her direction.

'She gets like that. Artistic temperament. Don't take it personal.' Dolores stuffs Janna's discarded Eccles cake into her mouth. 'As long as your young friend keeps her wits about her.'

The following day, with Orage nowhere to be seen, Rose looks round the corridor and deliberately closes the dressing room door.

'Bibi told me a story last night.' She sounds perplexed. 'Two stories, actually. I mean, she often tells stories but this one was different. Not just the story, but how she told it.'

Chrysanthemum looks up from an apricot sleeve that has already been unravelled twice, and puts it down gladly. 'What do you mean? She was in ever such a peculiar mood after you went out.'

'We were in the vardo, and normally I just drift off, but I was thinking about Mervyn, and our afternoon out, so my head was full of all sorts. And then out of the darkness there came this whispering voice, so low that I really had to concentrate to hear her saying "sas tai nas". So I knew she really wanted me to hear this, because she was making it difficult. And it was this story about a man called Ivan, or Yanko, she said it didn't matter which name, but he had a sister, and when he got married, he wanted to get rid of the sister, and he was too mean to give her any money, except for one miserable kopek, so he arranged for her to be married.'

'Go on.'

'So she goes to the market, and instead of spending the miserable kopek on a new scarf, or an embroidered handkerchief, she sees a little, old, grey, talking cat. So she buys him. And the wedding takes place, and when the groom appears, he puts the necklace with a bell round it that Russian brides wear around her neck, and they get married. But it turns out that although he's wearing a coat like a man, really her new husband is a bear. And the bear takes her deep into the woods, and he tells her that they're going to play a game. So he blindfolds her, and tells her that the game is blind man's buff, and he gets to eat whatever he catches.'

'So then what happened?'

'And then Janna whispered so low that I could hardly hear her: "And do you know how she got away, Rose, from this husband of hers? That wanted to eat her." And I didn't know what she could have done, so I just lay there, and didn't say anything. Then eventually, I heard a rustle, which was strange because usually she's so silent, you can't hear her move. And the vardo was filled with this strange glow, which couldn't have come from outside, because there was no moon. So I moved so I could see her sleeping platform, and I could have sworn that she was sitting upright, but floating above it. And she gave me this look, as if I was very stupid but that she really cared for me, and she said: "The little old grey talking cat told her what to do. And between them, she tricked the bear. She put the blindfold on the bear, and she danced. He followed the noise of the bell, and she danced so well, and so fast, that she danced him into the dust. And she got away."'

'And then it went dark again and in her normal voice she said: "In Russia a long time ago, in a café in a very smart part of St Petersburg, the people would come late at night to hear that story. They were very fine people in very grand clothes, and the most fine and grand thing that they could think of to do, after their night at the opera, or the banquet, or the soiree with the Tsar, was to come and hear my people sing, and tell our tales, and watch us dance. So after this story was told, I would dance the sister, and Medved would dance the bear, and he would pretend to be so fierce and try to eat me, but I would dance so fast that he couldn't catch me. Always we would get very much money for that show. My plaits were very heavy. So much gold.'

'Medved the bear?' Chrysanthemum's curiosity was piqued. She'd been so busy that the doll and the bear had slipped her mind. 'And did she say anything else about the café, or Russia, or what she used to do?'

'I went to sleep after that,' said Rose. 'What do you think she was on about? I don't know which story she meant me to think about, and I hadn't told her about him asking me to be a double act with him and go on the road after this season because I needed to think about it. I wasn't going to tell anyone until I'd decided. Well, I have decided. Oh gosh, I've told you now. Do you think she guessed?'

'Oh Rose.' Chrysanthemum feels her temples prickling. There is a third story, she can feel it, and somehow it relates to the unrelated stories that Janna has told Rose, and Rose has now told her. But she doesn't know how the pieces fit together, or how many more pieces of story there might be to find before she can make a sense of it. 'You never told me or Orage about this either, did you? About the double act. You can always tell us, Rosie. Please do. You will keep your wits about you, won't you?'

Janna sets off the next morning, before Rose is awake, and without telling her where she is going. Chrysanthemum, who is up early and sitting on the trailer's steps with a gasper watching her fire and waiting for the pan of water to boil, hears the vardo's door creak slightly as it opens, and the ghost of a whisper of cloth on wood as Janna slips down the steps and into the woods. Chrysanthemum, thinking the old lady is about her ablutions, waves, but Janna vanishes between the trees into the morning mist.

She doesn't come back by midday, and at two o'clock, His Gillpots sends Maurice up to Wardrobe with a message. The old fortune teller may be no-where to be found but the people who want a glimpse into the future have to be provided for.

'Chrysanthemum can hold the fort in Wardrobe,' decides Dolores. 'I'll do the dukkering til she comes back.'

'Won't they feel a bit weird when they realise it's not… her?'

'They'll never know. And if they do they won't care. It's not the first time, and I'm sure it won't be the last.' Dolores rolls her eyes and gazes stagily into the far distance. 'Just you watch. Now go fetch me the cold cream, then you can sit on the steps to make sure the coast's clear.'

Chrysanthemum does as she's told, and when the door opens it is to a veil-swathed figure that, despite the yashmak arranged artfully so that it conceals her lower face, is unmistakeably Dolores.

Yellow eyes glows like coals over the yashmak as she raises a combative eyebrow at Chrysanthemum. 'Not convinced?'

'You're a bit too… substantial.'

'Ooh, get her having an opinion,' retorts Dolores, faster than a snake. 'It's dark in that tent. Like I always say, people see what they want to see. And don't you get any ideas on your own in Wardrobe. If anyone wants an emergency repair just sew them into their costume and I'll do it properly later. You can be getting on with those matelot outfits, and don't go poking about. I know where everything is.'

The veiling shrouding her face only intensifies the glowering of her yellow eyes. 'And I mean: everything.' The eyes flare a warning and with that, she turns on her heel, takes a deep breath and sashays down the stairs as if she is about to battle her way across the desert sands to her star-crossed lover, Rudolph Valentino.

Chrysanthemum has never been left on her own in Wardrobe. She drifts proudly round what small space is available, letting her fingertips touch this piece of fabric and that. Amazed at her own daring, she pulls out a basket overflowing with sepia-toned sequinned items and ostrich plumes. She catches her breath as she gently lifts out a glittering headpiece, half-expecting that its previous owner might materialize, but nothing happens. Emboldened, she glances at her reflection in the mirror, and places the gorgeous thing on her head. Still nothing happens. A rare smile lights up her face. *I am almost beautiful. What a shame there is no-one here to see me. Perhaps I could be like Rose, a little bit. Perhaps I'm not so different. Perhaps I could be like Orage too.* She smiles at her reflection in the mirror, and pulls herself up short. 'No, not like Orage.'

But she does look nice. She begins to pick out the footwork of the little dance to Flanagan and Allen's Umbrella song.

'Drat her,' she mutters. The footwork, which had seemed as natural as walking when she fell into step beside Janna, is devilishly tricky when she tries to do it on her own.

She finds herself next to the samovar as if she has been magnetized, staring at the polished brass, willing the mist to appear and the images to form. But all she can see is the reflection, unflatteringly distorted by the curve of the brass, of her own frowning face, topped by the heavy headpiece, now drooping at an unflattering angle.

'Oh bloody hell. Now I look like me again.'

There's a sharp rap on the door and Maurice comes in before she can rip the headdress off. His flushed face makes his spots stand out even more.

'Ooh I say. You're a sight for sore eyes.'

Chrysanthemum tries to look nonchalant, as if she'd been just about to polish the samovar, but her cheeks are hot and, she's sure, the colour of beetroot.

'It suits you.'

As if anyone would polish a samovar in a spangled, feathered headdress. Well, somebody might. But not her. And now everyone would know.

'No really. A proper sight for sore eyes.'

When Chrysanthemum raises her head, Maurice's eyes are very kind. 'You do, honest. But I won't let on. I know she doesn't like her things being meddled with.'

'You mean she wore this?'

'That and not a lot else, by all accounts. My dad's told me all sorts.'

Maurice flashes her a smile, teeth glowing white against the livid red of his spots. Poor thing. Chrysanthemum feels herself warm to him, at least a little bit. He can't help being spotty, just like she can't help the things about her that are different. She doesn't want to be like Muriel, so she smiles back.

'I just dropped in to say hello. I won't always look like this you know.' He sounds more grown up than he looks. More than that, he sounds wise. 'And you won't always be stuck up here, either.'

Funny what you can see when you look again. Chrysanthemum is on the brink of asking him what he means when her name is bellowed up the stairs.

'That's His Gillpots.' He's the Chairman. Unless it's showtime, His Gillpots rarely leaves his office.

'Dad?' Maurice leans over the banister. 'She's up here.'

'Well get her down here.' It's a voice that carries. 'At the double. Dolores appears to have taken leave of her senses.'

A voice that you don't argue with. Maurice helps Chrysanthemum tear off the showgirl's headdress and she gallops down the stairs as fast as her legs will carry her, just in time to see the veiled apparition that is Dolores marching towards the gentlemen's lavatories with a desperately wriggling figure attempting to escape from the headlock under her arm.

'Fortune? I'll tell your bloody fortune.' Her voice carries thrillingly. 'I can tell you in advance that you're not going to like it. I've scraped better than you off the bottom of my shoe.'

It seems as if everyone in the theatre has gathered to watch, but no-one dares go any nearer. Dolores brandishes her victim – a gentlemen of retirement age - at the spectators. He wriggles in her grasp, eyes pleading for help.

'Put him down Dolores,' ventures His Gillpots, stepping forward with the air of a man about to beard a lion in its den. His voice does not carry quite so far now. He may as well not have spoken. Pushing the yashmak to one side, Dolores bares strong teeth, inhales, and heaves her victim into the lavatory. The door closes, firmly, from the inside, as the entire theatre holds its breath.

There are a couple of thumps and crashes, what sound suspiciously like whacks, then the sound of running water.

Finally the door opens, and Dolores poses, grandstanding, arms akimbo and eyes glittering triumphantly above the yashmak, which is back in place. She takes in her audience, and pauses momentarily, dramatically unrolling her sleeves, until it falls silent.

'I will not have it. Filth, at my age. I've tanned his hide and washed his mouth out with soap and water. And the toilet brush. Which is no more than he deserves. Trying to sample the goods.'

His Gillpots shakes his head. 'Oh Dolores. We've had this out before. You can't just take the law into your own hands like that.'

'I can,' she replies. 'I have done, as well you know, and I will again. Do I need to spell it out?' She scowls directly at His Gillpots, who tries to meet her glance, then appears to find something interesting on his jacket that requires his attention with a handkerchief. When he raises his head again, he's in full ringmaster mode.

'Haven't any of you got work to do?' he blusters. 'I have, and I'm going to do it in peace. Dolores, the girls will be shortly be preparing a new number, which will require new costumes. That should keep you out of trouble.'

Dolores gives Chrysanthemum the filthy look that is really intended for His Gillpots. 'What on earth are you still doing here? Get back upstairs.'

Unrepentantly queenly, Dolores sweeps back up the stairs, and by way of acknowledging both her audience and her sense that justice has been done, as she reaches the landing she wiggles her bottom, turns her head, and winks.

In Wardrobe, so pleased with herself she is looking for more trouble to cause so she can keep the fun going, she takes stock of her domain. Her eyes light on the abandoned headpiece, earning Chrysanthemum a withering look.

'New costumes eh? I can see you haven't been getting on with the matelots. You can't hide anything from me. I've got eyes in the back of my head. And there's no use mooning over that samovar. I'm surprised you didn't realise. You won't see a bloomin' thing if Janna's not there.'

Two days later, Dolores is stony on the subject of Janna's continuing disappearance. 'She'll turn up,' she says shortly. 'She likes wandering off.'

If Dolores knows where Janna has got to, and Chrysanthemum strongly suspects she does, she isn't telling.

At first forlorn – 'the vardo feels really empty without Bibi' – Rose becomes increasingly distraught. 'I don't even know if she's got her ration book,' she frets.

'Well I can put you straight on that one,' says Dolores through pins. 'She hasn't got one.'

Rose's face tells a story of its own, so Dolores is unnecessarily merciless as she continues. 'She hasn't got a gas mask either. In fact as far as anyone official is concerned, there is no such person in this country as Madame Anna Ludmila Maximova, also known as Janna Kalderashka, also known as Nellie Khelitorka, also known as Zingarina and sometimes, when it suits her, Rosina Lee or Annie Fox. She doesn't exist. So don't you go stirring up trouble asking questions about her whereabouts.'

Orage looks at her nails, then at Dolores. 'Why has she got all those names?'

'She'd say one was just as good as another.' With a flourish, Dolores draws out a long running stitch.

Rose sits silently and chews her lip. Orage reaches over kindly and squeezes her hand. 'She won't have got far. She can't have done.'

'I wouldn't bet on it,' says Dolores cruelly. 'She walked here with that bear all the way from the Carpathians. Mind you, it was a long time ago. She's not as young as she was.'

'I'm not sure,' says Orage thoughtfully, 'that you aren't enjoying yourself rather too much, Dolores. I think perhaps the three of us might go to the tea-shop. Actually, I might go see if Mervyn's free. He might like to join us. Especially as Rose – who he cares about – is upset. Come along Chrysanthemum.'

'What if there's an air-raid?' moans Rose, allowing Orage to help her to her feet. 'She might not be able to find a shelter.'

'She wouldn't go in it,' says Dolores, with the relish of someone who knows she is having the last word. 'She'd rather be buried alive. Enjoy your tea, girls.'

Twenty-four hours later, the sirens wail. Sid and Joey, the two elderly Augustes turned odd-job men who spend the period between every matinee and evening show lounging outside the Red Lion in full clown face paint and costume, smoking and passing remarks at female passersby, turn into strict ARP wardens and hustle the show's entire cast into the reinforced shelters under the theatre.

'Where is she? Dolores, where is she?' Rose moans and plucks Dolores' sleeve and has to be dragged down to the shelter by Orage and Chrysanthemum. 'I'm not going in without her!' she wails.

'Any more of your nonsense and you'll be getting a thick ear.' Dolores picks up Rose as if she weighs no more than a parcel, lifts her over the threshold of the shelter and places her on one of the bottom bunks, where she crumples in as forlorn a heap as any pile of discarded showgirls' stockings.

'I wish Mervyn was here,' Chrysanthemum whispers to Orage as they settle in next to Rose. 'He went straight back to his digs after the matinee.'

'Hmm. Take her mind off things. Or at least give her a cuddle in the dark.' Orage winces as she pulls off her gas mask case and opens it. Inside are two lipsticks, something flimsy in peach satin and a bar of chocolate, which she snaps into three.

'Chryssie, here.' She passes two of the thirds to Chrysanthemum, whose mouth begins to water. 'Make her eat some, and don't give her yours.'

'Come on Rosie. Stop carrying on, she'll have tucked herself away somewhere I'm sure. You don't want to miss this, it's a proper treat.' She puts the chocolate in Rose's limp hands, and gratefully eats her own.

'Ooh, that was lovely. Thank you. Where did you…?' She leaves the words unspoken as Orage's expression changes, and turns back to Rose.

'It'll melt in your hands if you don't eat it.' Rose looks blank.

'I'll take it back if she's not going to eat it,' said Orage. 'You don't know what I had to do to get that.'

'Another word out of either of you and I'll lamp the pair of you. Chrysanthemum, get on with your knitting.' Dolores plucks the chocolate from Rose's fingers.

'I'll conceal your ill-gotten gains,' she snaps, and pops half in her mouth.

Sid, standing by the door, looks round the shelter through the fug of cigarette smoke.

'Is everybody in? No-one not accounted for?'

'Bibi,' whispers Rose disconsolately.

'One more.'

Even over the murmur and chatter, the voice – the faint, accented, insinuating croon - is unmistakeable. The shelter falls silent, and then, as Janna pushes open the door and struggles through, her arms clasped round the bulging brass body of the samovar, and makes her way to where Dolores and the Three Graces sit, a round of applause breaks out.

'I'll go to the foot of our stairs,' mutters Dolores. She glares at the Graces. 'Budge up then. Where d'you expect her to sit, on the floor?'

Janna wedges herself and the samovar into the small space next to Dolores. From across the shelter, Maurice catches Chrysanthemum's eye and winks.

'Are you lot playing sardines?'

'Come on Chryssie.' Orage is gathering her things. 'Rose can stay with them if she likes but I think we'd be better off keeping Maurice company. There's room over there.' Chrysanthemum remembers how kind he was when he caught her trying on the headdress.

'My dad's nodded off, I've got a torch, a bag of toffee and a pack of cards. Rummy?'

Several hands and a lot of giggling later, there's a stirring from the bench behind Maurice.

'Dad? You were spark out. Shall I deal you in?'

His Gillpots raises his head and his eyes swivel round, adjusting to the light and finally fixing on the two dancers.

'A pleasant pastime, whiling away these dangerous hours. Some sit with their hearts in their mouths in terror of aerial bombardment by the enemy forces but my own flesh and blood choses to pass the time with two of our delightful terpsichorines and a hand of cards. You make the right choices, my son. A sight for sore eyes and a credit to our boards. Fankes will have to make the most of them.'

His Gillpots props himself up on a elbow and takes in the assembled Fankes cast crammed in the shelter: Sid and Joey, propped against each other; Dora asleep with her head in Duckie's lap; Stella Maris glowering in the far corner, Dolores snoring with her mouth open. And Janna, gazing watchfully into the darkness, with a sleeping Rose tucked under one arm and the other round the belly of the samovar.

## THE SONG OF THE SAMOVAR

*You think that samovar's all about Janna, don't you? You've fallen for it hook line and sinker. Seeing isn't always believing in our line of work, and the faster you find that out, the better.*

*And maybe it is about Janna, in a way, but what you aren't seeing, because you're so wrapped up with looking, is how much it's about Dolores. Just as much, if not more so. And she's the one who's keeping her secrets close to her chest.*

*Dolores never told anyone where she got the samovar.*

*If someone asked, and not many dared, she'd give them a tight-lipped look and pass them off with a tart 'mind your own' or if she was in a better mood, 'look where curiosity got poor old pussy.' If anyone persisted they'd get short shrift and their gussets liable to come adrift at a crucial point in their number. It didn't matter where they were on the bill either. Dolores didn't believe in airs and graces, or only when she was the one putting them on.*

*But stories are like plants. They grow from roots, and roots grow from seeds, and seeds have to be planted in fertile earth. So we need to look where the story of the samovar might have sprung from, because nothing comes from nothing. We need to look back, so a good place to start might be Jeffcocks. And it might have been called Jeffcocks and it might have had old High Lee's name on the signs, but it was Miss Maude who ruled it from the inside, even if the flatties never got to see her seeing as how she'd put the willies even up Christ himself. They made a funny pair, High Lee being so short and round and smiling in his ringmaster's coat, and her like a beanpole in black and never a sight of her face behind that mourning veil. Like everyone else, he never dared to go against her but the one thing he wouldn't stand for was cruelty, said it turned his stomach and how could he go out there and make nice for the kiddies knowing that he'd made some poor creature's life a misery.*

*Miss Maude was an entirely different kettle of cold fish. Janna might have been her investment but she never forgot the way Janna fought back and she'd have beaten Medved for the sake of bringing the dancing girl down a peg or two. High Lee put his foot down for once. He was clever with her and said that an animal that's used to force will never look happy in the ring, which means the punters won't like it, which means they won't come back. But everyone knew it was out of the kindness of his soft heart and that he was taking the bear cans of condensed milk on the sly, and playing cards with him after hours.*

*Miss Maude always chose her battles and she knew that one wasn't worth fighting. And High Lee was right, because Janna might have fought Miss Maude every inch of the way but when High Lee asked her to dance – asked her, mind, not told her – she put on a show that* no-one who saw it would ever forget. Her and the bear. And she did it night after night, with the big top so full that there were tentsmen posted all round to make sure no-one tried to crawl under the canvas to sneak a glimpse without handing over the readies.

It was Dolores that made the costume. Janna wouldn't let Miss Maude go anywhere near her, not even with a tape measure in hand, but she and Dolores were as thick as thieves right from the get-go.

'All the flowers of the forest, all the way to here,' she said, raising her hands so they met above her head. 'And an edge which look like fire when it move.' How Dolores did it no-one ever knew, or where she found the material, but that's what it looked like when she'd finished it. Janna's still wearing it, though these days it looks more like autumn leaves than fresh flowers.

And Miss Maude? I hope you haven't forgotten we were talking about her. Always remember, never forget, and she never forgot that bite. She got her revenge, and she made sure it was served cold. When the war broke out in 1914, and the call went out for volunteers, she sent them Medved. She said that with his strength he'd be of great service behind the lines, and anyway with a war on how were they supposed to feed such a creature when there was bound to be rationing? She was right on both counts of course, but it was a bitter and cruel thing that she did and though Janna was too proud to grieve in front of people, it took something away from her and anyone could see it when they looked at her. She'd smile for the punters, but not for anyone who wasn't paying, and if she talked, it would be about the old country. She never mentioned the people, which is the way of her sort, when folks have died, but she'd talk about the things she missed: the flowers, the forest, the fires, the dancing. And the samovar. She kept coming back to the blasted samovar, as if it was something sacred, like a cornerstone or shrine.

And in the meantime Dolores had grown into – well, Dolores. She was a growing attraction herself, as the Hirsute Stunner for the matinee and evening shows with her stomach dance that was only for after hours. There's always those who like things that are on the strange side, so you could say her star was in the ascendant and there was always a lot of interested gentlemen, and we're not saying any more on that side of things. But she was her mother's daughter, in that you knew not to mess. And whenever Dolores was finished with whatever bit of adventuring she was up to, she'd seek out Janna and their two heads would be stuck together.

And then there was the trouble, and it was in the papers, and they upped sticks. Dolores first, and then after she'd gone, there was nothing to keep Janna. She took herself off. At first no-one thought anything of it – you know by now what she's like for wandering off. But she didn't come back, and after a while High Lee took both of them off the posters.

It was years later when they waltzed back into camp, Dolores bold as brass like she always was, all folded up in a velvet wrap. She marched straight into High Lee's trailer and unfurled herself, and under her arm there was this splendid great brass samovar. And there was Janna standing just behind her, grinning from ear to ear so that you could see the thing reflected in her gold teeth.

It was a beautiful thing, not an everyday sort of urn, at all, and obviously expensive, so everyone wondered where you'd find such a thing in the first place. One after another Dolores *was asked and asked where it came from, where she got it, who she got it from, and she never let on. Not a muff. No, much as everyone begged her to let them in on the secret, Dolores has never told the story of where she got the samovar.*

*Maybe that secret is at the heart of this story. And maybe it isn't. Perhaps it's a story in itself. Or a red herring. Or perhaps a flourish, a bit of decoration for another, bigger story. Or perhaps it is important, but not in the way you think it might be. Sas tai nas, as Janna would say. It was and it was not. The truth is in there somewhere. Your job is to find it.*

*Think about Janna's little Russian doll. She's faded with age — and there's another story, the journeys she's travelled, the places she's been — but still painted and decorated on the outside for all that she's shabby now. So quaint, so pretty. Then look inside. Within her there is another, also painted, but less worn. The patterns are a little less lavish. And more vivid. Unscrew her and there's another, and another, each one with less and less specific detail... until finally you get to the last one. She's tiny, and the painted patterns on her are bright and simple like child's drawings, but for that very reason they're definite, too. And unlike the other, hollow dolls, she's solid. You can't break her open. A tiny kernel beneath the decorative layers.*

*Stories are like that. As time goes on, each story becomes wrapped in another, and the stories build up. But where is the story that joins them together? What about that? Sas tai nas. It was and it was not. All stories have their own truth, or truths. And a tiny kernel of something solid and bright and true at the heart of them, that has to be unwrapped, a layer at a time.*

Chapter 17

His Gillpots having asked for it, the new number – Orage playing to type being languid, love-lorn and lovely, Rose and Chrysanthemum as the cheery dancing girls who perk her up – results in new costumes: gaudy, moth-eaten and sticking out all over the place.

Rose and Chrysanthemum, in mismatched magenta and lime brocade underlaid with mangy beige and yellow tulle, adorned with ribbons and pom-poms, embellished with bows on wrists and insteps, and topped off with enormous, drooping tulle headdresses, are already wearing theirs when Orage turns up.

'I'm not putting that on. I'll be a laughing stock. You two look like an explosion in a gas factory.' Orage puts down her nicely shod foot.

'Oh yes you are.' There is an ominous note in Dolores' voice. 'You'll wear what you're given. I've been up all night cobbling those together. There's Chu Chin Chow from old Peking, half of a Widow Twankey and four oriental dancing girls gone into that lot. Get it on. Now.' Her amber eyes glow a warning.

'Just wear it,' hisses Chrysanthemum. 'Remember the pins in your gusset.'

'She must have got out of the wrong side of the bed,' suggests Rose appeasingly.

Chrysanthemum shakes her head. 'There's only one side she can get out of. Her bed's wedged up against the wall.'

Dolores looks daggers and thrusts the gathered net underskirt into Orage's face.

Scowling, Orage takes it, flinching and wincing as her fingers encounter the dingy, tacky fabric, stiff with caked-on dirt and ingrained sweat. Dolores has crafted the outfits from what is available: remnants of pieced-together costumes from times gone by that have been worn and performed in until the fabric could do the routine on its own.

Orage shucks it on, trying not to let it touch her skin. With each layer, her colour deepens until her china-doll face is almost the puce of her frayed brocade overskirt. The cockade, pinned grimly into her hair by Dolores with a bulldog clip, is not the final humiliation.

Dolores, an Abdulla dangling from the corner of her mouth, ties a string of trailing pom-poms round her waist and stands back. Orage looks down at them in disgust.

Dolores shoots her a withering look and deliberately blows a mouthful of perfumed smoke into Orage's eyes.

'It took me 30 minutes to make each one. They're staying on. It'll do you good. Now off with you.'

'It does make me look a bit broad in the beam, Dolores.'

'Rubbish, Rose. There's nothing of you. If anyone looks like a house side it's me.' Chrysanthemum tries to pat down the skirt a fraction but the beastly thing has a life of its own and springs back up, wider than before.

A wheezing, cawing noise from the corner makes them all turn round.

They haven't seen Janna, in her chair, until now. She is bent double. The tears that stream down her face highlight deep wrinkles.

'You make so nice for this dance,' she cackles. 'You look like many fairies from Christmas tree. But in hell I think. You maybe go to Las Vegas with the chocolate money. And of course the wallets of gentlemen who do not yet know they have lost them.'

The new number gets a lot of laughs, and not the unkind variety. 'Maybe it's not too bad after all,' suggests Chrysanthemum as they catch their breath in the wings.

'It's much worse than that and you know it.' Orage rips off her headdress and hurls it savagely into the props basket, followed by the detested pom-poms. 'Never mind costume scraps, she made those costumes entirely out of spite. When this war's over and you can get decent clothes again I am never – I swear this on my life – going to wear cast-offs and hand-me downs again. It will be couture all the way…'.

Chrysanthemum raises an eyebrow.

'Well, at least, I'll make sure there's a genteel lady tailoress who can run me up nice new things that fit.' Temper restored, Orage smiles sweetly. 'Come on, let's get our civvies on and see if we can find a cuppa before we have to make ourselves look like frights again for the evening.'

'Where's Rose got to?'

'Oh lord, how should I know? She's probably snuck off to see Mister Magic and his wand. Come on, let's get backstage. I'm gasping for a ciggy.'

Chrysanthemum has completed most of the crossword and Orage has worked out a new way to do her hair from the latest Hollywood styles in Picturegoer before Rose, still in her costume, turns up.

'Hello.' Pink in the face, she plonks herself next to Orage. 'Got any Wild Woodbines?'

Chrysanthemum fishes in her handbag, then stops.

'Rose. Your pom-poms. Where are they?"

All three girls look down at Rose's ragged costume, then up at her headdress, tilting at a tipsy angle, then back at her waistband.

Rose's mouth opens as wide as her eyes.

'Oh golly I'm going to be for it, aren't I?' She scrambles to her feet.

'Don't worry. You can have mine. Here, I'll give you them.' Orage's hands go to her own waist.

'You will not.' Materialising in the doorway, Dolores is a wolfish apparition with her lips drawn back in a snarl. 'You will find those bleeding pom-poms or you will have me to answer to.'

Slinking away as silently as she appeared, Dolores leaves hanging in the air the unspoken threat of what might happen if the pom-poms are not recovered.

'No rest, is there? Come on then Graces, let's scour the bowels of Hades for the devil's own pom-poms.' Orage gets to her feet.

'Rosie, you ought to be more careful, really. I know they're dreadful costumes but she did spend all night making them.' Chrysanthemum, knowing that she will bear the brunt of Dolores' ire because living in the trailer makes her a sitting duck, tries not to sound fed up as they trudge round to the back of the stage.

Rose nods guiltily, and tucks her chin down and her shoulders up.

'I didn't mean to.'

'I know. We just need to find them. They're bound to be somewhere. Where did you go when you wandered off?'

'She'll have been lost in a dream of tall dark and not very handsome conjurors and their unconvincing box of tricks,' mutters Orage. 'You do behind the stage, I'll do the wings on this side and you, Rose, do the other. And don't forget behind the flies. I once found half a crown under the fringe.'

It's Chrysanthemum who finds the pom-poms. They are trailing from the doorknob of one of the men's dressing rooms. The door is ajar. Pushing it open, Chrysanthemum discovers it is empty apart from a top hat, a wand and a pack of cards scattered all over the floor. Chrysanthemum pulls at the string of pom-poms and they come away, trailing in their wake six knotted silk scarves that have got tangled up in the plaited wool attaching the pom-poms.

Chrysanthemum carefully unknots the silk and the wool. 'Oh Rose, what are you up to?' She looks at the top hat as if waiting for something – a rabbit? an answer? – to emerge from it, but nothing does. She shakes her head, and makes her way back to her dressing room. The pom-poms swing from her hand in tune with the line from a song that pops into her head: *Run rabbit, run rabbit, run, run. Run.*

'What's that, Rose? Have you been in the wars?" Rose is wriggling out of her costume in the corner of the changing room when Orage, standing to pull up her stockings, catches sight of the raw patch at the top of her arm.

'It's nothing.'

'What do you mean, nothing? That looks sore.' Orage bears down on her and drags her into the light for a closer look.

'It's just a scratch.' Rose wriggles angrily out of her friend's grasp.

'A scratch from what? Chrysanthemum, look.'

'Mervyn's box. He misjudged.'

'Misjudged what?' Chrysanthemum winces at the rubbed raw patch at the top of Rose's arm.

'Me. I wasn't quite fitting in properly.'

'And you didn't say anything? You idiot, that could go septic.'

'He didn't mean it.' Rose is red in the face. 'He wouldn't hurt me.'

Chrysanthemum's face darkens. 'Whoever said he… Rose, what happened?'

'Nothing.'

'Rose, it's not nothing. You need to get some Dettol on that.'

'It was an accident. The box was a tight fit, that's all.'

Chrysanthemum and Orage exchange glances.

'What box Rose? Everyone's seen you get in his case. You fit just fine. Is this a different box?'

Rose's head jerks up and her eyes widen.

'I shouldn't have… yes of course it's that box. What other box could it be? He's only got that one. I misjudged it a bit, that's all, and it scraped me.'

'Rose, you should have said. Come on, let's get you cleaned up. Orage, do you know where the first aid kit is?

'I think it's in the box office. I'll go get it.' Orage belts her kimono round her and strides off down the corridor.

Rose turns her back to Chrysanthemum and, head down, fusses with her shoes and stockings.

'Rose.'

'You've no business interfering.'

'Rose, we're only trying to help. You should have told us.'

'Just don't tell anyone. About the box. Don't let Mervyn...'

'You aren't scared of him, Rose, are you?'

Rose shakes her head.

The door rattles open, but instead of it being Orage with the first aid box, Janna's face materialises round the crack in the door frame.

Rather than going to Rose, she looks around her, her skirts seeming to fill the cramped dressing room, until she settles, resting back on her heels as if she was by the fire outside the vardo. Janna waits like the veteran performer she is until she has the complete attention of both girls, and then, slowly, she begins to peel away her layers of shawls – first the fringed, flowered red woollen one whose point reaches to her knees, then a smaller one, with a pattern of blue roses, and then the cobwebby grey knitted lace that is folded and knotted around her body. Finally she sits there in her wide-sleeved, wide-necked blouse, revealing the gold coins and jewelled chains festooned round her grimy neck. With a swooping gesture whose grandeur is in no way diminished by the tarnished embroidery and faded cloth of her blouse, Janna pulls down one side of her neckline. The flesh of her scrawny shoulder is marked – in just the same place that Rose has been scuffed by Magical Mervyn's box – by four thick, white scars.

Still Janna says nothing, and the room is silent apart from the chinking of her necklaces and bracelets as she carefully rearranges her layers of shawls. Then, rocking slightly, she draws out her pipe from a pouch round her waist, lights it carefully, and draws on it. Finally, exhaling the words with her pipe-smoke, she says what she has come for.

'I came from the Carpathians with a bear, who we shall call Medved, because that is the Russian word for what he was, although it was not his name. I will not tell you all of this bear because there are many stories and only one of them needs to be told now. But you need not to think badly of Medved for all of his history, because of only one story, but just to know that every creature is what he is, and if a creature – for instance, a bear – has claws, there may come a time when he will use them.'

Janna pulls deeply on her pipe, not looking at Rose, but above the heads of her audience – even Orage, who has sidled into the dressing room.

'So Medved was a bear who danced, and in St Petersburg he was a bear who was famous, but in this country he became tired of being teased and being made to feel that he was butt of the jokes of the men in Jeffcocks who were glad of him when they needed his great strength to put up the big top or to pull it down, but thought he was less than them because he could walk on four legs, not only on two. And more and more with each joke or snub that the men would make, Medved would growl and be less kind. And one day, he growled at the person who cared for him most and trusted him. And she did a stupid thing, which was forget that when a creature has claws, it is in its nature to use them. So, when she turned her back on him, because she was upset that he had snarled at her, Medved struck her with his claws, and left the marks that you have just seen.'

Janna closes her eyes, as if the pain is new and hard to bear, and sucks on her pipe.

'And though he had been my companion for many years, and many, many miles, I never turned my back on him again, or trusted him enough to do so.'

She pushes herself to her feet, and makes her way out of the room, patting each girl absently on the arm or shoulder in passing.

'Well,' says Orage, finally. 'That was entirely peculiar.'

'You can put some Dettol on my arm, if you like' Rose offers herself as a peace offering to her friends as if she is a doll they might want to play with. 'Shall we stay here, just the three of us, and play cards?'

'I think that's a jolly good idea.' The scratch cleaned and re-dressed, Chrysanthemum can't help doing up the buttons on Rose's cardigan.

'Orage?'

'I think this is one of those nights that calls for cocoa. Back in a jiffy.'

For the second time, Orage sashays down the corridor, leaving Chrysanthemum and Rose alone.

'You will take care, Rose, won't you? Don't turn your back, will you?'

'I don't know what you mean, Chryssie.' But instead of turning away, Rose comes into her arms and lays her head on Chrysanthemum's bosom.

'I wouldn't ever turn my back on you,' she says finally. *Of the Graces, she is Faith, remember. Living on a hope and a prayer.* 'No matter how long we live, I will never have friends like you and Orage.'

And Chrysanthemum *who is Charity* pats her friend's shoulder and thinks the words of a prayer.

# Chapter 18

'His Gillpots liked the new routine.' Dolores' mouth has something like a smirk round the edges. *That doesn't bode well.* 'He liked the pom-poms and he's asked me what else I could run up in a jiffy. He must think you've improved, though I'm not sure what gave him that idea.' The smirk slides into the expression of a tiger licking its chops.

'And look what I've found.' She reaches behind her to one of Wardrobe's heaving shelves for the reveal: three be-ribboned tambourines. *I don't know. Could be fun. What was I worrying about?*

'It's not as easy as you think. You'll have to learn to catch them.'

Because of the tambourines and not entirely displeased by the ruffles on the violet gowns Chrysanthemum has sewn under her supervision for an incoming sister act, Dolores produces a packet of pink wafers from the pockets of her pinny.

'Don't say I don't treat us. These'll do very nicely with a wet while we listen to Workers Playtime.'

'Why she bother I don't know, she never like.' Janna gives her pipe a baleful suck. 'Always she have heard better.'

'I like to keep my ears in tune.' Dolores chunters her way though each half-hour's programme of variety acts. She's out of sorts if she misses it and plays to the gallery when it's on and today's no exception. Installed round the wireless with tea and biscuits, as the singers and comedians go through their paces it's business as usual, tin ears, call that a tune and don't give up the day job, she's heard funnier on people's deathbeds.

'And now we've got a treat for all you variety lovers out there.'

'He's got a good voice, for radio, I'll give him that.' Chrysanthemum wonders if Dolores might be harbouring a secret, late-life pash for Sylvester Sheridan and his dark, matinee idol good looks.

'She's a sparkling newcomer with a brilliant career ahead of her. And though you can't see her over the airwaves, let me assure you, she's as pretty as a picture. Ladies and gentlemen – for the first time on BBC World Service, it is my pleasure to present Miss Orage Meacham, singing...'

The song's title is drowned out with Chrysanthemum spluttering as she chokes on pink wafer crumbs.

'No – listen.' Janna, no longer baleful but quick and eager, leans over the wireless as Orage's voice transforms the popular hit Sentimental Journey into something smoky, enticing; deeper and warmer than Chrysanthemum might have expected.

'She sing nice. She hide under shrub.'

'Bushel, Janna. Hide your light under a bushel. I've told you often enough. How long have you been here? 1911 I think it was. And you were covered in fleas. Turned a pillowcase black with them. Never seen the like. Bit Tira when she tried to scrub you. I knew we'd get on.' Crumbs sputter from her mouth but tea and wafer don't stop Dolores in her tracks when there's a mouthful to be given.

'With you, too long. Bush. Is same.'

'She never said... She's never sung... I never knew.'

'Well you do now. She's a sneaky cow and no mistake. Better have another wafer.' A faint expression of what might be approval creeps over Dolores' face.

'She sneaky maybe but she sing very nice.' Janna starts to waltz round the cutting table.

'Oh do sit down. I haven't got time for you wafting about sending things flying with your sodding skirt. At least she's gone and got herself somewhere. No more grubbing around at the bottom of the bill for madam. She'll never find herself on the bill beneath the talking sponge, that's for sure. Not that I approve of her sneaking off. I'll put one of these tambourines away then, shall I? She'll get a thick ear when I see her.'

'Every person you meet get thick ear.' Janna sounds as if she is trying not to laugh. 'She got two left feet but she sing nice. She never be dancer so why not sing on wireless? She do good. She maybe famous. I see.'

'Oh go count your gold coins.' If there's one thing guaranteed to rub Dolores up the wrong way, it's not being the first to know something. 'Did you ever tell Chrysanthemum that you once sewed a cricket medal into your plaits because you thought you could buy something with it? Isn't it time you went and charged for seeing into the future? You didn't see this, did you? You let me get those tambos out and you never said a word.'

'I maybe did. Anyway she do good. I go. Money not make itself.' Janna waves airily at the radio, pulls a face that uncannily resembles Dolores' narked expression behind her old mucker's back and swirls off in the direction of front of house.

'It'll be all change now. Just you wait and see.' Chrysanthemum is still staring at the radio as if it might offer her an explanation. Dolores carries on berating, banging on, full of herself as per. 'A double-act's a very different thing from three half-baked hoofers with bonny faces. You've sewed on that flounce inside out. You'll have to unpick it and do it all over. And leave those wafers alone or you'll only be able to get work as a roly-poly.'

She picks up the packet, extracts a wafer and crams it in her gob in one, then sparks an Abdulla as if there's nothing left to be said.

But there is, of course.

'Sorry girls, there's no nice way to say this so I'll just get it over and done with.'

Orage stands poised in the dressing room door as if she isn't sure if she's coming on or going out.

'I'm leaving.'

Chrysanthemum and Rose stare at her in silence.

'I'm going to make a record. And go on tour. Sylvester... Sylvester has arranged it all.'

'Oh. I see.' Rose's tiny, flat voice leaves her tiny, flat body like a sigh.

Orage's face floods. 'Oh girls. I really am sorry. At least, sorry to leave you two. I'll miss you so much.'

'You could stay.' Chrysanthemum puts all the persuasion she can muster into the words but she knows it won't tip the balance. She still has to say it. 'You could still sing. You could sing in the act. Now we know you can. Couldn't she Rose? We didn't know before. You might have said.'

'If I could I would.'

Tears glint in the sparkling sapphire of Orage's eyes. 'But when I said I was leaving... I really am. I'm engaged to be married. To Sylvester.'

She stretches out her hand towards the corridor. A man emerges – a man the girls have seen in the papers – and takes Orage's hand.

'Sylvester Sheridan, at your service. Orage has told me so much about you. Pleased to meet you.'

It is the first time Chrysanthemum and Rose have met a real-life celebrity, let alone been bowed to by one. As if that means anything when he is taking their friend away.

'So this is what you weren't telling us.' Rose's voice, still tiny and flat, is now accusing. 'Your secret.'

'I'm so sorry. I know you must think I've been awful, but we've been having such larks together I couldn't bear to spoil it. But I'll make it up. I'll be a better friend, I promise.'

'Congratulations. Rose, say congratulations. Orage is getting married.' *Muriel taught her well. Manners.*

'Congratulations.' Rose's fists are balled.

Chrysanthemum walks over to Orage. For the first time in their acquaintance, the taller girl flinches.

'Don't be a stranger.'

Orage bends down and hugs Chrysanthemum so hard it hurts her ribs. She doesn't let go for the longest time.

'So it's true then. What Janna said. Luck, love and luxury.'

'Yes. But you know, I'd got that already. The Three Graces.' The words choke Orage and she tries to laugh but instead she has to take a deep breath. 'Whatever comes next, that will be the top of my bill for the rest of my days.'

There are two occupied tables in the café and Orage is waiting for the other two Graces at the best one, sitting in the window so that the light falls prettily onto the newly washed and set peekaboo hair that hides one eye in the style of Veronica Lake. She waves the tips of her fingernails at her friends, showing off a fresh manicure.

As Chrysanthemum and Rose settle themselves in their chairs, Orage looks reflectively at the bun in front of her.

'I wish this was even half as spotty as Maurice's face. It's not really a current bun at all, is it?'

'I'll have it if you don't want it.' The unwanted bun is in Rose's mouth almost before it leaves Orage's plate.

'Good lord.' Orage reaches over and taps out a Wild Woodbine from the green packet in front of her. 'Anyone would think you hadn't eaten in weeks. Are you due on?'

'Due on what?' Rose mumbles through the last mouthful of the wolfed bun.

'Your monthlies, dear.' Orage wafts her cigarette in the air.

'I've only ever had two, and then I stopped. I must be a late starter.'

Orage peers through her cigarette smoke.

'When did you stop, Rose dear?'

'Well I suppose I never really started properly. I had one before I came here, and then one after. I remember that because it was awful dancing with cramps and Chrysanthemum got me an aspirin. And then I haven't had any more. I must say I am glad, it wasn't nice at all. And I am hungry all the time, but only for certain things. But other things seem make me quite off colour. Maybe I should just live on buns.'

Chrysanthemum's eyes meet Orage's as Rose bends her head to examine the plate for crumbs.

Chrysanthemum speaks first.

'Rose, how old are you? I mean really?'

'I told you I was sixteen, didn't I? How did you know? You won't tell anyone, will you?'

'Rose, this is important. How old are you?'

'Fifteen.'

Orage catches her breath. Chrysanthemum glares at her, halting whatever she is about to say before it is spoken. Rose's head droops and a tear makes its way down her cheek. Chrysanthemum passes her a handkerchief.

'You're frightening me Chrysanthemum. Is something bad happening to me?'

'I don't know Rosie. I don't know yet what's happened to you.' *The pompoms. Tangled up with the magician's handkerchiefs.* Chrysanthemum signals an appeal to Orage. 'Ask her,' she mouths.

Orage rolls her eyes, and takes a deep breath

'Rosie-Posy, have you done anything with Mervyn that you shouldn't have done?'

Rose turns bright pink, and doesn't say anything.

'Rosie, has Mervyn done anything to you in private that he's asked you to keep quiet about?'

Rose's chin tilts sharply and her nostrils flare.

'You rotten beast! How did you know?'

Chrysanthemum wants to put her arms round her but Rose flings them off and stands up, pushing her chair violently backwards.

'Whatever he did, it's none of your blasted business!'

Orage stands too, and looms over Rose, forcing the smaller, younger girl to sit down. When she speaks, it is in a whisper that, for once, isn't intended to carry.

'It is our business Rosie, because we're your friends. And seeing as it looks as if you're fifteen years old and in the family way, you're going to need all the friends you've got.'

Rose turns her back on Orage. 'I don't know why you're making a fuss, it's nothing to do with you, or at least it won't be, will it? You're leaving.' She can't hide the sobs. She doesn't try.

'I'm leaving the act, Rose. I'm not leaving you. Chrysanthemum, do you think it would be better if you stay with Rose tonight? I mean, all night.'

'I don't see that it would make any difference. It's done now, isn't it?'

'You          won't          tell          him          I've          said,          will          you?'
'Oh Rosie. No. Of course not. But you'll have to tell him.'

Oh the times you wish words that seem the right thing to say in the moment had never left your mouth. If only they were as easy to eat as cake. But that's easy to say, after the event. Less easy to mend and now Rose looks as worn out as an empty costume, discarded on the dressing room floor.

'I've got to go, I'm being picked up.'

Orage looks at the bill and counts coins. 'Rosie, listen.' She speaks to Rose but looks at Chrysanthemum.

'Chrysanthemum will keep her eye on you.'

Chapter 19

Dolores stands at the top of the steps and dismisses her lodger into the night with a lordly wave of a teacup full of gin. Janna's taken herself off on another of her expeditions and Dolores, left to her own devices, has had a few. 'If you're kipping in with Rose that gives me a night off. All sorts could happen. You never know.' She slurs her words and staggers slightly as she waves Chrysanthemum on her way. It's a relief not to have to explain.

At night, in the splendour of Dolores's showman's palace on wheels, the darkness is pierced by shards of moonlight reflecting off its bevelled glass interior. In the bowtop, the night has a different, musky, stuffy, enclosed quality, and once the door is closed and the heavy velvet drape pulled over it, once Rose has blown out the single candle that lights them to bed, the darkness is so complete that Chrysanthemum can't see her own hand when she holds it in front of her face.

Rose sleeps on the pullout – a child-sized bench that wouldn't make a bed for one adult sleeper, let alone two. Chrysanthemum wraps her coat around her and prepares to curl up on the scrap of floor next to it. 'No, get in Bibi's bed,' Rose encourages her. She hasn't mentioned the conversation in the café and neither has Chrysanthemum. For the first time since they met, they'd both rather the other weren't there but that's where manners come in. 'There's more room. Though I don't know if you'll be able to stretch out. But it's nice and snug, and better than the floor.' *It is the sensible thing, and I'm nothing if not sensible. No point making things worse.*

She clambers up into the raised bed, though not expecting to sleep. Used to the hard smoothness of Dolores' art deco chaise longue, it feels strange to plummet into a soft, yielding nest of feathery rags. She reaches out and pulls what feels like an old satin down-filled quilt over her body and it settles over her in the way a comfortable resting cat seems to turn itself into a bag of feathers. Her fingers make out a cord holding thick chenille that would curtain off the sleeping area, but the space already feels claustrophobic so she leaves it open.

'See? Much more comfortable.' *But it isn't. It seems as if she is floundering in a strange, unfamiliar element.*

Janna may be elsewhere but closed in under the shell of the vardo's canopy the smell of her, undiluted by her occasional quick washes in a biscuit tin, is practically an entity in itself. Thick and rank, it stinks like a ground-dwelling forest creature that marks its lair with its own scent. *Laying under Janna's rags, in Janna's bed, inside Janna's wagon, is like being inside Janna; I can't feel where I end and Janna begins.*

Easier to surrender to it than fight it. Chrysanthemum gives herself up, feels herself go under.

That's when they come through, a greased, vaselined blur of pictures, jumping from frame to frame. A bear, dancing; a campfire surrounded by elegant men and women glittering in diamonds; a ship's hold, tilting; the bear again, but chained; a veiled woman in black holding down a furious figure who bites and scratches as her hair is hacked off and the white pillow beneath it swarms black with insects. Two blonde girls, watching. One disdainful, the other curious.

She forces herself to swallow. She closes her eyes but it doesn't shut anything out. There's Dolores, in a white panné velvet cloak, rearranging her clothing as she saunters in the moonlight between her trailer and a big top. There is a mourning-shrouded figure holding Janna down. There's her mothe… No. *Breathe.* Her hands reach into Janna's bedding and grasp handfuls of suffocating fabric. On the pull-out, Rose sighs gently in her sleep and turns over. *Why isn't she awake with all this going on? Hold on. Breathe.*

Then it slows, sharpens. Comes into focus. There's Janna, in the dark and secret world of woods and trees – a world of mysterious scuffles and rustlings as small companionable creatures go about their business. With the nights drawing in she keeps close to the trees and shelters in their shadows, the faded reds of her skirts and the fading fire of the falling leaves becoming less and less distinct with each, shortening, day. She is a creature of fern and frond and leaf mould, her grimed fingers beetling in the earth to find the forest treasures: the roots and shoots and mushrooms that will make soup and sustain life as the days become shorter and the air nips harder so she wraps herself tighter in her shawls and curls herself into her nest of rags in the wagon where she sleeps.

The night world closes around her. She sighs and settles into herself, becoming bigger with each breath, so that soon she grows to the size of the tallest tree. As the moonlight turns branches silver and the fallen leaves to bronze she tracks the fluting twit-twoo of the owls, the flittering of bats, the crackle of hedgehogs rootling in the undergrowth, the clatter and chatter of the young foxes playing in the leaves. Now she's in her crone years, Janna, who in her younger days walked across the Carpathians with a giant bear, finds the company of the small, brown forest creatures, with their bright currant eyes and their searching, snuffling button snouts, suits her very well. She waits until, at last, the crow comes to her, settling itself into her high branches.

'You took your time.' The bird tilts her head and shrugs her wings. She'll tell Janna her stories when she's ready. She isn't ready yet.

'Nothing for nothing. You'll get your treats. There's berries with your name on them. Big, juicy blackberries, the first ones to fall and I'll keep them for you. But you tell me what you've seen.'

The crow shrugs her wings and hops from foot to foot.

'Whisper it,' Janna points at her ear and the bird's beak angles towards it. 'No smoke without fire,' says the crow, and Janna slips a berry in her beak.

The edges of the figures blur, fade, vanish. Under the canopy, Chrysanthemum gulps for breath, as if she's trapped under a thick, heavy blanket. On the pullout, Rose sleeps on, snoring gently.

The hooting of an owl wakes Chrysanthemum in the middle of the night. Too. Woo. She peers, blinking, into the unfamiliar surroundings. Moonlight streams through the vardo's tiny window, straight onto Rose's bed. Rose's empty bed. Suddenly Chrysanthemum is wide awake, and reaching for her clothes.

With great care, Chrysanthemum edges the massive flat deep within the wings in the darkened theatre. Then, tucked out of sight, she watches as Rose flies into Mervyn's arms. His glossy head bends over hers as he towers over her in a lover's clinch, clasping her tiny frame to his. Her eyes close as if finally she has reached a safe harbour.

'I knew you'd come.' Rose lays her head on his chest and sobs gently.

'Of course I did. You're my little bird, my Rosie.' He raises her head, presses his mouth to hers.

Taking the weight of the flat, Chrysanthemum pushes herself backwards into the warm worn velvet of the side-drop, and tries to make out the murmured words between the two lovers.

'We don't have much time, Rose. Now they know. We'll have to do it now. While we still can.'

He gazes lovingly into Rose's face and brushes her lips with his own. His eyes move down, assessing her body.

'While you still fit.'

Mervyn never takes his eyes off Rose's face. He removes his white buttonhole and for long, long moments lays first the flower and then his long hands on her friend's cheeks, caressing away her tears as he mutters endearments into her hair. Who supports her as she appears to swoon like a tango dancer into his arms.

Who holds Rose's limp figure in his arms.

*Limp. Rose's feet. Too limp.*

Mervyn picks her up and carries her towards the box set up at the back of the stage.

*The magic box.* The one in which Rose is jack-knifed, folded up inside like a piece of origami during the act as Mervyn's magical swords pierce the 24 holes before she emerges, radiant and unscathed.

He opens the lid with one hand and pulls out another box. Smaller. One she's never seen before. Places it on the floor.

With the magic box now empty Mervyn places the unconscious figure of Rose inside. He lays her out carefully, folding her, placing her arms on top of her chest. His magician's hands move too quickly for Chrysanthemum to be sure what he's done. Then he replaces the lid.

Chrysanthemum puts her hands on either side of the flat.

In her hands it weighs nothing. She's always wondered why other people make such a song and dance act about lifting things.

Sure the thumping of her heart will give her away, she pads on silent feet through the wings. Her hands are steady, though, as she balances the weight of the flat between them and judges her distance.

Mervyn is about to thrust the first sword through the hole in the top of the box, where it would have pieced Rose through her stomach, when the flat falls on him.

The crash of the falling flat in the empty theatre sounds like the end of the world. Chrysanthemum stands, rooted to the spot. *Knowing what I've done and not believing it.*

Two eyes glow in the darkness of the wing where she's been standing.

'Don't just stand there.'

Dolores, in her coat. More owl than human in her leather flying helmet. Eyes swivelling, taking it all in. Sashaying across the stage without making a sound. All Chrysanthemum can see of her are the prehistoric eyes that have seen everything and hold its secrets trapped in their yellow depths.

Dolores passes her a pair of leather gloves. 'Lift it up.' A stage whisper that for once doesn't carry.

Chrysanthemum obeys. Picks up the flat and tries not to look at the mess of blood and brains on the painted wood. Dolores swabs it with a towel. It doesn't even occur to ask what she's doing there. *She's brought a towel. She knew.* Dolores raises an eyebrow.

'Now put it back. Quietly.' She watches like a hawk as Chrysanthemum moves the heavy wood back into the wings and leans it up against the wall.

'Where you found it. Look at the marks on the floor where it went.'

Chrysanthemum does as she's told.

'Now him.'

'Rose.'

'Leave her. She's out cold. He's chloroformed her. Sleight of hand. I saw it all. It's him we've got to get rid of. Unless you fancy a spell in chokey.'

Chrysanthemum can't make her brain think of words. Is there a word she for what she's done? There must be. She can't think of it.

'Let's get these on him.' Dolores has another towel, a bath towel, which she wraps around Mervyn's head, and a sack, which she pulls over the top half of his body.

'Pick him up.'

Chrysanthemum bends to obey, then halts.

'I can't. He's warm.'

'Pick him up.' The yellow eyes flash a warning. No arguing.

'Take him out the back and put him in the sidecar. Then wait for me while I clean this.'

'Rose.'

'Janna will come for Rose. Now shift.'

*It will be impossible to sit with the sack in the sidecar without touching it. There will be no choice but to touch it, although it will only be with my feet. Which are walking….* Away. *So there are blessings to be counted. And Rose is alive. And it was Dolores standing watching as I …as I …* but there isn't a word for that. Not yet. Not one she can say to herself, and there is nothing that can be said out loud until… *this is a getaway, after all. And we are breaking the blackout, so we risk getting a tug, and then it will be game over, and the evidence in a sack in the sidecar and no explaining that away.*

So without a word being spoken they push the bike between them, easing it over potholes, Chrysanthemum holding it steady when the going is rough so there is no clanking until they are well away from anywhere the sound of two women transporting a dead body in a motorcycle and sidecar might be heard.

Dolores motions Chrysanthemum to get in when they are well clear of houses and on the edge of the wood. She tries to keep her feet clear of the sack – *of Mervyn* – but as the sidecar lurches and bumps on the cinder path to Devil's Kitchen, she has to plant her feet on it to stop herself being thrown out.

Dolores manoeuvres the BSA into its lean-to. The sack – *Mervyn* – is stiffer and heavier – colder – *deader* – by the time Chrysanthemum heaves it from the sidecar and hefts it to the clearing. By the time she reaches the trailer it is a dead weight in her arms. Fingers full of pins and needles and shoulders frozen into a ball of pain, she drops her burden unceremoniously between the trailer and the vardo.

The brown vixen has been sidling in the undergrowth, darting out of sight as they approach but there is no sign of Janna until Dolores whistles. A mottled, flowered shape emerges from beneath the trees and glides to Dolores' side. The coal of her eyes burns black as Dolores whispers a few brief words to her and then she seems to disappear again, merging into the darkness of the way they'd just came.

Chrysanthemum sinks to her haunches.

'What do you think you're doing?' Dolores' voice is low and urgent. 'We've got work to do,' She disappears into the trailer and emerges with an axe and a saw. The axe was used for chopping wood. 'I used to play that.' Dolores juts her chin at the saw. 'In an act. It went between my legs. It'll do. Carry him into the woods.'

Chrysanthemum's legs buckle as she picks up the sack. Teetering, she lays it on the ground.

'I don't think I…'

'Don't you go soft on me girl.' There is no quarter in Dolores' voice. 'I used to think you couldn't hit a cow's arse with a shovel. Well, I've changed my mind. You did what you did and now we've got to deal with it.' As Chrysanthemum looks towards Dolores, the amber eyes glow warmly at her. *We.* She bends down and lifts the sack into her arms with no more effort than if it were a feather quilt. *Unwieldy, but not at all heavy.*

'He wasn't the first to have corpsed on that stage and he won't be the last. Come on, Tallulah, we've got a job to do.' Dolores leads the way as they move off the path and deep into the trees. 'Feather duster into a pigeon, that's the oldest trick in the book. He'd have done better leaving them as dusters. Much more use. Bloody pigeons.' Her voice is a trail of crumbs, enticing Chrysanthemum to follow her towards the execution of their grim task.

Chapter 20

The way the two old Augustes tell it, having a well-earned half in the boozer for a late breakfast, it took both of them to pull Janna out of Mervyn's dressing room.

'Screeching the place down she was. Mad old bat. Russian you see. D'you want Jerry to hear you, I said?' Sid tilts his chin in a way that suggests he's playing to the gallery. 'As for the girl, she was obviously drunk. Reeked of gin. Poor little sod. In my day we had a name for men who behaved like that.'

'A shower.' Joey nods wisely.

'Worse than that. A sewer. But even so. Couldn't hear myself with all that carrying on.'

*I have never once heard Janna raise her voice. And Rose was in the box when I left her.* But Chrysanthemum doesn't say a word, just listens in wide-eyed shock as the self-important Auguste sits in the snug and tells everyone who'll listen about his more than usually eventful ARP round.

'Lost what's left of her marbles, poor old thing.' Joey doesn't want to be on the sidelines if there's an audience. 'She's always had a screw loose. Mind you, what a rotten sod. Do a bunk on a young girl like that. Magicians you see. Slippery bastards at the best of times.'

'Slippery.' Sid enunciates the three syllables in a way that makes it clear he missed his vocation as a Shakespearean actor. 'And slimy. And you can bet that's not his real name. I wasn't taken in of course but that's young girls for you. He'll have pulled this one before, goes without saying. Have his fun, girl gets attached, does a moonlight flit as fast as his slippery little legs will take him. He'll be halfway to the middle of next week by now. Human vanishing act..'

As Sid exits the snug, he all but takes a bow.

Before the curtain goes up for the next day's matinee, the entire theatre is united in sorry disapproval that Mervyn has acted towards Rose in the most ungentlemanly fashion and run out on her. Probably to a wife and children somewhere else. Or one of several. Despicable of course, but it happens. Show people are used to comings and goings, and people who aren't always what they want you to think they might be. Mervyn's dressing room had been cleared out. They'd seen it all before. Taken everything, hadn't he? Hadn't left a trace. He wasn't owed any wages. Timed it nicely, going off with a bob or two in his pocket. There's a word for people like that. The only thing he left behind him was a box. It never occurs to anyone to wonder where he's gone.

It's business as usual with Dolores, holed up in Wardrobe. The left-behind box is filled with hairpieces and an assortment of eyepatches. *Who'd notice a few more costume scraps in the overflowing mounds?*

'Anyone with half a brain could see that one coming,' she sniffs if anyone mentions Mervyn's disappearance. 'Bloody conjuror gone and vanished himself. Good riddance to bad rubbish in my book.'

Janna cooks up a batch of pirogi – to try to tempt poor Rose to eat, she whispers to Orage, although Rose is too sunk in misery even to nibble at one – and for once they taste as if the meat in them is fresh, even if it isn't immediately apparent what it is. *Fresh rabbit. Fresh pigeon.* It doesn't occur to anyone to wonder about the whereabouts of Mervyn's live props. He's just done a bunk, and left that poor child with her heart broken. And, some whisper, a bun in the oven.

The days that follow are the darkest Chrysanthemum has ever known. She moves through her days as if submerged in dark, cold water, trying silently not to drown. Rose, shocked with grief and unable to comprehend the first betrayal of her life, is a rag doll that's lost its stuffing. The act is a shambles, with Orage and Chrysanthemum desperately trying to cover up for the fact that there are two dancers, not three, whilst Rose wanders the theatre corridors in tears.

'This will not do,' Orage says finally. 'She is not well and she is little more than a child. We must take her home.'

Chrysanthemum can no more imagine going home to Muriel with any troubles she might have than she could see herself flying to the moon.

'I don't know…'

'She isn't you, Chryssie.' *When did Orage get so to be grown up?* 'She was happy at home. I know it's hard for you to imagine, but there are people who are. She needs to be looked after. And not by Janna and Dolores. I know you and Rose have got rose-tinted spectacles as far as they are concerned but they are not fairy godmothers. Even now they could be conjuring some witches' brew and that is not a solution. Rose needs to be looked after by people who live in the real world of everyday people. At least until the baby comes.'

*The baby. Rose is such a child that it seems next to impossible that she could be having a baby.*

Rose's mother looks like Rose, or at least what Rose might look like after bringing up eleven children in a two-up, two-down on whatever she could earn hand-to-mouth. But it's Rose's sweet smile that twists her mouth upwards when she sees the Three Graces on her doorstep, though her face changes the moment she sees the glazed, blank misery on her daughter's face.

'Oh Rosie what have you gone and done?' She takes the unyielding girl in her worn, wiry arms and presses her to her apron.

'Is it a young man, sweetheart? I did warn you that you wasn't old enough for all that. But it'll come right, you'll see.'

*No it won't.*

'May we come in?' Chrysanthemum lets Orage do the talking.

'We thought we ought to bring her home.' Orage has a knack when she wants, she really does. Natural authority, but so charming and gracious that no-one realises they are being wound round her little finger. 'Can we come in?''

'My manners. I am sorry. Yes, yes, of course.'

Mrs Brown leads them down the narrow passage, negotiating a pram full of coal, in the tiny, overflowing house. There is nowhere to go that isn't spilling people, or stuff: an old lady and three blonde girls in the kitchen; four wiry boys in the yard.

'There isn't really anywhere to be private'. Mrs Brown shakes her head sadly. 'You three. Take Nanna upstairs. I've got visitors.'

'That's not visitors. That's our Rosie.' The old dear sticks her neck out like a tortoise.

'I want to see our Rosie,' chorus the girls.

'And her friends. They're visitors.' Even at the end of her tether, Mrs Brown's sweetness is undiminished. 'Now just this once, please, will you do what I ask and take Nanna upstairs so I can have a few minutes peace to talk to the young ladies. Please.'

Mrs Brown's imploring doesn't do the trick, but the look in Orage's eyes works wonders, and to soften the blow she produces a bag of toffee from her handbag and bestows it with a film-star smile that lights up the room.

Rose plonks herself at the table and stares at the wall opposite. She hasn't greeted her mother, or her grandmother, or her brothers and sisters, and she gives no sign of recognizing her surroundings.

'Mrs Brown.'

The poor woman jumps at the sound of her own name.

'Oh Rosie what has happened to you?''

Chrysanthemum looks at Orage, and Orage rises to the occasion.

'Mrs Brown. Rose is going to have a child, and the father has – unfortunately – deserted her. Rose hasn't taken it very well, Mrs Brown, and we – Chrysanthemum and I, her friends – have thought very hard about what to do – for the best. For Rose.'

Mrs Brown simply nods. She takes Rose's hand, but the girl doesn't seem to notice.

'It was a very great disappointment to Rose when her young man let her down. She had become very much attached.' *And now he is dead. By my hand. Even Orage does not know that, or even that he would have disposed of Rose as easily and thoughtlessly as…as a magician might casually kill the tiny birds that vanish forever when they turn them into flowers.*

'She's like this a lot of the time, Mrs Brown. And sometimes she wanders off, and then there is the crying.' *The endless crying, the noises in the night like an*

*animal caught in a trap, and Janna barring her in the vardo to keep her from wandering in
the woods at night. Chrysanthemum sometimes wakes and sees Janna, swathed in shawls and
her schoolboy's jacket against the autumn air, puffing clouds of smoke as she mounts guard
on the vardo steps to keep Rose inside.*

'We think it is the shock, and she is very young.' Orage sounds older, and
wiser, than her years. 'She cannot do her job, and in any case, as she is a dancer,
that is not a suitable occupation for a girl who is expecting a baby. And where
she is living…'

Orage's voice tails off.

'Doesn't her landlady… I mean, I know a lot of theatrical landladies would
have thrown her out by now. In her situation. But there are some that turns a
blind eye when a girl…'

'Rose is living in a caravan in Devil's Kitchen.' Chrysanthemum doesn't
mean to blurt it out, but there it is.

Realisation dawns in Mrs Brown's eyes. 'Down Egypt Lane? Not with
Madame Maximova? Or is it Mrs Pickles?'

'Madame Maximova.' It feels strange to refer to Janna by her formal name.
*One of her names.* 'You know them then?'

'I was a chorine. At Jeffcocks. I was only the age she is now.' Mrs Brown
points helplessly at Rose. 'But Janna – Madame Maximova – surely she
wouldn't… she was never… she was a strange one, I'll give you that. But she
was never unkind.' Mrs Brown shudders. 'Not like some.'

'Not unkind, not at all,' says Chrysanthemum firmly. She and Orage have
decided, between them, that it would be tactful not to mention how devoted
Rose has become to Janna. 'But Madame Maximova is an elderly lady, and as
you say, a strange one, and a caravan is a caravan, and Rose is going to have a
baby, and at the moment she is not herself at all, and Orage – Miss Meacham
– and I feel that the best place for her would be at home with her family.'

'With her family.' Mrs Brown wipes way a tear making its way down her face,
but as fast as she wipes, another follows it. She bends and tries to mop her face
with the edge of her pinafore. Orage passes her a clean, pretty handkerchief;
distracted, she looks at it as if she didn't know what to do with it, folds it quickly
into her pocket, and wipes her eyes again with her apron.

'Yes of course, with her family. Yes I quite see. She will have to sleep with
me, so Violet will have to top and tail with her sisters to make room.' She runs
her hands through the pretty curls that are so much like Rose's, only the soft
yellow is run through with silver.

'It will be a squeeze.' She goes for brightness and making the best. Just like
Rose. Pray there is a best, and not just less worse. 'But it will be nice to have
her home. And with the baby to look forward to, she'll soon forget her troubles
when it arrives.'

'We know it will be difficult for you.' It is hard not to love Orage at a time
like this. 'Rose is our friend, and we will help.' She digs in her purse, and brings

out two £10 notes. Chrysanthemum's eyes widen. 'She was owed some wages, so we have brought them.' *Liar. Where did you get that?* 'And we will come very often. We only want what is best for Rose, Mrs Brown, and we think that is to for her be here with you. With her family.'

Mrs Brown smiles bravely at Orage as she shows them to the door, but it is through tears.

'Goodbye Rose. We'll be back to see you shortly.'

Rose stares at the wall. When Chrysanthemum looks back down the passage, she sees that her friend hasn't moved an inch.

'It is for the best.' Orage's voice has the same kind-but-firm tone she used for Mrs. Brown.

'I know it is.' The sadness and stress of it all make Chrysanthemum snap. 'But in that case, why does it feels like the worst?'

Orage doesn't answer. When Chrysanthemum looks at her to see if anything is going to be forthcoming, she sees a crystal tear is gracefully sliding down Orage's perfect powdered cheek. *Am I the only person who isn't in tears? I don't dare start in case I never stop.*

Chapter 21

Afterwards, after Orage has gone and there is no act to be part of, when Rose is changed and Mervyn is dead and when it seems beyond belief that life could go on, or at least any kind of life worth living, there is a routine to existence in Devil's Kitchen and a kind of domesticity. That in itself is a surprise. But there are others.

For one, how warm the trailer is. After that terrible night in the woods – and though it wasn't been a cold night there had never been one more chilling – Chrysanthemum hoped the block of ice inside her would freeze her from the inside so she could never feel anything again. But the wagon is cosy, and she has a mammal's instinct to keep warm.

And even though there is no more dancing in the show, Dolores keeps her busy. In the theatre, she's put to use in Wardrobe and in the trailer there may be peace of a sort but there is no rest. *For the wicked.* There is a Queenie stove in the living area and the first job in the morning is to riddle it out and stoke it up. Ready to relight in the evening, the little woodburner emits a snug, dry heat. The physical comfort more than compensates for the choking mouthfuls of woodsmoke that billow out when she makes what Dolores calls a pigs' ear of lighting it.

There is always something to do: kindling and wood that need to be collected, water carriers that need to be filled, bedding to be aired and shaken. Whether she likes it or not, Dolores sends her out, sack in hand, to get firewood. And for all the apparent surface disorder of Dolores' dwelling, there is a place for everything and woe betide the unwary lodger who stacks the tins in the wrong order or folds the bedding into the wrong chest. By the time she's done it all there is always something else to be done, before the thoughts can crawl in and take hold.

It isn't spoken of. What happened that night is tidied away and never mentioned. Perhaps not for the first time. Who knows what went where in here? A place for everything and everything in its place. The trailer is spacious but ingeniously designed, with strategically placed hooks, cupboards and stowaways ensuring that not an inch of space is wasted. The terrible saw from that terrible night has never been seen again. 'Don't ask and you won't find out.' The words hang in the air but are never spoken aloud.

Not a scrap of surface is undecorated, either, and the images draw

Chrysanthemum into a world that's a retreat from the one outside the trailer, where the images are always the same: Rose; Mervyn, the falling flat. The glow of Dolores' eyes under her motorcycle helmet. The sack, and what became of its contents in the unlit glade. She couldn't think of it, and she couldn't not. So instead, she stands in front of the old artistes' calling cards, circus posters, music hall flyers, souvenir photographs, snapshots including Dolores resplendent in musquash and peacock-topped turban, holding Usnavy on a leash, or the oil painting of the back view of a meaty peroxide blonde in bias-cut flesh tones waiting to emerge from deep red curtain folds into a glittering big top.

Peering at it, this one is signed. 'Laura Knight. I've heard of her. Isn't she that war artist?'

'Well she might be now, for all I know, but she used to prefer the smell of greasepaint.' Dolores' face, reflected over and over in the refracted light of the myriad mirrored surfaces, is a repeat motif in the trailer's carny collage.

'She liked our sort – did a lot of pictures of show people at one time. Janna was in an exhibition. Kelly Torker Dancer it was called, we had a laugh about that because she thought that was Janna's name.'

'Maybe she wasn't to know. Janna's got quite a lot of names.'

'Don't show your ignorance. It means dancer in her language, that's all. We never put the great artist straight, we were having too much fun that she'd called the bleeding thing "dancer dancer." She always had a good eye for a backstage view, I'll give her that. She did me too but only from the back, or at least that she finished.'

After the unspeakable trip into the depths of the woods, Dolores makes her lodger more welcome but she does it in her own way. Like a bomb that might go off at any moment. Or a bad-tempered cat. In this closed-in space she's curled up but she might lash out. *She's like that stove. It makes you feel warm and draws you to it but you have to watch not to burn yourself on it.*

Tonight's no exception. Sitting on her chair draped with the tiger skin that had once been Usnavy, clad in the voluminous apricot nylon negligee that signals she's inside for the night, furiously knitting a sock by the light of three strategically placed oil lamps, Dolores, busily replacing accidental puffs of woodsmoke with deliberate Abdulla fumes, is in the mood for telling stories.

'Tira put it about that it was her in that picture but she wasn't fooling anyone. She could never fill a frock like that.' Dolores stops in her tracks to admire her reflection in the nearest glass surface, smiling as she caresses her beard.

Tira. Another secret that has been tidied away. But Chrysanthemum remembers what Maurice said about the cooch dancing. Dolores likes the tease, without there ever being a cat's chance in the warm place of a reveal.

'She did start the drawings for a portrait, but the show moved on and it never got finished. I suppose she thought the great viewing public might not be able to overcome their shock at the sight of the face that God gave. She did some of Janna, too. She gave me them all.' *I bet she had no other choice.*

But, sock nearing completion, gin to hand and following a satisfactory bollocking about the Queenie stove only smoking because Chrysanthemum hadn't raked out the ash properly, Dolores is in a good mood. 'Well, she made a lot of money from that picture of Janna and we weren't offered any. I'll show you another time, if you like, when there's more light, the ones that's left.' *And another time, you might bite my head off asking.*

Dolores bends over the sock and cast off in a flurry of clicks. 'There.' She holds it up. 'Halfway to a pair. It's time she had some new ones. The one's she's wearing now are mostly darn.'

Chrysanthemum reaches out her hand for the sock. It is small, the size of a child's foot, and made of strong, thick wool.

'Have you run out of wool? It's really nice, but it is a bit short.'

'It's how she likes them. How they wear them where she comes from. The socks I've knitted for her, over the years. She's never learned.' Dolores shakes her head, bares her teeth at the sock in an affectionate smile, and folds it into a workbag crusted with tarnished spangles that is evidently the last hurrah of what had once been a costume.

'It's lovely.' Dolores knits as well as she does everything else, which is better than other people.

Chrysanthemum's hand folds itself longingly round the sock. Muriel never made Chrysanthemum's socks, at least not since she stopped being a baby. Since she was a toddler – *since she decided she didn't like me* – she had never made her a cardigan, or a jumper, or even a scarf. Oh, she'd made sure she was nicely dressed, *of course she had, because what would people think?* But all of it had been made by other people.

'Would you knit me some, please, if I was able to get you the wool?'

The fuse has been lit and *I didn't even see the flame.* 'I would not. You can knit your own socks.'

Dolores pulls herself heavily to her feet, unzips six inches of the negligee, and withdraws a fresh packet of Abdullas. Lighting one, she inhales deeply, bends over Chrysanthemum, and blows a mouthful of smoke into her face.

'I don't knit socks for just anybody you know. You've got some nerve. Ooh look, your eyes are watering. You must be tired. Isn't it time you were asleep?'

Yellow eyes smouldering menace through the cigarette smoke in the lamplight, Dolores seems to blend into her striped seat as she glowers at Chrysanthemum until the girl stands up and retreats to her couch. *Yellow eyes. Under a leather helmet. Lighting her way every second of the way on the night that changed everything. There's a reason it feels safe in here. There used to be two tigers that lived in here. And I know for a fact that Usnavy would have been the one on his best behaviour. But this tiger, even though she flexes her claws and growls, has allowed me into her cage.*

Chrysanthemum waits until Dolores has stubbed out her fag and slurped up the dregs from her teacup.

'Dolores? What if I got some wool?'

Dolores makes a noise like a seal barking. 'One thing I'll say for you. You give up less easily.'

'So if I get...'

'I'm not doing it for you, if that's what you're thinking. You can knit your own bleeding socks. But God loves a trier. If you get the wool, once you've finished that cardigan, I'll show you how it's done. And while I'm at it, not that I'm thinking of anything in particular, what if you hadn't been there? Think on that, instead of dwelling on things it's too late to change.'

'The thing is though, I even got to liking him. I didn't at first but he grew on me. He did.'

'Give over. You'd need a very long spoon to eat with that one. It's not only bad hearts that do bad things you know, though you'd try the patience of the Almighty. He'd have had your Rose in that box without a second thought. And what about all those other poor girls? You've put a stop to that haven't you? So from now on, young lady, put a bleedin' sock in it. I've just told you I'll show you how to knit 'em.'

Chapter 22

Chrysanthemum is looking through Dolores' collection of biscuit tins, all containing mendings and makings, elastics and fasteners, buttons and bobs, when she lifts a lid to find herself confronted with a severed hand. She gazes at it in incomprehension – it is, as she looks at it, obvious that it is fake, not flesh, but still, quite horrible. A queasy blackness comes over her.

'I've gone all giddy,' she manages, and then slumps to the floor as if her strings had been cut. As she crashes down, the tin shoots upwards and the hand flies across the room.

Dolores picks up the pallid, flabby thing from where it lands. Ignoring Chrysanthemum, she holds it to the light, and examines it, delicately picking off some carpet fluff with a yellowing fingernail. 'If I leave it by the window and let it catch the sun, it'll be glowing in the dark by bedtime. I think that must be why I hung on to it – she used to give us the spoiled ones to play with after she'd cooked them.'

'Play with?' You couldn't imagine a less likely child's toy.

'I don't know where to start. It was an education, the way we was brought up. When we moved on to a new place, she used to send me to the drapers to match up the ectoplasm. We wasn't like most kiddies. What we learned, when other kiddies was doing their kings and queens, was that seeing is believing, but seeing depends on all manner of jiggery-pokery, and there was no-one to beat Ma in that line of work.'

Dolores looks almost kindly at Chrysanthemum. "He might have vanished an elephant off the stage – which was impressive, I'll give him that - but even old Houdini got his tricks from somewhere. And there he was, claiming to be the scourge of the spiritualists. Will you get up you stupid girl? What do you think it's going to do to you? You've gone a dreadful colour. You haven't been eating Janna's pirogi have you? More fool you if you have.'

Chrysanthemum drags herself onto her knees and makes an effort to fight off the sickly waves that make her spine prickle and her head reel. 'You mean your mother... made that?'

'My mother couldn't cook to save her life but she knew a lot of recipes.' Dolores holds out the disembodied hand. 'She used to make them for what you might call spirit fingertips – people don't do it now but it was all the rage. It was a difficult job and she wouldn't do it for just anybody – she wouldn't do anything for anyone unless she could help it. Come on, up you get.'

Chrysanthemum tries, but when she does she feels worse. The floor swims, the bones in her legs seem to have dissolved and her muscles turn to soup. 'Dizzy' she manages. It feels as though a black cloud has sucked out all the air from the room.

Dolores stoops over her, grappling her under the armpits and hauling her upwards, then lifting her onto the couch and draping the red sideshow cloak over her. Chrysanthemum feels herself sinking into the couch, unable to resist, feeling as if the life is being slowly pressed out of her by something shapeless and clammy bearing down on her chest. At the same time, though, she feels herself moving, the sensation of riding on an omnibus, so tired that you keep dropping off, even though you somehow realise the thing is out of control, rattling through the darkness. She makes out vague outlines of faces she recognises as she shuttles past them – Tagalong, Tizzy, even Usnavy the tiger – peering at her through the other side of the glass as the omnibus hurtles forward. Tagalong smiles through the window, and beckons, and she tries to wave to him but her hand won't obey.

She's surrounded by death, she knows that much. Death. It covers her like a clammy, hairy blanket. No, like a flat falling in an empty theatre. Mervyn. Dead in a sack. Rattling in the sidecar. She's brought it with her. It'll always be with her. She tries to lift her hand. A finger. Nothing.

Time passes – minutes, hours, she didn't know – and eventually she manages to move her head. Just enough to see Dolores, sitting in her chair, in her apricot negligee, darning. There are mists gathering round her... no it's just the smoke from one of her Abdullas, smouldering in the ashtray next to her. She lifts it to her lips, sucks in a good lungful, and tilts her head.

'Back in the land of the living are we? Janna really must have put something rotten in that last batch. You was ever so poorly. I put a po next to you just in case.'

'They were waiting for me…'

'To pass over?' Dolores snorts. 'Give over. But you've had a right turn. Missed two shows. Matinee and evening. Mind you, you wouldn't want to see the act they've got in to replace you lot. The Shiteley Sisters. Never was anyone better named. And breakfast this morning. Lovely it was. My favourite. Fried bread and black pudding. I had yours. It would only have gone stale, otherwise.'

'What…happened? To me?'

'You remember telling me about your mother? How she never has a good word for you?'

'What?'

'If you're looking for a nasty piece of work, though, you'd go a very long way to find worse than the woman who gave birth to me. And it seems, in her own truly unpleasant fashion, she's just made herself known to you. She has that effect on some people.'

Dolores stubs out the Abdulla with particular vim, grinding it ferociously into the ashtray. 'Had, I should say. A lot of people like going to the spooks but there never was a one of them spookier than my dear mother. Miss Maude the Mysterious Materialisation Medium Brings Your Loved Ones Back to Life. Well, she did if you could make them out of a vest. At least in the cabinet you couldn't see her face, what with her being locked in and there only being the one red light. It was all ooger-booger and she wasn't actually any good at it but she did have one singular talent, my old Ma, which is that she knew to a T whenever someone's dearest had departed, and for an extra five shillings, the manner in which they had shuffled off their mortal coil. It was uncanny really. Not that I want to be the voice of doom, but I should prepare yourself to be on the receiving end of some news you don't want to hear.'

Chrysanthemum feels the shroud of bewilderment lift, to be immediately replaced by certainty with panic hot on its heels.

'I was on a bus.' She struggles to her feet and, grabbing her coat and thrusting unsteady legs into her shoes, blunders to the door.

'Where do you think you're off to?' Dolores was on her feet. 'What do you mean, omnibus? You've been spark out on that couch for almost 24 hours.'

'No, it's my mother. I don't know what your mother's got to do with it but something's happened. I know it.'

Dolores, tutting, lays her darning to one side. 'Put your coat on and help me get the bike out. I'll run you up to the telephone kiosk. And then wherever else we need to go.'

Muriel had been crushed by an omnibus in the fog. It happened her way home from her shift at the Forge in the evening blackout, the nurse tells Chrysanthemum before they take her down to the mortuary. It would have been instant. 'That must be at least some consolation,' the nurse says kindly.

The nurse peels back the covering to show Chrysanthemum the face. It is Muriel, her disdainful, pinched expression captured as if in wax, but with the hair arranged on the wrong side. Chrysanthemum reaches out to rearrange the grey curl, and then thinks better of it. *Why can't you just leave things alone? Let me be.* She doesn't want those to be the words she can hear her mother saying, but they are.

Chrysanthemum looks down at the body on the gurney and tries to feel more than she did. *I've never been able to make things right. It's too late now.*

'I'm sorry, Mother.' She says it in a whisper but it carries more than she intends. 'I know I wasn't the daughter you wanted. But I did try.'

Dolores, waiting by the door, is still wearing her flying helmet.

'We've got a ride ahead of us but we'll pop in the Crown across the road and get a brandy inside you. Come along.'

There are a lot of things Dolores could say about mothers, and not seeing eye to eye, and maybe even being in the same boat, but she doesn't. But she is there, and as a swaying, grief-stricken and slightly tiddly Chrysanthemum is loaded into the sidecar for the return journey, it strikes her that it is not for the first time.

Chapter 23

Chrysanthemum hasn't thought about the magic lantern for years. But now she's sitting on the stairs holding the box of slides in her hands, she sees it in her mind's eye.

There he is, her father, sitting in his worn tweed waistcoat that smelt of mothballs and tobacco and him, with the old camera obscura that was bought when he was small and then brought out again when she was a girl. He'd sit there as if there was nothing in the world more important, nothing he'd rather do, than be with his daughter, taking out the boxes and patiently threading the heavy glass slides into the projector, reading her the stories because she loved to hear them in his voice long past the time she was old enough to read them for herself. They were old fashioned even then, relics of a past generation of children, but she remembers how much she loved them, loved the stories, loved the transparent painted rectangles with their coloured bindings of red, pink, green and orange paper, loved watching them come to life as pictures on the wall, Cinderella and Alice in Wonderland and Grimm's fairy tales.

After her father died, her mother gave the lantern away. *You might as well let some poor children play with it, you've got your schoolwork to be getting on with.* It didn't make any difference that the lantern was a link with her father. *I've only got to dust it.* And that was that. Until after Muriel's funeral.

Clearing the house is awful – awful – but her clothes are far too small for her daughter and Muriel hadn't kept much in her life for Chrysanthemum to take away to remember her by. The empty suitcase Chrysanthemum brings with her only contains a couple of framed photographs, some napkins and a tablecloth, a small leather jewellery case, a copy of Little Lord Fauntleroy and a Book of Common Prayer, and, found discarded at the back of the bathroom cabinet, a bottle of good eau de cologne that has never been opened. *I gave her that so she could smell nice after she got back from the Forge and she never even used it.* That gives her a pang, and the tears come. She unscrews the top and breathes in the clean cologne scent, so different from the fug of Abdulla and stale Ashes of Roses that envelops her every time she gets home. Home. When did this house, as cold as charity, ever feel like home? 'Who were you?' she asks Muriel's empty hallway. Out of nowhere, there is rage. A torrent of rage. 'Who were you and who am I and why was that always, always the wrong thing? What was it that you couldn't love? And now you'll never tell me, will you?'

There is no answer. Chrysanthemum has learned, over the years, not to expect one. 'Why should I want anything from here?' she sobs, beyond minding that there is no-one to there to hear. Or to care. 'I'm something you could never love now.' Remembering why, she halts, shudders, and stops herself.

And then, once she has taken some very deep breaths, wiped her eyes and blown her nose and pulled herself together, she feels under the sink and there it is. A box of glass slides. All at once she remembers sitting by her father, entranced as the fairytale images fell onto the wall. *Perhaps there is something for me after all.* She picks up the box and carefully places it in her gas mask case.

Back in Devil's Kitchen, Chrysanthemum finds the trailer empty. She takes out the box of slides and lifts the lid. Picking the first slide, she holds it up to see what it contains. But this isn't a painted picture of Cinderella, or Alice, or even Rapunzel. This is a picture of a young woman. A young woman that she has never seen before, but whom she recognises. She picks up the next slide and there she is again. And again. Other characters come and go but Muriel is in each one.

Chrysanthemum puts the slides in order, holds them carefully in front of her and takes a deep breath. Then she picks up the first slide and holds it to the light.

*Muriel wants to be a good mother. All she ever wanted was that. A wife and mother. She has begun to think it will never happen. There was Terrence, of course, but Muriel was only fifteen and he was two years older, and it wouldn't have been right if he'd promised anything when he set off for Flanders, but he wrote to her, and she wrote back, stilted little notes filled with hope and a growing fondness, not just for the idea of him, the handsome young solder, but for what Terrence revealed of himself. And then nothing, and she was told about it as if she was just another of his old school friends. Which, in a way, she was: they had never so much as held hands, let alone kissed. But she mourned him sorely, and the chances that had gone with him, which with each year that passed became a more pressing source of loss than the absence of Terrence himself. Ten years after the ragged remnants of the Pals regiment limped back from the trenches, Muriel barely remembers his face but she feels acutely that he has done her a disservice by getting himself shot in the Somme, and that she has been cheated of what her life should have been. So when Ronnie, with his curly sideburns and travelling salesman charm, seeks her out, she is in an unseemly haste to give him more, even, than he asks for. And then he moves on, no forwarding address, and she is left to pick up the pieces.*

Chrysanthemum's heart is hammering as she picks up the second slide.

*When Muriel is 27 and an old maid and damaged goods, and has all but resigned herself to the life of the spinster daughter who will eke out her days caring for her mother, along comes Ernest. Much older, and a widower, and not what she might once have chosen for herself, but he seems kind, and is established, and Muriel quickly sees that he's a better option for her than being on the shelf for the rest of her life. Ernest offers Muriel a chance to scratch back some of her abandoned dreams of being someone. Of being respectable. Of being a Mrs, not a Miss.*

*Ernest has moved to the town as its chief librarian, which is how Muriel makes his acquaintance, when she is changing her mother's library books, and due to a staff shortage, Ernest is manning the counter. At home, he is placid, predictable and implacable about routine. He spends his spare time reading, and prefers quiet. As Muriel has expected, he is kind. He is appreciative of her housekeeping skills, respectful, and courteous.*

The third slide contains a picture of a man and a woman, in their bed with their heads on their pillows and the eiderdown tucked up to their chins.

*Every night, before he turns out the light, he places his book on the beside table, turns to Muriel in their bed, and kisses her on the forehead. 'Goodnight my dear,' he says, and then lays back on his pillow. On Saturday nights, he gently lifts her nightdress and asks politely if he might make so bold, or if she has no objection. As he drifts off, snoring gently, Muriel lies beside him, eyes wide open, hungry for something she can't give a name to, and wonders if, with Terrence, there might have been something more. The something she gave to Ronnie. She tries not to let herself think about that.*

*'You'll soon be in the family way,' her neighbours smile. But she isn't, and after a while, people stop mentioning it, and avoid the subject of children. She looks at Ernest, sweetly snoring in his striped pyjamas next to her, and wonders how a child might come. Night after night she listens to the gentle snores and imagines the child she might have. A girl. A dainty, pretty little girl who would worship her. A neat, quiet little girl, just like she was. They could be everything to each other. People would stop in the streets and admire her little girl for being so nicely brought up, and her for being such a good mother. No one would look at her with pity in their eyes, once she was a mother. She wonders if the absence of a child is a punishment for what happened with Ronnie.*

The fourth slide is a picture of a circus parade, with a neat figure in a cloth coat and cloche hat in the bottom left-hand corner, watching.

*And then Jeffocks Jollies comes back to town. Muriel is sniffy about the parade, with its horses and elephants and clowns cavorting in the street, and doesn't join the throngs who come out to see it pass by. She remembers Jeffcocks from the Ronnie time, and looks the other way. But then she overhears a women in the haberdashers, who mentions that she'd heard there is someone — not on the posters, and by private appointment — who could look... who could see a person's most secret desires... and the idea takes hold that this person, who after all is with the circus, and will be moving on, and knows nobody who might breathe a word... might... help. Again.*

Tears come to Chrysanthemum's eyes as she sees the fifth slide. In it, a woman is looking down at the baby in her arms, and her expression is full of love.

*For a time, when Chrysanthemum is tiny, Muriel thinks she has found more happiness than she has ever dreamed possible. The tiny hands! The dear dimples and the darling curls! She takes to mothering like a duck takes to water, and Chrysanthemum, who smiles easily, waves her hands and cries only when she is very tired, very hungry or needs changing, makes it an easy task. 'What a beautiful baby,' say the neighbours. 'Isn't she good?' 'Isn't Mrs Landry a lovely mother,' she hears one of them say. 'Aren't you Daddy's girl?" says Ernest fondly, cradling the child next to his Fair Isle pullover.*

In the sixth slide, though, the child is older and the woman looking down at her has frown lines etched into her face.

*When Chrysanthemum starts to speak, though, things begin to change. Her first words aren't 'mama' and 'daddad' but 'who's that?' as she points at an empty corner. 'Puppies,' she says next, although there is no dog in the Landry household. She insists on the puppies although she has never met one at close quarters, ignoring the dolls and teddies Muriel buys her, sitting happily for hours in her room, playing with her imaginary furry friends. 'There are no puppies,' Muriel insists. 'You must stop saying things that aren't true. You don't want to grow up to be a naughty girl, do you?'*

*'Puppies,' replies Chrysanthemum. 'Not naughty. Five. Look.' She holds out her little hands in the precise shape of a child who is carefully cradling a puppy.*

*Muriel finds that she can't bear to look at a daughter who plays with imaginary animals, and as she gets older, mentions people Muriel had never heard of.*

*'But Elizabeth lives here. It is her house too,' the girl insists.*

*Ernest is no use. 'She's just got an imagination,' he says. 'It'll be different when she can read. And of course, when she goes to school. Then she'll have other children to play with.'*

The woman looks even more angry in the seventh slide, in which the child is standing by the door.

*Chrysanthemum is a friendly child, but with the wrong people. She waves gaily out of her stroller at the chimney sweep and hoots with joy when she sees the rag-and-bone man. One day Muriel opens the door to a gold-toothed peg-seller and Chrysanthemum, instead of hiding behind her mother's skirts like a nice child would have done, nearly flies into the woman's arms. Muriel slams the door in her face before she slaps Chrysanthemum.*

*'They steal children.' Muriel spits out the words as if they contained poison. 'And sell them. They'd get a lot of money for a blond girl like you.' She gives Chrysanthemum's upper arm a sharp pinch. As the child howls, Muriel writes out and pins a note on the front door. 'No hawkers.'*

The eighth slide is a dramatic image of the child holding up the weight of an iron mangle that dwarfs her with a single hand, as the woman looks on in horror.

*And then there is the business of how strong she is. At two and a half, Chrysanthemum will toddle back from the shops with Muriel, cheerfully lugging heavy groceries — coal, potatoes — as if they weigh nothing. When she is three, Ernest is resetting the grandfather clock when he slips and falls into the clock's case, sending it off balance. It would have crashed to the floor — except that Chrysanthemum, holding it up with both infant hands, stops it from falling. When she is five, Muriel finds her in the cellar, dragging the mangle to the other side of the room.*

*'I don't know where she gets it from,' says Ernest.*

*Muriel's eyes narrow. A conviction has been growing in her and now it is confirmed. 'She's doing it to spite me.'*

*'Dearest!' Ernest blinks at her through his spectacles. 'She's only a child.'*

*And Muriel lets it go. This time.*

The ninth slide shows the mother looking disapproving as the daughter, wrapped in diaphanous cloth, dances round the back yard.

*The sight of Chrysanthemum, kicking up her heels in the back yard with a table cloth wrapped round her, dancing to a tune only she can hear, makes her bite her lip.*

*'Stop that right now.' She can hear the panicked note in her voice that undermines the authority of her words. 'What will people think? Get inside.'*

*'Dearest. It's just high spirits. Perhaps she should have lessons.' Ernest pats her shoulder and she tries not to flinch. She doesn't want to be calmed, to be gentled.*

*'Even so.' Muriel folds her arms. 'She is. She's doing it on purpose. The little dolly. She's doing it to spite me.'*

There are only nine slides. The set's not complete. There are so many, many things that Chrysanthemum does not know. So many pieces that have yet to fall into place before the picture is complete.

Chapter 24

Since the Shiteley Sisters were given their marching orders, Chrysanthemum's back in the show, jitterbugging with Maurice, who picked up some very flashy moves when the GIs were stationed at a base outside town in the run up to D-Day the year before and jumped at the chance to show them off when His Gillpots made noises about the lack of youthful acts on the bill. Dolores, who rather approves of the new rude American dancing, runs Chrysanthemum up a jive dress with a flippy skirt that shows her legs.

It gets the thumbs up from His Gillpots, too. 'We need to look at the future,' he tells Maurice. 'War'll soon be over and we'll need a few new tricks up our sleeves. Something kushti for the young ones that'll bring in the dinari. Not this load of all old cobblers. Time they was all sent to the knacker's yard, poor old sods.'

Everyone knows it's coming. Dolores has been fudging scraps of red, white and blue into bunting ever since the Battle of the Bulge, and there's enough to do a loop around the auditorium. But when Mister Churchill makes his quiet announcement in the evening of 7 May, it's like popping a giant bottle of champagne, with fizz, pops and bangs going off all over the country.

Duckie and Dora are bringing the house down with Nobody Loves A Fairy When She's Forty when Maurice, who's been tuned softly into the wireless in the wings, leaps on stage. 'It's over!' he bellows, all eyes on him, punching the air, his voice carrying all the way up to the gods, and as one the whole theatre is on its feet, stamping and hollering.

'I've never been so upstaged in all my life,' cries Dora, tears painting tracks of black down her powdered cheeks. 'And I don't mind even the slightest bit. All those poor lads coming home!' She chokes and hurls herself into Duckie's arms without a care for the crushing of her gauze wings and tutu.

'Be brave, darling girl.' Duckie is trying to keep a stiff upper lip, but it keeps wobbling.

'For you? I will!' sobs a distraught Dora, and clamps her lips to Duckie's as His Gillpots, full of himself in his role as Mister Chairman, strides out on to the stage and spreads his arms.

'Tomorrow night will be a Victory Show! Open house! Free for all!'

It's all so wonderful that Chrysanthemum doesn't mind being besieged by Sid, Joey and Albert Emery, all anxious for victory kisses, before Maurice appears at her side, bows gallantly and then sweeps her off her feet and onto the boards.

'It'll be all eyes on us tomorrow, kiddo'.

The stage is given over to dancing, and the lights burn on well past closing time. Maurice brings out his gramophone and audience members get up and shake a leg. Sid and Joey roll a barrel of beer back from the Red Lion, and drinks are on the house. When she staggers back down Egypt Lane on wobbly legs, Chrysanthemum is far too excited to sleep, which is a good job because Dolores keeps her up all night getting the bunting ready to hang.

'That Stella Maris had the brass neck to tell me she thought bunting was vulgar. I put her right in her place. "We've just won the war, you silly old bag," I told her. "And we're in a theatre. We're expected to put on a show." Not that she'd know about that.' Dolores gives Chrysanthemum a more than usually appraising glance.

'People will look back on what they did and what they saw tomorrow night. You put on a good show for 'em. Give 'em something so when they tell their kids what they was doing the night peace was declared, you're what springs to mind.'

She hands the girl some folded cloth. 'I've made you these. Make sure you wear them.'

The pubs have run out of beer and at the Victory Show it's standing room only when Chrysanthemum and Maurice take to the stage. There are whoops and cheers as they strut through their entrance and their syncopated moves gain pace. Chrysanthemum's flippy skirt flies out to show her legs, sending the temperature a good few degrees higher. The excitement mounts as the tom-toms take over from the brass and the insistent rhythm hooks its way into the tune. The dancers step up to the beat, getting flash as the rhythm gets fancy, and no-one in Fankes Musical Hall on VE Day will ever forget the moment when Maurice flips Chrysanthemum across his shoulders to reveal a glimpse – just a glimpse, but that is enough – of what are, unmistakably, a pair of close-fitting, modesty-concealing, patriotic Union Jack knickers.

'Good lord.' Chrysanthemum, preoccupied with the prickling suspicion that two new hairs are growing through on her chin, is stopped in her tracks as she rounds the corner and sees the charabanc parked by the stage door. The war has finally ended, the theatre was packed to the rafters for the Victory show, and now this! A racketty old thing to be sure, with high wheels, low sides and not a roof to its name, but still. A charabanc! All the way to the seaside! Next to it, the entire cast and all the theatre staff including His Gillpots are lined up, all in their best, clutching sandwiches in brown paper bags, waiting for the driver to usher them on board for the outing to Blackpool that has been announced as a treat to celebrate the end of the war.

'This is a right bus-load.' Dolores, swathed in musquash despite the spring weather and topped off with her turquoise turban, swans up to the front of the queue and pushes in behind His Gillpots. 'What makes you think I'm getting in that old boneshaker? Come on Janna, we're going home.'

'You go home pull sulk face if you like. Wind change maybe you stay like that. I go sit front like with horses.' Janna hops up and arranges herself and her skirts behind the windscreen before anyone else has a chance to bag the seat.

'I suppose I'll have to make the best of it. I'll just cock a leg over this.' Chuntering, Dolores hauls herself up next to Janna and makes a performance of digging herself into her seat.

'Good of you to turn up,' she snarls at Orage, who wafts aboard in a cloud of Je Reviens. 'Seeing as none of us were good enough to invite to the wedding.'

'How could I possibly keep away? I mean, such illustrious company.' Orage backhands Dolores a pack of cellophaned Abdullas and a brand new Tangee. 'It's not everyday I get to gaze on such splendour. That's a new shade. Don't get it in your moustache.'

'You can bugger right off back to where you crawled out from you cheeky cow,' honks Dolores, but she budges up just enough for Orage to step onto the bus without stumbling.

Orage makes for the back of the bus and sweeps Chrysanthemum along with her. 'Come on Chryssie, Graces to the rear,' she orders, commandeering the long bench seat. 'Age before beauty. Swine before pearls. Ooh I do feel queasy.'

'Have you eaten something? You do look a bit green around the gills.'

'I've been like this for a few mornings.' Orage's voice has a wonderful carrying quality. 'Let me sit down, I'll be fine when I've had a biscuit.'

She makes herself comfortable as various people turn round to look at her, and then pretend they haven't.

'It's only powder,' she mouths at Chrysanthemum as soon as they've all turned to face the front again. 'But it'll get them all thinking.' She winks and links her arm with her friend. 'If anyone asks about me, tell them you think something must have disagreed with me. If you say it for a week or so they'll have made up their minds without us having to do anything. And at least we get a day out together. I'm so sorry about your mam. Was the funeral awful? I know you weren't close but somehow that makes things worse, or at least as bad. I do miss you, you know.'

'It was a bit grim. Small. It was sad. Dolores came with me you know. It was good of her.'

Dolores, now slurping from her hip flask, seems an unlikely Good Samaritan. She's well away by the time the charabanc sets off. 'It was a train show,' she can be heard boasting, holding court at the front. 'A long one. It was a very big show.' The girls peer to down the bus to catch a sight of her pausing, preening, curling a finger into her moustaches, dirty diamonds glinting through the whiskers.

'It had elephants and tigers and a dance troupe of wild men from Borneo and cowboys. And because of the cowboys, because they were their natural enemies, the train was held up by Red Indians. They captured me and took me to their reservation as a prisoner. I was tied to a totem pole and their medicine man, all over feathers, tattooed me from head to toe. Not an inch of me he left. I didn't make a sound, though of course it hurt like very devil. I wasn't going to give him the satisfaction.'

'Gosh it's like a foghorn, you can hear it through the mists.'

'I expect she's making it up. Anyone who captured her would give her straight back. Anyway, I didn't come to talk about her. I came to see how you were. And Rose.'

'Rose is the same.' Chrysanthemum's lip trembles. 'She lets on as if she doesn't know she's going to have a baby. She won't talk about it. She hardly says a muff, just sits there with a face like thunder, and her Mam says it's all the time, not just when I go round. Can we not talk about her?'

'Let's not.' Orage links her arm through her friend. 'Anyway, I've got something much more interesting to ask you. A little bird told me all about you and your smalls stealing the Victory Show. Have you been keeping up morale, Chryssie? Duckie told me she'd spotted you. Who was that last night?'

'Just a johnnie. A nice one, though.'

A lot of johnnies wait for Chrysanthemum by the stage door these days. Most of them are returning forces boys or soldiers on leave and no-one special to share it with. They're nice boys, mostly, and if they aren't, Chrysanthemum learns to move on swiftly to the next one – and there is always a next one, waiting hopefully outside the stage door for the chance to spend a few sweet hours with a smiling dancer. The shy ones have damp hands and offer bags of sweets. The bolder ones might bring flowers they've pinched from the park, or sometimes just a handsome face, a glad eye and cheeky grin. There's something good in each of them if that's what you're looking for. Chrysanthemum takes it for what it was, and takes precautions. It isn't love, but it's nice.

'No-one special?' Orage's eyes shimmer.

'No-one like your Sylvester, no. I'm not that sort of girl I think.'

'Well whatever sort you are, you're my sort. Now, what shall we do when we get to Blackpool?'

'I don't mind. As long as it's just us two.'

The two Graces give the rest of the cast a wide berth when the charabanc disgorges them all in front of the Ballroom, going in the opposite direction from Duckie, Dora, Albert, Stan, Joey et al, who nip straight inside to use the conveniences.

It's a golden day when they arrive, and it stays that way, one of those perfect spring days on which the sun never sets. The sort of day that makes people look back and say 'do you remember?' Seagulls whirl overhead, the sun shines on the sands, and the two friends walk on the pier, sit in the sunshine, eat fish and chips out of newspaper and although it is far too chilly to swim, take off their shoes and paddle, squealing with happiness as the cold, frothing Irish sea swooshes between their toes and over their ankles. Peace has come, the war in Europe is over, and the future stretches out as vast as the rolling sea in front of them. Deliberately, Chrysanthemum turns her face to the sun and her back to the shadows. She knows they're there. They're never far away, but they can do without her, just for a few hours.

'You know that song? Pack up your troubles?'

'In your new handbag, that Sylvester bought you?'

'That's the one. It feels as if we have, rather.'

'Shall we have our fortunes told?' Arms linked, they wander towards the Pleasure Garden to see if they can stretch to a knickerbocker glory.

'We shall not. You've found your fortune now you've got Sylvester, and I'll make mine. You'll see. Anyway, today's our day off from all that.'

'It is. It's just for us.'

'Anyway if we'd stayed with them they couldn't be gossiping.'

'Thinking what a hussy I am. Couldn't wait to get a ring on my finger before getting a bun in the oven. Well, I am I suppose. Mind you, if I'm a hussy, so are you.'

Chrysanthemum finds, on this golden day, that she wouldn't mind at all if they thought that. *Sorry Mother, but I don't. They go away with a smile on their faces, and leave me with a happy memory. Did you ever smile at a man, Mother? Did you ever smile at anyone?* She turns to Orage and beams.

'They'll be thinking the worst when you're about to do something completely kind.'

'We couldn't very well leave it with Rose, could we? And poor Mrs Brown. When we suggested it she practically kissed my hands. There aren't enough chairs in that house for everyone to sit down. And I do get something out of it you know. Without losing my figure.' Orage smooths her skirt over slim shanks. 'Sylvester and I won't be able to have our own, you know.'

'No, I didn't know,' says Chrysanthemum, although as soon as the sympathetic words are out of her mouth she knows it's a lie. That there is something that Orage has never said but that she's known since she saw her for the first time at the audition. And that this is the closest Orage will ever come to revealing her secret.

'You'll be wonderful.' She means it. 'I mean, you are. But you really will be wonderful.'

'Me in all my glory. You do go on. Well, I suppose we'd better make tracks. Was it in front of the Ballroom?'

They leave by the back entrance of the Pleasure Gardens. A low-lying sea mist has rolled in, bringing with it a close, foreboding atmosphere familiar to Chrysanthemum, if not a friend. Getting their bearings, she and Orage run smack bang into a small knot of passersby standing at arms length from

Dolores. Drunk as a lord and with her turban wildly askew, she's bellowing Ta-ra-ra Boom-de-ay at the top of her voice, waggling her rear suggestively, as Janna clatters out a syncopated beat on the spoons. In front of them is a rusty tambourine containing screwed up fish and chip wrappers and some loose change.

Orage's eyes rise into her hairline.

'We could just leave them.'

'They haven't seen us.'

As they speak, Janna turns her head and fixes the two girls in her sights like a hawk just as His Gillpots rounds the corner and takes in the spectacle of the two smashed old carnies busking in the street.

At the sight of such an evidently authoritative figure, the little gaggle of people surround His Gillpots.

'She threatened our Ethel.'

'With that tambourine.'

'That thing's lethal.'

'And the language.'

'Never heard anything like it.'

His Gillpots picks up the tambourine and thoughtfully fingers one of the cymbals. Blood blossoms where he touches it. The edge has been sharpened. His face gives nothing away as he glances first at a glowering Janna and sullen Dolores, then hands it wordlessly to Chrysanthemum.

'Come along ladies, back to the charabanc. I have an announcement to make. You two, make sure those two don't go anywhere they're not supposed to. I've got my eye on all of you.'

His Gillpots waits until the entire cast, giddy on unaccustomed sun and sea air, is assembled and seated. Then he tells them that he will be closing the theatre. It is going to be converted into a dancehall. All those young men coming back from the war will want somewhere to take their sweethearts. He's signed the contract. The last show will be next Saturday's evening performance. They've all been marvellous. He is very grateful for everyone's hard work, especially in wartime, when the show has done so much for morale. But times are changing and he needs to move with them. They'll be paid until the end of the month, as a gesture of goodwill. And he'd wanted to give everyone this smashing day out, as a personal thank you.

As they drive home in darkness and a stunned silence, the only thing that can be heard over the rattle of the engine is Dolores, snoring.

By the time the charabanc pulls up outside the theatre and its cargo of passengers, chilled to the bone and numb with shock, have disembarked, Dolores is at the stage of drunk where she's on her dignity. She sails down the steps as if she is on a red carpet, and swans off without a backwards glance, not even at Janna.

'Best be off then.' Chrysanthemum totters after them, blowing a kiss to Orage, who is being whisked away by Sylvester's driver.

As the trio tramps down Egypt Lane and through the dark wood to Devil's Kitchen, Janna increasingly camouflaged and less visible against the foliage as the woodland shadows deepen, a glint grows in Dolores' eye that doesn't come from gin. By the time they reach the trailers her jaw is set at an angle that suggests she's ready to take on all comers.

'That's it then. Time for us to jal orderly. Pack up. We're pullin' down, in a manner of speaking, and atching.'

Only slurring slightly, she glowers at Chrysanthemum, her eyes still bleary from the contents of the hipflask.

Chrysanthemum looks blank, and turns with pleading eyes to Janna for help. It's been a long day. *And she must still be drunk, because I don't understand half of what she's just said.*

Janna, partially rematerialised in the form of sharp eyes, a headscarf and a beak of nose, hunkers down on the vardo's steps. She strikes a match, inhales and puffs out a cloud of pipesmoke before speaking.

'Put that bloody light out? I say go ppft. She mean it time for us to take down show sharpish and go somewhere else.'

Chrysanthemum's heart plummets. *So this is it then. Closing time at the inn.* Her out on her ear. On her own. *I thought this was my home.* It's strange to realise, just as you are about to leave it, that you have felt at home for the first time in your life.

She bites her knuckle, hard, and tries to think where she might go. Orage will help her, surely, but Orage is already helping Rose, and she has her own life to lead.

Janna looks impatient. 'So why you waiting? You understand?'

Chrysanthemum nods dumbly.

'How long, do you think?'

Janna cackles. 'Yoyoyoui. She think you throw out like rubbish.'

'Standing there. Like Marsden's monument.' Dolores only hiccups once, gently. 'When things need doing. We're used to moving on. You better shake a leg if you don't want to be left behind.'

The relief that floods over Chrysanthemum at not being discarded is replaced by a swell of exasperation at her charmless benefactor.

Dolores reaches the trailer and after several fumbling passes with the key, holds the door open for Janna, then shoves Chrysanthemum after her. Stumbling into the midden of costume scraps, she gropes around for a while then thrusts a boudoir doll that has seen better days into Chrysanthemum's hands.

'Make yourself useful, chava. Under her skirts... Young eyes are better than mine. Count that.'

Chrysanthemum puts her hand up the doll's legs and finds a bulging pouch.

It's stuffed with paper money.

'Where did you get that? What are you going to do with it?'

'My ill-gotten gains you mean? Now that would be a long story to tell on a dark night. Copper it up and tell me what's in there.'

Dolores pours gin into three teacups, passes them round and sparks up an Abdulla. 'Cheers, my dears. And I've got eyes in the back of my heads so no sticking any of that up your knicker leg. You know I'd play Hamlet and anyway it's all spoken for. We're opening a boarding house.'

Chapter 25

His Gillpots may have sold the theatre but until its conversion to a dancehall is complete, the new owner sees no reason to turn away either customers or anything that might bring them in to look at his advertising for future attractions – and that includes Janna's booth. A new notice has appeared outside the booth since the boarding house back garden incorporated – after a couple of trips in the sidecar from which Janna appeared with chickens emerging from under her skirts – a hen coop. Beneath the sign advertising her professional services, another, written in curly block capitals, reads 'also eggs.'

'They not always buy,' she complains, as Dolores concocts a late supper of scrambled eggs seasoned with Abdulla ash for what seems the hundredth time. 'Why is it they not buy my so nice eggs?' She gulps from a teacup and Chrysanthemum catches the distinct whiff of gin.

'I don't know Janna.' Chrysanthemum bites her lip and tries to look helpful *Perhaps it might be because they want their fortunes told, not groceries?*

'Is so nice eggs. Maybe I place sign higher.'

'Yes, you do that. Get them sold.' Dolores, settled by the fire with a green glass bottle by her side and a glass to hand, in her apricot negligee, musquash coat and a fox-head tippet that matches her beard, is in an excellent mood. The other boarding house in the street has suddenly sold up and shut up shop, leaving its clientele – longstanding regulars – with no choice but to decamp to Dolores'.

'Apparently there was something nasty at the top of the landing.' Her ths, which she pronounces as vs, and the long nasal vowel in nasty, give the impression that whatever it was had been memorably unpleasant.

Having had a few, Dolores preens. 'A smell, or suchlike. I can't think what it might have been.' She rolls her eyes. The fox round her neck appears to blink in agreement. 'Not to mention other irregularities.'

She examines yellow, stained fingers encrusted with dirty diamonds and waves them airily in Chrysanthemum's direction.

'I know what you're thinking, dearie.'

*She's got the same shaped hands as me.*

'Usually when there's something nasty at the top of the stairs, you're thinking, it's me.'

Janna shakes her head, setting the coins in her plaits jangling. She covers her mouth to conceal the laughter – a rusty, creaky sound.

Dolores throws back her head in a brazen, insolent guffaw, her beard a furry circle round red lips, a tongue glistening with gin and spit, and strong teeth. *Murderers' hands.*

'But where's the proof? Here I sit. Broken hearted. Went to shit, and only farted. Oh don't look at me like that. Here, Janna, tell us a story.' The s-sounds slur. *How much of that gin have they got through?*

'I have no stories to tell.'

'Don't you come the dog with me.' *Ver dog.* 'That's for the punters. Here, I'll start. Once upon a long dark night, three smugglers sat in cave.'

Janna's hands move down to her skirt in a well-practiced move.

'Don't you shake your skirts at me.' Dolores is well away. 'Anyway, where was I? One smuggler said to the others, come on Bill, tell us a story.'

'I'll tell you a story.' Janna pounces on the green bottle. 'Once upon a long dark night, two young womens shared a wagon.' She pronounces it 'vagon.' And 'vomens.'

'And more than the wagon, they shared also other things. Nas drovje!' She unscrews the bottle and drinks directly from it. 'A mother. And an other.'

Dolores raises an eyebrow.

'A man.' Janna slurps from the bottle again, and bends over, coughing and cackling. 'Is like sandwich. Two womens one men in the middle for juicy filling.'

'I don't think this is the sort of story that young ladies ought to hear. Chrysanthemum. Hop it. It's well past your bedtime. Boarders' breakfasts at seven, remember.'

Two sets of old, beady eyes bore into Chrysanthemum's back as she leaves the room. The hall echoes with laughter – rude, drunken laughter – from behind the closed door as she makes her way up the stairs. The noise insinuates its way through the floorboards so that she resorts to pulling the pillow over her head to try to get some sleep as the two old carnies relive their glory days. *Something they know, and don't want me to find out. Something nasty at the top of the stairs. And something nasty at the bottom.*

Days and weeks go by. A routine, restless and watchful, imposes itself: boarding house, booth, grief made up in equal, anxious parts of worry about Rose, mourning what was and now never will never possible in her relationship with Muriel, playing over and over again in her mind the night when Mervyn… when she… . That's all there is, day in, day out. There is no space, or time, for anything else.

As often as she can, she visits Rose and Mrs Brown. Partly because it helps the guilt, to do what she can, to make up for… *what? Saving her friend's life? Or killing the person she loved?*

But life goes on. A plan has been agreed, and it needs to be set up, and staged, and played out as best it can be. Dolores always makes sure she never goes empty-handed, and there are messages to and fro from Orage, which need to be relayed. It hurts, being with sullen, silent, furious Rose, Rose who sits in the chair by the fire, hair all over the place like a crown of sticky feathers, cramming everything that Dolores sends into her mouth uncaring if the crumbs fall in her lap. She grows as round as a ball and scowls more and more as she gets bigger and bigger, so her face peering over her distended body looks like a hen's bottom. Chrysanthemum is drawn back to her like a magnet even though every time she visits it reinforces how different this Rose is from her Rose, who made everything better just by being there. This Rose sits, and eats, and stares, and scowls, and has nothing to say about any of it whatsoever. Although nothing is happening without her knowledge, it is as if her mind has taken itself out of the equation while her body grows and grows and grows. *And some of that is because of what I did.* And that thought goes round and round in Chrysanthemum's head, battling with the other thought that *if it hadn't been for me it would have been Rose, not Mervyn, who was dead. And I can't tell her either of those things.*

'She'll be more like herself when the baby comes,' says Mrs Brown 'Won't you, Rose?' Every time she says it, Rose's eyebrows meet further in the middle. 'The wind'll change, cajoles Mrs Brown, 'and you'll stay like that.' But Rose refuses to be jollied along.

'I don't know why poor Chrysanthemum comes to see you.'

Rose rouses herself from her torpor to glare at her mother. 'No-one asked her. She doesn't have to.' Chrysanthemum doesn't know whether to recoil with hurt or rejoice that Rose has responded.

Mrs Brown shoots a look of anxious apology at Chrysanthemum.

'She's been ever such a good friend to you Rose. Don't be like that. He couldn't have been a nice gentleman, if he could get you in this state to begin with. You won't stop coming, will you, Chrysanthemum? She'll be herself again when the baby arrives.'

'Of course I'll come.' It would never occur to her not to.

And partly, more and more, she goes for the company, and the stories. There's always a space for her in the cramped little house, and always a brew, and maybe because it's a distraction, Mrs Brown tells her things from the old days, when she, and her mother before her, picked up bits of work from Jeffcocks. Tales of Dolores, and Tira, and the characters from the cabinet cards and posters that lined the showman's wagon's walls.

The stories are like scraps, and Chrysanthemum painstakingly pieces them together and adds them to the scraps she already has to try to make them into something that makes sense. A collage that forms a picture. It's Janna and the samovar all over again, she thinks. It was and it was not. And as the pasts of the people she has become connected to pull her into their puzzle, it pushes the pain and sorrow of the present into a place where it becomes sufficiently distant for her to deal with it.

# WHAT MRS BROWN SAW

*'Maude had the twin girls, and they was both terrors, which is only what you'd expect, and as like as two peas if it hadn't been for the fact that Dolores took after her mother in having the beard, whereas Tira's cheeks was as smooth as a newborn baby's bum. She was a looker and no mistake, a real golden girl, but her twin sister was more than a match for her, facial hair or no facial hair. Dolores had the moves, she had the voice, and whatever else she had, the gentlemen seemed to like it, so they was round her like flies round a honeypot.*

*'They earned their keep at Jeffcocks, as well. Miss Maude saw to that. She may have been out of sight, but hers was a reign of terror from that backroom, and her girls were at the top of their trade the first time they ever stepped out in front of an audience.*

*'At first, when they was just nippers, they were The Heavenly Twins, and a more angelic pair of moppets you never saw. That all had to stop when they became young ladies, of course, which is when Dolores started sprouting the beard, and Miss Maude separated them, with Tira singing on the music halls, whereas Dolores was sent to the US, where she kept with the circus. Folks came to the sideshows to see the human curiosities, but your bearded lady was usually more in the way of a human statue; nicely dressed and always very ladylike, whereas Dolores had trained as a song-and-dance act, and she knew she was good. So she combined the two, which was unheard of in them days. She went down a treat – where she learned some of them moves no one ever knew, and she never had what you might call a family act – but the gentlemen loved it, and once she came back to this side of the pond, if a lady wanted to be considered fast, then all she needed to do was mention that she'd been in the audience when Dolores did her turn. Divine Dolores who defies what mere mortals are capable of, that was how she was billed. And she got paid for it as well: one of the highest-paid performers under canvas she was. On her own terms you see. There wasn't another one like that so if you wanted it, you paid the going rate.*

*'And that's where all the trouble started. Tira didn't like it one bit. As far as she was concerned she was the looker, she should be the star. And it wasn't working out that way.*

*'Now you'd expect both of them to be spiteful – they was Miss Maude's offspring and there was many that said that one didn't have a heart, at least not of the human variety – but what Miss Tira did next – well, it might have been meant as a bit of fun, but it was wicked all the same. There was some business with a young man on the show they both liked. She must have put something in her sister's nightcap, and then she crept in whilst Dolores was asleep – and shaved her.*

*'Well, that meant Dolores couldn't work til it grew back – she'd lost her trademark, hadn't she? Who's going to come and see a dancing bearded lady without a beard, no matter what kind of tricks and contortions she can do? So she went away. For some time, I might add, to get it back to its full luxuriant splendour – and when she did, she made sure that she'd never again be without something special that set her apart. So she had herself tattooed – from top to toe, so they say. And every prick of that needle was like a prick of hate for Tira, who might have been a beauty, but she was just an ordinary beauty, whereas with every new line of ink, Dolores became more exceptional. Now you consider how many pricks it*

takes to cover every inch of a person in ink. Dolores was that poisoned with loathing for her sister that there was never going to be anything but trouble.

But Tira was so swept up in her own success that what she never reckoned on was that Dolores was cleverer than she was. She waited. She smiled sweetly when Tira went to America and said she was pleased for her when Tira started to get parts in the movies. She made nice when Tira came home draped in furs and dripping pearls, so that Tira never thought there was anything up. Dolores had her own place as the attraction – sideshow, not main stage – and as far as Tira was concerned, it was all in the past and she was in her rightful place as the star. And Dolores let her have her place in the sun.

'At this point, I ought to point out that although Dolores had never been short of gentlemen callers, there was one in particular who had his eye on her. Mustapha the snake charmer. Well, there wasn't a female in that show that wasn't a-flutter at the thought of him and his smouldering eyes and his curly moustache, and we'd all have given him the chance to play his pipes, should he have asked, even when we found out that his real name was Albert Pickles and he came from Barnsley. But we all knew to keep our hands off, because she had her eye on him, and like I said, she was a terror.

'Not that she was ever nice to him – she treated him like muck, leading him up the garden path and then like as not, throwing her washing water at him and worse if he said a word out of place. But everyone on that show knew he was a marked man – that is, until Tira clapped eyes on him.

'Just like the rest of us, she was smitten, and she set her cap right at him. She was going to take him with her to Hollywood, she said, she was going to get him in the films, they were the coming thing and what they couldn't do together, her all golden and him all dark and handsome, they'd set the silver screen alight and the world on fire.

'Well, you wouldn't have blamed him if his head was turned, and it looked as if she'd got him eating out of her hand – and a whiter, more jeweled hand you've never seen. And when Miss Tira made her cow eyes at him, he made them right back, and it was noticed that his slinky way of walking was becoming much more of a swagger.

'And Dolores watched, and she waited whilst Miss Tira mooned after him, and she never said a word that Bert was mooning right back, and not at her. All anyone could have said of her at that point was she spent her days minding her own business and that the queues outside her tent were longer every night. Something to do with a new costume, and how it set her off. The word got round that some of her tattoos took on a life of their own when she did the shimmy and shake. An eye on her elbow that used to wink at the gentlemen, for a start. And she made sure that whenever Bert clapped eyes on her, she was minding her Ps and Qs, though she'd given word that neither he nor Tira were to be allowed inside the tent when she was performing. You could tell he was torn though. One night he slipped inside, paying like a punter and dressed in a cap and muffler, but she knew it was him and she stopped the act and said that if the audience wanted her to continue to the finale that the gentleman familiar with reptiles – she said that very pointed – would have to take his leave. The crowd was all fired up and Mustapha didn't want pulling limb from limb, so off he went.

'Then out of the blue one afternoon, Tira and Mustapha sailed into the big top, arm in arm with a bunch of flowers between them. Tira announced, as sweet as pie, that they'd got *married that very morning and her name was now Mrs Albert Pickles, and Dolores could put that in her pipe and smoke it. And that she'd have to move out of the trailer and find somewhere else to live because Bert was moving in, and she'd heard all about ménages a trois but it wasn't going to happen on her watch. Oh and by the way, she said, it was just for the time being because after the summer season she was shipping stateside and that Bert would be going with her because he'd got himself a contract too. In the films.*

*'And of course Dolores never forgave her for that. And Tira should have learned her lesson there, but she didn't. It made no difference that Bert never got as far as the ferry, because he choked on a beetroot sandwich. That was two strikes: first the beard and then Bert. It made no difference that they'd shared a womb. Dolores was her enemy now. She was just biding her time.'*

Chapter 26

There are things about living in a house that don't sit right with Janna. For a start, she isn't happy with the doors shut, and whatever the weather, rather than sit in a chair in the living room, in the evenings she makes a small fire out of twigs and squats on the back step, with the door wide open, wrapped up in her tweed jacket and extra shawls, puffing on her pipe and alternately gazing up at the stars or eyeing the chickens.

'You're letting in a terrible draught,' grumbles Chrysanthemum, earning a more than usually filthy look from Dolores, who rather than desert her old friend, has taken, rather grandly, to wearing her turban and the fox collar over her apricot negligee to keep out the chills, and staying with her in the kitchen.

Dolores doesn't permit the boarders to enter the kitchen or the back parlour that she uses as a sitting room where the samovar has pride of place on the sideboard – their access to the house is limited to the dining parlour, the bathroom and their own rooms. If they want so much as a glass of water, they have to ask for it and have it brought to them, which means extra work for Chrysanthemum, but it is better by far than risking their using china that isn't earmarked for their particular use. Even Dolores loses patience when she discovers Janna, rather than risk eating from a dish that has been contaminated by being used by a stranger, has smashed the entire set and stashed the pieces in the dustbin.

'She can't help it, it's how she was brought up,' is all she says when Chrysanthemum shows her what Janna has done, but words must have been said, because after that the boarders are kept away from Janna, and she from them, and their dishes are returned to the dining room – from which Dolores denies Janna access – as soon as Chrysanthemum has washed and dried them.

And then there are her ablutions.

'Janna, where are you off to?' Chrysanthemum has been wakened by a scratting at the back door, *like a fox trying to escape*. She's come downstairs in her dressing gown, brandishing a poker *just in case*, but when she gets there, it's only Janna, fumbling to reach the bolt at the top of the door with one hand and clutching her biscuit tin to her side with the other.

She casts an embarrassed, anxious look at Chrysanthemum, and bends her body over the tin, as if trying to conceal it.

'Are you trying to get out? What are you doing?'

Janna shakes her head furiously.

Chrysanthemum rubs her eyes. There is barely any light in the room; dawn must just have broken.

'Here, I'll do it.' She reaches up and draws the bolt.

The moment the door is open, Janna scuttles through it, holding her tin in both hands. Chrysanthemum hears the sound of liquid splashing against its metal sides, and Janna moves up the path. *Poor old love, she's been caught short.* But Janna beetles past the outside lavvy and out of sight. *Might as well put the kettle on now I'm up.*

As she fills it from the tap and sets it to boil, it strikes Chrysanthemum that she has never once seen Janna visit the bathroom. But when they lived in Devil's Kitchen, she'd occasionally observe Janna carefully pouring a measure from the water-holder into that very tin, which was kept carefully beneath her sleeping area. And when she thought no-one was looking, gliding off into the forest with it. *A quick wash in a biscuit tin. That's where she's off to. But where? Where, in a residential street, can she find where she'll be private, and unobserved?*

Just as they inhabited Wardrobe, and Devil's Kitchen, Dolores and Janna now inhabit the boarding house. It is as if there is a boundary between their world and the rest of the world, and Chrysanthemum is the go-between. But, for all she is more shadowy and peculiar with every passing day, Janna decides that it is time for one of her excursions. Time for her to visit Mrs Brown.

'Why don't I tell her that you'd like to come and see her next week? So she can expect you?' Chrysanthemum can hear Muriel in her voice, clinging to the remnants of propriety. Manners. But Janna has already put her tweed blazer on, and shrouded herself with an extra shawl.

'Pft. For Rose is nearly time. And for her mother too. And she maybe tell you story of me, from the past, but now it is the present and if I come now, her mother will remember me, not some stranger.'

Carefully, Chrysanthemum tries to assemble her expression so that Janna will not be able to see her words had struck home. There will be no place for stories of the past in this visit.

'Stop putting on the dog. It's not the bleeding Queen she's paying a call on.' Dolores, Abdulla in mouth, looks up from a batch of pies she's constructing and waves a rolling pin. 'You want to get a move on before I decide to come an' all.'

As they hurry through the streets to the Brown's house – everyday streets, full of everyday people doing everyday things, some of whom take one look at the little cavalcade as it progresses on its way and hurry their children indoors – it strikes Chrysanthemum as strongly as it did the first time she saw her what a sight Janna makes. *I have grown so used to her I do not see her any more. Or, for that matter, smell her.* In the theatre and in the woods, even in the boarding house, she is simply herself, and there. But here…here, out of her environment, in these workaday streets, with her watchful hawk face, lined skin and jewelled claws, orange plaits glinting with coins and topped off with the scarf drawn tight above her brows, her golden ornaments and layers of flowered clothing in faded colours, she is thrown into relief. *They loved her in the theatre. She was... contained. She was part of something... apart.*

Chrysanthemum feels a protective pang that sharpens as the old woman, who for all her years still walks with the poise and grace of the dancer she once was, freezes slightly so that her old face becomes a mask of itself, as one passerby deliberately swerves to avoid her, and a woman averts her eyes rather than meet Janna's. *They're frightened of her out here, she makes them feel threatened.* A young man spits at her skirts but when he looks up he puts his hand over his face. *He's terrified. He thinks she might curse him. Is that defiance in her eyes or fear? Or dignity? Or is she meeting what she has met all her life? It does not make it any better because she is used to it. It makes it worse. And it is worse even than that, because we are going to Rose, because it is almost her time. And after that, nothing will ever be the same. The first act was Mervyn, and he is gone, and I will live with that because Rose is still here because of it. The second act is what happened afterwards. The third act is the future, and how it is joined to the past, and everything that is not yet understood, and yet to be revealed.*

When Janna arrives at Mrs Brown's house she stands aside to let Chrysanthemum knock, and then allows herself to be ushered in by Mrs Brown, who tries not to show that she is flustered by this unexpected visitation. But as they cross the threshold they're greeted by an unexpected sight – Rose, round as an egg, standing to greet them. Eagerly holding out her hands in welcome.

'You came! Bibi! I thought you never would!' And with that Rose, who had been so light and spry, heaves herself across the floor to Janna.

'I can't do the splits any more,' she says. Her voice, that she isn't used to using, comes out as an uncertain crackle. She tries to smile, but her lower lip trembles. 'What's going to happen to me, Bibi?'

'You will do the splits again.' Janna takes hold of Rose's chin and her gaze is so fierce that it reflects in Rose's eyes. 'You will grow wings, and fly. I see it in the samovar, and I see it in your eyes. It will only be a short time to wait.'

'It's not my baby. It's growing in me, but it's not mine. I don't want it.'

Mrs Brown and Chrysanthemum lock eyes. This is the first time that Rose has mentioned the baby.

'This is not all your life.' Janna's fingers force Rose's chin upwards. 'You know before your act, before your music. You wait. And then you play your part. And then the show goes on.'

Something is transmitted from one to another, because Rose's blue eyes begin to glitter with the same spark as Janna's brown ones, and Rose arranges herself, for all the awkwardness of her body, as if she is once more waiting in the wings. Infused with Janna's presence, suffused with her perfume, the little parlour feels like her booth. Crowded with spirits, and secrets, and the things that needed to change, and have shifted. Janna looks around, evidently satisfied.

'And now we will have tea. We will sit, and wait. Soon there will be new life, and new ways. And also, more of stories.'

Chapter 27

Dolores unceremoniously flings back the eiderdown on Chrysanthemum's bed.

'What the heck?'

'Shift your stumps missy. The new arrival's getting ready to make its entrance.'

'I didn't hear...' Chrysanthemum rubs her eyes and tries to focus. The room is pitch black except for the snap and flash of amber eyes.

'As if you knew no better. Janna woke me. Said it was her time. Anyway we'll be off as soon as Miss Muck here has made herself ready to face a new dawn. Wrap up warm. It'll be a long day.'

With that, Dolores rips open the curtains and exits with the flourish of someone whose entire life has been geared to putting on a show. *Oh no, of course we can't hear about it because Rose's mam has sent a message. We've got to get up in the middle of the night and make a whole song and dance act about it because Janna has had a premonition.*

'And before you say a word.' Dolores rams her head round the door. 'We are going to be there for as long as it takes to make sure that no-one steals Rose's baby.' She is milking it now. Shamelessly grandstanding. Who is going to steal Rose's baby from the back bedroom in her mam's house, which is where it will be born?

'Now get down those dancers and get yourself to a telephone kiosk. And remind Orage what we said.'

Whilst Chrysanthemum is out telephoning Orage, Dolores makes up a flask, and fries up rounds of black pudding for sandwiches. Then, with Janna bundled in the sidecar and Chrysanthemum riding pillion, they arrive at the Brown's house as dawn is rising above the rooftops.

Not that there's much to do. Mrs Brown is upstairs with Rose. Chrysanthemum wraps her arms round her head and shudders every time she hears Rose wailing from above. Each cry feels like a direct hit. The war's over. This can't be worse. But it feels as if it is.

'You carry on like that much longer and they'll think you belong in the loony bin.' Dolores, having established herself in the best seat by the fire, is well into the making of a complicated matinee jacket. She waves her handiwork airily. 'Sit down and keep still. Anyone would think you'd got fleas.'

The wails go on and on as Rose labours throughout the morning. *I saved her life. I murdered Mervyn. For this. A life for a life. This life cost that life. All our lives have changed because of what I did. And if I could change it? Would I? It isn't that it all comes back because it never goes away. The wings, the dark head bending over the drooping blonde one. The flat, in her hands then crashing to the ground. The sack, in the sidecar. And after, with Dolores' saw in the woods, and later, scrubbing dirt from her fingernails until they were raw. So many holes we dug. Who'd have thought a musical instrument could have teeth that sawed through joints? The thoughts ran round and round. I should be the one paying for it. Not Rose.*

Dolores knits grimly on, and Janna folds herself into her clothes in the corner of the room, and becomes as good as invisible. Unless you know to look. She catches Chrysanthemum's gaze and her beady bird's eyes drill into the girl's. *He made his fate and his end came about because of that. If you were standing in the wings again, and you saw what you saw, would you have walked away? That way the death on your hands would have been Rose's. It was your fate to be there. Your secret is not your shame. Your fate is not your fortune.*

Then another voice. Strident and scornful where the other caresses and insinuates. *You don't have to like it. You just have to lump it. In case you hadn't noticed, you've done him in. Done him in. Done him in. Don't go soft on me. Feather duster. The oldest trick in the book.*

Dolores looks up from her knitting.

'Fancy a cold black pudding sandwich? You look a bit peaky. I've cut it nice and thick, you want to know you've eaten something. Tuck in.'

Orage arrives at lunchtime in the Bentley. Sylvester ushers her into the Brown's front room and the pair of them are so glossy and elegant that the little room, in the little house, seems to become darker and damper and dingier than it was before they arrived.

It's a long wait. Chrysanthemum rocks, and shudders, and stares into the fire, sporadically galvanised into life by calls from upstairs for hot water and towels. Sylvester stands by the fireplace smoking, or prowls up and down the shabby length of hearthrug. The sandwiches run out and Orage murmurs gently to Sylvester, who leaves immediately and returns with a mountain of fish and chips that only Dolores eats. Dolores finishes the matinee jacket, which is intricate and surprisingly, perfectly white, and starts on a matching bootee. Janna begins to sing under her breath, and snaps her fingers in time to a tune only she can hear.

Rose gives birth as night falls. Mrs Brown comes downstairs in tears, cradling the blanketed form of the new child. She goes to Orage and places the baby in her arms.

She only manages a faint whisper. 'A girl.'

'This baby will have a good life.' It is the first thing Janna has said out loud all day. She rises from the floor and is suddenly standing next to the baby. 'Family is who love most. Look. She eat her with her eyes.'

Joy and wonder turn Orage's beauty into something luminous as she gazes at the child in her arms. Sylvester joins her, peering down at the tiny form in the blanket.

'Rosemary.' Orage stokes the baby's face with a gentle fingertip. 'Hello, Rosemary.'

'Rosemary.' Sylvester's voice shakes. 'Our little girl.'

'Your mother loves you dearly.' As the words fall from Janna's mouth she's looking, not at the new baby, or at Orage, but directly into Chrysanthemum's eyes.

Orage holds the baby without fear. *From horror and sorrow and terror. And now this… wonder. The wrongness of what I did can never be undone. But it is the past, and Rosemary is the future.*

'Our daughter.' Orage shifts the child in her arms. *As if she was born to it.* 'Let's take her home.'

Chapter 28

More and more, Janna prefers to spend her days squatting in the yard, tending a tiny fire of twigs and peering through the smoke at the sky. Each day she's more unsubstantial. More like the smoke. Chrysanthemum believes she's ready to blow away. *She's close, now. Close to invisibility. Practically transparent under her clothes. Almost, now, she is not here.* Dolores, ever pragmatic, installs Chrysanthemum in the booth.

'Might as well make yourself useful. Your first day, I'll keep an eye.' She sparks an Abdulla.

Chrysanthemum sits at Janna's table but she can't settle. What if someone comes? What will she tell them? What if no-one comes? What if nothing comes?

'I'm looking for a Nelly Ballash.' Despite the drapes, Chrysanthemum can hear every word from outside.

'Bollocks.' Dolores, standing guard outside the booth, inhales on her Abdulla and watches dispassionately as a trail of ash drops onto the clean floor.

'I beg your pardon?'

'Bollocks.' The woman flinches.

'That's what she's called.' Dolores stands, arms akimbo and chin in the air, as if she's spoiling for a fight.

'Look, this is the spelling.' The woman shows Dolores an envelope marked with the letters BALASZ.

'I think you'll find it's pronounced bollocks. Nelly Bollocks.' Dolores advances so that the woman can see the globules of stale yellow make-up caked in her stubble. 'That's who you're looking for. Now what would that be about?'

'She said it was something about eggs.'

'Well she's not here. And there aren't any eggs.' The boarders' breakfasts have taken care of that. The woman turns on her heel. Dolores stubs out the Abdulla to proclaim her victory.

Chrysanthemum sits inside the booth and wonders if there will be any other customers. She wonders until it's time to close shop, but no-one comes.

Dolores carefully lays the blue shawl across Janna's bed.

'This is the one, isn't it? The one you want?' Covered in a soft mound of faded scraps, the bed looks like a pile of autumn leaves. With the addition of the blue one, it seems as if the sky has fallen onto it, bringing down with it a carpet of bright-hued blossoms. Janna's hand moves slightly, stroking the blooms.

'All the flowers of Russia.' They are the first words Janna has spoken in days. Her body is so slight that no shape of it is discernable beneath the covers, but her rasp of a voice rings out strongly.

'All the flowers of Russia. That's right, dear. You brought most of them with you.' Dolores lowers herself into the Lloyd Loom next to the bed where she has slept upright for the last three nights.

'In this one I danced for the Tsar.' Janna's fingers stroke the blue wool again, and a smile flits across her face.

'Tell us, Janna. Tell us the story.' Rose turned up on the doorstep the night Dolores installed Janna in the bed, and has kept a vigil for two days, rarely speaking, sleeping on the blanket box.

'One more story. Please.'

'Don't be silly, Rose.' Chrysanthemum, standing by the door, bites her knuckle. 'She hasn't got any strength left for stories. Leave her be.'

For minutes, the only sound in the room is the gentle ticking of the clock.

'No I tell. One last story. Rose, come.' Janna beckons to Rose. 'Come.'

Chrysanthemum expects Rose to sit on the edge of the bed by Janna, but she lays herself alongside her. Janna moves her hand to Rose's head, and instead of stroking the woollen flowers, caresses Rose's hair.

'So pretty.' The once-soft yellow curls are still frizzy and awry, a garland of sticky feathers. Rose buries her face in the covers. *Like a child. Not like a woman who has had a baby.* Not like Orage, who from the very first held and handled Rosemary with graceful, natural confidence. *A born mother.*

'Janna, will you tell us the story, please? Of how you danced for the Tsar?'' Janna's closed eyelids flutter open.

'I don't tell you that story. It has been told, and will be told again. For my last story, I tell you one so that you remember. I tell you the story of my people.'

Janna's voice fades into a whisper.

'Don't stand there by the door like Marsden's monument, you great lump. Come here. And blow your nose.' Dolores holds out her hand and Chrysanthemum takes it gratefully, kneeling down by the Lloyd Loom.

'There was, and there was not, a time when my people were birds, and they could fly.'

Janna stops. Takes a breath as if she is preparing, one last time, to dance.

'And one day, flying, they saw a palace, glittering and gold in the sun, and it was so splendid that they flew down, to look. And when they landed, they were surprised to see that the inhabitants of that palace were turkeys and hens and ducks – birds that do not fly. And these turkeys and hens and ducks, who had no beauty, but desired it like all people, thought my people, with their graceful wings, were so beautiful that they begged them to stay, showering them with gifts of gold and jewels, which they draped around the necks of my people. All except one, who we shall call Lolo Chirikli, which means red bird, who saw what was happening and begged my people to resist the temptation of the shiny gold. Lolo Chirikli's heart was as heavy as the gold chains but his soul was full of wisdom, and sadly, seeing what was happening, he flew high into the sky and dashed himself onto the ground.

'When my people saw what he had done, and what he meant, they came to their senses and tried to fly, but the gold weighed them down and although they beat their wings, they were bound to the ground and could not leave the earth, and the turkeys and ducks and hens crowed in triumph because now they could keep my beautiful people as prisoners, in cages, for ever.

'And then a red feather fluttered from the sky, and as it landed at the bird's feet, the gold chains fell from their bodies. But although they could spread their wings, they could no longer fly, and as the feather fluttered down the road, they followed it on foot, and as they walked, their feathers turned to clothes and their birds' bodies turned to human bodies.

'But my people never forgot they once were birds and they knew how to fly.'

Janna closes her eyes again and her hand lays still on Rose's head. For a long moment, Chrysanthemum is sure that Janna has gone.

'I had wings, beneath my skirts.'

'You did. No-one who saw it will ever forget.' For once, Dolores' tone is gentle.

Janna's life hangs on, seemingly one breath at a time. Night falls, and the room fills with comforting darkness.

'It is my time to fly again. Take me outside.'

Janna's voice is imperious: a command, not a request.

'No!' Rose and Chrysanthemum wail in chorus.

Dolores stands up. 'It's time.'

'Where are you going? You're not leaving her?' Chrysanthemum stands up too.

'I'm going to get the wheelbarrow. She'll have to go in that. You can push it, Chrysanthemum.'

'No.' Chrysanthemum stands in front of Dolores, hands balled.

Storms gather in Dolores' yellow eyes. 'Don't you defy me, missy. She can die where she likes as long as she dies in peace.'

'No, I meant, no, not in the wheelbarrow. I wasn't trying to stop you. I just meant, I'll carry her. I'd rather. Please.'

A grim kindness settles over Dolores' face, and she pats the girl's hand.

'It's the way of her people. To die in the open air. Take her carefully.'

Together, Chrysanthemum and Dolores raise Janna and wrap her in her familiar skirts and shawls, finishing with the beautiful blue. Then Chrysanthemum lifts her, cradling her across her arms. Dolores lights a candle and leads out Rose, who can't see for sobbing. Then slowly, carefully, the sad little procession makes it way down the stairs, out of the door, and into the night.

Dolores goes first, holding her candle aloft with as she leads them away from the streets and houses. Guided by the little flame, they wind their way in the cold and darkness through the woods until they reach the clearing. A crow flies overhead, circling them as they make their way, but the vixen is nowhere to be seen. *Perhaps she died. Poor thing. She must have been getting on a bit.*

'It's where…'

'We used to live. Yes.' Dolores arranges piles of fallen leaves into a soft mound. 'There. Put her there.'

As Chrysanthemum lays her carefully down, Janna's fingers close round her wrist. 'The samovar. It has stories to tell.'

'I know, Janna. I'll always remember.'

'For you. Stories for you. Maybe you find there what you need.'

Chrysanthemum nods, and can't find any words, and bends over the old lady until she trusts herself not to cry out loud.

The three figures sit in silence only broken by Rose's snuffling until the candle burns down. The crow joins them and sits, solemnly, in vigil with the women.

Dolores gets to her feet, crouches over her friend's body, and whispers in Janna's ear.

'You are a bird now.'

There is a gentle sigh, and then nothing at all.

Chrysanthemum can't tell when she passes. It is fitting for Janna. As long as she's known her, she's inhabited a shadowy space between her world and everyone else's world. She'd just gone further into the shade. And yet, for a person so full of shadows, she burned with such brightness.

Dolores takes the blue shawl and drapes it over Janna, covering her face.

'I'll stay with her tonight. You two go home.' She says it kindly enough, but her subdued dignity brooks no argument. She reaches into the pocket of her musquash for a second candle, which she hands to Chrysanthemum with the lantern.

'That'll see you home. Make her some cocoa when you get in – for you and all. You're a good girl.' Tears running down her cheeks unchecked catch in her beard, glinting in the cold moonlight as if they are diamonds, and Chrysanthemum wonders if the old carny mourning her friend might be the saddest sight of all on that sorrow-filled night.

Dolores turns her back on them and Chrysanthemum draws Rose away, leaving the two old pals for their last night on earth together. The crow flaps into the air and caws, loudly, into the night, as if it is making an announcement. They watch it fly up into the trees. It's the first time they've been together, just the two of them, since… since that night. Chrysanthemum stretches out a hand and tremulously, offers it to Rose. Rose takes it. There isn't anything to be said, not at the moment, just the understanding that a bond will not be broken. They walk in silence, holding hands; each one lost in her own thoughts and glad that the other is there. They don't notice that the crow takes off again, and follows them, at a distance, while they go on their way.

The boarding house, when they walk through the door, feels full of strange electricity, *as if it's alive with something.* Chrysanthemum puts the milk to warm in a pan before the sense that there's a presence in the house draws her to follow Rose up the stairs.

'Chryssie, you won't believe this.' Rose's face, full of wonder. 'Look at this.'

The bed where Janna had been is covered in autumn leaves.

'And look.' Rose holds out her hand. 'There are these.'

She's holding two long, stiff, black feathers.

Chrysanthemum takes one, and strokes it gently. 'Do you know what these are, Rose?'

'Feathers. I know they're feathers. One for each of us.'

'They are. But they're not just any feathers Rose. Look at them, they're asymmetric, but a pair. One from each wing. They're flight feathers.'

The next morning, Dolores returns, then sets off in the direction of Devil's Kitchen with a shovel, a basket containing firelighters and a bottle of whisky and her face a mask of grim, grief-laden purpose. Rose slips into her coat and falls into step behind her, but Dolores turns round. She is a thing, almost, of horror, yellow eyes circled by red and then dark hollows in her gaunt, furred face, but almost kindly, she shakes her head.

'Not where I'm going. Take Rose back. To her ma.'

Chrysanthemum opens her mouth to protest but Rose stops her without a word being said.

'She doesn't need to. I'll make my own way.' Rose has already got her hat and coat on and is out of the door before you could say 'five minutes, ladies.'

Rose is washed out with sorrow and pale with lack of sleep but there's nothing frail about the look on her face when she turns back to Chrysanthemum. She looks at her steadily, for a long moment.

'I'll see you,' she says, as if nothing out of the ordinary has ever happened. Then she swivels round, and sets off down the road.

With a heavy heart, Chrysanthemum clears up everything that needs to be cleared. She washes the pots, scrubs the floor, sweeps the yard. Tries not to think of Janna. Wishes Rose had stayed. Eventually she plods upstairs with a heavy heart. In Chrysanthemum's room, her flight feather lies abandoned on the lino. How could she be so careless? She stoops, picks it up, and gently strokes its quills. *We give a little bit of our hearts to the people we love, until there is nothing left.* It might have been something Janna said. *And then we die. It is an everyday story, because it happens to all of us.*

Chrysanthemum holds the feather in her hand and makes up her mind. She can't sit there all day, in an empty house, hoping for ghosts. As if she was being pulled – *no, drawn* - she goes back downstairs, pulls her coat on, and walks, retracing last night's steps until the road gives way to the path that leads deep into the woods.

She smells the burning before she turns into the clearing and sees the flames engulfing what is left of the bowtop. Its canvas has gone, and the wheels have burned out so that it collapses sideways, but the shape of the hardwood frame and the dray hold their shape even as they smoulder. Next to it, a neat pile of overturned earth, topped with a makeshift cross: two sticks, tied with lamé ribbon into a gaudy crucifix. Nearby, where the showman's trailer was once parked up, Dolores is heaped like a bag of washing on a stump, drunk as a lord, her turban rakishly slipped to one side, the shovel at an angle by her feet and the whisky bottle dangling from her hand.

She raises it in salute as Chrysanthemum approaches and proffers it to her, swaying as she does so. It is nearly empty, less than an inch in the bottom.

'What you looking at. I'm having a rest, after all that digging. Drink.' Dolores' face, smeared and blackened with smuts from the fire, is slack, her eyes rheumy and her words slurred, as if she is having trouble getting them past her teeth. For all that, it is a command. 'Go on. Nas drovje.'

Chrysanthemum raises it to her lips, and gingerly sips.

'And now for her.' Dolores points an unsteady finger at the earth, and then, as if it's all too much effort to follow her point of focus, lets her arm drop uselessly to her side.

Not knowing what to do, Chrysanthemum looks about, at the burning bowtop, then at the grave. And then, as if it has been waiting for a moment of quiet, the little brown vixen pads quietly from shadows cast by the trees and sits, fixing its yellow eyes intently on Chrysanthemum. The creature has thinned since Chrysanthemum last saw it. Its muzzle has whitened and its eyes dulled, but its mask has a quick, intelligent expression. *It isn't afraid of me.* The thought fills Chrysanthemum with wonder, and strange comfort. *I know what to do next, although I do not know why I know or what it means.*

As still as a statue, the vixen doesn't move as the girl unscrews the whisky bottle, sprinkles a few drops on Janna's burial place, and then drinks a toast. It feels, at first, more than strange, to be standing in the clearing, singing a Flanagan and Allen song and marking out Janna's umbrella dance on the freshly turned earth of her newly-dug grave, but Chrysanthemum finds she is smiling, and singing and crying, all at the same time, until the dance is done, and the whisky finished at the same time.

Wiping her eyes, she stumbles over to Dolores, who is snoring, and squats down beside her. One yellow eye opens.

'I heard you. She'd have liked that.' Dolores' eye half closes, and her mouth falls open.

'Rose gone on her way?' The words come out in a slurred mumble.

Chrysanthemum nods. 'Poor Rose. I can see why you didn't want her to come. It'd have been far too much for her.'

Dolores slowly pulls herself semi-upright, and eyeballs Chrysanthemum as if all of a sudden she's spoiling for a fight.

'You think Rose is a fluffy little chicken.'

Dolores pauses for dramatic effect before letting rip.

'If you look you'll see that underneath her feathers she's a scrawny tough little bird, all muscle and sinew and sheer determination to go her own way. Cheep cheep cheep and you think what a cutie with her soft curls and her bright eyes, you want to stroke her and pet her and smile at what a funny playful little scrap she is but seeing isn't always believing and you don't get to turn yourself inside out and fold yourself back up again in a box unless you're made of steel. She may have laid an egg but she's barely a fledgling herself and now it's her who wants to fly the nest. She might have stretched her wings with that ghastly conjuror and his blasted red apple, just a babby really and all a-flutter with the attention and the having shiny things dangled, and to say she got them clipped is saying the least, but like I said she's made of will and wire and what with having got Janna's flight feather she's turned cuckoo now and someone else gets to keep the egg warm seeing as she's ready to take off. You mark my words.'

Having completed her monologue, she grabs the bottle out of Chrysanthemum's hand, drains the dregs, belches loudly and rolls off her stump onto the floor of the clearing.

She is a dead weight but Chrysanthemum pulls her to her feet, crams the turban as far as possible down her forehead so it won't fall off, and then slings her over her shoulders in a fireman's lift. She shifts her slightly to adjust the weight, feeling the old girl's head flop heavily against her upper arm. *She's going to dribble on my sleeve.* As quickly as she think it, Chrysanthemum is ashamed. *It's only a coat.* But still. *It's the only coat I've got.* It's wrong to be arguing with herself under these strange, sad circumstances.

'Goodbye Janna,' she whispers. Looking round, the clearing seems emptier than she'd ever seen it. *As if its spirit had departed.* She looks around but the old brown fox is nowhere to be seen. As she watches, the bowtop's dray collapses into the ground. *This will be the last time, here.* It is strange to think that she had felt so much at home in this desolate place.

She wraps her right arm round Dolores and sets off down the path with her burden.

Dolores' head bounces against her back but it doesn't wake her. 'Gilbert,' she mumbles, apparently content, then smacks her lips, and starts to snore.

Chrysanthemum looks back once towards the trees, just in case, but there are no transparent tightrope walkers, or insubstantial clowns. *Only hungry crows, and the winter is coming.*

Chapter 29

Janna has gone. Rose has gone, just a postcard stamped from the docks at Liverpool with the words 'wish me luck as you wave me goodbye!' to let you know she might have done a moonlight flit, but no hard feelings, though no mention either of where she might be going or what she's going to do when she gets there. Dolores' words stick in Chrysanthemum's mind: *made of will and wire*. Will and wire. *Ready to take off.* And now she's on her way. But the last words she said were 'I'll see you.' She'll be back. Sooner or later she'll make her way back to the nest.

Orage has gone, too, though in her case it's to Sylvester's elegant flat in Bayswater where there's room for a live-in maid.

'You could go too,' says Orage, sensibly, down the telephone. 'You don't have to stay there. You could come to London. Sylvester knows all sorts of people and you'd be able to see Rosemary. At least think about it.' It would be the sensible thing.

Chrysanthemum does think about it. She thinks about it a lot. But too much has happened in too short a time, and she's not ready to leave behind what she found in the world in the woods. She's walked out of one home already, pushed herself right out of Muriel's reach. She might not have liked the process but there was no looking back once she'd made up her mind and she can tell herself and anyone else all the stories she likes about Muriel but the fact was she was looking for an excuse to get out of there and when one came along she jumped on it faster than a kitten on a ball of wool. And then, what a strange home it was that she found but that was what it felt like. A place with people she could be herself with. A home.

It's an odd sort of home but she's not ready to leave it yet. It's riddled with stories and secrets and she knows she doesn't know the half of it yet. Perhaps Orage will always be the sensible one. And Rose is made of wire.

'You don't have to stay,' snarls Dolores through a mouthful of gin and Abdulla smoke. There's been a lot of that since Janna died, and not much else. The apricot negligee is covered in stains. Chrysanthemum has taken to carrying its wearer up the stairs in the same fireman's lift she used to bring Dolores back from Devil's Bottom, and putting her to bed each night.

Every night, passed out pissed and upside-down on Chrysanthemum's shoulder, she says the same thing. Just like she did at Janna's grave. Gilbert.

Who was Gilbert? That's a new one. He never got mentioned until Dolores was too befuddled to know what she was saying. How does he fit into all the other half-told tales? It's like completing a jigsaw puzzle. Once you get the pieces out of the box you have to carry on, bit by bit, finding out what fits where until everything is in its place and then there's a picture. That's what her father used to tell her. He wasn't the kind of person who would abandon a half-finished jigsaw; he'd sit there, patiently, piecing things together. And now she's in the middle of her own puzzle. There are so many bit and scraps and she needs to put them all together. Stories are no use if they've only got beginnings.

Dolores can still put the dog on even through the booze fumes. 'But if you're stopping here you can make yourself useful.'

'I'll clean that then, shall I?' The samovar, forlorn in a corner of the kitchen, is dull and tarnished. 'She'd be turning in her grave at the state of that.' And besides, what might it have to say to her? Some scraps of story to impart? You never know, until you try.

'Not on your Nelly.' Dolores is suddenly bolt upright and belligerent with a tigerish glare in her amber eyes. 'You keep your nose out. If anyone's polishing that thing it'll be me. There's enough to keep you occupied.'

Chrysanthemum dutifully sweeps the hall and stairways, freshens the rooms, sets the dining table and irons the boarders' bed linen, but all the while her mind is ticking away. Why doesn't she want me to polish it? The jigsaw pieces are not yet fitting into place but perhaps a pattern is beginning to form. 'Tura lura', she sings, Janna's umbrella dance, and as her feet remember the steps, the broom makes a reasonable partner to waltz round the kitchen. Maybe I'll see something when she's not looking. Something she doesn't want me to see. *Tura lura. I'll try to mend the umbrella but I'm not going on my way.*

Later, when Chrysanthemum goes upstairs to bed, there's a pair of socks, hand-knitted, folded on her pillow. They're almost as much of a treasure as Janna's feather, and it makes her sure she's made the right decision. To stay, and be a part of this story, not the beginning of a new one. The next morning, she puts them on, and goes downstairs, where Dolores is sitting in front of the samovar, which has been polished to its accustomed high shine.

'Thank you!'

Dolores is still bleary-eyed but she's sober and as far as Chrysanthemum can tell, the cup in front of her only contains strong tea.

'I hadn't finished them when she passed and it seemed a shame to let them go to waste.' Dolores sounds a little bit more like her old self. 'I suppose you'll be stopping, then?'

Emerging from the hold of the barge, Dora's round face breaks into a smile at the sight of Chrysanthemum. Without her pencilled-on moustache and wrapped in a flowered apron, she has the look of a new wife adjusting to life after a honeymoon.

'Duckie, dearest, we have a visitor!' Chrysanthemum is ushered down the steps into the cosy, low-ceilinged hold, her coat whipped off her and a schooner placed in front of her, before Duckie emerges, in her fisherman's sweater, with a bucket of coal in her hand.

'Chrysanthemum. Welcome to our floating palace.' She stretches out a hand, looks at the colour of it and withdraws it. 'Black bright. Soap and water please my dear.' She bends to wash her hands in the water Dora pours from a painted ewer and when she turns round her face is solemn. 'We were sorry to hear about Janna.' She reaches out a clean, sympathetic hand. 'You will pass on our condolences of course.

'I will. It's a funny old time.'

'We thought as much. And Rose, without a backwards glance, so we gather. We hear things, you know, even living on the water. There's Sid and Joey in the Mallard's Tail every Friday lunchtime, and young Mister Fankes pops in from time to time to pass the time of day, and then Stella writes, though from what she has to say for herself you'd think she was staying with the Duchess of York rather than in her sister's back parlour. But then she always was partial to an air and a grace, old Stella. You'll have a snifter with us?"

'I'd love one. If you can spare it.'

'More than enough to go round. Pass the bottle, please, my dear.' The barge is so cramped that Duckie could reach out and pick it off the shelf, but a look of love passes between the two women along with the bottle.

'It's Stella I wanted to talk about. I want to get in touch with her.'

'I didn't think you were that fond of Stella.'

'Well...'

'No point putting it on with us, dear.' Dora's smile is sweet but her eyes are shrewd. 'Nobody's that fond of Stella. You want her to tell you about Jeffcocks, don't you? Janna's dead and Dolores is a spiky old clam who'd never dream of giving you the satisfaction and for reasons known only to you, you're like a dog with a bone.'

Chrysanthemum blushed. She didn't expect to have been seen through quite so quickly.

'I'm sorry. I didn't mean to be obvious. I'd just that there is...'

'Something you want to get to the bottom of. Concerning Jeffcocks.'

'There is. I...'

'You're a good girl and you've got the rest of your life ahead of you and I'm inclined to tell you not to go opening that can of worms, along the lines of what you don't know can't hurt you.' Duckie's tone is measured. 'But from what we hear there has been quite enough happened to hurt you recently, and if you think a chat with our dear, dear Stella may be of use, I will point you in the right direction, if only because you will do it anyway, whether Dora and I help you or not. Though I warn you that there's often very little point in digging up the past. It is always better to look forward. Here we are, on our barge, looking forward to the next part of our lives. We've called her The Ship of Good Hope. It's a big name for a little boat but it suits our purpose. Did you see the sign? We'll take life one lock at a time from now on.'

Dora nods, and her smile becomes sweet again. 'Well said, dearest. We don't turn away friends in their time of need.'

'There is, though, a very good chance that Stella will. It's exceedingly likely that she'll turn on the dog and you won't get a muff out of her.' Duckie pours a cherry brandy into three schooners and passes them round. 'If, on the other hand, she sees a good reason to demonstrate that she's the privileged party to particular information, you may well strike gold. She was at Jeffcocks from a chorine and she'll know as much as anyone still living, but you'll have to play her like a very delicate instrument.'

Duckie raises her glass and licks her lips. 'I do like a drop of this. Cheers, me dears. Bottoms up. Mud in your eye and a toast to all the ladles and jellyspoons what so kindly bought tickets and so, indirectly, paid for us to set sail. For which we are truly thankful. Amen.'

'Amen. You are a wag.' Dora raises her glass to her beloved. 'She's right though. She should have been called Stella the Mare. Or Stella Nightmare, because that's what it was like sharing a dressing room with her. You'd think she was the Queen.'

'In all her crown jewels.'

'In case anyone comes along waving a sceptre at her.'

'In the middle of the night.' *And now they've started acting the giddy goat, that's the last bit of sense there'll be out of dear old Dizzy and Ada.* Chrysanthemum sips her drink and wonders if that might be the key to unlock the magic door. Duckie and Dora, giggling like teenagers at a whiff of cherry brandy.

'Does Her Majesty partake of the occasional drink?'

'Like a fish, but only for medicinal purposes.' Duckie can't keep a straight face and Dora snorts into a lace handkerchief.

'What's her favourite tipple?'

Dora's eyes crinkle with laughter as she looks up from her hankie. 'Whatever she can get her hands on, the old lush. But she's always been particularly partial to a nice bucket or two of crème de menthe.'

'I tell you what, leave it to me. Dora, the writing paper please. What say we invite Madame Maris to pay us a visit. She must be dying of boredom in her sister's parlour. It'd be a kindness, poor old soul.' A look of pure deviousness crosses Duckie's handsome face. She is, after all, a show person, and what show person likes to miss a good show?

Chapter 30

'Was there someone called Gilbert?'

'Gilbert? I'm not sure that there ever was dearie, at least not that I knew.' Duckie, substantial in the Guernsey that Dora has finished in time for her birthday, looks up from the fishing tackle she's tidying. 'We should have fish for tea tonight, Dora. I fancy a nice herring if there are any. What makes you mention that?'

'Just something I heard someone say.' Chrysanthemum tries to sound casual, but sharp-eyed Duckie pricks up her ears. Like all show people, she's always got an eye on the timing.

'As long as it's not a boot my love. That's what you caught last time.' Dora winks at Chrysanthemum and lays her hand on top of Duckie's.

'I threw it back in, if you remember Dora. Now hang about. Let me think.'

'I knew a Gilbert once.' That's Stella Maris. Here she is. Duckie sent her invitation, and Stella took her up on it with indecent haste. Maybe she thinks there's a free fish supper in the offing, and here she is, freeloading. Maybe word's got round that Janna's died and she's like an old vulture, circling round in case there are any scraps she can pick up. When she isn't singing her voice sounds like the faint rustling of tissue paper, and she rarely deigns to use it. Duckie, Dora and Chrysanthemum all turn round. The former Gibson Girl makes quite a show of patting her rouge into place before she condescends to turn around and pick up her schooner, full to the brim with crème de menthe.

'Handsome fellow, from Florida. Came over with Miss Tira when... well, when she came back.'

'You don't mean... with the tattoos... and the moustaches... ?'

'The very one.'

'Oh. Ow.' Duckie sucks her thumb, where a fly hook jabbed it.

'Yes, quite a stir, wasn't it?'

'Wasn't what?' Chrysanthemum feels her fingers itching with the desire to shake the silly old fraud and get the story out of her.

'All in the past, my dear. And before you were born, I'd say. Of course most people knew him by his stage name.'

'What was it?'

Stella flutters her eyelashes in case anyone might mistake her for 'most people' before taking an exaggerated sip of her drink.

'Oh it won't mean anything to you, these days. It's all film stars these days for you young people.'

'His stage name.'

'You're being boring dear. Is there any more of this? If you'd be so kind. These glasses are awfully small if you don't mind me saying. But have it if you must. He was The Incredible Lifto. The most famous strongman in the business. There nothing he couldn't lift, and that includes skirts. And he didn't half leave some trouble behind him.'

Chapter 31

Restored to its gleaming glory, the samovar takes pride of place on the sideboard in the front parlour, with an embroidered cloth over it at night to keep it from tarnishing. When she's on her own in the room, Chrysanthemum scrutinises it, lifting up the cloth, for the stories Janna said it had to tell her, but all she can see is her own reflection in the shining brass. Janna's prized tea glasses and saucers are under lock and key in the corner cupboard, but her little Russian doll and bear have vanished into thin air and are nowhere to be found, even though Dolores turned the house upside down looking for them.

Dolores' gilded, ornate and much-prized Crown Derby – 'Royal Crown Derby, I think you'll find' – is on display and in daily use by its owner, although the boarders and Chrysanthemum have to make do with utility china. In the kitchen, a kettle with a loud metallic whistle has taken over from the eerie, bubbling hiss and moan of the samovar.

Without Janna, the stories vanish, the quality of the tea distinctly declines, and Dolores, sunk in the doldrums, is trickier than ever. Mardy doesn't come near. Chrysanthemum pours herself and Dolores a cupful each from the pot Dolores put on the table. She takes a mouthful, and grimaces. *Blimey, I can't drink that.* It takes a great deal of will power not to spit it out.

'Dolores, what have you made this tea with?'

'Why, isn't it to madam's liking?'

Chrysanthemum takes a long, patient breath. It is 6.30 in the morning, all four rooms are occupied, and she has the boarders' breakfast to prepare for when they come down at seven. Commercial travellers, the lot of them. They aren't like show people, who get up late and are happy with whatever they're given as long as they can linger round the table, swapping anecdotes and bitching about last night's performances over a nicely stewed cuppa. This lot want all mod cons and a hearty meal to set them up for the day.

'I can taste the rubber in it. You've made it with the water out of your hot water bottle, haven't you?'

'No point wasting it. It's money down the drain.'

'You can't give that to the boarders, Dolores, or they'll complain. They'll want a proper cup of tea.'

'I can't taste anything wrong with it. Anyway, I can't be doing with wasting perfectly good water. It's only been boiled, that's all.' *At least it's not her bathwater.*

Dolores guards the bathroom like a hawk, keeping the bath plug in her bedroom. Anyone who wants a bath has to sign for it and leave a half crown deposit. She's painted a line three inches up from the bottom of the bath, and woe betide anyone she suspects of running water that goes over it. She isn't above standing outside with her ear to the keyhole, banging on the door when she thinks the tap has been running for long enough.

'Well if you want to drink your hot water bottle water that's up to you, but I'm making a fresh pot for the boarders. And for me.' Chrysanthemum pours her tea down the sink. She lives here now and it's not taking liberties.

'You throw your own money away my girl. Water doesn't grow on trees. And don't throw those tealeaves away. I can dry those out and use them again.'

'That wouldn't be very nice either.' *Anyone trying to read those would see it straight away. Mean spirit at work.* Chrysanthemum scrapes the leaves into the slop bowl.

Dolores huffily spoons four teaspoons of sugar into her cup before lighting an Abdulla to smoke while she eats her fried black pudding sandwich. Chrysanthemum tries not to look at the specks of greasy dried blood and congealed fat round her chops and in her beard. Dolores takes a noisy slurp of tea and smacks her lips.

'It's a lovely cup of tea. Don't know what all the fuss is about, Little Miss Tea's Not Good Enough. I bumped into Stella Maris the other day. While she was visiting. She said she'd seen you. You never said anything about that, did you?'

'Well I'm glad you're enjoying it. I'm still brewing another pot. No, I dropped in on Duckie and Dora and she was there.'

'You can't trust anything she tells you, she's a terrible romancer. Makes it all up to suit herself. Who's supposed to be paying for all this extravagance, then?'

'The boarders, I suppose. In that they're paying for bed and breakfast. They'll be down in a minute, and like I said, they'll want a proper cup of tea.'

'Fussy buggers.' Dolores takes another noisy slurp from her Crown Derby.

'Mr Whythenshaw was asking if there was any jam.'

'You can tell him where to stick his jam. There isn't any.'

Jam is another thing that has vanished from their lives since Janna died.

'He's just trying it on, Dolores. He'll be happy with his fried breakfast. And a nice cup of tea.'

Dolores takes a thoughtful sip.

'Now you come to mention it, is a bit stewed.'

'I'll get a fresh pot ready. Will you be wanting some?'

'Ta very much. Don't mind if I do.'

Chrysanthemum doesn't need eyes in the back of her head to know that Dolores is lacing her tea with a splash of gin. The rustle of the apricot negligee and the tinny squeak of the hip-flask lid give it away. But that suits her fine. Once the boarders have been fed and watered and Dolores is sleeping it off on the sofa, she nips into the front parlour. Softly, quietly, pulling the door and turning the knob so she doesn't make a sound. Padding across the carpet. Lifting the cloth.

'Sas tai nas,' she whispers. 'Sas tai nas.'

Is she imagining things or is the air thickening, infused with an odour that wasn't there when she walked in... a musky, smoky scent, a mixture of fallen foliage and pipesmoke? And is that what she hoped she'd see... the samovar's shining brass filming over? And who was she hoping to see? But there's something gathering, a picture, or a figure, just an outline, only vague, but as it looks, it can't be... no it is... it is... and it's not the past at all, and things she can only imagine. The figure in the samovar, the figure bending over a suitcase, is one she knows as well as her own reflection.

*Rose tucks Janna's flight feather into the corner of her case, underneath the cracked tap shoes and the battered ballet flats, and the tights and leotards and whatever she can cram of Dolores' costume scraps, the grime-stiffened nets and the reworked Little Egypts, the lampshade birdcage with the stuffed budgerigar wired to the light-fitting. She even keeps those bloody Pom-Poms and the memory of Orage's moue of disgust when Dolores forced them into such revolting get-ups, and then she remembers how luminous that face looked when they talked about the child — the child whose name had been given to her, but not by Rose, that Rose had never even looked at once it had torn itself out of her body, her elastic body that was already returning to its old stretch and sway, she could still fold herself up into that case if she needed to, she'd done it last night just to see and there she was, all tucked up just like she was in Mervyn's box, but she wasn't going to think about that, there was no need to think about that, or Mervyn, if there was any grief it was for Janna but what would Janna say? She'd look at the path and say 'Latcho drom, te aves baxtali, and 'good riddance,' Dolores would add for good measure, in that rancid sneering foghorn tone just to let you know she meant it too, and not saying a word about the used notes that she'd snuck in under the tights when she thought you weren't looking and glad this particular trick had been pulled off, a swap and a disappearing act, and no one any the wiser.*

*She doesn't look back once she'd gone. There's a train to catch, and then a boat, and then a name in New York where, if you can dance and fold yourself into a box and are pretty and blonde and fearless and perhaps give yourself a new name, there's a good chance they might be hiring.*

Rose, whose postcard had said 'wish me luck.' As Chrysanthemum watches the picture in the samovar, Rose turns to meet her eye. Chrysanthemum's heart lifts at the sight of her. Rose looks at her with great solemnity, then drops a curtsey, tips a wink. Right at her. Chrysanthemum lifts a hand to wave and the little figure of her friend waves back

'Bon voyage, Rosie,' she whispers. 'You must be there now, eh? Right in the middle of it all. But I'm not saying goodbye. Let's stick with au revoir, shall we?'

The little figure in the samovar nods, and smiles, and Chrysanthemum tears up and finds she can't see very well until she's wiped her eyes. The next time she looks Rose has gone, and the only thing she can see in the samovar is the reflection of Dolores' ornately gilded Royal Crown Derby, too precious for everyday use.

Chapter 32

With the rumour that chops are available as well as sausages, the queue outside the butchers is longer and more quietly frantic even than usual. Dolores, grim-faced, has got there early, with Chrysanthemum there as her skivvy, to hold the basket and carry home the spoils. The tension grows with each women served: will there be sufficient meat to go round? 'Coupons ready ladies, the next ten ladies only.' The queue erupts in mutterings and Chrysanthemum watches Dolores doing calculations in her head. She is number eleven in the line.

Suddenly there is a commotion as the woman in front of her jumps, and squeals, slapping her clothing. The women around her back away as she wheels round sharply in one direction, then another.

'Ooh.' Dolores is all solicitude. 'Have you been stung by a wasp?'

Her face is all innocence but Chrysanthemum could swear that was the flash of a hatpin disappearing inside the gauntlet of Dolores' glove.

'You better get home and get some bicarb on that.' The woman is still gasping in shock. 'You want to take care and get indoors because you probably swatted it inside your coat and there's nothing more spiteful than a wasp, I've heard of wasps ganging up when one of them's been swatted. She ended up in hospital, that poor woman did. They chased her, you know.'

'You're right.' The woman can barely speak for gasping. There's a sheen of sweat on her face and her cheeks are flushed. 'Golly, that hurt. I'd best be off.'

'And not a word from you missy.' Dolores plonks her feet bullishly on the pavement as Chrysanthemum heaves the basketful of meat back to the boarding house. 'There's a lots of wasps about, this time of year. If you've got anything to say I'll take it that you won't be wanting meat with your dinner, shall I?'

Chrysanthemum finds the baby owl in the garden when they get back, a bedraggled heap of tawny feathers that has fallen from a nest. She picks it up and carries it indoors with a sinking heart: the bird has a broken wing and is surely too young and frail to survive, and Dolores will doubtless tell her to wring its neck and put it out of its misery. Chrysanthemum wishes with all her heart for Rose, who would have conspired with her to hide the creature and care for it, or for Orage, who would have scoffed at her for being soft and then fetched up with a parcel of whatever luxury she thought the owl would need, and a twinkle in her eyes that hinted at the adventures she'd had in the process of procuring them.

But Dolores' face lights up in the first smile Chrysanthemum has seen on her face since Janna died. The broken wing is splinted with deft, sure fingers, and a box is found, and lined with scraps of shell-pink crepe de chine. After baiting every mousetrap in the building with cheese, Dolores sets the box by the fire and watches with evident pleasure, teacup of gin and orange in hand, as the little owl shreds the remnants of her old underwear and settles down. When she hears the ping of a trap, she heaves herself to her feet and returns to the room with a just-dead mouse in a saucer.

'Not squeamish are you? What did you think it eats?' Chrysanthemum turns away from the sight of her snipping off bits of mouse with her pinking shears and feeding them, skin, bone and all, to the owl. 'I don't expect you brought it in here so it could starve to death, did you?'

'I thought it might eat bread and milk, and maybe bacon rinds.' Chrysanthemum knows she sounds pathetic even as Dolores rolls her eyes. She's still sitting there, looking at the sleeping owl with a peaceful expression on her face when Chrysanthemum decides to turn in.

'Goodnight.' Dolores is too engrossed in the little owl to reply.

When she comes down the next morning, the owl is nowhere to be seen. Dolores emerges from her bedroom, bearing its box.

'Have you checked the traps? It wants feeding. Oh I see Miss Squeamish, this is a job I'm going to have to do myself.' Dolores shuffles off, backs of her carpet slippers slapping on the cellar stairs. Chrysanthemum takes a peek inside the box. The owl peers up at her, a fluffy mass of brown and grey feathers with two fierce, fearless eyes that return her gaze over its sharp, curved predator's beak.

'Goodness me, you do look like...' Chrysanthemum stopped short. The owl's box has been lined with what is – unmistakeably – Janna's diklo.

'Got one.' Dolores snips off a rodent limb with the pinking shears and pops it in the owl's beak. 'And yes it is. I should have burned it.' She fishes in her apron pockets for the Abdullas, sparks up and sticks her chin out. 'But I didn't.'

Chrysanthemum bends down and gingerly fingers the faded fabric, half anticipating that its former wearer's head might materialize

'I always knew she'd show up, in some shape or other. You might as well put the samovar on, this morning.'

Lifting the samovar as if it were as light as feather to take it into the kitchen, Chrysanthemum's heart beat faster at the faintest possibility that she might catch a glimpse of Rose.

'Sas tai nas,' she whispers, remembering the last time. But nothing happens. Not a puff of smoke, not a whiff of scent. Just, from the kitchen, the hooting of the rescued owlet, making the place feel spooked, and familiar, all at the same time.

'Pass us the scissors – not that pair, stupid – she's in the paper again.'

Dolores has taken to collecting pictures of Orage from the newspapers to put in a scrapbook. Chrysanthemum, waving the third-best scissors at the little owl, who, much recovered and poised over a saucerful of cut-up mouse, might be sizing her up for a peck, looks over her shoulder.

'I don't want your rotten mouse. I want a cup of tea and a bit of peace and quiet.'

It's not on offer.

'Look at her. She's a proper picture.' Dolores points to Orage, svelte and chic in wide-skirted, narrow-jacketed New Look, smiling lovingly at Rosemary as Sylvester, dark and suave with his arms round the elegantly coiffed blonde woman and the adorable baby with golden ringlets, beams proudly to camera.

> *'Fame is nothing next to family. On the eve of her new show at the London Palladium, light entertainment star Orage Sheridan welcomes The Post into her home, and tells us that once the show is over, she's at her happiest as a wife and mother.'*

Over the page there are pictures of Orage feeding Rosemary in a high chair, serving Sylvester with a tumbler of whisky as he lounges with a pipe in a comfortable chair, and, impossibly slender in slacks, opening a wardrobe door to reveal an array of fashionable confections.

'She must have got someone to tidy up after her. When we were in digs she was what my mother would have called a slattern.' The little owl gives Chrysanthemum a beady look. 'I can just see her, lying on the bed with her curlers in and her old nylons – and worse – all over the floor.'

'She's done well for herself. And she doesn't forget her friends, I'll say that for her too.' Dolores reaches into her handbag for her new enamelled Helena Rubenstein compact and pointedly dusts her nose and cheeks, then fastidiously flicks away any loose powder that might have drifted into her whiskers.

'She's sent tickets.' Dolores checks her bag.

'They're still there. You only looked yesterday evening and you haven't left the house since then. Except to go to the lav.'

'You can shut up, close the door and call me Mary. You might like to take a leaf out of her book. No-one's going to be pleased to see you moping round like a wet weekend. You can talk about slattern. You can stop coming down for breakfast in that dressing gown for a start.'

Chrysanthemum tries not to begrudge the former Grace the fame and fortune that's come her way. Orage's generosity – no, kindness – has no limits. But some mornings it's hard, having the difference rubbed in between Orage's charmed life and Chrysanthemum's existence. Mother deceased, friends scattered, and Mervyn... no, she can't – she mustn't – think of that. But here she is at the beck and call of a bearded harridan, terrorized by an owl who's the reincarnation of a dead fortune teller and the only light on the horizon the tealight in the booth. It's not that she'd swap with Orage, her bright glossy life, her illustrious singing career and her devoted husband and daughter, but perhaps it wouldn't have hurt, to be a bit more sensible.

She glares at the owl, and brandishes the third-best scissors at it, in case it gets any ideas.

'Bloody bird kept me awake most of last night, hooting.'

'It wasn't just her.' Dolores slurps her tea more malevolently than necessary. 'It was me, too. I was keeping her company. If you don't hoot back at them they think they're being neglected. It is mating season.'

'Bloody Ada. How long does it go on.'

'I've no idea. Weeks, I should imagine. It won't be for ever, she'll take herself off when her wing's strong enough. If you don't like it, you could ask Orage if she'll have you for a visit. That would be nice for both of you, I'm sure.'

'Yes, I'm sure it would. I could remind her of everything she's left behind. I'm sure she'd love that.'

'Look at you, clumsy clot. You've got jam all over that picture.'

Chrysanthemum prepares to exit in such a dramatic manner that, for once, she'll have the last word. 'In my life that seems like an achievement.'

'You're so sorry for yourself you make me sick.' From the tone of her voice, Dolores is thoroughly enjoying herself. 'You don't know the meaning of sorry until you've been abducted by Red Indians and tattooed from head to toe against your will. They had to bind me hand and foot and I still gave them as good as I got.'

She flourishes her wrists so her dressing gown sleeves fell back, and looks down with pride at the smudged blue patterns on her forearms.

'Red Indians my foot. You weren't abducted by Red Indians. You wouldn't know a real Red Indian if it came up to you and said 'How.' You made it up. You got them done yourself.'

Dolores' mouth falls open.

'How did you..?'

'Rose's mother told me. When we were waiting for Rosemary. We had a lot of time to pass. She was at Jeffcocks when you were there. She told me all sorts of things.'

With that, Chrysanthemum sweeps out of the room as quickly as possible, before Dolores notices the smile on her face. Closing the door behind her, she does a little war dance in the hall.

Chapter 33

As Maurice holds the door open for her, Chrysanthemum notices he isn't
spotty any more. He stops in front of her, turns round.

'I used to think Orage had the nicest bottom I'd ever seen. But I've changed
my mind. Yours is much nicer.'

With that, he doffs his trilby with a flourish, and leaves her standing there in
the Fankes lobby, red as a beetroot, not knowing where to put herself.

Maybe it's the colour of her new suit, or the way she's set her hair. Maybe
it's Maurice's unexpected compliment. Brightening her up. Turning her into
someone who attracts attention. Maybe it's just luck. Or fate. She looks at her
hands. Janna's voice. *This one's for fate, this one's for fortune.* Maybe it just boils
down to being the right person, in the right place, at the right time. Whatever
it is, when Chrysanthemum walks up to the booth for the matinee shift,
Sylvester is standing in front of the booth.

'Hello old chap.' He takes her hand in his and then leans in for a brotherly
peck on the cheek.

'To what do we owe the honour? Is Orage here?'

'No, home with the baby. Teething. Poor little mite, needs her attention.
Sends love of course. Says don't be a stranger, always at home. No, I'm here
on… hang about.' Sylvester looks at her properly. Then he looks her up and
down and when he looks her in the eye, Chrysanthemum sees the glimmer of
a chance.

'You…work, in here?' He gestures towards the booth. Janna's old sign has
been removed and a new one painted, that says straightforwardly: Your future
path revealed. And in smaller letters, 'the chosen successor of genuine Gipsy
Fortune Teller.' Although there is no name, next to it is a photograph – and
not a bad one either, even if it has been cut out of a larger picture of The Three
Graces, and stuck up in its frame a bit on the wonky side. Sylvester examines
it, then looks at her.

Chrysanthemum nods. 'Since… Well, someone had to and I… well it gives
me something to do. Otherwise I'd be stuck in the boarding house. I mean, I
don't mind, but it is nice to get out and about…'

'Yes, of course.' Sylvester isn't listening, she could tell. But he looks at her
again. Peering. Sizing her up. Then he smiles.

'Can you do it?'

'I… they talk to me. Tell me things. Stuff they're worried about. I tell them things that might help, if something occurs to me. It's not like Janna. But they come back so it seems to work. I quite like it actually. Helping people, I mean. It does seem to help. Well, it does if they want it to.'

Sylvester hasn't been listening. But he looks eager, as if an idea has sparked a possibility. 'Not that it matters. If you can do it, I mean, though I'm sure you can, or you wouldn't be here. The thing is, it might work. You might be the very thing. Could you – do you think – come with me to London next week?'

Which is why, a week later, Chrysanthemum, in her suit and with her hair done nicely, is met off the train at Kings Cross Station by Sylvester and driven, in the grey Bentley that used to meet Orage, to Fleet Street.

This is her first London visit that isn't a trip to visit Orage and see Rosemary. *Her first visit that might be an opportunity.* She doesn't want to appear unsophisticated, so she keeps her mouth shut and sits as elegantly as she can manage whilst a group of men in their middle years and a young woman in a narrow suit that is the chicest thing she has ever seen examine her, and talk about her. *Almost as if I'm not actually there.*

'I don't know. She's very young.'

'Precisely.' That's the woman. *She has a faint tang to her pleasant, energetic voice of …tea, and terraced houses.* 'She will appeal to the younger readers. You can't have the latest fashions on the women's page and then some dreadful old boot who looks as if she's spent her life in a booth on the pier. That wouldn't do at all. We want someone modern.' *She's got more life and ambition than everyone else in this room put together.*

'She's got a nice face. Good looking, but not so ridiculously lovely she's like a member of a different species.' *Like Orage.* Chrysanthemum and the woman both look at Sylvester, then catch each other's eye at the same time. *I think I like her.*

'I can work with her.' The woman's voice is warm, but also decisive. 'I'm Elizabeth Hix – women's page editor. How it will work is that every week you will answer a letter from a reader who has a problem and wants to know what the future has in store for them.'

Chrysanthemum folds her hands and nods.

'Have you actually got any letters? What will she write about, day in day out? Won't it all get a bit tedious?'

Elizabeth gives the man a withering glance.

'Edmund, you have no idea how many problems our lady readers have got, largely on account of men like you who don't listen to them. And you have no idea how much they will like the fact that there is somebody to advise them about what is in store for them and what is the best thing for them to do about it. And you will like it because everyone has an agony aunt but there will be something new and different about yours that will appeal to the readers. A novelty. You're always saying that readers love something new.'

She turns to Chrysanthemum.

'Don't worry about the writing. We will send you the letters and somebody from the desk will telephone you – we'll get you set up with a telephone if you don't already have one – and you will tell us what to say. Does that sound like something you could do?'

'Yes it does.' Chrysanthemum's dancing days have taught her poise, at least when it is called for, and this is definitely a performance. 'I like the sound of that very much.'

'Then we have it. Now, what do they call you?'

'Chrysanthemum Landry.'

'Oh golly. We'll have to do something with that.' That's one of the middle-aged men. *Assserting his authority.*

'It is a bit of a mouthful.' But Elizabeth Hix looks unruffled. 'Still, it's not all bad. Do you have a professional name?'

Chrysanthemum shook her head. *Janna had all those names and I've only got one. And it isn't good enough.*

'That's OK. You can be something special, from now on.' Elizabeth's smile is very feline. 'Chrissie. No. Pretty. But too ordinary.' *That gives her a pang. Chryssie is the name Orage and Rose call her.*

'Chris… I know, Crysta. With a Y. And no H. More exotic. We'll run it for a month and see if it takes off. And if you get a letter where you see bad things – I mean really bad things – then you must tell us, and we'll send you another one.'

The telephone is installed the very next day. And two days later, Chrysanthemum – no, Crysta – gets a letter. She takes it as far away from the front room as she can, and holds the first letter in her hands. She must have read it forty times, and she has no idea if it was written in Doncaster, or in the newspaper office, but she looks at the lines asking for her help, and does her best. Remembers what Janna told her. *Tell them what they want to hear, and one thing you can see that they'd never have thought of. Trust what you see. It might be a name, or a colour, or a warning. Just one thing.* A young man called Arthur carefully takes down everything she says.

'I heard all that.' Dolores' voice carries all the way down the corridor from the front room. 'I don't know why you're hiding. You didn't sound too bad at all. For a beginner. She'll go to America of course. Loverboy holds all the cards. Whether she'll regret it is another matter.'

Chrysanthemum hasn't got too much time to listen, because she doesn't want to run late. Maurice has invited her to the Gaumont for a dinner dance. For some reason she can't quite explain, there are butterflies in her stomach, but she needn't have worried. They fall into step very easily with each other.

'I told you I wouldn't always have spots,' he tells her as they walk home in the fog. She doesn't quite see stars when he stops her underneath a lamp-post and gently presses his wide, smiling mouth on hers, but the butterflies flutter more strongly than they ever used to with the johnnies.

Clairvoyant Crysta's first column appears in print the following week.

> *Dear Crysta,*
> *Do the stars see a journey for me, or will I stay at home? My fiancé has been*
> *demobbed and recently came back to Civvy Street. He is keen for us to get*
> *married, as am I, but what he does not know is that while he was away I*
> *made another a good friend who was posted here. He has returned to America*
> *where he lives but he has written to me and tells me he has feelings. I did not*
> *mean for him to develop these but we both feel the same. I have waited for my*
> *fiancé and do not want to hurt his feelings, but I am torn. Please help me.*

Chrysanthemum advises her to take the path she knows is right, and stay with her fiancé. When her pay cheque arrives, she blows all her coupons and spends it on a new dress because Maurice has invited her to the Gaumont again. It's money well spent to see the admiring look in his eyes. They find their feet in the foxtrot, and when he stops under the lamp-post, she leans in for his kiss and returns it. It takes him a while to draw breath. 'I always knew you'd be a cracker,' he says.

The next letter, she advises the writer to give her heart to the man in blue, and to watch the supervisor on her shift at work because she's up to something that could get the writer into trouble. She and Maurice win the audience's choice vote for the dance-off at the Gaumont and when she lets herself in at two in the morning she finds Dolores sitting in the kitchen, waiting up for her with a bootfaced expression. 'I suppose you think you've invented it,' huffs the old lady. 'Next time, you might want to wipe the lipstick off your face before you crawl home. You look as if you've been at the jam.'

The third letter, she suggests that 67 might lead to a windfall, and Maurice asks if she would like to go away with him for a weekend. The following week the writer of that letter wins the jackpot at bingo and writes in to say that if it hadn't been for Clairvoyant Crysta she would have picked another number.

Elizabeth Hix calls two weeks later.

'It's all going rather well,' she says, as casually as if she's just passing the time of day. 'I've got a sack of letters that have been sent in for you, a lot anyway, and I wondered if we could make it every day? And I've had a request. Do you think this is something you could do on the radio?'

'Actually, yes.' Chrysanthemum realises she has found a voice, as well as her feet. 'I'm coming down to London next weekend with my gentleman friend. Do you think it might be possible to set it up around then?'

*ACT THREE: TAKE A CLOSER LOOK*

Chapter 34

It's getting late and there might have been a port and lemon. Or three. Rose's eyelids are drooping.

'Right. Time to get you up those dancers. You can have your old room if you like. I don't suppose you've brought a nightie have you? I can always get you something.' Chrysanthemum is mentally going through her drawers to think what might suit.

'Someone might have died in it.'

'Someone may well have died in it but that's no reason for it to go to waste. Anyway I'll have washed it.'

'It wasn't one of Dolores' was it? Did she die in it?'

'She did not. She wouldn't go to bed. She sat in that chair, the one where you're sitting, for three days, with her coat on and her handbag in her lap, bolt upright, as if she was waiting for a bus. She never said a word until right at the end. She looked at me and she opened her mouth and I thought, this is it. The reveal. The prestige. The moment when everything becomes clear.'

'What did she say?' Rose leans in, all agog. 'Did she tell you everything? Did she tell you where she got the samovar?'

'Did she heck. She glowered at me for about thirty seconds, with me holding my breath in case I missed anything. "Why did you cook all that mince," she said. Loudly. Proper accusing me. And then she died.'

'She was a right bugger.' The way Rose says it, it's affectionate. 'She never would say a muff about that samovar. Anyway. Why did you cook all that mince?'

'It would only have gone off if I hadn't. It wasn't my fault she died before she could eat it.'

But Rose evidently isn't thinking about nighties any more, or Dolores, or mince, as her eyes are locked on Chrysanthemum's chin.

'How long have you...?

'After Maurice died. I wasn't bothered about anyone else looking and there didn't seem much point in buying razor blades after he was gone. He never knew, you know.'

Rose lifts the pencil line that stands in for her right eyebrow.

'Well, if he did, he never let on. I'll get you that nightie.' Chrysanthemum clumps off and returns with her hands full of winceyette. 'Come on. Up those dancers.'

'Me and Orage knew. We didn't want to hurt your feelings. But if you were in a room on your own and one of us walked in, you'd jump every time and there'd always be a pair of tweezers in your hand. We always knew and we never let on.'

'There was too much of that if you ask me. People knowing and no-one saying anything. A bit of plain talking would have saved everyone a lot of trouble.'

'Maybe so. But seeing isn't the same as believing, as you should know as well as I do after all those years round show people. And what you see isn't the same as what you get. You'd still have had to find it out for yourself. We all would.'

'That's what you found out on your travels?' Chrysanthemum gives the eiderdown a vengeful shake. 'Janna told me that the first time Dolores had me sit in with her. And she taught me a dance, to boot. I can still remember it. I'll do it for you now if you like. *Any umbrellas, any umbrellas, to mend today.*'

'Don't fall out Chryssie.' No one does bedraggled like Rose. 'I wish Janna had taught me that dance. Ooh I missed you all.'

'Surprised you had enough marbles to miss anything. You'd forget your head if it wasn't sewn on. Where did you get to? After the postcard? I can do Ovaltine if you'd like.'

'I was in a show. A travelling one. We went all over America and I met a cowboy in a bar in Texas. He picked me because I was the smallest in the line and he liked my English accent. I married him you know.'

'How could we know? We never heard from you. Orage and I, we talked about you all the time. Wondered what had happened to you.' That was the truth. But though there'd always been a nagging ache at her absence, it had been a good life. What with the column in the paper, and the ballroom dancing, and Maurice raking it in with his car dealership, and all the lovely times with Orage and her family. Time had passed. It was only when she looked back that she realised how much of it.

'I sent you a letter. He was a very nice man but it was no life, more miles from anywhere than you could imagine. It wasn't like here, it was a long drive even to a shop. He'd have liked kiddies but that wasn't for me. And after he died, I went back to New York and I went to Coney Island. And do you know, there were all sorts like me, old hoofers, and I talked my way into a show? It was the first time I'd danced for years and I still could. They were very surprised when they saw me. I wasn't though. With milk?' *A letter that never arrived. Oh Rose. Any sins of hers would weigh less than a feather. We missed her. Me, and Orage. Thought we'd lost her. Lost her once, and then lost her for good.*

'All milk.'

'When I started to dance again I remembered all of you, and how much I missed you. I wish I'd known you'd never got that letter. I thought you'd washed your hands of me, what with all the trouble I caused. And then we had someone clever who found us funding so we got to be an actual theatre company and went all over the place, with people paying for tickets. We did have fun, but I never forgot the Three Graces. So I gave them the slip and came looking. And here I am. Milk and a nip of brandy?' Rose always could tell when she'd been forgiven.

'And a nip of brandy. And I'll get you a nice hot water bottle.'

Chrysanthemum lumbers back up the stairs with the bottle under one arm and two laced Ovaltines on a tray to find Rose, wearing all her clothes, has made herself a nest in the middle of the bed where the springs dip, and curled up in it. She stretches out her hands for her bottle and snuggles it to her.

'It's in the bones, these days. Cold all the way through. Do you remember, we used to go out with no stockings and a thin frock and we never felt a thing?'

'You might not have. I was always happier with a bodice. And Orage couldn't have been happier when Sylvester bought her first fur coat. A beautiful black seal it was, with a swing to it. Set her hair off something lovely.'

'She was the most glamorous person I ever met in my whole life.' Rose has got hot milk on her lip. *Just like when we were in digs.* 'She won't have changed. I know it. I'm so excited about seeing her again. Do you think she'll be pleased to see me? What time does she wake up? We can telephone her after breakfast. Won't she be surprised?'

'Rose.' *There is no easy way of telling you this.* 'We can't call her, I'm afraid.'

'What do you mean we can't call her? You haven't fallen out with her have you? Oh, Chryssie, you haven't, have you? *No. I never fell out with her. All those years and never a cross word, for all that there were a lot of sarcastic ones.*

'I didn't. I miss her every day.'

'You don't mean it. She's not is she? She can't be.'

'A couple of years ago.' *Deep breath, Chryssie. Chin up. Look 'em in the eye and don't let them have anything for free. That's what she'd say.*

Quick tears pool down Rose's crumpled face into her Ovaltine. Chrysanthemum bites down on her own lip and takes a deep breath before clasping her old friend's hand.

'I never thought I wouldn't see her again.' Rose is hiccuping. 'I thought she'd walk into the room where I was one day and it would all be just the same.' *Oh Rose. Nothing's the same, and everything.*

'She was very brave. Well, of course she was. It was in the papers, afterwards. Because she'd been famous. You know how they are. She and Sylvester kept themselves to themselves – they had a beautiful bungalow, in Eastbourne – but after she died, there was a piece in the papers. It was very hard on Rosemary. She'd always thought the world of her mother and it came as a bit of a shock.'

'What, her being dead? It must have done.' Rose wipes her nose on her sleeve. 'It has been for me. Not expected.'

'No you daft ha'porth. Well, yes, but it wasn't that. Or even that she found out that Orage wasn't her real mother, though that was hard enough.'

'Wasn't she? Though she always could be a dark horse. Remember when she used to disappear to see her mystery boyfriend that she couldn't tell us about until it turned out to be Sylvester and she married him?' *I could shake her but it wouldn't put any sense back into her.*

'Let's just put it this way. They found her secret. After she died. The one she wouldn't tell anyone. Not even us.'

'What, that she was a fella? I always knew that. Like you and the tweezers. I didn't want to hurt her feelings, either. I never said anything because it was as plain as the nose on her face. Don't you remember her great big feet? Dinnerplates they were like. And she could pee faster than anyone. Didn't need to sit down I suppose. Didn't you realise? It never made any difference to me and now I'll never see her again.'

Rose dissolves into tears and wails like a heartbroken child into the ancient pink satin eiderdown. Chrysanthemum pats her gently on the shoulder as she weeps, and with the other hand crossly sweeps away the tears that drip from the end of her own nose. Eventually Rose raises her damp face and puts out her hand for a tissue.

She gives her nose a terrific blow and looks up through wet eyes.

'Rosemary. You said Rosemary. How is she?'

It's a hasty goodnight because Chrysanthemum doesn't know what to say. Rosemary, dear Rosemary, and Rose, who seems quite chipper, much more on top of things than you might expect and not as if she's been gone for an adult lifetime, but there's this great hole between then and now, and what to say to fill it, when she's just found out her dear friend is dead and then why would you put the tin lid on that by rubbing it in about Rosemary when you don't know the first thing about how she feels about the daughter that she gave away without even looking at her?

'Sleep tight Rose' is all that springs to her lips and then she shuts the door and makes for the room behind the shop where she stores all the clothes, which is where she always goes, when she needs to think about things.

So many secrets, and usually by the time she's found out the truth of them, none of it comes as a surprise. Mostly it comes from the clothes. Get your hands on what they used to wear and there's nothing you can't find out, if you put your mind to it. Gentle Tagalong, the clown with his foot perpetually in his mouth to stop him from saying the wrong thing, was a girl. It was the bandages that gave it away, to strap up his chest so that no-one could ever take him for what he was, and take him against his will, which he'd put up with all his life from his drunken father before he ran away to Jeffcocks. Tilly the tightrope walker, who had lost first her wits and then her life to alcohol because of her unrequited love for Gilbert, the Great Lifto, that she was too ashamed to confess to, so that it wasn't even between herself and her God. Poor Tilly, who was never able to lose her balance because she'd learned to walk the wire by concentrating her thoughts on the blessed Virgin, until Gilbert came along, and then the booze. It was in the tutu, with her, once it had gone all droopy, like a flower that's been cast aside.

Janna's veiled mysteries were no secrets at all, but stories told so many times that they became the truth whether they were or not: the dances for the Tsar, the flight from the Carpathians, the bear in the coat who danced with her in the woods and accompanied her in the hold of a ship disguised as a human in a Cossack's coat. The stories that were too good not to go on believing even after Dolores died and there it was in her things, that she'd kept all those years, this moulting old bear-suit complete with head and paws.

Rose's secret she'd kept all her life, because it was hers too, and the most important secret she was keeping was her own. But she knows that all stories, if they get told at all, must have an end, and sometimes there's a twist in the tale so the story doesn't end the way you thought it would.

Like Orage's story. The undertaker went to the rags with the information that the one-time household name he'd just buried, light entertainment's epitome of gracious elegance, had turned out to be more, in certain departments, than he'd expected. He'd have got a good price, for that. And then they'd ferreted out a birth certificate, and for a while you'd think there was nothing else to talk about. At the height of it, Rosemary turned up at the shop after dark with her mother's old costumes, and her stage shoes, in a holdall.

'She always kept them. It meant a lot to her. But now they've found out... It's enough that they know. I don't want them picking over her remains and making her out to be something extraordinary.' Broken hearted and bewildered, Rosemary, so beautifully brought up, was never less than Orage's child.

'She was entirely extraordinary. But perhaps not in the way that people who didn't know her would like to make her out to be. You can leave all your mother's old things with me. I'll keep them safe for you.'

'My mother.' A shadow crossed Rosemary's face. *One of many, I dare say, in these sad days.* 'Chrysanthemum... do you know who my real mother was?'

'Orage was your real mother. You were put into her arms when you were less than an hour old. If love has anything to do with it, not to mention a lifetime of looking after, you couldn't have had a better.'

'That's what I think too. But I'm glad you said it. I wanted you to say it.'

'It's only the truth. And don't let anyone persuade you otherwise. Not everyone has that kind of love from their mother. I certainly didn't.'

Even in her own grief, Rosemary is kind. 'Oh that's sad. I'm sorry.'

'It's a long time ago. But it taught me that family is who you love, and loves you most. And Orage loved you.'

But of course it is not quite that simple. Families are blood as well as the ties that bind, and Rosemary is Rose's blood. And now what is she going to tell Rose about Rosemary, and Rosemary about Rose?

There are some secrets that should be kept. Silent as the grave. Mervyn.

She'd buried that secret as deep in her past as he was in the ground. Looked for him out of the corner of her eye for a long time but now it was as if he never existed. Most of the time anyway.

Some secrets reveal themselves. Some are never secrets, only mysteries.

And one she'd never got to the bottom of, and that was the one she most wanted to find out, before she was too old and it was too late.

The one that always did her hiding in plain sight.

She'd have known what to do, about Rose.

It's no use. Back to kitchen she goes, where the samovar, set out to welcome Rose, draws her over. She rubs it gently.

'You'd never let on where you got this, would you? Even if you'd bought it in a shop like anyone else you'd be buggered if you'd give anyone the satisfaction. I cooked all that mince to make a shepherd's pie because it was your favourite, you horrible old woman. Not that I expected any thanks. And when I laid you out, there were tattoos all over you and I wished I knew if they were just for decoration or if they added up to a story. There was something you didn't want me to find out, wasn't there? Your secret that you took to your grave. All your life you never gave me a clue. And you might have put me out of my misery. But all the same, I wish you were still here. You were always the one that kept an eye out for me.'

And what, indeed, was she to say to Rose? The weight of it bears down heavily on Chrysanthemum's shoulders as she makes her way back up the stairs to her own room. I am an old woman, she tells herself. I ought to know the answers by now. But how can I, when the question itself is not simple?

Questions. Secrets. Much the same thing really. A lack of information. She came of age in a time of secrets. Different from nowadays, where everyone talks about everything. Muriel concealed information from her and she soon learned that she, in return, had to camouflage everything that mattered to her from Muriel if she was to have any chance of keeping it safe. And then she grew up when the world was at war. Careless talk costs, and all that. Minding your own business was more than manners in wartime, it was vital. And then at the theatre, no-one ever let on what they were about, not really. Let them see the performance, not the rehearsal. It spilled over, offstage as well as on. Skeletons in every closet you cared to open. It was the way of things, and she fitted right in, too bloody right she did. Second nature? She'd had good teachers but… First nature more like. Walked right in. To the manor born. The missing piece slotting into the jigsaw. Seeing may be believing, but that's for the punters. She'd done alright. Earned a pretty penny, been able to put on a good face, when it came to her own secret. Not that it would have served anyone, to let that cat out of its bag.

But. This.

Rose is the only truly innocent person she has ever met. All the decisions were made on her behalf. The only thing she did was to walk away from it all.

Not one bit of this is her fault. *Yes it is. If she hadn't been such a trusting idiot none of this would have happened. No it isn't. She was young. She met a man. She made a mistake. Anyone can make a mistake. But anyone didn't. Rose made it. Made it and paid for it. And yet here she is. So pleased to be back. So pleased to be home. And here I am, legging it away from her as fast as decency and my old legs will let me.*

It's a relief to be back in her own bedroom, *that's right, get your dressing gown on*, but she needs something else. *A slug of brandy, that'll put me to rights.* She keeps a bottle on the bedside table. For the nights when she can't sleep. Not that there are many of those. There isn't anything on her conscience. Maybe there should be. But what else should she have done?

The shadow people never quite vanished, though over the years they came less and less, but she's pleased to see them when they pop up. Old friends, mostly, or familiar acquaintances more like. The ones who really matter never put in an appearance. Maurice. Orage. Janna. Dolores. She'd be pleased to see them. More than. The single one who haunts her is Rose, and she's the only one left alive. All those years, and not a bit of it her fault. And now there are only the two of them left, and she has to do the right thing by her. But she has to do it by Orage and Rosemary as well. The second brandy slips down even more easily than the first, and the third more easily still. But she can't get into bed, or even sit still. From bed to window she walks, and window to wardrobe, and back again, and to the dressing table, and still there's no settling.

There's no-one left who could offer advice. Orage would put her finger on a solution. Maurice wouldn't know at all, but he'd be able to make her feel better. Janna would look at her with those unfathomable eyes and see exactly what needed to be seen. Dolores… She'd know precisely what to do. She always did.

But she was dead. They're all dead. She and Rose are the only ones left.

She hardly ever touches the music box on the dressing table because it's old, and fragile, and she's scared that if she winds it up too tight, it will never sing again. She brought it back for Dolores, from the weekend in Blackpool that was her honeymoon. It was only a plastic powder box, but it had a jewelled lid and played *Dark Eyes*, and in a sentimental moment – she had been on her honeymoon, after all – she thought it might be a momento for Dolores of her old mucker.

'Why would I want that,' was all she got in the way of thanks, and the box was spirited out of sight and forgotten about. But when she'd been clearing out Dolores' things, all those years later, she found it in the drawer next to the bed, carefully wrapped in the ragged remains of French knickers in peach crepe de chine. She'd lifted the lid to find, in the powder puff tray, a tiny nest of feathers. *If only it was not just me, on my own.*

She picks the box up and holds it in both hands. The way you'd hold a bird or a nest, but not a box. *If only someone would talk to me.* Turning it upside down, she twists the tarnished little key until it resists. Then she sets the box down and opens the lid.

Over-wound, the cheap, plinking notes trip out in a wonky waltz. Da-da-da-dada…Funny how the words of the Al Bowlly song spring so readily to mind. After all those years. *Gypsy love of mine… Is there ne'er a sign… On your path to show…The way that I must go…*

*Ne'er a sign?* Learn to look, Janna told her. Then you will see more than other people, and they will pay you for what they could have told themselves. It was a good lesson and she learned it well. But she's at a loss now. *What is left to me is just a memory…* Should she look backwards for answers? And if so, how far? Back to the first time Rose clapped eyes on Mervyn? To the day Rosemary was born? To the day of the audition? Or the day she met the lady in gold with a tiger on the end of a string, and knew for the first time where she would belong? To the night she stood in the wings of the theatre holding a flat in her hands? They were all the beginnings of the stories that make up a life. *Or for me, perchance, just a broken dream…* But this is Rose's life, not hers, and she holds it in her hands too, as fragile as a nest. What would be the right ending – the good ending, the ending that made sense of everything in the rest of the story – for Rose?

The tinny tune slows down, the notes bending and warping just where the song should have speeded up for the *whirling dance*. Grabbing it, Chrysanthemum winds it fiercely until the mechanism crunches, gives a sharp, protesting ping that's followed by the unmistakeable sound of something snapping.

Chrysanthemum feels her heart fall through her stomach. *I can't have.* She lifts the lid but there's nothing. Not a note. *It's only a box. It doesn't matter. It's not a person. No-one's hurt.* She shakes it. Not a sound. A tiny grey feather, downy as a dandelion clock, flutters to the floor.

She's broken it. *It's only a box. But it's not. Not only.*

Chrysanthemum lays the box in her lap, puts her hands to her mouth, and weeps. She pulls open the dressing table drawer, and places the box inside. And then, just as she's about to slide the drawer shut, something catches her eye, and she gasps. She hasn't thought about it for years; in fact she'd forgotten about it completely. But it's there. One of the two flight feathers, one each for her and Rose, that she found on the bed the night that Janna died. And now, here it is again. Almost as if it's been waiting for her. To remind her. *It has stories. For you.* Except it hasn't told them. All those years of looking, and nothing. But Rose has returned, and she's fished the samovar out of the glory hole. Maybe it was time to see if it would fulfil Janna's promise, and tell some more of its stories.

Chapter 35

Chrysanthemum lets Rose sleep in but it's a shop day so even though she's got a thick head from all that booze she's up and about. It isn't like her to let things slip her mind but since Rose's came back – only yesterday – her mind has been so crowded with remembering – no, reshaping – the past, that she completely forgets about the parcel that arrived with Rose, the one she left in the footwell under the counter, until a customer asks her if she could leave her bag of bargains there, to be picked up later. As Chrysanthemum puts down the customer's bag, her finger brushes against it. Later on, when she takes stock, it will seem that it drew itself to her attention.

'I'm losing my touch.' Chrysanthemum mutters under her breath as she drags it onto the counter. 'First sign of you know what. That and forgetting things.' There is no-one in the shop to answer her and she shakes her head. 'Talking to myself. Maybe I need something to perk me up. Hair of the dog.'

The parcel is bulky, but not heavy, wrapped in an old-fashioned way with string, brown paper, and sealing wax. Chrysanthemum's name is written, in precise lettering, in dark blue. Ink, she notices, not felt-tip or ballpoint.

She carefully unpicks the knotted string and detaches it from the brittle red blob of dried wax. *You don't often see that these days.* Curiosity piqued, she winds the string round her fingers and then loops it round the middle so it won't unravel.

Under the brown paper is a bundle. Wrapped in heavy linen; fusty-smelling and spotted with age; tied with yet more string. There is something peculiarly repellent about it. Chrysanthemum halts, reluctant to investigate further.

'It's just stuff for the shop.' She gives herself a talking-to. Out loud. Playing to the gallery even if she's the only one in it. 'The stuff people bring. Not even sorted. Get it open and then whatever it is, if it's dirty I'll run it through the washer and if it's not nice it can go in the bin.'

Even so, her fingers are tentative as she peels pack the heavy old linen and gingerly unwinds it. A small, black, claw-like thing emerges from the fabric and Chrysanthemum startles – it couldn't be a hand, surely? A tiny, mummified hand? And yet that is what it looks like.

She pulls back the wrappings until the thing inside is revealed on the counter: an ancient, dessicated figure less than two feet long, with a scaled fishtail, a human torso, two mannikin hands and a face. If face is the right word for this grotesque thing. For all that it is twisted into an expression unmistakeably of grief or pain, it is not the face of a person, nor any other creature Chrysanthemum has ever seen

'A mermaid.' The thought comes into her mind although the dreadful thing in front of her isn't like any mermaid she'd ever imagined.

But why has it been sent to her? The parcel had been addressed to her, in person. She picks it up again: her name has been precisely lettered, and the address, but not that of the shop.

Someone wanted her to have this poor, sad, horrible creature.

But who?

But why?

Chrysanthemum bends to rewrap the mermaid, as much to conceal it from herself as hide it from view in case anyone comes in the shop. As she does, the room seems to darken.

'That's given me a bit of a turn.' *Aloud again. Maurice would have something to say about her talking to herself. Darker, and colder. Must look at that light fitting. The air seems to be moving. And it's nippy in here.*

As she looks around, particles in the air shimmer and Chrysanthemum hugs her cardigan tightly round herself, arms goosebumping against a chill in the air that wasn't there a moment ago. *Maybe I'm coming down with something.* She starts to feel queasy and the glowing specks gathering before her eyes might be a symptom of food poisoning. *You're having yourself on. You and Rose had far too much to drink last night. A hangover. At your age.*

The shimmering in the air turns to a swirling in the rapidly darkening shop as more and more glowing particles gather into a mass. Nausea sweeps over Chrysanthemum in a hot-and-cold rush that makes her skin prickle as her stomach leaps. And then she remembers. All that time back, when she picked up the spirit hand in Dolores' trailer. And then found out that her mother had died. She sits down, gripping the sides of the chair, and concentrates until the giddiness passes and she can stand without her head spinning.

And as she looks up, the phosphorescent specks coalesce, between the men's rack and the shelves of bric-a-brac, into a glowing mass rapidly taking the shape of a woman. A woman in negative, clad in luminous white garments from the turn of the century, black where her skin should have been white and white where her hair...and her beard...would have been black, when she was alive. *Oh that's the giddiness, that's what it is, I'm seeing things.*

Seeing things. Well it's been a while. When she was alive. And now Rose is back. Reminding her of that teenage energy. All that life, just waiting for us. Only now we're at the other end. Nearly at the point where death's waiting in the wings.

The apparition settles its hands – mittened in white mesh against dead black flesh – on its stomacher and gives Chrysanthemum a look that, even if it hadn't been for the facial hair, bears a resemblance to Dolores.

'Usually, they run screaming.' The voice has that fairground intonation. *Vey.* 'But you're not like most people, are you? We all have our crosses.'

Chrysanthemum holds on to the sides of the chair.

'You're shivering,' remarks the figure.

'It's got…colder.'

'Yes.' The apparition couldn't look more complacent. 'I couldn't do that in life. People thought I could but that was just fear. Do you know who I am?'

Chrysanthemum shook her head.

'I came with the mermaid.'

Chrysanthemum looks at the grotesque creature with mounting distaste.

'I knew I should never have opened that parcel.'

'It wouldn't have done any good. It made it more convenient, but I'd have found a way.'

'Found a way?'

'Through.'

Chrysanthemum nods. She's beginning to understand.

'I think…are you a relation of Mrs Pickles?'

'You mean Dolores.' It isn't a question.

Chrysanthemum grips the chair even harder to stop herself falling from it.

'I've come to show you something.'

Chrysanthemum shook her head. "I'm not coming any nearer.'

'You don't need to. Just look.'

'I don't want to know. Whatever it is. Go away. Please.'

'You let me come in here. You thought it was you, didn't you? A gift you had, or something special. There's no such thing. You was just the doorway. That's why it came and went, and you never worked out why. You let things though that wanted to come. Strong things. Stronger than you. You were just a channel, if you like. A rat will find its way, you know, when it sees a clear run up a drainpipe. Like this. You touched… my handwork. I was always handy with a needle. But I've had my eye on you. I was biding my time. And I think you do want to know. It's all you ever wanted, to find out the secrets. And you did, in the end. All except one. Now watch.'

Chrysanthemum shakes her head and tries to screw her eyes shut but is compelled to watch as the particles that comprise the apparition appear to rise, separate, then reassemble into another shape. The chill in the room works its way inside her, into her very bones, as she realises the forming shape is the corpse of her mother. Muriel.

'That was what she looked like when she passed.' The disembodied voice comes first from one side of the room and then the other. 'An accident with an omnibus. Very sudden. There was nothing you could have done.'

The dreadful sight fills Chrysanthemum with a familiar deep sorrow that she has never been able to love Muriel. She's never missed her or mourned her, though after her death she grieved bitterly the relationship she'd never had with her. But it isn't the first time she's seen it. She remembers as if it were yesterday, standing by the gurney in the hospital mortuary, looking down at the figure that was once Muriel. 'That's not a secret.' Chrysanthemum feels her voice grown stronger. 'You're a fraud. You can't frighten me. It's time you slung your hook, whoever you are. Go on. Bugger off.'

'There was no love lost.' The voice sounds conversational. 'Not on either side, I'd say.'

'You should mind your own business. She was my mother.'

'She'd have been a better mother to a cat.'

'How dare…'

The room echoes with a chilly laugh. 'Oh she fed you and clothed you and made sure she brought you up right. But like I said, there was no love lost.'

'You're a liar and you're not real. I want you to go.'

'Not real? I've been called worse. And she wasn't your mother, either.'

'Oh get lost. I've had enough of you, you spiteful thing. And who the bloody Ada are you, anyway?'

'She wasn't your mother and I should know. I gave you to her the night you were born.'

'Who are you?' Chrysanthemum looks wildly round the room.

The particles shift again and form themselves into the apparition's face, which scrutinises Chrysanthemum until the old woman feels that she's falling down – or up, can you fall up? – into a cold, clammy tunnel of infinite length and darkness.

The white lips in the black face move, and the cold white eyes gazed into hers, and Chrysanthemum isn't sure if the voice spoke or if the thought – 'I'm your grandmother' – has just been pressed into her unwelcoming brain.

'I brought you into the world. Three in the morning on October 31$^{st}$ it was – that's the hour when the soul is weakest on the day when restless spirits walk the earth. The time most people die, you know, but that was when you chose to come into the world, just as the souls that had grown most tired of it was taking their leave and there wasn't another living creature to welcome you on such a bleak October night apart from me that they always said was never quite alive – well, as you can see, I never quite died either. So if you ever wondered why the living and the dead use you as a passage, in and out, in and out, coming and going without a by your leave…well, now you know why.'

'My mother…'

'My daughter didn't want you and she didn't so much as look at you. You came into the world in blood and pain and your birthright was shame and guilt and worse besides, and she thought that if she looked at you once, she might love you, and every time she saw you, you'd remind her of the blood that she had on her hands as a result of getting you. So I did my best for you, because you were my blood too.'

*Murderer's hands.*

'Who are … no … were… you?'

'My name was Maude. And there never was any love lost between her and me, but even if it's bad blood, blood will out. She may not have wanted you when you were born, but your real mother loved you dearly.'

Chapter 36

She's still sitting there, with the poor mermaid in its brown paper coffin in front of her, trying to make sense of it when all of a sudden there is Rose, pattering down the corridor in her nightie, bearing two cups of tea.

'You look a bit done in.' Chrysanthemum had never noticed Rose, noticing. Turns out she'd been so busy looking there were a whole lot of things she hadn't noticed.

'I put sugar in it. Nice and strong. I'll put the closed sign up. I suppose you've been seeing things again and this time I'm not going to say it was cherry brandy. Come on, you can't just sit there all day. You'll soon warm up in the kitchen.'

She remembers Rose making cocoa, all those years ago, after she saw the figures in Janna's fire. And now she's here. But this time she isn't frightened by the things she's seen. Shaken, yes, and shocked too, but not scared.

'There was another parcel. And I was so caught up with you turning up that I forgot about it. And then I opened it.'

Rose looks inside and shudders.

'I think the kindest thing might be to bury it,' she says at last. 'I don't know what it is or how it came to be here but perhaps the best thing to do is to put it to rest and leave things in peace.'

Rose, talking sense. Perhaps she always did. Perhaps this was another thing she hadn't noticed.

'All those years. So many secrets. All that shame, and sadness.'

Rose wraps her hands round her cup of tea. Her eyes fix on the box and an expression of resolve settles on her face.

'Chryssie. If we're talking about secrets. That box. With old newspapers in. Mervyn's box.'

Chrysanthemum inhales sharply at the sound of his name. First Maude, and now Mervyn.

'The one I used to fold myself up inside.' Rose's voice is quiet but determined. 'You've kept it all those years and you've kept me too, on your wall and in your heart, without ever knowing, so you've got a right to know. I was supposed to vanish. That was the whole point. But he couldn't get it right. That's when things started to go wrong. He was working on a box. A new trick. It was going to be the big one – the one that made him famous. He'd got the box – we'll, you've got it now. That's why he chose me, you know. I was tiny and bendy and I could make myself fit in his box. The whole point was that it was supposed to look impossible. The box was too small to fit a person and yet a person got in. And then once that impossible thing had happened, you disappeared. You were supposed to climb inside and then it's spun around and when he opens it there's no-one to be seen. No-one at all. And then it's spun around again, and there they are. Back in the box. But there was something he couldn't get right. The vanishing wasn't a problem, but when it came to bringing them back – that's the bit he couldn't get right. Once he made them disappear, they vanished for real. And he never got them back.'

'Did he tell you all this?'

'Just bits. But I worked it out – I mean, all those stories about the girls who vanished. And I put two and two together and it made sense – they'd worked in the same towns, even if they weren't in the same shows. But he chose the dancers because they were like me – they were young, and they were gullible, and they had flexible bodies. But something about the trick never went right. He could do the prestige but there was something about the twist he couldn't master. And he thought it was his last chance to be the Magus, and not just someone who did parlour tricks. By the time he got to Fankes he was desperate – that's why he made me swear I'd never tell anyone about what he wanted to do with the box. Once he knew I was right for what he wanted, he did everything he could to make me want to leave with him, so we could go somewhere nobody knew him, and get the trick right. It was the only thing he wanted, really. The other thing was just to get me under his spell. And then, when we'd done it, he'd look at me with those beautiful dark eyes he had and he'd stroke my hair and he'd say it. "It's just a box, Rose. Just a box." That's what he said. "If you love me. Get in the box." And I did. I did love him and I did get in the box. But I never let him go so far as to spin it. I promised you I'd keep my wits about me, didn't I? And I did – well, as far as that was concerned. I never even thought about any consequences from the other thing. I only kept my eye on half a deck, didn't I? I was little Rose, silly and inexperienced and far too young to know what happens to dozy young dancers who let flattery go to their heads – just like you all thought. But when it came to show I wasn't a bit daft and I was never foolish enough to let him do that trick. He didn't reckon on that. And that must have been when he decided I knew too much and he'd have to make me vanish in another way.'

'Where did all those other girls go, Rose? Did he ever say?'

'In the box. They got in the box, like he said.'

'And then? Did they ever come out again?'

'He said they didn't come to any harm. But no. No, they didn't.'

'Did you believe him? What do you think happened to them?'

'I wanted to believe him. I did believe him, at the time. But I do know that no-one ever heard of them. But they heard of me, and that's thanks to you. If it hadn't been for you, Chryssie, no-one would ever have heard of me again. I do know, you know. I know what you did that night. And for a long time I wished you hadn't. But if you hadn't done what you did, all the rest of it wouldn't have happened, would it?'

Rose fishes in her pocket and brings out Janna's flight feather. Silently, Chrysanthemum reaches into her own pocket and brings out its double. The two Graces sit in silence, each clutching her feather, before Rose plucks Chrysanthemum's from her fingers and lays the pair of them in front of the samovar.

'And I'd never have come back, and we'd never have made it all right again, would we?' she continues. 'There wouldn't have been Rosemary, and she wouldn't have had such a lovely life with Orage and Sylvester. And you might not have stayed and there'd never have been Maurice. And I'd never have taken Janna's feather and gone off to see what there was in the world for me. And it was a world, I can tell you. I saw some things, Chryssie! And one of these days, I will tell you. But that's another story, isn't it?'

'It is.' Chrysanthemum sits up straight and strokes her fingers across the surface of the samovar. 'And talking of stories. It's been a day of them, hasn't it? Let's get this thing lit. She never told anyone but after everything else today, I want to know where this blasted thing came from. Once and for all. Or it's going back in the glory hole for good.'

'Janna would be turning in her grave. You know it was her pride and joy. Do you know, I think Dolores knew you could, and she was scared you would find out.'

'She wasn't scared of anything.'

'We're all scared of something, Chryssie. We've all got secrets.'

Slowly, carefully, Chrysanthemum stands up, fills the samovar, and sets it to boil. As it begins to hiss and sigh, she looks into its surface. And there it is. The same and not the same? What she's been looking for? Or what's been waiting, all these years, for her to find?

*IT WAS. AND IT WAS NOT.*

*Far away from home she may be but these are customers she understands. In their way – a different way from the way she lived before, but she sees it for what it is - they are as much show people as any she's known.*

*They live completely inside their music. It comes to them as naturally as breathing and means more to them than food and drink – and they eat and drank as if each meal was their last banquet. They're flashy, stylish, concerned about every detail of their clothing. Each polished stud, every last button. When they're in the money they pay her, handsomely in fact, because she welcomes them and many don't. When there's no money they repay her with loyalty, and play for the customers, drawing them in off the streets with tunes so irresistibly jaunty that they immediately suggest liquid accompaniment.*

*They're itinerants, their roulottes parked up and ready, no matter how settled the camp* seems, to pull off, should circumstance suggest that hitting the road is a better bet than staying put. They live in the moment, which means what she's been before this part of her life is of no interest to them.

That suits her. She keeps her secrets close to her chest. All of them. Tattooed on, the stories of her life, there on her skin in blue ink, for anyone brave or foolhardy enough to venture there, and with the wit to read them. She's had three new ones done since she got here. A leopard, crawling its way up the inside of her thigh. The heavenly twins, Castor and Pollux, under her navel. And a tiny skull – a miniature death's head. But they're wrapped up tight under her liberty bodice, and there aren't many who'd dare, she thinks, giving the zinc a rub with her pinny.

All in all, it's not a bad life. For a bad lot.

There's the café, which may not have been what she'd in mind for herself in the long term, but it serves a purpose and who'd think of looking for her, who'd earned a living and fame of a certain sort in the lurid limelight of a sideshow spectacle, behind a counter?

She keeps her head down, her nose clean, and – just in case – a knife in her knicker elastic. The local villains give the place a wide berth, she's seen to that from the beginning. The last thing she wants is the attention of the local gendarmerie.

The café came her way in a game of cards where the pastis flowed just that bit too freely and no-one noticed the Englishwoman who didn't speak the lingo was dealing from a deck made up entirely of the ten of clubs. That hadn't been too long after she'd fetched up in Montparnasse with nothing to her name bar a shaved face, a single case and a pressing need to put a lot of space between her and the scandalous affair of a minor film actress, blonde, discovered deceased in suspicious circumstances in the caravan belonging to The Great Lifto, an American strongman who'd attached himself to a British travelling circus. The strongman's body had been found the next day, suspended from the high trapeze by his own leopard-skin body suit. The coroner later passed a verdict of suicide.

Passion, murder, suicide and a cast of carny outsiders is a heady mix of ingredients, and the sensation had been reported widely, even on this side of the pond. Crime passionel, the regulars chuntered, reading the papers over their pastis. He'd been driven to it. She'd been carrying on with all and sundry. Even, while she was alive, her own sister's husband, it had been rumoured. She'd pretended not to understand a word but she'd picked up more than she let on and after she locked up that night she took the papers to the pokey garret behind the café which was her bolthole, read them intently, burned them in the grate and drank half a bottle of brandy out of a mixture of relief, self-congratulation and – at first she thought it was indigestion - a pang of sorrow. You should never believe everything you read, but other people doing so worked nicely in her favour. If only Bert hadn't choked on that bit of beetroot in his tuba. Things might have been different. She always stops herself from thinking precisely how different because it's a waste of time.

The main thing, though, is that she won't be staying, which is a good job because in her book, life on this side of the pond leaves a lot to be desired. She'll wait it out until the coast is entirely clear, and that won't be until the whole business has been long forgotten.

And she has to admit that as life in exile goes, this one has its moments. There's company if she wants it. There are the long summer nights of booze and syncopation, all centred round the dark, smiling figure of the moustachioed Belgian who wears workmen's boots and whose crippled hand, far from restricting his guitar playing, has twisted it into genius by making him find a new way. A new sound. She likes it. It sounds easy, and free, but she knows, because behind her zinc she watches the men working – the gypsy way, playing and watching, listening and watching and playing again until it goes beyond fluency into a whole new expressive language – that it takes the same kind of single-minded determination that you need to be a good trapeze artist. Or magician. Or cooch dancer.

She never follows them on the nights when they play in Pigalle. On those evenings she presides over a quiet café, and locks up early. She knows the places where they play and more to the point, there might be people in them whose memories stretch back to her own appearances. Notorious appearances, even if it was a decade earlier.

The Apache dancers of Pigalle were known for the violence of their duets that acted out the relationship between a prostitute and her pimp, but there'd been one particular mean-eyed Jo-Jo who'd made the mistake of thinking he could wipe the floor with the English dancer. It was an unforgettable show. Janna took the knife off her just as she was about to relieve him of his manhood on the dancefloor. They'd toasted her in champagne that night and the offers from the specialist establishments had been tempting, but the next morning she and Janna were on the early morning express from Gare du Nord.

Besides, why trail across the city to hear what's there all the time? The boys don't make a difference between practice and performance – where they are, so is the music. They play it in the roulottes, in the street, on trains. In the café. Regardless. There are times when she comes out from behind the counter, shakes a leg; a tail feather. Gets into the swing. Shows them what she's made of. Not that they know what she is. But she can still show them a trick or two. There isn't a one to touch her. Not their own dark, lipsticked beauties with their flowered blouses and rolled hair. Blondes – this blonde anyway – may be a long way from home but she there's still more fun to be had.

That was how she hooked the one they called Baro. It's not his real name, but his nickname – big man – suits him. There's gusto in his eyes, his clothes, his great, feline maw of a smile, his playing. Some say he's a match for the Belgian, but the truth is he doesn't care as much, he has gold-ringed fingers in other, more dangerous pies. He comes and goes, as he pleases, flashing his cash, his smile, his charm, knowing she's a handful, liking the challenge. He never knows if she'll purr or turn nasty, and she likes that he enjoys that about her. It suits her. When he gave her the samovar, he mentioned – quite casually, as if the shining urn wasn't valuable, or something that loved ones gather round in the darkness, and as if he didn't really care either way – that she might like to share his roulotte on a more permanent basis. She couldn't say she wasn't tempted, as much by the familiar trailer existence as the big, brash, beautiful man who made the offer. But it wouldn't do to get close to anyone, not even here, so she laughed him down and shook her head. 'Ah, Dorotée,' he shrugged, 'you know how to kill a man.'

She hasn't told him her real name. Another of her secrets. She didn't back down that time, just climbed on top of him and showed him what she was made of. He's a worthy adversary, the big man. Didn't ask for his gift back. Might have made a decent lion-tamer, if he'd been born into her world.

*Still, she's been restless recently. Ever since she read the papers and knew there'd be a time when she could go back. She'd murder for a proper cup of tea, and a fried black pudding sandwich, dripping with grease. It's harder every day keeping her Montparnasse persona intact. She'd been the attraction, not the skivvy, even if she owns the place. She'd like to see her own face, beauty and the beast magnificently merged, when she looks in the mirror, and not have the bother of shaving every day. Like a man. If there weren't three workmen waiting for café-cognac she'd have spat. And most of all, if she's honest about it, when she looks into the shadows, there is an empty space where her sidekick should be.*

*That was a hard parting. She hadn't minded the night-flight, before Tira's body was discovered. There'd been exhilaration of a kind, and companionship too, and if she's honest she wasn't entirely herself, hormones raging and her body so sore after its ordeal that it was weeks before she was able to sit down properly. Janna did everything, concealing her until she was strong again in the woods, where they hid out whilst the police crawled nearby towns and villages interviewing everyone they could find that would testify that Miss Tira had been no better than she should have been and the Great Lifto had bitten off far more than he could chew.*

*The days passed in a blur, until the evening Janna returned with a resolute expression and she knew that a tide had turned.*

*'Today I hear the gavvers talk to Miss Maude.'*

*She'd shuddered, and tried to suppress an image of the shrouded figure, moving silently into the shadows, carrying the bundle away from her. 'It can never belong to you,' Miss Maude said. She'd never held it, or even seen it.*

*'They won't get anything from that, apart from the willies.'*

*'So there it will end.'*

*Under the trees, and in the moonlight, Janna shaved her and cropped and tinted her hair, eventually producing a slip of mirror from her skirts.*

*'No-one know you now.'*

*She'd looked at the woman in the mirror, still handsome for all the changes, and tried to find herself, and just for one moment, had not been able to.*

*'Except me. I always know you. And now we go.'*

*At the edge of the wood they went their separate ways. There were no goodbyes.*

*They stood beside the path and looked at the fork in road.*

*'Good journey,' said Janna. 'I see you along the road. When it is safe.' That was four years ago, and not a word.*

*No, the hardest thing is the empty space. She can do without everything she left behind. She can do without Janna, if she has to, but the truth of it is she doesn't want to.*

*In the meantime, though, there are tables to be served, and pots to wash, and the tradesmen to berate for the appalling quality of their produce, because it wouldn't do for one second to let them think she's satisfied with what they sell her, or standards will drop and she isn't having any of that.*

*And now, too, there's the Belgian, limping in, sitting in the corner, on his own for once, stroking the neck of the guitar that goes with him everywhere, twisting the keys in his powerful fingers to tune it, signalling for his usual – a double expres', Armagnac on the side – with a flash of his dark eyes and a grateful half-smile that lifts his ever-present cigarette under the dandy moustache that looks as if he drew it on with a pencil. Dapper, he is. She approves of that in a man. Baro goes beyond that, just as Gilbert did, to a flaunting peacock flair. She likes that too, but she knows it for what it is and where it can lead you, if you let it. Here, for a start, living on her wits a long way from home with a set of marked cards and a knife in her drawers.*

*She let it happen, with the Florida strongman, but it isn't a mistake she's going to make twice. Funny, though, even if sometimes she wonders about the result of their dalliance, she's never missed him. And if she gives Tira a second thought it's along the lines of good riddance.*

*She fixes her lipstick – the same dark shade that makes the manouche women's mouths maraschino cherries in their swarthy faces – as the coffee boils, then takes it slowly across, well aware of the eyes she draws as her hips roll in the lascivious lope that had hints at the promise her act used to fulfil.*

*As if in time with her movement, the Belgian starts to strum. Gently, almost drowned out by the street noise, the traffic, the calling of children, neighing of a horse and the bipping of a car horn that are the sound effects of a café next to a busy crossroads.*

*And then she hears it, just faintly. A raw, joyful female voice. A familiar voice, singing an unfamiliar song. She moves to the door, craning her neck. The voice whoops, once, twice. The hairs prickle on the back of her neck.*

*The Belgian hears it too, and it must call to something in him, because he picks up his playing, not to match the chanting nursery rhyme rhythm of the song, but to counter it with his own. Five lilting chords, on the offbeat.*

*The voice comes louder, the words clearer. The Belgian strums, to the same tune, then as the singer pauses, he begins to pick out his own jazzy runs.*

*Her feet begin to tap, and her hands slide down the edges of her giant flowered pinafore, wrists curling into shapes that match the music.*

*That's when the singer comes into view, leaning backwards, dancing forward, leading with her right hip, her face concealed beneath a giant spangled veil which she holds aloft, still singing. She bends, arranges the veil behind her neck, picks up her wide, striped, mirrored skirt and, as the Belgian reprises his licks, teasingly moves the skirt and her hips up and down as she turns in a circle. Picking up the veil again, she dances on bare brown feet right into the café, still singing her sweet, harsh, gutteral song.*

*She dances right up to Dolores and as the Belgian finds ever-more syncopated variations on his riff, the two women dance round each other, taking it in turns to show what they can do to the music until he speeds up in a display of the virtuoso improvisation that draws crowds from all over Paris, and the veiled figure spins round and round in a whirling blur of skirt and gauze whilst Dolores kicks up her heels in a flurry of fancy footwork until the three of them have to stop because they are laughing too hard to carry on.*

*The singer lifts her veil, revealing for the first time her face – her dark, familiar face, the skin stretched tighter than ever over the cheekbones, making a beak of the long, curved nose. She looks at Dolores with bright black bird's eyes.*

*'So. I come.' Her smile reveals a mouthful of uneven brown and gold teeth.*

*'You took your time.'*

*Dolores makes for the counter so Janna can't see how pleased she is.*

*'I took the right time.'*

*Spurning a chair, Janna squats on her heels.*

*'Where d'you get to then?'*

*Janna spreads her skirts proudly, and smooths them with dirty jewelled claws. 'India. With the snake catchers in the desert. They people like me. Like him.' She gestures toward the Belgian, who raises his coffee in salute. 'And then I come back. In India many cows, all holy. All cows get special treatment in India. But for some reason I want different cow from Indian cows. Bloody rude old cow. And time pass and now it the right time, and I find.'*

*She looks round, critically at first, and then appraisingly.*

*'This you make nice. I like. People come. You do good, for a cow.'*

*'Well don't get too used to it.'*

*Dolores reaches behind her and unties the pinafore, hanging it up on a hook behind the door. She's made up her mind. 'Just a few days, and then we'll be off. I've got a few things to sort out.' Another card game, where she'll lose the café, or at least liquidise it. A last hurrah of music, and dancing. And Baro. A bit of special treatment. He deserves a good seeing to, by way of being seen off. But she's had enough of watching someone else put on a show.*

*'This samovar. We keep with us. It has stories to tell.' Janna has moved behind the counter and is stroking the gleaming brass with an acquisitive fingertip. As she does so, a mist seems to come over the surface of the samovar. Janna bends, and peers, and when she looks up her face is an unreadable mask. 'Stories to keep too I think.'*

*Janna's back. Secrets are safe. It's time to go home.*

'I've been thinking.' Rose, now wrapped in a pink candlewick dressing gown, has crumpled petal creases in her soft-skinned face. She's picked up the flight feathers; hasn't let go of them since Chrysanthemum lit the samovar. 'Orage could not have had a baby of her own. And I had a baby that I didn't want. And I wonder, if perhaps I should meet Rosemary. Not as the child I gave away, but as the daughter of my dear old friend. I expect I will love her dearly, and perhaps she may learn to love me.'

After all the day's revelations, Chrysanthemum cannot think of a single thing to say, so she busies herself with the samovar, giving it a final, gentle polish.

'My mother didn't love me.' She blurts it out. A whole lifetime and everything clear except the one thing that matters most. A whole lifetime of not being the right person.

'Oh she did. You were like Rosemary. Adopted. Everything you told us about the woman who brought you up. You were nothing like. Your real mother loved you dearly.'

The second time she's heard the words in in one day. And the third time in a lifetime.

The two old ladies huddle over the table, hands pressed round cooling glasses of tea. '"Your mother loves you." Janna said that the night Rosemary was born. No-one had ever said that to me before. No-one's ever said it since, either. Until today.'

'She was always right.' Rose lays her hand on top of her friend's. Even more of a comfort than the hot tea. 'I always knew she loved you. Look how she took care of you. You're living in her house.'

Just for a second, Chrysanthemum could swear she hears the distinctive sound of a derisive snort as the missing piece of the jigsaw of her life slots into place.

'I think I did know. We both did. We even had the same hands. We never said anything though. Neither of us. We never let on.' Leaving Chrysanthemum's mouth, the words have a distinct echo. Almost as if they are being spoken by two people. *As if I didn't know who you were. I knew it the first time I ever clapped eyes on you.*

Who said truth will out? Some secrets go to the grave. Like where that blasted samovar came from. Some secrets are buried deep in the woods, and there they can stay, because there are things better left uncovered.

But if the picture is completed to everyone's satisfaction, it means the show's over, and the audience can go home.

And just before our curtain falls, a faint scent, Abdulla tobacco mingled with Ashes of Roses, insinuates its way into the room.


THE END

About the author:

Tina Jackson is a writer and journalist. In addition to The Beloved Children she is the author of Stories from The Chicken Foot House (Markosia, 2018), a collection of grungy transformation tales illustrated by Andrew Walker, and Struggle and Suffrage in Leeds: Women's Lives and the Fight for Equality (Pen & Sword, 2019).

She has an MA in Creative Writing from Sheffield Hallam University and her short stories and poems have been widely published in journals and anthologies.

Getting her start in journalism at the radical independent Leeds Other Paper/Northern Star, Tina has worked as an award-winning writer and editor specialising in the arts and books for The Big Issue and Metro and her journalism has appeared in many publications including the Guardian, the Observer, the Independent and the Mail on Sunday. She is now Assistant Editor of Writing Magazine.

Tina is also a dancer and variety performer. She brings her experience of show life to writing about secret lives, liminal spaces, everyday magic, and the borderlands between reality and imagination where extraordinary transformations take place.

## Acknowledgements

This book would not exist without the passion, commitment and sheer bloody-minded awesomeness of Fahrenheit's own His Gillpots, the inspired rebel ringmaster Chris McVeigh, Max Grey and everyone at Fahrenheit who championed it, so beautifully designed it and brought it into the world. Thank you.

I'm indebted to the two exceptional crime writers who are Hull Noir's ace faces. Nick Triplow read the manuscript and provided not just editorial support but faith, belief and unfailing encouragement. Nick Quantrill is legendary for his support for new writers and generously extended this to The Beloved Children and me. Thank you too to Fahrenheit's stellar line-up of authors, who have welcomed this debut novelist into their ranks with such big-hearted warmth.

At Writing Magazine, thank you to my terrific editor Jonathan Telfer, and to Helen Corner-Bryant of Cornerstones Literary Consultancy for her advice.

At Wide Open Writing, thank you to Dulcie Witman for raw, powerful truth finding, Nancy Coleman for deep wisdom and everyone at the retreat I attended in Tuscany in 2018 for one of the most joyful, transformative creative experiences of my life.

Storyteller and dance historian Jo Hirons, thank you for the story of the little grey cat, which brought a tear to my eye as I was waiting in the wings. Simona Jovic, Katjusha Kozubek, Anna and Natalia Debicka and Rada Boguslawa, thank you for teaching me Janna's dances. Marcus Von Cudworth, thank you for shows, signs, and also eggs.

I've had the best people in my corner while I've been writing this. For particular support, take a bow Patricia Jackson, Marc Jackson, Chris Bradshaw, Andi Walker, Maria Woods, Michaela Noonan, Jane Cornwell, Julia Bell, Golnoosh Nour, Adam Macqueen and Michael Tierney.

A very special thank you goes out to Dancers Bizarre: Karen Ingham, Joanna Ferguson, Naziya O'Reilly and Sarah Selwood, and past members Hayley Jeffcock, Helen Nightingale and Sam Saxby. And in particular, Dancers Bizarre's magnificent wardrobe mistress, the real-life Dolores – Kirstin Ramskir, co-conspirator, partner in crime and travelling companion, to whom this book is dedicated.

More books from Fahrenheit Press

## The Transit of Lola Jones by Jackie Swift

Debut author Jackie Swift brings some playfulness to the Fahrenheit list with this first book in a series featuring her eponymous hero Lola Jones.

It's fair to say Lola Jones' life is not turning out the way she expected it to.

As the book opens we find Lola recovering from the breast cancer that threatened to prematurely end her life and languishing in a police cell, the main suspect in the murder of businessman Daniel Blain.

As the truth begins to unfold about the events leading up to the untimely demise of the dashing Daniel, we learn more about the journey that brought the normally infectiously vivacious Lola Jones to such an unsatisfactory pass.

But is she guilty, and even if she is guilty, is she to blame?

This is a funny, smart, sexy, modern romp of a book and Lola Jones is a character that you'll instantly want to be your best friend. If you're a fan of Fahrenheit legends Derek Farrell and Duncan MacMaster we guarantee you will absolutely love this book.

## Souljourner by Paul Steven Stone

Where to start with Souljourner? Let's start with the author - Paul Steven Stone is either a madman or a genius – probably both – and he's written one of the most gripping and enjoyable books we've ever come across.

The novel, if it is indeed a novel (the narrator insists it is in fact a warning letter from your soul's previous incarnation and aimed directly at you dear reader) - as we will discover though, this narrator is often unreliable - so frankly warning or novel, you pays your money you takes your choice.

One of the central premises of the novel/letter is that our souls make their eternal journey towards enlightenment in the company of a single unchanging 'karmic pod' of companion souls who take on different roles in each of our incarnations.

In one life a soul may appear as your mother, in the next your best friend, in the next your sworn enemy, in the next your lover and so on for eternity. The identities of the souls in your 'karmic pod' are hidden from you in life – this letter/novel seeks to wise you up to who's who in your karmic pod to help you avoid making the same mistakes that landed the narrator, David Rockwood Worthington in prison serving a life sentence for murder.

## Deer Shoots Man by Tyler Knight

It's a much over-used phrase, but this book by Tyler Knight really is one of the most extraordinary debuts we've ever published.

Set in a near future Los Angeles, jobbing cage fighter and man about town, DeShawn Trustfall finds himself in a high-octane chase to track down the genetic code that could cure a disease that threatens the lives of hundreds of thousands of people, including himself and his son.

Set against a background of a global pandemic, a corrupt government pushing a cure for its own self-interest, genetically altered CRISPR babies and civil unrest in the streets you could be forgiven for thinking the author Tyler Knight is part writer, part Nostradamus.

The writing in this book is razor sharp and the flights of tech/cyber creative inventiveness are right up there with the very best authors in the genre and as if all that wasn't enough, Tyler Knight writes noir like he was born to it...

Sound Of The Sinners by Nick Quantrill

In Sound Of The Sinners we find Joe Geraghty leaving his new home in Amsterdam to attend the funeral of his former business partner and mentor Don Ridley who was found dead shortly after asking for Geraghty's help.

With a heavy heart and weighed down with guilt, Joe returns to Hull, a city he thought was in his past.

Don's death points to his days with the police and an off-the-books investigation into the unsolved 'Car Boot Murder' decades previously. As Geraghty investigates the circumstances of his friend's death he uncovers dangerous secrets and a conspiracy of silence - Hull might have had a makeover during Joe's absence, but clearly some things never change in the northern seaport.

With his own life on the line, and with a debt of honour to be repaid, Joe is unable to stop in his quest for the truth, but powerful people with vested interests will always seek to ensure some stories never see the light of day.

*"Crime fiction done right. Realistic, human, and relatable"* – Jay Stringer

9 781912 526932